Acclaim for the Dana

Forsaken Oath is "clever, immersive... K(
and exposition, keeps the reader engage
evidence. There is a lived-in feel to Bureau 90 that sets this work apart from
lesser legal thrillers." — *Kirkus Reviews*

Homicide Chart "is a law buff's delight, with intelligent discussions of
unusual legal situations and excellent courtroom combat... Kemanis is an
excellent writer..." — Jon L. Breen, *Mystery Scene Magazine*

"*Forsaken Oath* is a terrific legal thriller, written by a prosecutor who knows
her way around the legal trenches. Kemanis's expertise brings wonderful
authenticity to a twisting plot." — Allison Leotta, author of *The Last Good
Girl*

Homicide Chart is "a page-turner, expertly written and well crafted, deftly
plotted with characters that portray real, human emotions... Kemanis is a
writer of high caliber worth noting..." — *The U.S. Review of Books*

Thursday's List is "engaging and thought-provoking... Well-written, with a
plot that is complex and presented in a way that will keep you captivated."
— *The Kindle Book Review*

In *Homicide Chart*, "Kemanis meters out the suspense in compelling
fashion... A well-paced, polished, and highly enjoyable read... Highly
recommended." — Carmen Amato, author of *Diablo Nights*

Forsaken Oath "really shines. A powerful book... Dana Hargrove is a
beacon of light, a modern idol..." — *Mystery Sequels*

Thursday's List is "a true page-turner." — *Kirkus Reviews*

"In *Homicide Chart*, [the] characters are well-defined, very authentic,
painted with a deft hand. This is Ms. Kemanis' real talent. She makes us
care for the characters."— *Online Book Club*

"*Thursday's List* has some qualities of mystery, legal thriller, and the police
procedural... A plot that is different, with qualities that would appeal to
fans of any of those genres." — *Books and Pals*

Forsaken Oath is a "legal thriller meets murder mystery ... The reader is
thrust into the dizzying world of the legal profession at a running pace and
never slows down." — *The U.S. Review of Books*

Also by V.S. Kemanis

Dana Hargrove Legal Mysteries

Thursday's List
Homicide Chart

Story Collections

Dust of the Universe, tales of family
Everyone But Us, tales of women
Malocclusion, tales of misdemeanor

Anthology Contributor

The Crooked Road, Volume 3

Visit
www.vskemanis.com

To Anne,

Forsaken Oath

a Dana Hargrove legal mystery

V.S. Kemanis

V.S. KEMANIS

ISBN: 099659096X
ISBN-13: 978-0-9965909-6-9

ℒ Opus Nine Books
• New York •

For the Decision Department,
the best and the brightest

CONTENTS

FOIL

COUNTDOWN. Nine days to go. Escape!

Hard work deserved a reward, and Dana was aching for hers. The desk calendar was marked. On Saturday, June 30, she would be on her way to the Jersey shore with Evan and the kids. They'd stuff the family Toyota with sand toys, paperbacks, and beach towels, pile in, and trundle across the George Washington Bridge, singing songs.

Two whole weeks of freedom. No criminals, witnesses, cops, judges, or attorneys. Nothing but salt air, white sands, ocean mist, and the soothing murmur of the surf.

Patience. That day would come.

For now, it was quitting time, already past six o'clock. Dana picked through the mess of papers on her desk, making piles for tomorrow in order of priority. Exigent, Pressing, Necessary, and Would Be Nice. She was tired and headachy. As her fingers worked, she was elbowed by a recurring doubt: A year ago, what had possessed her to accept this position? Bureau Chief of Trial Bureau 90, the busiest bureau in the busiest prosecutor's office in the country.

Whenever that doubt surfaced, it afforded a little escape of its own. But indulging it was a mistake. The question was satisfied with a simple answer: *just this*. She loved this place, the people, the heartaches and triumphs. She belonged here. This life was her third baby.

Today, like every other day, there'd been the usual trumpeting march of crises. A few unsettling dilemmas lingered in her thoughts.

This morning: The rookie she assigned to arraignment duty, in a panic, called her from the courtroom. He'd botched a bail hearing, tongue-tied, unable to find the DA's write-up in the morass of case files on the table. Then, mysteriously, it appeared ("I don't know *how*") moments after the judge released the defendant—a dangerous armed robber—on his "own recognizance."

This afternoon: A senior assistant district attorney, near the end of a month-long murder trial, burst into her office. Moments before, a juror was discovered entering the jury room with a tote bag full of news clippings about the notorious case. The judge called a recess—exactly fifteen minutes!—for the attorneys to prepare their arguments for and against a mistrial.

Never a dull moment. With sixty attorneys to supervise and thousands of open cases, Dana's job was a revolving door of surprises.

She stuffed a few draft indictments into her briefcase for late night reading at home and clicked the clasp shut. A knock sounded on the door jamb. She looked up to see Leticia Townes standing in the open doorway. Dana wasn't surprised to see her secretary still at work. Five o'clock was swipe-out time for all support staff, but Lecia—as she liked to be called— was a dedicated young woman of thirty-one who thrived on public service. Lucky for that, because a private law firm would jump to hire anyone with half the talent and pay twice the salary.

"This just came for you by messenger." Lecia stepped forward, holding out a manila envelope, larger than business size.

Dana took the sealed envelope and flipped it over and

back again. There were no preprinted markings or return address. More or less in the middle, someone had written: "Assistant District Attorney Dana Hargrove, Bureau Chief, Trial Bureau 90." The childish block letters in blue ballpoint gradually shrank and tightened up toward the end, as "Bureau 90" threatened to fall off the edge of the envelope. "Who brought this?"

"A kid named Oliver Fliegler. I've seen him before, so I buzzed him into the reception area and met him out there. He's one of those law students who volunteers at Justice Restored. The skinny one with the bad haircut and pimples."

Dana and Lecia exchanged a knowing look. Justice Restored had been very busy these days, serving papers in every trial bureau of the office. J.R.'s mission was to free all wrongly convicted prisoners, and lately, part of that mission seemed to include a takedown of District Attorney Patrick McBride. In court papers and statements to the press, J.R. insinuated that all of McBride's five hundred ADAs were hell-bent on obtaining convictions at any cost, spurning their oath to uphold the law.

"Why the unmarked envelope?" Dana mused. "Perhaps J.R. has a new, secret investigation up its sleeve?"

Lecia suppressed a smile and shrugged. "The search for justice continues."

"It's amazing how much paperwork a single attorney can generate with the help of a few pro bono lawyers and a handful of law students."

"They have a lot of passion going for them."

"And so do we. Along with a healthy measure of restraint and reason."

"One of the girls over in archives tells me she's been working a lot of overtime, just to answer all the FOIL requests from J.R." Lecia was referring to the Freedom of Information

Law, a means to obtain discovery of any non-privileged files of a government agency like the Manhattan District Attorney's Office.

"Speaking of overtime, you've done *your* share. It's time for both of us to go home."

"I'm just trying to get everything in shape before your vacation."

"Well, everything can wait until tomorrow, including *this*. Here." She handed the sealed envelope to Lecia. "Whatever it's about, you'll have to look up the case tomorrow and forward the papers to the assigned ADA. If the case is closed, it goes to the Appeals Bureau. And if it's a misdirected FOIL request, it goes to the FOIL unit in archives." Dana grabbed her briefcase.

"Will do," said Lecia, already ignoring her boss's orders to postpone the task. She hooked a neon-orange fingernail into the small opening at the corner of the envelope, threatening to use it as a letter opener.

"Have a good night," said Dana. She walked out the door and started down the long hallway.

"You too," said Lecia absently.

Dana passed the office of her deputy, Ernest Chin, who'd just left for the night. Along the remainder of the hallway were the offices of a dozen senior trial attorneys. As she strode past, she glanced here and there on both sides. Most doors were open, and a few ADAs were still inside, hard at work. Those who noticed her looked up and waved or said "good night."

Eric Trumble's door was wide open, the room dark. He was usually one of the last to leave, but tonight he was on homicide chart. No doubt, he was resting at home to prepare for a possible all-nighter. Eric had the constitution and ease of mind that allowed him to drop off to sleep at odd hours as needed and jump up again, fully refreshed. Dana was the opposite, wound too tightly to adjust her sleep schedule at will. That's *one* good thing about being the boss, she thought. No more graveyard, no more chart. Still, she made herself available by cell phone 24/7, in case one of her ADAs in the field needed advice.

Dana was about to open the locked door at the end of the hall and step into the reception area when Lecia called her name. Dana swiveled around to see her secretary at the other end of the hallway, still standing next to her work station outside Dana's office door. Even from thirty yards away, Lecia's stiff stance seemed odd. It conveyed a note of alarm. She held the opened envelope in one hand, its contents in the other.

Dana retraced her steps and, halfway there, said, "What's up?" She would have preferred to feel annoyed or angered by Lecia's interruption, but all she felt was an inkling of dread. She knew Lecia well enough to sense that all the blood had drained from her face under the dark complexion.

"I'm sorry…"

"Don't be sorry."

"I shouldn't have called you back. I just thought you would want to see this." They were face-to-face again, Lecia handing her the paper. "Just tell me how to handle it…" Dana took the document and stared at it, as Lecia's voice faded into the mist. "…tomorrow I can make any calls you need…"

A subpoena. The caption said: "The People of the State of New York against Ramón Pineda, New York County Indictment Number 2456/1992." Underneath the caption, Dana read: "YOU ARE COMMANDED TO APPEAR in the Supreme Court of the State of New York, Part 96, Honorable Theodore Deal, J.S.C., presiding, at the date and time below, to testify in the post-conviction proceeding in this case."

Her gaze dropped to the writing in bold: "Monday, the

2nd day of July, 2001, 9:30 a.m."

The signature line: "Ellen C. Fortier, Justice Restored, attorney for the defendant."

"...what a pain! On your vacation! I'll give her a call tomorrow and say you have to reschedule..."

Ellen, you've really done it this time. Dana opened her briefcase and shoved the paper in. "Thanks, Lecia. I'm glad you told me. Don't worry about it. I'll handle it myself."

"Okay. Just let me know if there's anything I can do."

Slowly this time, Dana turned around and made her second attempt to get out of the office, to go home to her family. Her movements were deliberate and careful, a mirror on her thoughts.

Mary Poppins, we will meet again. But not on Monday, July 2nd. Not if I can help it.

1 »   BATTERED

ERIC GOT THE call at 12:38. Refreshed from an early-evening nap, he was sitting at the kitchen table, eating a midnight snack of organic oatmeal and chopped dates, with a sprinkling of sesame seeds and oat bran. Some of his best recipes were created in the middle of the night, on the chart, waiting for a call. His fiancée Jessica was to blame for this health food craze.

She was sound asleep in the bedroom, undisturbed by the few words Eric spoke into his cell phone. He agreed to be downstairs "in five." Minutes later, Senior Investigator Gilbert Herrera from the DA's squad pulled up in front of the apartment building in the East Village. Eric hopped into the passenger seat of the battered 1998 Mercedes-Benz 300E Turbodiesel, a prize Gilbert had acquired from the forfeiture program. Tax dollars were not available for body work on the deep scratches along the driver's side and caved-in fender on the front passenger side. Gil didn't mind. The dings were a source of pride and a good tale to tell about the chase and crash preceding his takedown of the former vehicle owner, a cocaine kingpin.

"What've we got?" Eric asked.

Gil turned onto Third Avenue, heading north. "Gonna love this."

"You know me, the thrill junkie. Always love a good murder." Eric glanced at Gil's profile, but the investigator didn't crack a smile. Must be my delivery, Eric thought.

"The vic is a fashion designer. Loránd Kallay. He peddles

7

high-end clothing on Madison Avenue."

"Well, fuck it. I'm not dressed for the occasion." Eric looked down at his khakis and short-sleeved dress shirt, the compromise he'd made for the sake of a professional look. Suit and tie were not required for the graveyard shift on homicide chart, but Dana drew the line against his preferred garb for a warm summer night: muscle shirt and cargo shorts. "What else do we know about Loránd?" Eric teased out an accent on the name.

"Multi-millionaire. Hungarian by birth, age fifty-two by death. He was shot more than once. Happened on the ground floor of his townhome."

"Any suspects?"

"Nothing yet. Possible home invasion and robbery. That's what the wife says. Frances Kallay. She called it in about midnight." Gil fell silent after this bit of information, a signal that he had nothing further to tell. He was a man known for his frugality with words.

Any stranger peeking in on the unlikely duo in a banged-up Mercedes would wonder about their acquaintance. Eric was thirty-five, with a sunny smile, inquisitive face, and curly, flaxen locks, now cut closer to his head than in former years. In his ninth year as an ADA, he had matured since the early days, when the combination of puppy-dog innocence and suburban-kid foul mouth—an attempt to fit in with the cops—was often a source of humor around the office. Gilbert was forty-nine, a veteran of undercover work with an underworld aspect to his face, deep acne scars, hollow cheeks, and a broken nose. His eyes were changeable, with the power to inspire fear in street thugs or the affection and respect of his colleagues. Gil's over-the-collar hair, now thinning and streaked with gray, was pulled back in a short ponytail.

Traffic was light, and Gil made good time up Third

Avenue to the posh Lenox Hill neighborhood. He took a left onto East 69th Street and drove a few blocks west, crossing Madison Avenue. The crime scene was a four-story townhome close to Central Park, easily worth more than a million a story.

Gil pulled up behind a line of five double-parked vehicles: three blue and whites, an unmarked Ford Fairlane, and an ambulance. He left some room behind the ambulance, although there wasn't any apparent need for its speedy getaway. The medical profession was of no help to the victim, who was now serving his postmortem duty as the subject of photography, physical examination, trajectory analysis, and fluid and fiber testing while his temperature slowly descended.

There were three shallow steps up to the front door. They walked into a grand entry hall, where the ambulance crew had left a collapsed, wheeled stretcher, and a uniformed officer was monitoring foot traffic. The activity was concentrated in the den on the left side of the hall. Just inside the door, Frances Kallay stood in the company of two paramedics. She was deathly pale, her absence of color accentuated by the deep aubergine shade of the Loránd silk robe she wore. Eric was no fashion expert—he would have to learn more. For now, his keen interest was focused on the woman's behavior.

"Just to check things out…," one of the paramedics was saying, touching her elbow. She resisted their attempts to get her to sit in a wingback chair. Her eyes were vacant and dry. Intermittently, she expelled spurts of muted jabbering under her breath. Shoulder-length, unruly locks fell over her face as she hugged her abdomen and hunched over, draped in the luxurious material that covered most of her body. Signs of vulnerability were to be expected under the circumstances, but something about her appearance seemed off. On the other side of the den, face down on the carpet, was the body of her husband, Loránd Kallay.

At least ten cops and crime scene investigators were milling around, doing their jobs. The digs and identity of the deceased signaled the importance of this case, but the presence of the inspector from the 19th Precinct confirmed it. He was a tall, broad-chested man of fifty-five or sixty, scrutinizing the scene from his stance about halfway into the spacious den, an equal distance between husband and wife. The gold eagle medallion on the shoulder of his white, short-sleeved shirt identified his rank.

Eric walked up and introduced himself and Gilbert. "Craig Bitters," said the inspector. No handshake. Inspector Bitters kept his arms folded across his chest, nodded in the direction of the deceased, and said, "That's Kallay. House of Loránd." Perhaps Eric seemed young and uninformed, in need of the basics.

"Right," said Eric. "Big name in fashion." He glanced around. Mahogany furniture, ivory statuettes, original oil paintings, heavy crystal glasses on a wet bar in the corner. "A lot of money here."

Gil said, "I'll go take a look," and wandered off toward the body.

"You ever had a murder case out of the 19th, counselor?" asked the inspector.

"This would be my first."

"We haven't had a murder in more than a year. We don't have trouble like this here. People in the neighborhood know how to protect themselves from home invasion. Burglar alarms and video cameras."

"Any video footage here?"

"No such luck. They were between systems, installing a new one. That's what she says." He nodded toward Frances, who'd finally been convinced to have a seat. A paramedic was putting a pressure cuff on her arm. "It checks out," continued

Bitters. "The alarm and video system are brand new but only partly installed, wires not connected. The missus gave us a signed consent to search the house, so be my guest."

Eric kept his eye on Frances Kallay as he spoke with Bitters at a level that couldn't be overheard. "What else did she tell you?"

"Hard to get much out of her. She's real shaken. Smith spoke with her directly." Bitters indicated one of the uniforms. "What I know of it, she's on the fourth floor in the bedroom and her husband's alone down here in the den, working. She hears noises, and right after that, shots fired. She comes downstairs and it's just like you see it. Weapon over there." The inspector gestured toward the desk.

Eric visually scanned the items on the surface: a flat screen monitor and keyboard, brass paperweight, cordless phone, opened bills stacked in a letter box, Cartier pen set—and a handgun. Eric knew handguns better than he knew fashion. This one looked like a Browning semiautomatic, .22 caliber with a wood grip.

"Seems too neat," said Eric. A gun nicely placed on a desktop. Everything else on that desk nice and neat too. In fact, the rest of the den was very orderly, except for the body on the floor and the roll-away desk chair that lay on its side next to the victim's head. "Very considerate of the perp to leave his piece behind."

"Frances says it's her husband's. He keeps it in the desk drawer." Bitters nodded toward the upper left drawer, which was partially open. "Only way it makes any sense is this: they struggle for the gun, the killer uses it, then he lays it on the desk so he can get what he wants out of the safe."

Safe? Where's the safe?

"He's nervous, so he forgets it," Bitters continued. "Or maybe he left it on purpose. Didn't want to risk having the murder weapon on him before he could get rid of it."

Behind the desk, Smith and two other uniformed officers stood in a cluster with their backs to Eric. They moved away, exposing the object of interest: a wall safe, open.

"What's in the safe?" asked Eric.

"Nada. Zilch. Everything taken."

"Did she say what was in there?"

"Kallay's designs for the spring show."

Eric furled his brow and mused, "Designs? Spring is over, everyone's seen them. What's so valuable you have to lock it up?"

Bitters smiled in a fatherly manner: "Spring 2002, the new designs. Top secret until the collection is shown in September, a couple months from now." Perhaps Bitters had just learned this tidbit of fashion smarts himself. Eric couldn't tell.

Just then, a crime scene investigator standing at the desk called out to Bitters: "We've got all the photos and measurements we need. You don't mind if I...?"

"Go ahead. I want prints *and* DNA."

"You got it." The investigator caught Eric's eye and they exchanged smiles. He recognized her from a previous case. Nicole Verona. It was about five years ago, right around the time he'd finally made peace with his unrequited love for that older woman, Dana Hargrove. Up until then, all his contacts with the opposite sex had been purely medicinal, "good for him," far from nirvana, inadequate to meet his perfect vision of that unattainable woman. Dana's marriage and motherhood only made his longing worse. But, sometime after the birth of her second child, the fog lifted and the world of women opened up for him. Nicole—Nicki—was really a fun person, and he'd been getting up the nerve to ask her out on a date when he met Jessica. Everyone else was forgotten.

Nicki's question to the inspector showed concern for an

accurate recording of the gun's exact location. She wouldn't touch it before that recording was complete, and only with the inspector's approval.

"When you're done," Bitters instructed her, "work with Smith to preserve the chain. I made him arresting." He turned to Eric and said, "That is, he'll be the arresting officer *if* we find our guy."

"The place to start might be Kallay's competitors."

"Already on it. I've got a detective back at the precinct drawing up a list."

Nicki pulled latex gloves over her delicate hands before taking the first step, looking for any fingerprints made visible by foreign substances on the surface. She peered at the gun through a magnifying lens, then gently picked up the gun by the edge of the handle, turned it over, and peered at it again. Then she searched for latents with the aid of a blue light.

Eric was still wondering about the perfect placement of the gun on the desk. The inspector's theory suddenly made no sense to him. The killer put the gun down so he could empty the safe? Did he know the combination? Maybe he forced Kallay to open it first. Eric examined his mental snapshot of the gun, taken before Nicole started to work. The barrel was pointing out into the room. Very awkward for someone to hold the barrel toward himself and lay the gun down that way. So, the killer must have been behind the desk, in the area where a person would sit, holding the gun by the grip when he laid it down. Viewed from that perspective, the person had to be left-handed since the gun was laid on its right side.

And another thing. Inspector Bitters seemed to assume that this was the murder weapon, but maybe it wouldn't test out that way. Maybe Kallay took out the Browning to defend himself but was convinced to put it down when the killer pulled out his own gun.

Eric made a mental note to find out if Kallay was left-handed. And the wife. He didn't quite understand her yet. He'd seen all kinds of reactions to murder, and not every woman cried immediately, or even an hour after discovering the body of a loved one. Did the inspector consider her a suspect? Apparently not. She didn't look capable of the deed, at least not in her current state.

Eric asked the inspector to submit an order for expedited treatment of the DNA samples. Fingerprint comparison and ballistics came back quickly, but DNA could take a few weeks. "You got it," said Bitters. Eric thanked him and handed over his business card.

Ready to move on, Eric was torn between joining Gil over by the body or Officer Smith next to the safe. But first, he thought it best to squeeze in a conversation with Frances. The paramedics would have to give him a few minutes alone with her.

Just then, a slight man carrying a black leather case walked up to Inspector Bitters and said, "Kei Tajima, OCME." The investigator from the Office of the Chief Medical Examiner had arrived. He would need to clear the area around the body—another reason not to go over there.

As tough as he liked to appear, Eric really wasn't so tough. Getting close to dead bodies wasn't his favorite pastime. There was the smell, the blood, the dread of a sudden lightheadedness he hadn't been able to vanquish. He'd never humiliated himself by fainting or vomiting, but he'd come damn close. As for this body, it was on the far side of the room, about ten feet from the desk, and he'd seen enough of it from a decent distance. He already had a mental picture of its position and would rely on the OCME investigator to tell him the rest.

Eric went in the opposite direction to one of the paramedics, the one still standing. The other was kneeling next to the wingback chair, at eye level with Frances, talking to her in a low, calming voice.

"Eric Trumble, Assistant District Attorney," he introduced himself. "How is Mrs. Kallay? Any chance I can get a word with her?"

"She's not very coherent. Her pressure's low and her pulse is rapid and weak. Could be emotional trauma, or something else, hypovolemia or hemorrhagic shock. We're taking her in for observation and a few tests."

"Can you give a hand?" asked the kneeling paramedic, sending the other one off to retrieve the stretcher in the entry hall. Frances Kallay was shaking her bowed head. She didn't want to go, but didn't have a choice.

Out of luck here. Eric could see this would be a long night. He'd be taking a trip to the hospital later, hoping they'd stabilize her enough to allow him a visit.

He went over to Officer Smith and introduced himself. Martin Smith was about forty with an accessible face and a proud bearing. Definitely the most senior officer present, an obvious choice for the "arresting." Everyone around him simply addressed him as "Smith," apparently his preferred nickname.

Eric related that he'd gotten some background from the inspector but still had a few questions, and Smith was the best source, having spoken with Frances Kallay directly.

"Sure. Fire away." Unlike the inspector, who constantly surveyed the scene while talking, Smith looked Eric straight in the eye.

"Did she say whether the front door was locked before she went upstairs and her husband went into the den?" In his peripheral vision, Eric saw the paramedics wheeling the recumbent lady of the house out of the house.

"She didn't. But they were home all night. She said she

was supposed to go to a charity event but it was cancelled, so she was home all evening and started getting ready for bed a little before midnight. Her husband was still working in the den. He was alone. He wasn't expecting any visitors as far as she knew. I didn't ask her if the front door was locked. I just assumed it would be."

"Is there any evidence the lock was jimmied?"

"No. We checked."

"So that means the door was unlocked, or else he let the person in. Did you ask if she heard a doorbell or a knock?"

"No."

"No, she didn't hear?"

"No, I didn't ask. She said the first thing she heard was a commotion, some voices, maybe some furniture banging around, then the shots. She was scared. She waited a minute and then came downstairs."

"Did she hear the front door close before she came down?"

"I didn't ask."

"Did she use the phone on the desk to call 911?"

"Didn't ask. Say, you know, the lady was pretty much a basket case."

"Damn straight—"

"I'm lucky I got what I did out of her."

"And I'm glad you did. The paramedics wouldn't let me near her! Maybe later tonight or tomorrow."

"Maybe."

"Thanks, Officer." Eric hoped he hadn't ruffled Officer Smith's feathers too badly. He handed the officer his business card, stepped toward the safe, then paused and turned back, as if remembering something. "She wouldn't have said whether she knew the combination to the safe?"

"Couldn't get that far with her. The most she said about

the safe was that it held her husband's designs for the spring collection. He sketched all his designs himself. He was an artist, 'a visionary artist,' she said. 'Anyone would want to steal his designs.' After that, she started mumbling and pulling away—you saw it. I couldn't get any further."

"Okay, thanks."

The safe was on the wall behind the desk, a few feet from the area where a person would sit in the rolling desk chair. The camouflage was a framed oil painting—a bucolic scene of soft green hills—which was now pulled open on hinges, perpendicular to the wall. The door to the safe was also opened out on its hinges. The area inside the safe was about a foot square and two feet deep. Nothing inside. Eric peered around the outside of the door and saw the round dial combination lock. He was careful not to touch anything, although he was fairly sure that a crime scene investigator had already dusted for prints and swabbed for DNA.

Was Kallay working on the designs when the killer entered? This den looked more like an office than an artist's studio. Was the safe already open? If the safe was closed and hidden behind the oil painting, did the killer know it was there, or did he have to threaten Kallay to find out?

At his back, Eric felt Nicki's presence at the desk. She was still busy at her job, and he didn't want to interrupt her. But when he turned around, she lifted her eyes to him in a way that signaled she wanted to talk.

"Hey you," she said.

"Hi Nicki, how's everything?" It was nice to see her again. It had been four years since she testified at a burglary trial he prosecuted. Since then, they'd had occasional phone contact to discuss other cases that eventually pled out.

"Good." Their eyes locked, and she said "good" again. Was she asking for something to happen? Eric wasn't in a position to consider it. He asked, "How's our gun looking?"

"Nothing obvious showing, but that's to be expected." Visible fingerprints on a gun were rare. The finger would have to be soiled with blood, dirt, ink, or another visible substance to leave a patent print. "I'm taking the gun back to the lab to process the latents and DNA. We'll do superglue first." She couldn't swab for DNA now—it would wipe away any latent prints. The first step would be to place the gun in a testing chamber for cyanoacrylate fuming, or "superglue," which left a white deposit that could be seen under certain light sources. After that, human cells in the latent prints could be used for DNA testing. As a third step, even where latents weren't found, she would swab the areas that were less likely to hold prints, hoping to catch skin or sweat cells trapped in grooved or uneven surfaces, like the wood grip.

"Okay, let's hope for some blood, sweat, and tears."

"Or skin."

"Maybe an eyelash."

"*If* ballistics says it's the one."

"A lot of 'ifs' here. Anyway, you'll let me know?"

"Sure. The minute *I* know, you'll know."

"You still have my number?" Instantly, Eric regretted the suggestion in his voice. It was so easy to joke with this girl. What he really meant was his office number. Quickly, he pulled out his business card.

"I have it," she said with a wink.

"Great. Nice to see you."

"You too."

He took a step in Gil's direction and heard her say, "Just one more thing." He turned around, and she was standing there with a big smile on her face. "I understand that congratulations are in order. When's the big day?"

There were a hundred ways she could have heard. It was

a small world they lived in, even with thousands of players. Nice, though, that she was interested enough to remember the news. "September 8," he said, unable to control the pie-eating grin on his face.

"Lucky girl."

"I don't know about that. More like *I'm* the lucky one."

"Then make sure you show up at the church on time."

He laughed, and when he turned around, Gil was right there. "You'll make sure I get there on time, won't you Gil?"

The senior investigator gave one of his famous crooked grins.

Eric put a hand on Gil's shoulder and led him over to a clear area of the room, somewhat closer to the body but not so *very* close. Though Eric towered over Gil, his superior height was easily outpaced by Gil's advantage in years of experience. Eric glanced sidelong at the body while they talked. The OCME investigator, Tajima, was kneeling, making his provisional examination of temperature, rigor, and lividity. The body would likely confirm that the time of death was shortly before midnight, as Mrs. Kallay had stated. From this angle, Tajima was blocking Eric's view of the bloody torso, but the legs were visible. One knee up, the other leg almost straight. Kallay's slacks were made of an exquisite fabric, the fit perfect, the cuffs crisply pressed above his ankles. A photo of those legs could be published in the WSJ Men's Style magazine.

Except that Kallay's feet were bare.

"Three holes in him that I could see," said Gilbert, "one in the side, an entry and exit in the back. But there's a lot of blood. They picked up three casings and dug a bullet out of the wall over there." He pointed. "Recovered the slug, .22 caliber. Probably the first shot. It went through him, into the wall, and the others went into the body. I'm guessing one in the chest, one in the side, and one in the back."

"Okay, wiseass. You wanna tell me how you know all this?"

Sarcasm was Eric's typical gift wrap on his profound respect for any of Gil's theories. The veteran detective had a true eye and infallible instincts. He usually called it right, even before the autopsy and crime scene reports were in.

"Okay. This is the way it happened. The perp comes in when the safe is already open, or he orders Kallay to open the safe and tells him to stand back."

"What if the drawings are already on the desk when the perp walks in?"

"Maybe." Gil was humoring him, he could see. "Doesn't quite fit with the chair, though. But if the drawings are on the desk, the killer doesn't want blood on them, so he tells Kallay to move away from the desk. Maybe Kallay bumps into the chair and it rolls a little. When Kallay's at a short distance, the killer plugs him in the chest. The impact makes him step backward, and he starts to turn..."

"A defensive move."

"You got it. He takes the second shot in the left side and stumbles some more, pushing that rolling chair with him. He keeps turning..."

"It's instinct."

"He's stunned, still turning to get away, takes the third bullet in the back. He falls on the chair and it tips over, landing on its side near his head. The corner of the room stops the chair from sliding and farther."

"Okay, but you forgot one thing."

Gil looked at him, eyebrows raised.

"The killer needs a gun to threaten Kallay and order him around." Eric nodded in the direction of Nicki, who was packing up the evidence. "That's Kallay's gun. How did the bad guy get it out of the desk drawer?"

"Because that isn't the murder weapon. Or, if it is, something else is going on here."

"How about the inspector's theory?"

"What's that?"

Eric glanced at Inspector Bitters to make sure he couldn't hear. "Kallay takes the gun out of the drawer, they struggle for it, the killer overpowers him, shoots him, and puts the gun on the desk so he can get the drawings out of the safe. When he leaves, he forgets the gun, or he decides he doesn't want to risk carrying it."

Gil's expression said, *That so?* He deadpanned, "Sorry. Didn't go down that way." In other words, the inspector's theory was ridiculous. "Look at this place," said Gil. "You see a struggle here?"

"It's possible."

"Anything's possible. All I see is blam, blam, blam. From a certain distance, not too up close and personal."

"Why's the gun on the desk?"

"Two ways that could be. The killer had a different .22, not this one. Kallay took out the Browning, and the shooter made him put it down. Second possible, it's the murder weapon, but he didn't need to put it down so he could get the drawings. If he used Kallay's gun to pop him, there must be another reason it's on the desk."

Before Gil could elaborate on the second possibility, OCME investigator Tajima stood up and came over. Eric introduced himself to Tajima, who'd already met Gilbert earlier, over by the body.

"The man was shot three times," said Tajima, "and he was standing when he was shot, but moving in between each shot. One entered the front around navel level, exiting out the back, one to the left side just under the ribs, and one to the upper back, about heart level."

Eric and Gil exchanged looks. Gil's eyes said, *see?*

"I didn't note any exit wounds on the last two," continued Tajima, "but I didn't want to move the body either. We'll know more on autopsy."

"Time of death?" Eric asked.

"He's been dead about two to four hours." Tajima looked at his watch. "It's one thirty now, so that puts it between nine thirty and eleven thirty."

Not quite what Eric expected to hear. Of course, Tajima was not aware of the wife's statement about the time of the gunshots. "Could it have been closer to midnight?"

"Possible. But I would put it earlier. It's not an exact science. I'm factoring in his current body temperature, height and weight, clothing and temperature of the room, lividity, among other things. But it isn't more than four hours ago. Rigor has just started in the face."

"I see," Eric said, clenching his jaw. Without looking at the corpse, he could imagine it well enough. "Thank you." He gave his card to Tajima, who promised to call when the autopsy was completed.

Before leaving, Gil and Eric decided to accept the inspector's offer to take a tour of the entire premises. There would be no objection from the residents, one of them dead, and the other a party to a signed consent form. They left the hubbub in the den and crossed the entry hall. Under the stairwell was a half bath, and on the other side of the hall was a combination living room and library. While poking around, they discussed whether a trip to the hospital later would be wise or productive. It might take some time before Frances was up to talking.

Not much else to see on the ground floor, so they took the first set of stairs up into the hushed sanctuary of serious money. The second floor held the kitchen, formal dining room, powder room, and a parlor comfortably arranged for entertaining. The third floor held a guest bedroom with attached full bath, a smaller bedroom with a half bath, and an artist's studio with two large drafting tables, both empty. The fourth floor held an enormous master bedroom, two walk-in closets, and master bath with sunken tub and Jacuzzi. Eric noted the clothing laid out on the bed, a summer dress, light sweater, and underthings.

"That bed's gotta be bigger than king size," said Gil.

"I wouldn't mind stretching out in it," said Eric.

"With that *fine* lady..."

"Shut your sick mind!"

All of a sudden Gil froze, stock-still. Something about his face made Eric do the same. They remained silent for a full ten seconds, eerily encased in a vacuum, the complete absence of sound.

"What?" Eric broke the silence.

"She was up here getting ready for bed."

"Clothes are right there," Eric pointed.

"She hears something."

"Right. A commotion, furniture banging around maybe."

"*Before* the shots were fired."

They fell quiet again, listening for the sounds of a dozen cops and investigators, the bark of the inspector's orders, the squeal of handheld radios, the thud of NYPD-issued footwear on the marble floor in the entry hall. Inside this retreat in the sky, every bit of the outside world had melted away.

So quiet, it could be heaven.

Two hours later, after a few more conversations at the murder scene and a coffee break at an all-night diner (Eric ordered herbal tea), the duo walked into Lenox Hill Hospital and inquired about the patient, Frances Kallay. Gil flashed his shield and persuaded the receptionist to surrender some basic information. Frances had gone through triage in emergency and was now in a private room. Gil coaxed out the room number.

In the hall outside her room, the resident in charge of her care refused to answer Eric's questions about her condition. "Confidentiality. I'm not at liberty to say. You'll have to ask the patient." He paused and stared at Eric a second too long, a look that implied the significance of the facts he wasn't willing to divulge.

"You know that the woman's husband was just murdered?" Eric pressed.

"I'm aware."

"If you have any evidence relevant to the investigation…"

"I know the law," the doctor cut in. "Her symptoms don't fall into any category I'm required to disclose." Again, his expression was full of meaning. Like any smart medical professional, he wanted to avoid private lawsuits or license revocation for divulging patient information. A doctor was legally obligated to report a patient's injuries to the police only in a few situations: gunshot and knife wounds, or evidence of child abuse. For anything else, doctors typically stood behind the patient-physician privilege.

"May we go in?"

"You can have a few minutes with her. She's mildly sedated. We'll be moving her out for more tests shortly. Now, excuse me please." Something down the hall caught the doctor's eye. "Here comes the radiologist now." He remained anchored to his spot until the woman in a white lab coat walked up to him. Gil and Eric seized the opportunity to keep their ears open while they made a show of stepping a few paces away. They could hear every word.

"The woman in 534," said the radiologist. "X-ray is

negative for broken ribs. FAST is inconclusive for intra-peritoneal blood. We should do a CT to be sure."

"Okay. She's hemodynamically stable for now, so the bleed could be minor and might resolve on its own. I've got her on prophylactic antibiotics."

Without another look at Eric and Gil, the doctors parted company and rapidly walked off in opposite directions.

"Was that obvious or what?" asked Eric. "The doc didn't even try to lower his voice. I'm glad he was so concerned about patient confidentiality."

"Did that lady say 'fast'?" asked Gil.

"Focused abdominal sonography for trauma."

"Now who's the wiseass?"

"They were looking for internal bleeding."

"No shit. I knew something was up. Let's go in." They entered the room and stood for a moment just inside the door.

Stripped of her luxurious Loránd robe, Frances Kallay was looking very ordinary in a faded cotton, cap-sleeved hospital gown. She was on her back with eyes closed, propped up with pillows on the raised head of the bed. The ties on either side of the top of her gown were undone, and the two sides were flapped open, exposing the first few ribs of her upper chest. Both arms lay on top of the bedspread. An IV line was connected to her left arm, and a nurse stood at the IV pole, adjusting the drip.

The first thing, the obvious thing, drew their eyes immediately. Then came the second thing, not quite so obvious, but it was still there after another good look and a shake of the head to remove any doubts.

Eric tilted his head down to Gil and whispered. "You see that? Both her arms. That sonuvabitch."

"Finger bruises. And an ugly purple mark on her chest."

They were squinting hard at what appeared to be evidence

of a battering. Still, the patient's eyes were closed, her breathing deep and regular. The nurse finished her adjustment of the IV and walked toward them, on a path to the door. When she was two feet away, Gil said to Eric, "Finger bruises on her arms," and glanced at the nurse.

She returned a blasé look that didn't contradict him. "Visiting hours are long over."

"Yes, ma'am," said Gil, flashing his shield. "But the doctor said we could have a word."

"She's sleeping. And anyway, she won't say much."

"What did she tell you? That her husband did this to her?"

The nurse glanced behind her at the bed and turned again to Gil. "Look, I heard what's going on, and I can't talk to you." Her eyes burned with conflicting desires: the need to speak candidly about the patient and the urge to lash out against Gil's audacious attempt to extract confidential information. She stepped toward the door. "If she wakes up, don't get her overexcited." The nurse left the room.

"Everyone's very helpful around here," said Eric, "wouldn't you say?"

"Very helpful."

"Let's wake up the patient and see how helpful *she* can be."

2 »   ABORTION

FROM THE MINUTE Dana saw that subpoena, her single-minded plan was to get out of it. Nothing, least of all Ellen Fortier, deserved priority over family time at the shore. Ellen's signature—her lack of professional courtesy—was written all over this procedure. A call would have been polite. Instead, she served a subpoena, treating Dana like any other hostile witness on her list.

Dana would get an adjournment, but for the moment, nothing could be done. At home that evening, her cherished time with Natalie and Travis was tainted by the disruption. Thoughts of testifying (about what?) cropped up in the middle of play, bath, and story times. Later, when Grandma Brenda recounted her day with the kids, Dana heard only half of it. When Evan launched into an update of his class action lawsuit, she just felt annoyed.

Not only had Ellen picked the wrong time, she'd picked the wrong case. Everything about the prosecution of Ramón Pineda, as far as Dana could remember, made him the least likely candidate for a get-out-of-jail card. She hadn't yet seen his petition and didn't know his arguments, whether he was claiming his innocence or a deprivation of due process. Either way, the petition would fail. Pineda's trial had been fair, and he was guilty of the charge.

Maybe this was really about the fairness of the felony murder statute. A lot of people didn't like it, and if Ellen was one of them, she should lobby the state legislature. Under the law, armed robbers and their accomplices were guilty of murder whenever an innocent person was killed during the course of a robbery. The timeworn debate was about the fairness of a murder conviction when the killing wasn't intentional. Proponents of the law said it didn't matter who pulled the trigger, why, or how, because death was always a foreseeable consequence of a robbery involving guns.

If Ellen was planning an assault on the statute, the Pineda case wasn't going to harvest any public sympathy for her cause. The proof was in the physical evidence. The bodega owner was standing helplessly behind the counter with his hands raised when he was shot. A bullet from Pineda's gun killed him.

Friday morning at 8:30, Dana walked into her office, itching to take action against the unwanted summons. Impatiently, she worked through the half hour remaining until the start of the business day. At 9:01, she picked up the phone.

"Justice Restored," said the person on the other end, most likely one of Ellen's volunteer law students. His voice had the inappropriate self-assuredness of a hatchling just freed from the nest, flying off on a mission to save the world.

"Ellen Fortier, please," Dana said.

"Who's calling?"

"Dana Hargrove."

"Can you spell your last name?"

Yes, I can. Can you? Dana suspected that this law student was the very one who'd typed up and delivered the subpoena to her. But she spelled her name for him anyway.

"Hold one moment please."

The line went dead. Dana played piano on her desktop, examined her wedding ring, looked out the window, and moved the "Would Be Nice" pile over to the credenza.

Suddenly, that voice was in her ear. "Hello, Dana." The sound of it brought back those rookie days and the four-attorney office they once shared, Ellen's desk neat as a pin.

"Ellen," said Dana, pausing mid-breath to hold back the automatic greeting, *How are you?* She didn't want to know how Ellen was. "I received your subpoena yesterday."

"Good. Then I'll be seeing you in court."

"Yes, certainly, but you'll need to ask for a two-week adjournment. I'm sorry you didn't call me first to arrange a time. I'll be away on July 2nd."

"On business?"

"Business or not, I'm out of town."

"Well, I guess you'll have to arrange to be in town. Ramón is giving up his summer vacation to be there. In fact, he hasn't had a vacation for more than eight years of the twenty-to-life he's serving."

Dana breathed in deeply and side-stepped the provocation. "It's impossible to change my plans," she said in a matter-of-fact tone. "If we can't agree on an adjournment, I may have to file a motion to quash the subpoena. What's this all about?"

"I think you know. You convicted him. And you have full access to all the files. I only recently got the few things I'm allowed to see as a mere member of the public. What I found was shocking enough."

The innuendo was hard to ignore, but Dana kept it cool. "You're right about that. A hard-working store owner was shot and killed, leaving a wife and three young kids. It was shocking, and very, very sad."

Ellen emitted a delicate "tee-hee" that matched her petite, finely-etched features and diminutive bearing. Dana hadn't seen her since 1994, except on TV news clips, and she imagined her face as it looked years ago. If anything was shocking, it was the unexpected transformation of such an unlikely person into an assertive advocate for convicted felons.

Ellen's bitterness and restiveness—now that Dana thought of it—had always been there, under the surface. "You were always good with a comeback," said Ellen, explaining her momentary mirth. "Of course it's sad. I'm not blind to the victim. But you can't let sympathy blind you into pressing bogus murder charges either."

"Sympathy isn't the only reason to prosecute when there's overwhelming evidence of guilt." Dana paused for just a moment, but spoke again before Ellen could jump into the void. "You know, it's interesting that it took you so long to express doubts about the murder charge against Pineda. I seem to remember that you handled the pretrial motions when I was on maternity leave. Your client might not like that."

"If you're implying that I have a conflict of interest, there is none. You tried the case. This is all about what happened at the trial, not the pretrial motions. Look, I'm not going to litigate this on the phone."

Ellen clearly didn't want to surrender the element of surprise, her chance to see Dana's face when confronted with whatever "shocking" evidence she'd uncovered. "Okay," said Dana. "I'll see you in court." There seemed to be nothing more that could be said. After an exchange of terse goodbyes, they hung up.

Well, so much for that idea. The next step was to consider a motion to quash, or maybe simply an application for an adjournment. She should just walk into Judge Deal's courtroom and ask for a new date. What was she missing here? Maybe this was something to bring to Patrick's attention. But as soon as she had the thought, she dismissed the idea. The District Attorney was much too busy with more important things than her little problem. Plenty of ADAs were dealing with subpoenas from Justice Restored these days. Besides, even if Patrick granted her a sixty-second meeting, she could predict what he would say: "You have to comply with your legal obligations as a subpoenaed witness." She had no intention of not complying. She simply needed a postponement.

Still, it would be nice to discuss this with a senior ADA. The logical person was her best buddy, Jared "Denzel" Browne.

She made a quick call to be sure he was available before jumping up from her chair. "I'll be across the street in Mr. Browne's office," she told Lecia on the way out. "Back in fifteen."

Dana and Jared were now in different buildings, where they'd landed after last year's game of musical chairs. Dana was still getting used to their separation, after thirteen years in the same bureau. Hired straight out of law school in 1987, they started as rookies in Trial Bureau 90 under Patrick McBride. When Patrick won the election for District Attorney in 1994, Michele Seidman took his spot as bureau chief, Jared was promoted to deputy bureau chief, and Dana continued as senior trial counsel. In 2000, Michele left to become a judge, and Dana took the job of bureau chief. Patrick promoted Jared to the title of executive assistant district attorney, and Dana gave Jared's deputy spot in TB 90 to Ernest Chin.

All of this meant that Dana now had to take a trip across the street to the Criminal Court building, where Jared enjoyed a very large office in the executive wing of the DA's Office, a few doors down from McBride. Jared no longer worked in the courtroom but directed programs on the proactive side of reducing crime and developing intelligence against crime. His current favorite project was the Safe Neighborhoods Program. He also headed a project to review the cases of incarcerated prisoners who advanced credible claims of actual innocence. More than anyone, DA McBride wanted to prevent and rectify any wrongful convictions.

The Criminal Court building, an art deco monstrosity with a granite façade, was known for its unique stepped tower like a ziggurat, rising to twenty stories at its center. The two main entrances in the front of the building were each flanked by a pair of massive, three-story tall granite columns. Dana rarely passed through those symbolic gatekeepers. Instead, like today, she used the DA's entrance on the south side of the building. She took the elevator to the eighth floor and used her card key to swipe into the secure area of the executive wing. Without asking the secretary to announce her, Dana strode into Jared's office and blurted, "I've got a problem, Denz."

"Just fine, thank you, and the kids are also doing well."

"Sorry I'm being such a pig."

"I'll forgive you this time. What's up, Dorothy?"

"Attack on the Emerald City."

"Who's the invader?"

"Justice Restored."

"Also known as Ellen Fortier, also known as Mary Poppins."

"She isn't Mary Poppins anymore."

"That we all know. Stop pacing around and sit down." He motioned to a chair. "When you look at her now, it's hard to believe we gave her that nickname. She was so prim and tidy over in her perfect corner of the office. All that quiet compulsion turned into ... what would you call it?"

"Strident compulsion? She's a different person. Remember the way her eyes used to roll up to the ceiling every five minutes? I always felt we were being judged. She was joyless."

"Very true. Joy there wasn't. More like angst. It got worse after her fiancé left her. She was always dusting those photos of her fiancé and her nieces. Then the photos just disappeared."

"You won't believe this, Denz. She subpoenaed me to testify at a post-conviction hearing on July 2nd. That's the first Monday of my vacation. We rented a house on the Jersey shore with Melanie and Noel. My two kids, Melanie's three kids, grandparents, the whole thing."

"That stinks. Whatcha gonna do?"

"I was hoping you'd tell me what to do. I already called her and asked for an adjournment. She refused. I'm considering filing a motion to quash the subpoena. I could argue she has a conflict of interest and shouldn't be representing this client."

"Why's that?"

"She worked on the case when she was here. I picked it up on homicide chart in the summer of '92, right before my maternity leave with Travis. Ellen did the pretrial motions while I was gone, and when I came back in '93, I tried the case. Felony murder, that bodega in Spanish Harlem, you remember."

"I do, indeed. Hmm, this is interesting." He paused to think. "Is this some kind of vendetta?"

"She's targeting everyone these days."

"But this case ... she was pissed that it wasn't given to her, don't you think? She never made it onto homicide chart, even though she was also class of '87, like us. By '92 we were already on the chart, but Patrick held her back."

"I think ... I've never asked Patrick, but I think he was giving Ellen a chance to show her worth on the Pineda case. She didn't pass the test. I remember the Don was on this case..."

"Sure miss him."

Dana didn't have to voice her agreement on that—Jared knew how she felt. They'd both worked dozens of cases with the legendary Detective Paul Donegan before he died of lung cancer in 1995.

"Yeah. Well, you know the Don. He never crossed the line when he questioned Pineda. The statements were admissible, but Ellen botched the pretrial hearing and the judge suppressed some of the evidence. When I talked to Patrick about it—"

"Aha! You complained to the boss about her! I knew this was a vendetta."

"No, Jared, it wasn't like that—"

"More proof! You only call me 'Jared' when you have something to confess."

"Be quiet a minute, *Denzel*, and I'll tell you. I didn't rat on her. Patrick, of course, great bureau chief that he was, knew all about the pretrial before I came back to work. He said he was taking the case away from Ellen and asked me to handle the trial because ... well, he didn't say it in so many words, but..."

"He wanted the best attorney in the bureau to handle it."

"Someone good, anyway."

"The best. Felony murder is always tricky."

"After that, the chip on her shoulder just got bigger. That's the way it seemed, anyway. Remember? We had no idea what was going on in her life. She was a mess all through '93, and her work was bad. She left in '94 I think, sometime before Patrick was elected DA."

They fell silent, locked into a gaze with their eyes opened like windows on each other's thoughts. They were remembering the same things.

"Right," agreed Jared. "We found out about it later."

"The Fortier family secret."

"I suppose she was worried about losing her job, tiptoeing around, in dread of being found out. We're supposed to be spotless, after all."

"And she was always spit spot."

"On the surface anyway." Jared thought for a moment and asked, "What's her argument in this case? The Pineda case? Why does she think she has a chance at getting him out?"

"I don't know," Dana said. "I haven't seen the motion papers. They may have ended up somewhere in the post-conviction unit of the Appeals Bureau."

"Whatever it is, she's gotten better, you know."

"Better? How?"

"As a litigator. It's got to do with all that passion behind her cause. She started J.R. with the vision of filling the gap left open by other innocence projects that search for untested DNA samples as a way to exonerate the wrongly convicted. Her methods go beyond that. At first, she had very little success, but this year, she won two cases within months. Nazarov and Blakely. She did FOIL requests, found something in our files, and convinced the court that it was exculpatory evidence we wrongly withheld. She was very persuasive—I watched her argument in the Blakely case. These two men may have spent years in prison for something they didn't do."

"I don't know much about those defendants. They weren't TB 90 cases."

"Well, she successfully argued that the evidence she found raised a reasonable doubt as to their guilt and convinced the court to vacate those convictions. After she won the second case, Patrick started treating all of the J.R. cases more seriously. He's not taking this lightly."

"And I don't take them lightly either. I'm not suggesting that reasonable doubt should *ever* be taken lightly. But look at what Ellen's doing! Based on a few wins, she increased her filings exponentially and now has dozens of post-conviction motions pending. A lot of these are solid convictions. This is all about racking up the numbers for her trumped-up media blitz: 'DA McBride is out for blood at any cost!' And you say that Patrick is quaking in his shoes?"

"You know Patrick."

"Yes I do."

"He's given us our marching orders. We must quietly answer each of these petitions. Truth, reason, and justice will win the day."

"Hard to be quiet when Ellen isn't. Anyway, I'm not trying to get out of this, just postpone it. Justice *will* prevail here because she doesn't have a leg to stand on. That's what makes it so galling. It's idiotic not to give me an adjournment, because it won't change anything. Mr. Pineda isn't going anywhere for many years to come. So, I'm back to my first question. How do you advise that I proceed, Mr. Executive Assistant DA?"

Jared leaned back in his chair, folded his arms, and said nothing.

"What...?" She felt more than ever that she'd missed something.

"In 1993 you tried the case," he said, stating the obvious. "You were the lawyer for the People. Today, you're being summoned as a witness in the case."

"Sure, but..." Then it dawned on her. Emotion, if unchecked, will find a way to cloud reason. "I guess I have a fool for a client," she admitted.

"I wouldn't go so far as to say that. For one, you're not exactly the client. You're a witness. And for two, you're not exactly—or you shouldn't be..."

"...the attorney for the witness. An ill-prepared, naïve attorney, just like rookie days."

"Gee, Dorothy, too bad you don't have Toto...," he cleared his voice in jest, "I mean, Eric, as your personal trial prep assistant on this one."

Her face broke into a huge smile. "I just remembered one of your favorite lines from that time. Whenever you felt unprepared or made a mistake, you always said, 'I just love looking like a fool in court.'"

"Ah, those were the days."

"We've both come a long way, but today *I'm* the fool. Sorry, Denz. I knew better. I shouldn't have called Ellen."

"It's not the end of the world. I'll assign someone to the case. He or she will have to write a response to Ellen's motion papers and appear at the hearing."

"Assign someone good. Please. Not a second or third year ADA."

"Don't worry. We won't send you in there unprotected."

"And the first order of business is to get me an adjournment."

"You bet."

As Dana walked back to her office, the memories came flooding in. June 1992. Seven months pregnant with Travis. The late-term abortionist, Dr. Grant Spellman.

Heavy and slow, Dana felt, for the first time, slightly out of place in the courtroom. A voice whispered low in her ear: *This isn't natural.* Hormones were feeding professional self-doubt. When Travis kicked her in the stomach, she wanted only to stop and enjoy the moment instead of forging ahead in one of the toughest prosecutions of her career. The evidence was heartbreaking. The photographs were enough to reawaken the nausea of her early months of pregnancy. The impassive face of the "doctor" haunted her dreams.

In office talk and good-natured jest, her colleagues dubbed it the "battle of the bellies." Dr. Spellman's attorney was also seven months pregnant. Was there a point to be made here? It just happened that way. Dr. Spellman's finances had been wiped out in a civil malpractice lawsuit, and he was poor enough to qualify for legal representation at taxpayer expense.

On the day of his arraignment, Legal Aid attorney Vesma Krumins was picking up cases and landed the assignment. At trial, Vesma cozied up to her client at counsel table, sending the message to the jury that women did have a choice. Vesma had made her choice, and Dr. Spellman's patients had made theirs.

The indictment charged two counts of murder, two babies, close to term. The result was an even draw, one guilty verdict, and one not guilty. For one of the murdered babies, the evidence did not definitively prove that the baby was born alive.

What did this have to do with Ellen? Before the murder trial started, sometime in early 1992, Ellen indicted Dr. Spellman for assault. The victim, one of his patients, had suffered permanent sterility. Several months later, after Dana indicted the murder case, the assault victim in Ellen's case became reluctant and difficult. Ellen didn't have the skill to win her cooperation, and the only way to drag her into court would have been under arrest on a material witness order. Patrick, their bureau chief at the time, told Ellen to dismiss the assault indictment, betting that Dr. Spellman would be convicted in the murder case. The unspoken insurance underlying this bet was his assignment of a top-notch prosecutor. A prosecutor who happened to be seven months pregnant, the age of the murder victims. If asked, Patrick would have said that Dana's pregnancy wasn't a factor in his choice. Like Vesma, Dana picked up the case purely by the luck of the draw. She happened to be on homicide chart when the murders were reported.

The day after Patrick's decision, Ellen didn't look happy. Quick on its heels came the Pineda case, Dana's maternity leave, and Ellen's incompetence at the pretrial hearing. Soon after that, Ellen was hit by a personal crisis, which she concealed from the outside world. The emotional toll impaired her ability to function, and slowly, she turned against the people she worked with and for.

Maybe this wasn't a vendetta, as Jared supposed. But certainly there was a history of failure, despair, and envy.

3 »   KIDS

BRENDA GOODHUE SAT next to Natalie on the bed and
wrestled with her ballet outfit. There was a reason these
stockings were called "tights." She bunched up one of the legs,
inserted the child's toes, and unrolled the fabric upward,
yanking a bit. The angle seemed wrong. The result was twisted.

"Gramma?"

"Yes, pumpkin." She bunched up the other leg.

"Do I have to go?"

Brenda capped the toes of the other foot and pulled up as
she hummed *Camptown Races*. This would work better if she
could get down on her knees in front of the child instead of
leaning over sideways at the waist, but her knees wouldn't take
it.

"*Oh de doo dah day*. You don't want to? But you always
have fun at your ballet class."

"I don't want to. I'm tired."

Was that a devious smile on Natalie's face, an ulterior
motive for her request? How can a five-year-old be tired at nine
thirty in the morning? At breakfast, she was full of energy with
her usual smiling face as they sang those nonsensical lyrics
together. Dana had asked Brenda not to sing that particular
song, but the nature of the objection had slipped her mind.

Certainly Brenda was tired. It *was* Friday, and she was
always tired by the end of the week. Ballet should be banned
on Fridays. And maybe ballet should be banned in the summer
as well. It was getting too hot to put form-fitting nylon clothing

on a child. But, after today, it wouldn't matter. Today was the last paid-for class. School was out for the summer, and this week had been filled with "fun" classes and activities, enough to keep Brenda hopping. Next week the kids were going to day camp, and after that, they'd be on vacation at the shore.

"I think we should go," said Brenda. She'd succeeded in getting both legs rolled up to the thighs. "Okay, jump down and we'll pull it up the rest of the way." The child hopped off the bed, letting weight and gravity do the trick. The tights were now up to the waist, just under the round belly, although they still seemed to sag at the crotch.

Brenda examined the result. Hardly a ballerina that one, with her chubbiness and pudgy, sturdy legs. So far, Natalie's physique was mimicking her father's at that age. Throughout his childhood, he'd always carried a little extra baby fat. Come to think of it, Evan had some extra padding going into young adulthood too, until he met Dana and started his exercise regime. What he wouldn't do for his lovely wife!

"Now for the leotard."

"Grandma!" Travis yelled from his bedroom. "Where's my mitt?"

"Is it in your closet?"

"No!"

She heard objects being tossed around in the next room. "Hold on a minute, Tally. I'll be right back. Try to put on your leotard." She handed the garment to the girl and said, "This is the back and this is the front." Natalie had been known to put it on backwards, with the larger rear-end area in the front. A comical look.

Brenda walked into Travis's room, navigated the books and toys on the floor, and went straight to the closet. The mitt was in its designated spot—hanging on a hook inside the closet door—but Travis had draped a shirt over it, hiding the mitt from view. She took the mitt and turned around to Travis, who was looking handsome in his Little League uniform.

"Right where it's supposed to be," she said.

Travis reached for it.

"Not so fast, Buster. You don't get the mitt and we don't go anywhere until you pick up your things."

"We'll miss the game!"

"Still plenty of time. And there's always time for good habits." She started singing the *Clean Up* song they'd learned years ago from a toddler videotape.

"I'm not a baby!" Travis pouted and crossed his arms but quickly abandoned his show of anger and jumped to the task. The whole package—facial expression and body language—reminded Brenda of Dana. The boy looked so much like his mother, tall and slender, athletic, dark hair, and intense, unmistakable energy. Just like her, except for the eyes. Blue-gray with flecks of gold. Those were Evan's. Travis Ulrich Goodhue, or Tug as he was sometimes called, was a very good looking boy.

Every time Brenda noted a familiar behavior in one of her grandchildren, she marveled at the random but organized system of reproduction that made offspring in the images of their parents—except backward. Natalie was Evan, with sandy hair, plump cheeks, an easy laugh, and a relaxed nature. But the brown eyes were Dana's. That's it; each child had everything of the parent of the opposite gender except for the eyes.

Brenda returned to Natalie's room to see if the girl had forgotten her attempt at manipulation. Far from it. Natalie was in her underwear again, having reversed the painstaking application of the tights in less time than it took to put them on.

"Natalie! What's going on, young lady?"

"Just today."

"But today is the last day."

"I don't mind."

Well, I don't mind either! If it were up to Brenda, she would let the girl out of the obligation. She'd been to ballet twice this week already. But Dana had already paid for the class. "Does this have something to do with Aunt Cheryl?"

Natalie answered with a giggle and a collision, running up and throwing her arms around Grandma's waist.

How could Brenda say "no" to that? The usual plan was to drop Natalie at ballet during Little League, and after her class, take her to the field in Central Park to watch the end of the game. The whole game was too much—Tally wouldn't last. But today, Dana's sister Cheryl was coming to watch the final game of the spring season. Aunt Cheryl loved to attend the children's events and showed up whenever possible, often at the last minute. Her nightly schedule on Broadway allowed her to be a true doting aunt when Dana and Evan were at work. This week, she'd already watched little Tally's ballet class, and today it was Travis's turn.

The girl clung. Brenda stroked the top of her granddaughter's head with the hand that wasn't holding the baseball mitt. Should she overcome the girl's will, fight with that outfit again, yank the comb through those curly blonde locks to make a ballet bun? "You want to be with your Auntie Cheryl at the game?"

The head bobbed up and down.

"The whole game?"

The head bobbed again.

"Okay. Why not?"

"Yippee!" Natalie let go and skipped around in a circle.

Oh my Lord! Giving in to a five-year-old! Brenda glimpsed Dana's disapproving countenance, an image indelibly stored in memory. Schedules, rules, and discipline must be enforced. But not without love. *I'll just pay Dana back for that missed class out of my nonexistent paycheck.*

She replayed that thought and discovered the nastiness. Had she meant it that way? The lack of a paycheck was her own doing. "I absolutely can't be paid 'wages' for being a proper grandmother!" It wasn't "work," caring for these delightful children, Tally and Tug, her own flesh and blood.

There were times when she accepted Evan's offers to pay this bill or that. He also paid all of her "on the job" expenses, the food while she was here during the week, her transportation with the kids in the city, and her train fare back and forth from her home in Westchester County, where she stayed Friday and Saturday nights. Was she being inconsistent? Money was complicated. She believed she had enough. Most likely. Her house in New Rochelle was paid for (except for the yearly property taxes), she received monthly checks from her late husband's pension fund and Social Security, and she'd made a few investments. Very small down payments with the promise of return. These were her proudest accomplishments, made all on her own, without any help. She had some winnings and interest coming her way.

But things can happen. Banks can close, markets can crash, checks can stop coming. Frailty, ill health, destitution. Abandonment by grown children who turned heartless. She'd heard of things like this. She'd heard. Anything can happen. Anything … *Camptown ladies sing this song, doo-dah, doo-dah!* When the voices got too loud, the music saved her.

"How's this?" Brenda believed in color. She pulled a purple tee-shirt and orange shorts from the drawer, and Natalie had no trouble at all putting them on. When everyone was ready to go, she found her own sun hat in bright teal with plastic daisies on it.

They made their way downstairs from the eleventh floor

of their building on West 65th Street, near Lincoln Center and Central Park. Evan and his family had been living in this apartment for more than six years now. They moved after that awful time with the au pair in 1994, when Travis was two and Natalie was only a glimmer in Evan's eye. Had they stayed in their former apartment higher up on the West Side, the arrangement with Brenda would have been impossible. That place was too small. Here, everyone had a room. There were three bedrooms and a "den," which Brenda used as her bedroom Monday through Friday.

The space was more than adequate, organized and clean, but Brenda still felt there was something "hotel-ish" about the building. Marble-floored lobby with tall, leafy plants. Elevators. Uniformed doormen. Kids needed a real house with a backyard, didn't they? She'd suggested it once or twice. Maybe more than that. When would Dana and Evan come to their senses? It was useless to hope for it. Dana was so invested in her career, in love with this dangerous city and the battle in the courtroom.

At least the park was nearby. As they approached the playing field, the team was already warming up.

"See!" Travis exclaimed. "We're late."

"They just got started, Tug."

"Grandma!"

Oops. She'd forgotten his new embarrassment whenever his nickname was uttered in public. Sometimes, he would adopt a lawyer-like manner and pose the question: "Why don't you ever call Tally 'Nirg'?" Natalie Rebecca Goodhue. It wasn't the same. An alternative, "Nats," was sometimes used on those rare occasions when Travis was being less than loving toward his younger sibling.

This time, there was no one near enough to have heard Brenda anyway. "Go on and run ahead."

Travis needed no further encouragement. Focused on his teammates, he ran right past his aunt without noticing her. Cheryl stood as Brenda and Natalie approached the bleachers, where she'd been saving seats for them in the front row. Natalie ran up to her.

"Hello sweet girl! No ballet today?"

"Uh-uh. I'm not going."

"You're not going? But I thought you loved ballet."

"I do!" Natalie would never admit otherwise. She was keenly attuned to anything her beautiful Aunt Cheryl loved. Ballet was at the top of the list, along with every other form of dance. Cheryl had been the one to find the best dance classes for Natalie.

"She wanted to be with you," Brenda explained, looking up. Cheryl was at least six inches taller than Brenda and half the width.

"You little devil!" Cheryl bent down, and with all of her mighty, magical strength, picked the girl right up, as if she were still just a toddler. Natalie wrapped her legs around Cheryl's waist, hugged her neck, and ducked under the cascading fall of thick, fragrant chestnut-colored hair. Under that private tent, Cheryl pressed her nose into her niece's and said, "You know what? I want to be with you too! So there!"

Cheryl kissed the girl's cheek, and with a small groan, set her back down on the ground. "Sorry, sweetie. Don't want to throw my back out before the show tonight."

They all sat down in the space Cheryl had reserved, and good that she had, since the rest of the bleachers were filled with nannies, mothers and fathers. It was summer, and more parents were taking a break from work to be with the kids.

"How *is* the show going?" asked Brenda over the head of squirming Natalie, who sat between them. The girl was trying very hard to get onto Cheryl's lap but was gently pushed away and had to be content with sitting close alongside.

"Absolutely great. I couldn't be happier with the part." Cheryl was playing Peggy Sawyer in the revival of *42nd Street* on Broadway.

Brenda was thinking, what if...? What if her own life had taken a different course, her talents developed and shown to the world? True, she'd never had a svelte body and long legs, but she certainly knew all the Broadway tunes from the fifties by heart and could have run off to an audition at any time... "What a *marvelous* life! You're certainly going places, young lady."

"But I'm not so young anymore."

"Pshaw! Not so young? Wait until you're my age to say that!" Nowadays, sixty-nine wasn't considered very old, but that didn't change the fact that everyone else looked so very young.

"For the role, I mean. My agent moved a mountain to get me this part. At thirty-three, I wasn't the most likely prospect. Peggy is supposed to be twenty-one."

"You have that fresh look, my dear, not a day over twenty-one, and you dance up a storm! Take advantage of it while you can."

Natalie jumped to her feet in front of Cheryl, thrust her pointed finger into the distance, and yelled, "Allentown!" A few people around them giggled.

Cheryl laughed and declared in a high-pitched voice: "I'm *not* going back!" She hugged the girl while avoiding the eyes of those around her. It wasn't unusual now for people to recognize her. "Sit here, Tally. Look, the game is about to start. There's Travis." She pointed for Natalie's benefit. Travis was first baseman.

Brenda started singing exuberantly with a sway, right and left: "*Take me out to the ballgame!*" She pushed Natalie and Cheryl into the rhythm, and their voices merged, "...*buy me some peanuts and Cracker Jack...*," until the first batter hit the ball. It was a pop up, easily caught by the outfielder. They cheered as Travis's team made the next two outs, the second a strikeout, and the third a dramatic catch by Travis and tag at first base.

During the change of teams, Brenda asked Cheryl, "How's things with that boyfriend of yours?"

Cheryl laughed. "About the same."

"No proposal yet? Maybe you should bring him down to the shore. These little ones will win him over!" She ruffled Tally's curls and immediately thought, with regret, that she'd just said something stupid. Why would a man who didn't want to propose be impressed with a happy family and well-adjusted, bright children?

Natalie perked up. "Are you coming with us, Auntie Cheryl?"

"I don't think so, sweetie."

"Pretty, pretty please?"

"Well, maybe there's a small chance I'll come for a very short visit for one overnight. The theater's dark on Mondays. What about you, Brenda? Did you decide to go?"

"Oh, well, no, I've told them no..."

"But they'd love you to come, and Mom and Dad are going to be there too."

"I know, I know, but you see, I have so many things to catch up on—" Her little home office was jammed with correspondence, and there would be inquiries to make about the down payments and taxes she'd sent off.

"Look! Travis is up to bat!" Cheryl jumped to her feet. "Go Travis! Woo hoo!"

Brenda clapped and turned to look admiringly at this vibrant woman, so very young looking. Was she really thirty-three years old? *Not so young anymore.* Brenda thought back to when she was thirty-three. *Let's see...* She had to count on her fingers. Albert Jr. was nearly ten, and Evan was already eight. It was tough being such a young mother. Think of it ... what if her life had taken a different course? The songs and romance, the magic, the adventure! But when would the children have come? Was it Cheryl's plan to tap dance away the rest of her life? *Take advantage of it while you can.* What kind of advice was *that* to give a young woman of thirty-three? Turn around and youth is gone. Turn around, no husband, no children, no grandchildren.

But it wasn't Brenda's place to say anything. She really didn't think it was her place. Let Cheryl's sister say something. Let Cheryl's mother and father say something. Brenda's own children had blessed her with grandkids, two each, smart and beautiful, such a joy. Her own two boys had done just fine, including her in their family lives, letting her care for their children while they worked. Eleven wonderful years with Al's kids, Kelly and Ian, the last five years with Evan's kids, Natalie and Travis.

She wouldn't trade her place for anything, but it was true that she needed a bit of a break. She didn't want to go to the shore with them. She wanted to be on her own for two weeks, maybe take an occasional visit to Al's family, but mostly to putter around her own house, lonely as can be.

She needed to do some planning of her own, without Evan's and Al's voices in her mind. "Did you make a doctor appointment for that pain in your knees?" "Let me go over your finances with you." The music wasn't working as well for her these days. The voices were getting louder, clashing with the lyrics. Maybe the time away from the boys would bring out her own voice. She didn't want them to worry about her. She was perfectly capable. There were resources. Calls to take and make, envelopes to open, inquiries to send, people of her own choosing to help her.

Doo dah! Time for herself. *Oh de doo dah day!*

4 » CLASS

"ALL NATURAL REMEDIES. Who could argue with that? Corporate America, that's who! Pharmaceutical companies. They eat your tax dollars in research grants. They patent their drugs for *years* and get away with charging outrageous prices. Who gives them these grants? Who writes the patent laws? Your congressmen! It's a massive government conspiracy to keep you sick and keep you paying!"

A passionate delivery. A youthful, attractive face. The man on the television screen had a hypnotic effect on his viewers, especially the sick and the suffering, the lonely and the gullible. Anyone who watched and listened for too long ended up reaching for the credit card and calling the toll-free number.

Darren Tripp, infomercial mass marketer, was worth an estimated half billion. He was also well on his way to financial and personal ruin. It started when the FTC sued him for deceptive advertising and won a permanent injunction. Tripp defied the court order, kept running his infomercials, and wound up indicted for criminal contempt. This was no longer about money and injunctions. It was about prison.

The criminal prosecution was a matter for the U.S. Department of Justice. The money was a matter for Evan Goodhue and his law firm, Belknap & Rose, PC. Evan had filed a whopping big class action lawsuit, *Henrietta Edmonds, et al, versus Darren Tripp*. The goal was to divest Tripp of his assets and compensate the scammed viewers who'd bought his "all natural" cures under the brand name "Life Source." So far, the

litigation team had identified about a million victims across the
country and sent them notice of the lawsuit. A much larger
number remained unidentified. For Evan, these names on
paper were brought to life by the face and personality of his
client Henrietta Edmonds, eighty-two years old, the lead
plaintiff who was the named class representative.

B & R's top associate on the team was Joel Bachmann. At
thirty-nine, five years younger than Evan, Joel had a solid track
record in the litigation department. Energetic, dynamic,
brilliant, hard working. For all these reasons, Evan tried very
hard not to let Joel get on his nerves.

It was Friday afternoon. Evan and Joel sat in the small
conference room, watching the infomercial that had earned
Tripp a federal indictment. They'd seen it before but wanted a
reminder, a way to get riled up anew about their fight. Tripp's
lawyers had placed a settlement offer on the table, and a
conference with the supervising judge was scheduled for
Monday.

"You've heard about the court order," Tripp was saying
to the camera. His tone and expression conveyed wry
amusement. "The FTC is trying to shut me down. Who's
behind *that?* It's part of the same conspiracy between
government and big business. Corporate executives and their
lawyers. They don't want you to hear the truth about proven
natural cures for cancer, obesity, diabetes, arthritis, and back
pain. They don't want you to get well. Natural treatments can't
be patented. Natural treatments don't attract billions in tax-
dollar research. Curing disease doesn't pay. Forcing you to buy
chemicals, at twenty dollars a pill, *does* pay."

Joel slapped a hand on the conference table. "What a
huckster!"

Evan pressed the pause button. "He's a trip, all right. But
I understand the appeal. People love a whistleblower. And they

especially want to believe any message that could improve their lives." He was thinking of Henrietta's arthritis, the chronic pain. And something else was at the back of his mind. An image of vast America, its independence and isolation, houses with closed doors and television screens, ill defenders against a persistent intruder.

Joel sprang to his feet, crossed his arms, and paced dramatically while examining the floor as if gathering his thoughts to address the jury. He stopped and looked up, directing his gaze at a distant point above Evan's head. "He thinks the injunction is a joke? His offer is a joke. 'Here's five million out of my five *hundred*.' Very generous!" Joel turned and pointed at the distorted face on the screen, a frozen Cheshire Cat smile and half-closed eyes. "Wipe that smirk off your face! Offer rejected! We're not taking it!"

Fight fire with fire, Evan had thought when he picked Joel for the team. Bachmann's intensity easily matched Tripp's, but in a good-versus-bad way. That was the hope. Still, Evan never felt entirely at ease with Joel's style of communication. Absolutes and truisms. No questions, no dialogue—although it was clear that Joel implicitly listened to his senior colleague and held him in very high esteem.

However it was said, Joel was right. "No, we're not accepting the offer," Evan agreed. "And I doubt that Judge Friel will buy it either. With a million class members, even if half of them opt out of the settlement, they'd still get only a few bucks each after expenses and attorney fees. We'll make that point to the judge on Monday."

"We'll use Mineko's chart to drive that point home. The court will be impressed by the actual financial and social costs to the victims." This comment was further evidence that Joel appropriately gave credit where credit was due. Senior associate Mineko Inoue had made significant contributions to this case before the start of her leave of absence last month. Just yesterday they'd heard the news of the birth of her second child. Already Evan missed her, and he couldn't be certain of her return. She was considering taking a prolonged break from the law to be a stay-at-home mom.

Evan and Mineko went way back to a time in the late eighties when they worked together at the DA's office. Their professional association had been successful and full of fun. Now that she was gone, there would be no more bantering, that playful exchange of Minnie Mouse taunts and bald guy jokes. Mourning this realization, Evan absently rubbed the top of his shaven head, the site of his new experiment. He figured that, if he got tired of the daily electric buzz, he could always go back to wearing that ear-to-ear runner of hair, small tuft in the front. Very attractive.

Mineko was a hard act to follow, especially when it came to her intuitive ability to gain the trust of their clients and gently draw them out in ways that benefited the case. "Henrietta" missed her. By tacit understanding, Mineko was the only person allowed to call Mrs. Edmonds by her first name. Joel couldn't fill those shoes, and so Evan was now the holder of the arthritic hands. It wasn't going so badly. With his open face and sunny smile, Evan garnered trust in all who met him. Mrs. Edmonds liked him, it was clear, and he liked her back, with a deep feeling of compassion for her plight.

Still standing, occasionally pacing, Joel continued his overview of Mineko's research. "The initial outlay of $79.99 for the product is only the beginning for half of these victims. There were other consequential expenses. Sickness, doctor bills, missed days of work. Some of these victims bought second and third courses of Life Source, thinking they just hadn't taken enough of the crap! Averaged out, the costs come to $350 per victim. That's three hundred fifty million we've proved, just for the million victims we've identified. And that group is only the tip of the iceberg. We may never locate all of the victims."

"That's another point we can make. Tripp's customer records were incomplete and unreliable. The real victim count is likely triple that number. So, three fifty it is. That'll be our counteroffer, and it's a compromise—"

"—because we also have a theory for five hundred. His entire estimated net worth, all from sales of Life Source. He has no other income."

"Exactly. Two measures, five hundred if we go to trial, three fifty if we settle. Either way, we're not going to find a middle ground on Monday. Tripp's lawyers are so completely off the mark. I doubt Rajani will go any higher while the criminal charges are still pending. She's playing that card, saying we won't be able to prove our case without a criminal conviction."

"Who's she kidding?" Joel started pacing again, hands in pants pockets. This is how most of their conversations went. Evan comfortably seated, Joel in motion. "The FTC injunction *alone* proves our theory of deceptive advertising. We don't need the criminal conviction! But there's still no way that Xavier is going to get an acquittal. Look at this." He laughed and gestured toward the television screen. "Tripp conveniently made the criminal case against himself! He's openly taunting the federal injunction. He *asked* to be indicted for contempt!"

"Still, they're a tough team, Joel. We can't get too comfortable."

Tripp's attorneys were the high-powered defense team, Choudhary & Asante, PC. Civil litigator Rajani Choudhary was handling the class action. Evan had squared off against her several times, the most notable a defamation lawsuit in 1994, when she put Evan on the defensive. Rajani's partner, Xavier

Asante, handled the white collar criminal defense in their law firm. If there was anything that could be done for Darren Tripp, these two could swing it.

Joel halted mid step, crossed his arms, and regarded Evan dead on. "Who's looking comfortable?"

Irony? Self-awareness? There wasn't even a hint of a smile on Joel's face.

"Good," said Evan, hiding his amusement. "I didn't think you looked too comfortable."

Friday night was, by tradition, pizza night. At seven o'clock, the family was at the dining room table, Dana and Evan on one side, Natalie and Travis on the other, paper plates and napkins all around, and a monstrous, square box in the middle. Pepperoni and mushroom.

Grandma Brenda had declined an invitation to dine with them and was then on a commuter train home to New Rochelle. Her confession to the missed ballet class hadn't been a cause for censure or even a harsh look from Dana, who was distracted and easily swayed by a competing principle of parenting. Dana encouraged relationships with family members and accepted the occasional interruptions in schedule caused by Cheryl's unpredictable appearances. There was value in a surrender to spontaneous, healthy impulse—an aspect of personality that didn't come naturally to Dana. Evan and his mother were better at it. Cheryl, even better.

There'd been exciting stories of the day's events—Tally's fun and games with Aunt Cheryl, Tug's home run and skillful plays at first base. Now, stories told, the mouths were stuffed and busy chewing. Tally had carefully picked the mushrooms off of her pizza and piled them on her plate. "Here, Daddy," she said with a full mouth. "These are for you."

"Thanks, Squirt!" Evan reached across the table, grabbed

her plate, and unceremoniously scraped the pile onto his own plate, using Tally's half-eaten slice. "Hmm... You don't want this bit of pepperoni, do you?" He pointed to her dinner, dangling in his hand.

"*Daddy!*"

"Just one?"

"Your diet! I'm only giving you the *mushrooms*. You can eat all the vegetables you want!" She was repeating Evan's wisdom, frequently stated out loud as a reminder not to let his weight creep up again. In the days before he met Dana, he might have scarfed down more than half of this huge pizza pie all on his own. The effort grew more difficult as he approached middle age, even with his intense regimen of jogging and calisthenics.

"I'm glad you're looking out for my midriff!" He returned her plate and shoveled the mushrooms into his mouth with a plastic fork.

"They're not vegetables," said Travis with authority. "They're funguses."

"Is it fungi or funguses?" Dana asked no one in particular.

Evan pretended to gag.

"Don't worry," Travis assured him. "I don't think they put the poisonous kind on pizza."

Evan grabbed his stomach, rolled his eyes up into the sockets, and slumped forward, letting his forehead drop onto an empty spot of the table. The kids screamed with laughter.

When the merriment subsided, Dana caught Evan's eye, and they exchanged a look that said it was time to make her announcement. They'd formulated a backup plan in case an adjournment didn't come through. A week from Saturday, they'd all drive to the shore. Dana would stay over Saturday night and part of Sunday, drive home Sunday night, go to court Monday morning, and drive back to the shore Monday afternoon. A mere three hours each way. But the plan didn't take into account any possible snafus, the kinds of hitches that were endemic to the court system. Interruptions and postponements of every imaginable kind could extend a hearing beyond its anticipated schedule.

"Kids, I might have to miss part of the vacation."

Animal sounds of chewing, heavy breathing, and swallowing met her ears. No one looked at anyone else. Natalie found a stray piece of mushroom embedded in the cheese and picked it off. Travis rolled up a strip of pizza and jammed half of it into his mouth.

Dana explained. "I hope it won't be more than a day or so. I might have to go to court on the first Monday of our vacation."

Natalie sat up, her eyes gleaming, the wheels spinning. "Monday?"

"Mm-hmm," said Dana.

"That's okay, Mommy. The theater's dark on Monday!"

What was *that* all about? "The theater?"

"Aunt Cheryl can come instead of you!"

Dana's shoulders sagged just slightly. The air was suddenly dry and hot, making her eyes sting. She had nothing more to say. She lifted her slice of pizza and put it back down without taking a bite. Travis was still chewing, but slower and quieter now. Natalie's eyes searched her parents' faces.

Evan put his arm around Dana's shoulder and kissed her temple. Keeping his arm around her, he directed his gaze at the children, one at a time. "Listen here!" he said in a stern voice.

Immediately, they abandoned their slices. Daddy *never* sounded like this.

Dana made a grimace of a smile, but her eyes couldn't meet any of theirs. The sting wouldn't go away. She let Evan take control.

"Aunt Cheryl can come. We love Aunt Cheryl. She's always welcome. But no one, ever, may come *instead* of your mother. This is *her* vacation."

Natalie's lower lip started to quiver violently, and her eyes were pools of liquid. Travis, the stone statue, gazed in horror at his mother's face.

"Mommy!" Natalie screeched and burst into tears.

"Come here," she said, turning sideways in her chair.

Natalie ran around the table and jumped into her mother's lap.

Travis stood. "Are you okay, Mom?" His voice broke.

"You too," she said over Natalie's head. "Come here." He came around the table and put his arms around Tally and Mom both. At her back, Evan leaned over, his arms just making it around the entire group that was his family.

"I love you guys so much," Dana whispered.

Breath, hair, skin, warmth, tears. Heart. This family had everything it needed—except, perhaps, a long overdue vacation.

5 »   ALONE

SATURDAY AND FREEDOM. It was a nice feeling in so many ways, until that point in the afternoon when it got just a bit too quiet. Sometimes, she invited friends over for cards or lunch or tea. Today would be different, marked by a special occasion. Alone this morning, family this afternoon.

Brenda sipped her tea and glanced up at the wall. The hands of the old kitchen clock pointed to the eight and the three. In this house, the kitchen clock had always been the kitchen clock. She remembered the day that she and Albert purchased it at the Sears store downtown (now long gone). The boys were very young, and they were at her sister's that day. Errands. In those days, this is what young parents did when their children were being looked after by family or sitters.

They brought the clock home to a quiet house. Albert measured the electric cord, tapped a nail into the wall at the correct height, hung the clock, and plugged it into the outlet near the floor. Encased in brown cloth, the electric cord still made its presence known against the yellow wall. Five years ago, when Brenda hired painters to apply a fresh coat of bright yellow, she took the clock down but instructed them: "Don't remove that nail! I need it!" Now, the clock hung on a nail thick with yellow paint. Sturdy nails and good workmanship lasted forever. From time to time, the boys suggested that she purchase a battery-operated clock, but why would anyone want to worry about changing batteries?

Her medication, taken at seven o'clock, was doing its job,

and the pain had dulled to the level of background elevator music. At any moment, someone in the building could pitch it up again to full volume, with static and a screeching treble. She gazed out the kitchen window into the backyard. It was a sunny morning, with a ray of light hitting just so on the red bird house hanging from a low branch of the Japanese maple. Albert hung that bird house in the spring of the year he died, 1983. Cruel for a person to die so young. A massive heart attack at the age of fifty-three, when she was only fifty-one. After the years of grieving, she might have found someone to marry. But by the time she thought of it, the idea seemed absurd and more of a burden than it was worth. She'd been alone now these eighteen years.

But of course she wasn't alone. She had Al, Evan, and their families. Her family.

Her boys had grown up in this house, where they'd moved when Evan was just a baby. These walls had gone through many transformations. She glanced around the kitchen and admired the way she'd decorated it, the yellow walls, the chintz curtains, the rack of shining copper saucepans she rarely used, and on the counter, a set of matching glazed pottery containers labeled for flour, sugar, coffee, and tea. White with blue letters. So pretty.

Oh, what a beautiful morning! But there was work to do.

Singing her song in full voice, Brenda took the cup of tea along with her into the study. Her song stopped at the threshold. The space was tight and dark, overflowing with books, files, and papers. She turned on the overhead and the desk lamp. That was better. In the far corner of the small desk was a computer that Evan had bought for her and installed, giving her a short lesson in its operation. Now, the monitor was nearly hidden behind a stack of old mail. A few years ago, Al showed her again how to use it, but she hadn't turned it on since. The black rotary dial phone on the near corner of the desk was more useful.

"Running out of room," she said to the four walls. There were many piles on the desk and on top of the file cabinet. This week's mail was teetering on top of the middle stack, right where she'd put it upon arriving home last night.

She found a small empty spot for her tea cup and started to sort through the pile, looking for new opportunities, but mostly checking up on the old ones. There was one in particular she was looking for. There should be an envelope containing a check with her winnings. She'd lost track of time, but the check had to be past due. How long had it been? About a month since she paid the taxes? She sorted through once, twice, but it wasn't there.

It was time to make an inquiry. The boys would see—she was on top of her personal business. After squaring away this particular matter, she'd do some more thinking about that investment advisor who contacted her last week. It seemed a good idea to hire someone like him.

The thing to do would be to find the first mailing, the one she'd answered with the return envelope provided. Certainly the letter would have an address, and maybe even a phone number to call. Most likely, it was in that pile toward the back of the desk. She wanted to find it and take care of this business now so she could turn to the task of wrapping Ian's gift. It was waiting for her in the basement, on the craft table, with a little box to put it in and the wrapping paper. Finding a graduation gift had been a perplexing task. She'd gone to a hundred stores, but the effort had paid off. She ended up with the perfect thing! A wallet made of Superman comics. So clever, the comics were somehow laminated into a stiff fabric and sewn into a wallet. Ian always loved it when she read the comics to him, and he'd been Superman more than once for Halloween. To sweeten the gift, she'd put a crisp twenty dollar bill inside.

The phone rang. She sat down and answered it. Al was calling. "Hi, Mom. Did you have a good week?"

"Just wonderful! Those babies sure keep me hopping. How's Ian? Ready for the big day?"

"Sure is."

"Can't wait to give him a big hug and congratulations!"

There was a pause. "That's great, Mom, but just don't be too disappointed if he's more interested in his friends today than any of us. You know how teenagers are."

"Oh, I know, I know…" She laughed.

"A number of his friends will be at the party later."

"Teenagers! I know."

"Can I pick you up at one? Commencement doesn't start until two, but the high school will be mobbed. I want to get there early."

"One o'clock, yes, very fine. And Kelly…?"

"She'll be with us." Kelly, now twenty years old, was home from college for the summer. "Christine and Kelly will be in the car with me when I pick you up. Ian is going separately, and Evan will meet us there with his family."

"Yes, and Evan said they'll come over to your party afterward. You have a good day for it."

"We'll be in the backyard. I've got hot dogs and hamburgers to barbeque. It's going to be 75 or 80, so wear something comfortable."

"But I'll be dressed for the ceremony!" She'd planned on the purple suit, nylon stockings, white pumps, and the hat with the baby's breath and miniature pink roses. Now there was a barbeque to think of.

"You don't need to dress up. It's a high school auditorium. No air conditioning, miserable, "Pomp and Circumstance" off key. Shaky bleachers. That's another reason to be early, to get you a good seat. We don't want to be climbing up those wooden risers."

Heavens. She hadn't thought of any of this. Another task. Rethink the outfit! Al was right. She was not the person to be climbing up wooden risers, not with these knees, but she wasn't about to admit it. "Thank you for the warning."

"Just trying to keep everyone happy."

"Alrighty, then. See you at one."

She hung up and had a funny, instant certainty that she'd failed to say goodbye. But of course she had. And here! Just under her right hand, as she hung up the phone with her left, was the paper she'd been looking for! Maybe that's the reason she'd been in a rush to end the call.

The outside envelope had been sliced open neatly at the top with her letter opener. The letter was folded up again and placed sideways inside, along with its funny enclosure. All that was left of the enclosure was a slick, square piece of waxed paper edged in silver with the outline of a star where she'd peeled off the sticker. The instructions were very precise, as she recalled. The silver star was to be affixed in the box on the return postcard, next to the words, "Yes, I want to claim my winnings!" In the return envelope provided, she'd placed the postcard and her check for the taxes. Sealed it, mailed it ... but failed to write down the address for future reference. Oh, well, it must be on the letter or on the large, outside envelope.

She looked, and looked again. Must have missed it. She looked, and looked again.

The telephone rang, and this time, she felt a bit irritated by the shrill sound. The volume was turned up loud, in case she was elsewhere in the house when it rang. What did Al want now?

"Hello?"

"Mrs. Goodhue?"

"Yes, speaking." She recognized the voice, silky and gentle like a warm bath. But she waited for him to say his name to be sure.

"It's Mike Lane, from Guarantee Trust."

"Well, hello Mr. Lane." She'd told him last time that she was home only on weekends. He must have remembered.

And then he began to talk. His knowledge and experience were evident, and his manner was reassuring. This was the kind of person she needed, and he was having little trouble convincing her to make use of his services. And why not? Why not get her house in order and make her financial future secure? There was nothing to pay up front. Why not guarantee she would never be a burden to anyone, free of worry and doubt, every contingency planned for?

By the end of their conversation, she agreed with his suggestion to arrange a meeting.

"Later today, perhaps?" he asked.

"Oh, no, no, I simply can't! My grandson is graduating high school. I'm busy all day."

"Congratulations! That's a milestone! You must be very proud."

"Thank you, I am. But tomorrow I'm free. Are you available then?" Maybe this was presumptuous. Hard to think that a busy investment advisor would be so accommodating, willing to work on a Sunday. "You could come by tomorrow after church. I'll be home about twelve."

"That suits my schedule just fine."

"Alrighty. I'll put the coffee on and have a light lunch for you."

"Please, Mrs. Goodhue. Don't go to any trouble."

She gave him the address and directions before hanging up. This time, there was no question. She hadn't forgotten to say a proper goodbye.

She stood up and navigated the narrow passage between the desk and the file cabinet, on her way to the door. Her previous mission was forgotten, replaced by the music in her head. It was time to wrap Ian's present and dig out something to wear for a barbeque. *Everything's going my way!*

6 »   BROTHER

SING SING SUNDAY. That's what Ellen called her weekly hour with Antoine. As his attorney, she was allowed to visit her brother at the state prison any day of the week, but Sunday was her usual.

She met with him in the common visiting area like any other family member. Lawyers had an easier time than the general public getting through the door. Less arduous and humiliating. She didn't need to wait in line with mothers and sisters and brothers and lovers, impatient children and crying babies. Still, she was required to go through the metal detector, and although the guards knew her, they demanded her ID and logged it in.

There'd been other attorneys before her, the one who represented Antoine at trial, and the one who handled his appeal. The losers, the ones she'd hired, making it all the more galling. Back then, Ellen was a prosecutor and couldn't represent her own brother. Maybe it wasn't a strict conflict of interest—Antoine was being prosecuted by the Westchester County DA, not by her employer, the Manhattan DA. But it was against her employment contract to represent private clients, so she took out a loan to pay for his lawyers. Antoine's legal troubles started in 1993, and she resigned her job in 1994, on the day he lost his appeal and started serving hard time. She'd been fighting for him ever since and had nothing to show for it, making her just as much a loser as the others.

On this particular Sunday, her favorite guard escorted her

inside. He was a burly man of about forty with a big smile. She'd gotten to know him by name. Victor. "Hate" was tattooed, one letter per knuckle, on his left hand, "Love" on his right. She'd asked him once about the left because his personality leaned so prominently to the right. "A mistake of my youth," he said. "I thought I was tough. But I'm gonna burn it off one day. Make it into double love."

Her brother had spoken of special correction officers, people like Victor, who were more than just guards because they cared about the prisoners, showed them respect, mentored, and provided the encouragement to keep going, keep trying. Victor winked at Ellen as he unlocked the visiting room door, showing his "Love" with a flash of the card key. "Stay as long as you like," he said. "I'll be here all day." Another wink and he was gone.

It was early, and the visiting area was nearly empty. There were no private rooms, just one big place for everybody, guarded by correction officers and security cameras on the periphery. There'd never been an incident on her Sing Sing Sundays. The prisoners looked forward to visits and were on their best behavior. She'd been here plenty of times when it started out quiet and empty, the faint scent of industrial-strength ammonia hanging in the air. Gradually, the space would fill with human bodies, their voices sad or falsely optimistic, and their ever-changing combinations of odors— cheap perfume, Cheetos, sweat, curdled milk, hair gel, dirty diapers. It was one giant family picnic, without ventilation.

The vast, linoleum-floored room had puke-green walls and thick metal screens over the windows, dozens of orange plastic chairs, and a few tables reserved for group visits. Ellen found two chairs that weren't broken and placed them in the usual corner to wait for Antoine, where she gathered her thoughts. What news did she have for him today? Nothing.

Five minutes of quiet desperation ticked off before "Love" brought him in.

"Hey, baby brother." She stood and hugged him.

"Sis. Thanks for coming." He said this every time—never took her for granted. She was so proud of his attitude that she told their mother about it one day, a few years back, when she stopped home after a visit to Sing Sing. Their mother had this to say: "He's manipulating you. Nice words just to make sure you'll keep coming." Mom hadn't been to see him even once.

Anyone could tell that Ellen was Antoine's sister. They were both small-boned, thin, and relatively short. She was five-three, he was five-seven. They bore the finely-etched features and black hair of their French forebears. After so many years of prison, they'd acquired another common attribute: a jittery, simmering frustration beneath the intelligent exterior. The main difference between them was Ellen's comparatively better-rested look. Antoine's eyes were sunken into purple-green shadows.

"Heard anything about Brittany and Heather?" One of Antoine's weekly questions. His twin daughters, the result of a brief romantic liaison, were twelve years old by now. He'd never married the mother, but she'd given him visitation rights, and he'd made child support payments to the best of his ability—before his arrest. The mother's reaction to Antoine's legal troubles was immediate. She got a protective order and cut off all contact during the time he was out on bail, fighting the case. Then, just to be sure he'd never bother her again, she moved, keeping the new address a secret. Ellen tracked them down, but was not allowed to visit. She missed her nieces and the many sweet times she'd spent with Antoine and the girls when they were small. What little news she had of them now was acquired by adopting various imaginative ruses when contacting their school, friends, coaches, or church.

"Sorry. Nothing new. I'm not sure what they have planned for the summer." She quickly changed the subject. "Only five weeks to go," she said, putting a lilt in her voice. They both anxiously awaited his upcoming parole hearing. The first. Antoine was serving an indeterminate prison term of seven to twenty-one years. If the parole board thought he was a good risk for release, he could serve the balance of his term on the outside, under the supervision of a parole officer.

"No guarantees."

"But they won't deny you. Even if the fools are blind to your innocence, they can't ignore your prison record. It's stellar. No infractions. Doing your time in peace. Earned your place in the honor block." After the first five years in a cell block with the general population, Antoine was transferred to the coveted special housing unit for prisoners with the best institutional records, where he was granted additional privileges and extra time out of his cell to roam freely in the common areas of the unit. "There's no reason for them to turn you down," Ellen insisted.

Antoine didn't move or speak for a moment, examining the floor as he sat bent over with elbows on knees. He lifted his head and looked at her askance, like she didn't know the half of it. "The victims. It's always the victims." He dropped his gaze again, letting his head dangle from a limp neck.

"Hah!" She shook her head in disgust. "Those people are someone else's victims! And you're *one* of them!" The torment of this thought wouldn't let her go. Her vision went to the scene she'd imagined a thousand times. Nine years ago, a pernicious con man dug his talons into Antoine, a bright, tender, confident young man of twenty-six, a recent graduate of business school. It was 1992, a time when Ellen was preoccupied with her own life. She let this villain use her baby brother for months. Antoine was now thirty-five, and she was thirty-nine. Irretrievable years were gone. Every day of his incarceration was another day wasted in two lives.

He raised his head and matched her look. "You have no idea how many inmates think they've got it made before their parole hearing. Then they find out that everyone and his cousin has something to say to the board. The victims and their families write letters and get their priests and bosses and friends to write letters. 'Keep him in! Look how he ruined my life! Don't let it happen to anyone else!' You better believe the victims in my case are doing the same thing. They'll be sure to mention that everything was taken from them and their families and it was never paid back."

Ellen sprang to her feet. She couldn't bear this. "How can you pay them back when you never took anything?" She paced around his chair until she saw one of the guards eyeing her. Better cool it.

"Sit down," Antoine whispered.

She sat. "Okay. Look, I'm writing my own letter to the parole board. I'll show you next week, and you can give me your suggestions. We'll put everything in there. The whole story."

As if the whole story hadn't been given before. Backed with nothing. No hard evidence. No soft evidence. It was still Antoine's word against what the prosecutor called a "mountain" of documents proving his commission of multiple counts of grand larceny and scheme to defraud.

There was no need to speak of it now, the evidence they'd gone over again and again, year after year, the truth that Ellen believed was buried under the surface and hadn't been able to prove in a court of law. The irony was that they didn't have to prove his innocence. They only had to raise a reasonable doubt, and she'd failed even at that.

During the jury trial in 1993, Ellen's word hadn't counted

for much. She'd testified for the defense, truthfully, about her memories of what Antoine had told her when he was first "hired." He was excited about his new job as a loan officer for a mortgage lender in White Plains, a company named Security National. He worked closely with his boss, Mason Landers. Ellen intentionally added a certain detail to her testimony: the way Antoine had uttered that name with a look of reverence in his eyes. The prosecutor objected on the ground that her description was an unsupported opinion and not a fact, but the court overruled the objection. Ellen testified that the manner in which Antoine spoke of his boss made it easy for her to remember the name. He gave it a theatrical sound. She also told the jury that her brother described Security National as a thriving business. Antoine met with clients every day, very often in their homes, and he attended all the closings with Landers, three or four per week.

This was as far as Ellen could go, repeating Antoine's words to the best of her recollection. Her testimony was admitted into evidence over the prosecutor's vociferous objection that all of it was hearsay. This was the single, small victory chalked up by Antoine's unimpressive trial attorney. He convinced the court that Ellen's testimony was admissible to prove Antoine's state of mind. It wasn't hearsay because it wasn't offered to prove the "truth" of what he had told Ellen. Antoine wasn't trying to convince the jury that he actually worked for a legitimate mortgage lender, but simply that this is what he thought. He was duped by Landers.

Ultimately, the jury couldn't see past the "mountain" of paper evidence that investigators had seized at Security National's "headquarters." Of course, Landers was long gone by the time they entered that tiny office with a search warrant in hand. The mastermind of the scheme alluded capture, leaving behind plenty of tangible evidence connecting Antoine to dozens of crimes. Contracts he signed in his capacity as a loan officer. Titles to residential real property in the names of Antoine Fortier and Security National as co-owners. A post office box key and checks payable to Security National, mailed to that box. A bank account with deposit slips in Antoine's handwriting and checks he had signed, payable to their "clients."

Security National was a "full service mortgage scammer," argued the prosecutor. Creative con artists Landers and Fortier victimized distressed homeowners, the elderly, and anybody who simply wanted to save money on interest payments. Refinancing a mortgage through Security National required the payment of an upfront fee to cover "administrative costs" and the homeowner's signature on "modification" papers, including a deed to the property disguised as a "security interest" agreement. Reverse mortgages were offered to retired homeowners on fixed incomes who wished to receive monthly checks based on the equity in their homes. They also entered into "security interest" agreements, signing away their ownership to the property, only to find that the checks stopped coming after a month or two. Other victims were told that their current mortgage lender had assigned their loan to Security National for collection. The homeowners would start sending monthly mortgage payments to the post office box address, only to receive a default notice a few months later from the actual lender.

This "mountain" of evidence proved that, over the course of six months, the Security National team received hundreds of thousands of dollars in illegal upfront fees, two million in proceeds from flipped properties, and titles to scores of other properties, cumulatively valued in the millions. Whose pockets were lined with all of this plunder? Investigators failed to uncover any eyebrow-raising sums in Antoine's possession, although they were convinced that he had, somehow, squirreled away his share of the loot in a place beyond detection. Money like that simply didn't vanish.

Oh, yes it did. The money disappeared on the day Landers left town.

If the documentary evidence wasn't enough, the prosecution had the case sewn up with a parade of hapless victims. One by one they testified: the young, the old, nervous, scared, confused, angry, or destitute. They related visits to their homes by a handsome, intelligent, vibrant young man who was sometimes alone, sometimes accompanied by a distinguished fellow of about forty-five with salt-and-pepper hair. The victims had given everything away to these two scammers, never to be made whole again. And yes, they all recognized Antoine in the courtroom and pointed a finger at him when prompted to do so. "*He's* the one who came to my home."

In the early days of their nightmare, Ellen's abiding faith in her brother wasn't consistently pure. After his arrest, during the terrible buildup to the trial, the limits of her loyalty and belief in him were tested. She would never forget the day when she and Antoine were at the office of his trial attorney, and she learned, for the first time, the extent of the evidence against him. The prosecution had disclosed the documentary evidence, and a big box of it sat on the table before her. Ellen pulled out one document after another, dumbfounded, incredulous. She asked the attorney to leave the room, to give her a few minutes alone with Antoine. She knew her brother better than anyone, and she would get to the bottom of this.

When they were alone, she asked him in a voice barely above a whisper, "Why is your name on all the deeds?"

Antoine was fighting back tears, and suddenly he was the little boy she'd grown up with. "These aren't meant to be deeds," he said stubbornly.

"They look like deeds to me."

"Not when you read them together with the other documents in the deal. You have to read it all together."

This was hard to take. Her brother couldn't see the documents for what they were. It was easy to understand how a homeowner could be duped by a fast-talking loan officer from a company named "Security National" as he handed over one document after another, explaining that each was an integral part of a security agreement. An average person could be tricked by the fine print and legalese. But her brother was intelligent. Her brother had an MBA from a high-ranking university.

"Landers told you this?"

"Yes."

"And you believed him?"

Antoine tried to meet her eyes and failed. He turned his head but couldn't hide the small quiver in his lip or the tear hastily brushed aside. She didn't need his answer to that question. She saw it. Still, she persisted. "Why is your name on all these deeds—or security agreements, as you call them?"

"Mason said the deal wouldn't work without a name. If anything happened to the corporation, one of us would still hold the security interest. We backed everything up, to guarantee that the transaction wouldn't fall through. These were my clients." Antoine pointed to the deeds. "Mason put his name on other documents for clients I didn't help him with."

"So, where are *those* documents?"

"I don't know. They should have been in the office when they executed the search warrant."

"Well, apparently they weren't."

He shook his head. "Mason…"

Sure, Mason wouldn't be dumb enough to leave anything

with his name on it lying around. As for the money in the bank and the properties that had already been flipped, Mason cleaned up and took off with the cash.

That afternoon in the lawyer's office, as Ellen confronted her brother with the evidence, her incredulity turned to anger and then to overwhelming regret because, how could she not believe him? *Look at him.* Crestfallen expression, shoulders slumped in defeat, visibly engaged in his internal battle with emotion. Hating himself. To be so naïve and gullible. He was taken. He was a victim. And he was, after all, still a boy, her little brother.

When they were children, Ellen created a fantasy world of espionage, replete with messages in secret code. An impressionable little boy looked on as she "discovered" the notes she'd hidden under rocks in the backyard and inside crevices in the foundation of their house. Antoine's eyes were wide and unquestioning as she translated these notes, describing the dangers and threats that would befall them. Their enemies planned to kidnap their cat Snowy if they didn't send a return message of surrender, signed in blood. The enemy commando would force their mother to fix liver and onions every night for dinner if they didn't cooperate with his demands. Ellen had convinced her brother of many things. Landers had done the same.

Her faith was tested but never lost. Now, after hundreds of prison visits, brother and sister were fully steeped in bitterness. Ellen's had always been more pronounced than Antoine's. She couldn't fathom how an innocent person serving seven to twenty-one years in prison, one day at a time, could keep his spirits from sinking dangerously low. But on this day, as they spoke of his first chance at parole, he seemed different. Usually she found a glimmer of buried hope in his eyes. Today, he exuded pure despondence and a willingness to pin the blame outside himself.

"Go ahead and put everything in that letter to the parole board," he told her. "It'll get us nowhere. Nothing has worked."

This was the most stinging indictment of all—his slipping confidence in her ability to help him, the resignation to fate and loss of all hope.

"We have to go in with confidence," she persisted.

"We?" He emitted a sharp laugh. "You're not the one going in to talk to the board. I have no hope. But don't take it personally. You've done everything you could."

Maybe that was true. She'd done everything she could think of, and yet, there had to be something else to try. She'd gone through the complete case files at the offices of Antoine's attorneys, boxes of documents and the entire trial transcript. She looked for weaknesses in the testimony and possible falsehoods. There had to be something exculpatory, but all she found was more heartbreak. She made a FOIL request for the prosecutor's case file, but most of the papers were withheld from her as privileged work product. Even without any new evidence, Ellen filed a post-conviction proceeding, arguing that the trial evidence failed to prove Antoine's knowing involvement in these crimes. She lost. A year later she arranged a meeting with an executive ADA at the Westchester County DA's Office. He wasn't sympathetic and wasn't willing to reopen the investigation. Without any personal connections at that office she had no influence, no authority to get inside the door, to poke around in the record room, to sift through the files. She needed full access, and it was impossible.

"Go on now," Antoine said. "Go home and write the letter and don't think there's anything else you can do. You've done everything you could. You've done enough."

As he spoke, his voice was swallowed, its distinctiveness

rubbed out. They sat in a buzzing hive. She hadn't noticed it until now, the sounds and smells that invaded the small corner they occupied. The visiting room had been filling up. Antoine was speaking, his lips moving, the words apparently what she thought them to be, but his expression seemed to be saying something else. She looked into his eyes, and these were the thoughts she read:

You started an innocence project to free the wrongly convicted. But you haven't done anything for me, your own brother. I'm innocent, and you haven't set me free!

7 »   INVESTMENT

THIS WEEK, UNLIKE the last, Brenda would have more free time during the day. The children were signed up for "day camp" from nine to three. She didn't quite understand how something could be called a "camp" when it was headquartered on the second floor of a thirty-story building in New York City. There would be outdoor activities, to be sure, trips to a swimming pool and sojourns in Central Park. Trees and squirrels, anyway. And the children might even see a few city inhabitants that could be described as "wildlife."

When the boys were young, Brenda and Al used to take them camping. They had no money, and it was the cheapest vacation they could manage. The Ford was piled high with four sleeping bags, a tent, a Coleman stove, and a cooler with melted ice that sloshed whenever the car took a curve on a winding mountain road. A lake, a forest. Isolation. A campfire. *I love the fireside*... Her favorite camp song. *Boom-dee-ah-dah, boom, boom, boom*... She would direct the family in a four-part round, each voice starting up on a new line. She voiced her lead part in a heartfelt soprano while the others reluctantly chimed in. Al Jr. was the one who lost his place most often. When the round fell apart, he'd protest that the song was girlish, and the next time around, he'd sing it in falsetto. Evan mimicked everything his older brother did, and then Al Sr. would jump on the bandwagon. Before long, she was surrounded by a screeching mockery.

Perhaps it would have been nice to have a little girl. She

imagined herself—a younger self—in a different family with a sweet little girl or two.

Now, that was unfair. She really didn't mean it about the girl. Two healthy boys were more than anyone could ask for, and her boys had grown up to be wonderful men who blessed her with plenty of female family members: Christine, Kelly, Dana, and Natalie. And Cheryl, who evoked bittersweet regrets in Brenda about her failure to pursue a stage career. Oh well.

At the start of this new week, Brenda rose at six thirty. Evan was out on a jog, Dana was in the shower, and the kids were still sleeping. Brenda was in the kitchen making coffee, humming that tune, when Dana walked in. She was wearing a bathrobe, and her shoulder-length, dark brunette hair was still wet, making it look almost black. "What's that melody? I think I know it."

"An old camp song. 'I Love the Mountains.'" She sang the first two lines.

"That was my *favorite* song! I used to sing it in Girl Scouts!" Dana started the song anew, and they sang an entire verse in unison.

"Let's try a round! I'll go first." Brenda launched it, and Dana came in on the second line. Their round was holding up admirably when Evan walked in, panting and dripping with sweat. He chuckled with delight and began to sing in falsetto.

The women stopped short. "Oh, you're terrible!" his mother said. "You ruined it!"

"Sorry, Mom." He placed a flat palm on his chest and looked off into the distance. "I was transported to a time long ago—the camping trips of my youth."

"That song brings back memories for me too," said Dana. "Let's go camping!"

"Instead of the beach?"

"No. We'll take another vacation. Maybe in August? Let's

go to the mountains!"

"You're ready for it, girl. You're so miserable, you'd go anywhere. Let me take you where you want to go." He leaned in for a kiss.

Dana pressed her fingertips against his soaked tee-shirt. "I think you'd rather take a shower."

"I'm staying out of this," said Brenda. She started humming again and walked off to put some bread in the toaster.

While Evan was in the shower, the two women sat across from each other at the table and had their coffee and toast.

"Hopefully this week will be a little less crazy for you," said Dana. "More like the school year."

"Oh, but we had a great time last week."

"That's good. Did the kids behave? How were they, really?"

Dana, more than Evan, liked to ask these kinds of questions. How were the kids? Were they little angels or little monsters? And (the implied questions): Were they too much for Brenda to handle? Were they actually safe with her?

Now, that was ridiculous too! She knew Dana well enough to understand the true motivation behind the questions. It was a normal sort of motherly concern, with a bit of regret about her career mixed in. Dana wanted information about her children. She was missing so many precious moments and needed to envision their day. Hadn't Brenda been the same way about Al Jr. and Evan, the minute they started going to school?

"Last week was fun," said Brenda. "They were normal kids. Curious, bright, and excited. And cranky when they got bored. Testy and demanding sometimes. That's the way it is with kids. They keep you hopping!"

"You're a wonder, Brenda. I hope this means you're still enjoying this. They're crazy about you. I hear it from them all the time."

"And I'm crazy about them. They're full of love. I'm more than happy with everything. I wouldn't trade places with anyone. Not for the world."

"I'm so thankful you're here!" Dana touched her hand and gave it a little squeeze. "I have to get ready now. Thanks for the coffee." She stood and pushed away from the table.

A moment later, Evan came out, poured a cup of coffee, and took the seat Dana had vacated. A lone slice of cold toast sat on the plate in the center of the table. He claimed it, smeared strawberry jam on a corner, and took a bite.

"Let me get you something better than that," said Brenda.

"I'm fine, Mom." He took three more bites, and the slice was gone. Still chewing, he said, "What do you plan to do with your extra free time today?"

Evan's question was transparently innocent. Whenever she had a conversation with him, it never entered her mind that there might be something behind his words. He simply wanted to know. "Oh, this and that," she answered, wondering how much information she should impart. Evan would be proud that she was taking care of her personal financial business, and she wanted his respect and pride, but not his solicitude. Above all, he shouldn't take any time away from his family to help her. She was in control of her affairs, and she wanted him to know at least that much. "I brought some paperwork from home to go over this week."

"Paperwork?" He looked at her over the rim of his coffee cup. "What kind of paperwork?"

Evan had the friendliest, most trusting blue-gray eyes of anyone she'd ever known, family and friend alike. The warmest. She wasn't biased about this. Oh, no. People had been commenting on it for years, ever since his childhood. "I brought some mail and some files from the home office. It's just some information about investments, but mostly bills and statements from my accounts. I'm organizing everything."

"Hey, that's great! Let me help you. Maybe tonight."

"Oh, no, no, no, you're so busy at work you need to relax when you get home. You don't want to be going over this stuff. It's enough to make you pull your hair out!"

"Not a problem here. I already shaved."

She chuckled. "Looks nice. Did you put something shiny on your head?"

"That's my skin."

"Sure is shiny."

"I'll try not to stand under any bright lights. Or maybe I'll hand out sunglasses at the office."

"I meant it as a compliment."

He stood, leaned over the table, and kissed her on the forehead. "Thanks, Mom. I need all the compliments I can get. But promise me one thing."

"What's that?"

"We'll go over your finances together. Soon. I'll come up some weekend, right after the vacation."

"Alrighty then. If you want to."

"Okay. Good. Gotta go now."

She watched him as he walked away from her, down the hallway to the bedroom. A proud man, a family man, responsible and generous. Any minute, his children would wake up and demand her attention. She heard Travis stirring in his room now. Natalie was always the last to rise. She would stumble out of her bedroom in a daze, sandy hair pushed up to one side.

Brenda loved these mornings. A few hours of hubbub, filled with the routine of daily living. Then, suddenly, everyone would be gone.

This morning, at seven thirty, Dana and Evan left for

work.

At eight thirty, Brenda was out the door with two children and two backpacks stuffed with lunches, swimsuits, and towels.

At nine fifteen she was back in the apartment, all alone.

Brenda needed this time. She wasn't kidding. She'd brought a bushel of work along with her. A satchel full of unopened mail, brimming with new possibilities and opportunities, and maybe she'd find that check she was waiting for. If not that, then another letter explaining the delay, something with a phone number or an address so she could inquire, nicely, when she might expect to receive her winnings.

But the most important item in her satchel was the new manila envelope holding the brochures and applications that Mike Lane had given her. He was an impressive man, with a quality she always looked for and rarely found: politeness. So many people these days were rude. Brenda had grown up in a different time, when manners were the hallmark of good character. Mr. Lane wasn't exactly of her generation— somewhere between her age and the ages of her sons—but he knew how to treat a person with respect and thoughtfulness. All afternoon, they addressed each other as "Mrs. Goodhue" and "Mr. Lane." She wanted to look at the materials he'd given her and think about it carefully. There was a lot to fill out, and she'd promised him another meeting this coming weekend.

Yesterday morning, before church, she'd arranged everything for his visit. She prepared a light lunch, triangle-cut finger sandwiches and iced tea with lemon. The dining room table was laid with two place settings of sterling and china. The stoneware didn't seem quite good enough for the occasion— her first big step toward solid security and financial independence.

The effort paid off in plenty of compliments. After his first bite from a triangle, he said, "This is absolutely delicious."

"My goodness. It's only ham and cheese!"

"But very tasty, and far more than I could have expected for our business meeting."

"I'm glad you like the lunch. I know you're a busy man, so I appreciate you coming out here on a Sunday."

"Yes, I'm busy, but maybe not as busy as you! Tell me, what is this job that keeps you away from your lovely home all week long?"

His face was alight with interest, and so, she started talking. She didn't answer his question directly because it seemed to call for background information. Otherwise, how could he understand the reasons she was leading this kind of life? She talked for quite a while without any sense of time, and at the end of it, she'd covered quite a lot and they'd eaten their sandwiches. He was easy to talk to, and he listened attentively. She told him about her husband, his death, her sons, their careers, their families. She told him about her schedule, riding the train to the city every Sunday night, taking care of Natalie and Travis Monday through Friday, taking the train home again on Friday nights. His face was caring and receptive. He said things like, "Oh," and "What did your husband do?" and "They must exhaust you."

"Not so much," she said. "The children invigorate me!"

"You're a strong woman."

Yes, she was strong, wasn't she? Still, it would be easier if Evan and Dana moved their family up here, to Westchester County. She'd mentioned the idea time and again, though it seemed to fall on deaf ears. They wouldn't have to give up their careers. Plenty of people commuted from here to the city. "Thank you," she said to Mr. Lane.

"You're healthy and strong now, but are you prepared in

case something happens? If, God forbid, you become ill or disabled?"

"I've done some thinking about it. You could say I've been worrying about it, really."

"Worrying won't pay the bills, now, will it?"

"I guess not!" His question and her answer were suddenly, overwhelmingly comical. She laughed, and he joined in, and they laughed for more than a minute, to the point that she thought she couldn't stop. But she did.

"Then you must have done some thinking about what I said on the phone."

"Yes. Yes, indeed! Especially the part about Easy Street and the monthly payments."

"Good. Then I think it's time that we...?" He gestured toward the living room, where he'd left his briefcase. She looked out over the table and the remnants of their lunch, a few crusts and crumbs, the lemon rinds floating in melted ice.

"I'm sorry," she said. "I've been going on about a lot of nonsense."

"Not at all."

"You're very kind. Let's get started."

He pushed away from the table and quickly rose to assist her. He stood at the back of her chair and gave it a slight tug to pull it out. It was a charming, chivalrous gesture— something she didn't need. But she gave him a youthful smile and accepted his hand under her elbow. The touch of a man felt good. A man other than a son.

They settled into opposite ends of the living room couch. He pulled a glossy packet out of his briefcase, laid it on the coffee table, and opened it up like a folder. Inside were a number of forms and a brochure entitled "Getting the Most Out of the Equity in Your Home."

He handed it to her, and she leafed through. "This looks

interesting. Very interesting!" She would consider this very carefully, although she could already guess what her answer would be.

8 »   MISSION

DIRECTOR ELLEN FORTIER summoned the troops, her small, ever-shifting staff of law student interns. Monday mornings, Ellen liked to start the week with an inspirational talk and work plan. Today, there were five students. She could name two of them without a thought. Oliver and Janet. They'd been with her for the spring semester and were continuing into the summer. The other two boys and a girl were newbies, comprising a nameless lump of enthusiastic youth. All five were about twenty-three or twenty-four years old.

Ellen had been just like them at that age. Determined to build a better world. And what had she done with that dream? Bought into a false promise. "If you're thirsty for justice, go to the DA's office," advised counselors, professors, and recruiters. All lies. But her years at the DA's office hadn't been a complete waste. She'd learned valuable lessons. Working in their midst, she'd come to know exactly how prosecutors thought. Most of them were only in their twenties and thirties, yet they wielded their authority like sage elders, never questioning their entitlement to decide the fate of any suspect the police dragged into court. Did the defendant deserve a deal or an indictment for a heinous felony? This was the choice left to the whim of prosecutorial discretion, and Ellen was sickened by it. She'd come to know their thought processes, their practices and assumptions and prejudices and knee-jerk reactions. It was now part of her plan to use all of this against them.

She had no fondness for any of them, those people she used to work with. In her final months at the DA's office, she'd born the unbearable weight of her personal woes. Antoine's legal troubles and the finality of his prison sentence. A fiancé who called off the wedding, unwilling to marry into a disreputable family. Tough mothers. The mother who disowned her son, the convicted felon. The mother who built a brick wall between her twin daughters and their father, the jailbird, and the jailbird's sister, Ellen. It seemed she'd lost everyone. There was no one left for her.

As a new start, Ellen quit the DA's office and founded Justice Restored on the hope of freeing Antoine. The startup period was frustrating. She begged for funding and had to take on paying clients just to make a living. Her clients were all criminal defendants. She learned the ropes on the defense side and made contacts with the defense bar. Slowly, J.R. gathered strength and momentum. While working to free Antoine, she experimented with other cases, searching for the trick or procedure or design she needed to help her brother. She knew the Manhattan DA's office from the inside; but did the Westchester DA's office operate in the same way? She concentrated on cases prosecuted in those two counties, just to learn the differences and similarities. Victories were few and far between. One in 1996, another in 1999. Then, two in a row this year. Still, there was no help for Antoine.

By now, the organization had grown to the point that she needed a revolving door of interns just to screen the thousands of applications that flooded their offices every year. J.R. had the resources to accept only a fraction of these. Ellen was the sole fulltime attorney, aided by a continual rotation of private counsel, who volunteered hours to fulfill their professional pro bono requirement.

On this Monday morning, Ellen and her fledglings

convened in the "conference room" of their headquarters, furnished with secondhand objects: an overstuffed chair, a rocker, a lumpy couch, an easel, and an assortment of small, low tables. The furnishings and cheap wood paneling on the walls smelled slightly of mildew. Entirely dependent on contributions and government grants, Justice Restored wasn't able to afford any better. It had taken some getting used to, but Ellen enforced a regimen of cleanliness and order, a reflection of self-pride that overcame the trappings of poverty. Now, she couldn't be happier with the way the place looked and everything that it represented.

Ellen stood next to the easel as she spoke. At the top of it, some folded pieces of paper were clamped in place, not yet the subject of demonstration. Ellen was demonstrative enough with her hundred pounds of quick energy and dainty steps, soundlessly pacing here and there in front of her rapt circle. She wore her standard outfit, everything black. Knee-length dress, jacket, tights, and heeled, laced shoes. All of this, despite the warm, early summer day. She was in mourning, after all. For the past eight years, she'd been mourning the loss of her brother.

"At Justice Restored, we have to keep our eye on the mission. It's very popular these days to think that DNA evidence is the only way to exonerate the wrongly convicted. But just think of it. In most cases, the identity of the offender isn't proved or disproved by DNA evidence. In most cases, the jury has to decide if they believe the witnesses who testify about what they saw and heard. It's a matter of credibility. What do you think are some of the things we can look for to uncover falsity and injustice?" Ellen glanced around the room, her eyes alighting on one eager face after another. She loved these kids, but in a way, their inexperience was an irritant and a source of frustration.

Oliver piped up first. "You won two cases this year without any DNA evidence. You found papers in the prosecutor's files that weren't disclosed."

"Right. The cases of Ivan Nazarov and Trevor Blakely. Two men wrongly convicted, suffering a living nightmare. Years were taken out of their lives, but they're finally free."

"Thanks to you!" Oliver said, excitedly.

"And they're suing the Manhattan DA for money damages. But money can't compensate them for the lost time. Oliver, tell our new interns the basis for the court's rulings in those cases."

Oliver's mouth twitched upward, a sign that he was enjoying the spotlight. He was the most ardent intern Ellen had ever worked with. "The prosecutor had a duty to turn over anything that could help the defendant. You found evidence that contradicted the trial testimony, but the DA didn't disclose it."

"Exactly. In all of our cases at J.R., the first step is to do a FOIL request for the prosecutor's file. That's the Freedom of Information Law. In the Nazarov and Blakely files, I found exculpatory evidence. In Nazarov, the ADA made handwritten notes of a witness statement that conflicted with the witness's trial testimony. In Blakely, it was a copy of notes in a police officer's memo book about another possible suspect who fit the description of the assailant. After checking the trial transcripts in both of these cases, it was clear that the prosecutor hadn't disclosed these things to the defense. The court agreed that the new evidence left us with reasonable doubts as to Ivan's and Trevor's guilt."

Janet raised her hand like she was in a classroom, and Ellen pointed to her. "I have a question about that." The student blinked her made-up eyes, sending a shiver into the childish blonde bangs that dangled into her mascaraed lashes.

"Nazarov was an old case, right? And you couldn't question the prosecutor?"

Ellen nodded. "Right. We looked for the ADA who tried the case and found out he had died."

"So, what would have happened if the prosecutor was still alive and he remembered handing those notes over to the defendant's—Ivan's—attorney?"

The girl's question annoyed Ellen. These kids couldn't imagine what she'd gone through over these notes—what she'd risked—and she didn't like this neophyte implying the existence of an alternate reality. "There was nothing in the trial record indicating that the notes were disclosed. I demonstrated this to the court. So, what do *you* think would have happened if the prosecutor had testified as you suggest?"

Janet was suddenly at a loss for words, and Oliver came to the rescue. "We would cross-examine him. The trial was years ago. He did hundreds of cases after that. How could he remember? That's what you did in the Blakely case with the police officer's notes. You questioned the ADA, and she ended up not remembering. She got all confused. And the police officer admitted it looked like his handwriting, but he really couldn't remember either."

"You were there in court that day, weren't you Oliver?" Ellen's eyes flashed at Janet who, as she remembered, had not attended the Blakely hearing.

"And I also read the trial transcript in the Nazarov case," Oliver went on. His pimply face shone with pride at having played a supporting role in Ellen's two victories. "In the part where the ADA handed documents over to the defense attorney, he didn't mention his notes of the witness's statement."

"That's right," said Ellen. "Nothing in the record shows it. So, that's your answer, Janet. If the ADA was still alive and testified that he made an off-the-record disclosure, we'd say his memory was faulty. More likely, he was covering up a deliberate sabotage of the defendant's case. We can tell from the record because, if the notes had been disclosed, any defense attorney would have used them to confront the witness. There was a glaring inconsistency between the witness's trial testimony and the previous statement. There's no cross-examination like that in the trial record."

"Maybe Ivan had a bad lawyer," suggested Janet.

Ellen took a moment to breathe in deeply. Hadn't that girl learned anything in the past five months? "If his lawyer was incompetent," instructed Ellen, "it would be another reason to overturn the conviction. Every defendant has a right to competent counsel. But I know Ivan's trial attorney, and he's excellent. Xavier Asante. He's the absolute best you can get. We worked together on Ivan's post-conviction motion. Xavier said he never received the notes. It's clear that the prosecutor withheld the evidence. Deliberately. It was right there in the file. I saw it! This, this *rampant* misconduct in the DA's office ... it's out of control!"

There was a moment of silence. Five pairs of eyes were opened wide, but Ellen wasn't looking. She lowered her head, crossed her arms, and traced an imaginary circle on the floor with her footsteps. Hmm... Wouldn't that be great? To get Xavier involved in the cause. His fiery rhetoric was always so convincing.

Ellen turned to face her audience. They would see. She started up again in a low-pitched, seething monotone. "When you work on enough of these cases, you'll start to notice it. Everywhere. We're uncovering the evidence of this misconduct, and it's becoming a huge problem for the District Attorney, Patrick McBride. I'm sure you've seen the articles in the newspapers recently. And that's why we're here. That's why *you're* here."

A few heads bobbed in hushed agreement.

"Now, let's move on to the Pineda case." Ellen unpinned the papers from the easel and opened them up. They were photocopies—originals were never released from the prosecutor's file—and she'd made other copies of these, locking them away, just to be safe. She wouldn't show them to the interns. These kids were so green and potentially untrustworthy. She wanted merely to hold the evidence in her hands and refer to it as she summarized the case for them. One look at these papers, and her pulse quickened from the emotion.

She waved the three papers in the air. "*This* is what I received from the FOIL request."

Her narrative omitted the backstory. Later, alone, she would cry. The mere mention of Pineda's name elicited memories of a shameful period in her life and stoked her determination to turn that name into a badge of victory. She would make it her third win this year, three for three. There would be headlines. People would have to sit up then and start listening to her. People in the Westchester DA's office, on the parole board, in Albany, the governor himself. Whatever it took. Because, even if Antoine won his parole in a few months, he would still be branded a felon, under constant supervision and the stigma of a criminal record. Every waking moment of his existence would be tainted until his conviction was reversed and the indictment dismissed. Full exoneration—that's what they needed.

With a series of wins under her belt, the world would start listening.

But for now, Ramón Pineda still signified her shame. It was that case, and the case of the abortionist Dr. Spellman, that had consumed her life at a time when she should have been paying attention to her brother. When she could have saved him from that villain at "Security National." But she was too busy chasing a false dream, obsessed with earning the respect of Patrick McBride. Even to be noticed by him. To capture the eye he trained on Dana Hargrove, the woman who seamlessly glided between planning for her baby and prosecuting murder suspects. What a wasted effort! The objective: to put a man in prison for life. To ruin his life. A man struggling to survive. Ramón Pineda. She was ashamed to think of it.

On July 25, 1992, Pineda was a young man of twenty-two with a heroin habit. Robbery meant the difference between easing his pain and being strung out. It was a Saturday morning, 2:00 a.m. Pineda walked into an all-night bodega in Spanish Harlem with a loaded gun tucked into his waistband, under his shirt.

Addicts are not the most careful individuals when it comes to avoiding detection. The physical urge is too strong. But Pineda waited, at least, until the store had cleared of other customers before he pulled out the gun and pointed it at the man behind the counter. After that, his luck wasn't the best. In a single moment, a passerby on the sidewalk looked through the front window and saw him pull out the gun, just as a police cruiser on routine patrol turned into the block. The witness flagged down the blue-and-white, and Sergeant Dean Habberly pulled the car halfway onto the sidewalk in front of the store.

The man behind the counter was staring down the barrel of the gun. He was the store owner, forty-two years old, a husband and father of three children, ages four, seven, and thirteen. His name was Felipe Bedoya. Ramón demanded money, and Bedoya opened the till. His hands shook and he dropped some of the cash, fueling Ramón's volatility.

The Sergeant's voice boomed from the loudspeaker

system in the car. "Put down the weapon!" Habberly stood on the far side of the vehicle, peering over the roof, holding the mike in one hand, his service revolver in the other. His partner, rookie cop Aurelina Vargas, crouched behind the partially opened passenger-side door with her gun aimed at Ramón through the open window of the cruiser.

What happened in the next minute was the source of heated debate at trial. The only eyewitnesses were Ramón, Habberly and Vargas—by then, the pedestrian who had alerted the police was long gone, running scared.

The officers testified that Ramón was pointing his gun at Bedoya. They could hear him shouting but were unable to make out the words. It looked like Bedoya was trying to duck behind the counter and Ramón was ordering him to remain standing, under threat of being shot.

By the time of trial, Ramón was detoxed and cleaned up. He took the stand and testified that he didn't intend to shoot anyone. He'd pulled the weapon just to give enough of a scare to get some cash. He testified that he didn't fire his weapon on purpose. He was actually lowering the gun, complying with the Sergeant's order, when the cops shot him first, hitting his shoulder and making him press the trigger accidentally.

The ballistics evidence showed that Ramón fired his gun twice. One shot was aimed at the front of the store, toward the officers. In the close quarters, Ramón's bullet ricocheted off a metal bar in the security gate on the front window and hit Bedoya in the head, killing him. The trajectory of the second bullet suggested that Ramón was aiming his gun over the counter, in Bedoya's direction. That bullet was lodged in the wall behind the counter, between shelves displaying cartons of cigarettes.

Officer Vargas fired her gun twice. Sergeant Habberly did not fire his weapon at all.

As standard protocol, a full investigation was conducted of the officers' actions. Officer Vargas was cleared of any wrongdoing. One of her bullets went into Ramón's shoulder, the other shattered a jar of extra hot enchilada sauce on a display rack behind him. The report concluded that she was trying to save Bedoya's life in the instant after Ramón discharged his weapon at Bedoya.

It was the defense theory that the cops were at fault, and Ramón was surrendering. He was lowering the gun with the barrel facing the front window when Officer Vargas started shooting, firing off two bullets in rapid succession. The first one hit Ramón's shoulder, causing him to discharge his weapon accidentally in the direction of the window, where the bullet ricocheted. The force of being hit in the shoulder changed Ramón's position and caused the gun to go off again, involuntarily. Bedoya was already down from the first shot, and the second shot hit the wall behind the counter.

ADA Hargrove gave the jury a different theory. When the police arrived, Ramón was about to collect his cash and wanted to get rid of the witness. Suddenly, the police were barking orders at him. His plan was already underway, and in the split second that could have made a difference, he lost all sense and panicked. He fired off the first bullet at Bedoya, missed, and spun around to the police, firing at the window, causing the second bullet to hit the metal bar and ricochet. While this scenario was the most likely one, it actually made no difference under the law who shot first. It also made no difference that Ramón was aiming away from Bedoya when he fired the shot that killed him. Felony murder was proved whenever a deadly weapon was used in a robbery and someone ended up getting killed. Death was a foreseeable consequence, and Ramón was responsible. Even if the jury didn't think he acted intentionally, they were obligated to find him guilty.

These details of the evidence were emblazoned on Ellen's memory. The conviction was heralded as one of Dana's brilliant victories. But Patrick never should have assigned this case to his favorite ADA to begin with. He should have removed that hugely pregnant woman from the homicide chart and promoted Ellen instead. Dana was always the superwoman, out to prove the impossible. So casual about her intimate collegial relationship with Patrick, she could never be accused of flaunting it. Their over-the-top mutual admiration. "Patrick, you can keep me on the chart. I'm up for it." Dana said this in front of everyone at a bureau meeting, her face glowing with maternal bliss. Think of it. What kind of mother, eight months pregnant, would want to visit a bloody murder scene in the middle of the night?

When Dana started her maternity leave in August of 1992, Ellen inherited the Pineda case. Temporarily, it turned out. In November, she handled the hearing on the defense motion to suppress Ramón's post-arrest statements. Funny. Looking at it now, she could say it was her first win for Ramón! But at the time, she was representing the opposite side, the People of the State of New York. And when the judge ruled in favor of the defense, the ruling hit her hard with the shock of a profound loss. Here was another test she'd failed. In Patrick's eyes, Ellen's work wasn't up to snuff. He never said this to her directly. But she felt it in the condescending tone he always took with her, and in the way he, so glibly, reassigned the case to Dana for trial, a few months later.

The suppression ruling really wasn't her fault. The issues at the hearing were close. It could have gone either way. The defense argued that the People shouldn't be allowed to use Ramón's words against him at trial. He'd said a few things after his arrest, when he was at the hospital, about to go into surgery for the wound to his shoulder. The interviewer was Senior

Investigator Paul Donegan of the DA's squad, the man everyone used to call "the Don."

Ellen never liked the Don, and he probably never liked her. But she asked him all the proper questions at the hearing, and the Don gave all the correct answers. Like always, it was the "truth" presented in the light most favorable to the People. She saw that now. Always a slight spin to it.

Donegan testified that he got to the hospital when Ramón had been there for about half an hour. A number of medical professionals were in the prep room, but they let Donegan into their midst to ask a few questions of the suspect. Donegan followed proper procedure to the letter, informing Ramón of his right to remain silent and his right to a lawyer. Ramón seemed lucid, coherent, and articulate—more than articulate. He said "yes" and "yes" again, showing that he understood his rights and wanted to talk without a lawyer. He blurted, "Who'd I kill?" and repeated it several times. Then, he just kept talking, spouting off about that *hijo de puta* bodega owner who kept dropping the cash and had it coming to him, and the "fucking cops" who set themselves up so pretty outside the window, "just asking for it."

When Ellen finished her direct examination of the Don, she sat down at counsel table, feeling satisfied that she'd done an adequate job. But then, the defense attorney hammered the witness on cross-examination. Wasn't Ramón shackled to the hospital bed? Yes. Was Donegan aware that Ramón was a heroin addict? Yes. Wasn't Ramón sweating profusely? Yes. Wasn't he screaming in pain? Not exactly. Speaking very loudly.

After that, the defense put on medical witnesses, a nurse and a doctor. There were medical charts and detailed descriptions of Ramón's wound, its location deep in the flesh and the kind of pain that would cause. There were descriptions of heroin addiction and withdrawal symptoms and the kind of agony that would entail. There were firsthand observations of the patient as he thrashed about, screaming obscenities.

Ellen cross-examined the witnesses, but she was thrown, ill-prepared, weak, and ineffectual. With every question, she seemed to draw out additional details of the physical horrors Ramón was experiencing.

The judge ruled that Ramón's "waiver" of his constitutional rights was invalid. He was in no state to make a voluntarily and intelligent decision to speak with Investigator Donegan without the aid of an attorney.

After the judge's decision, and for weeks afterward, Ellen's head filled with an incessant refrain: *if only*. If only she'd asked this question or that question, if only she'd assumed a more authoritative attitude, if only she'd phrased her argument to the court differently. It didn't help much to know that the suppression ruling actually had no effect on the DA's desired result in the case. Dana got her murder conviction anyway. The statements might have helped her to prove intentional murder, but the brilliant ADA Hargrove didn't need her cases handed to her on a silver platter. She executed the backup plan. She had him on felony murder, and she cinched it.

Won't Dana be surprised now?

A few months ago, more than eight years after Pineda's conviction, Justice Restored accepted the case. Ellen called on Ramón at the Green Haven Correctional Facility. He remembered her.

"You," he said. "I know you."

"How's that?" she asked him, testing his memory.

"You the one on the case. Against me."

"I was taken off, remember?"

"After we won the hearing. You lost it. For them."

"Right."

He thought a minute, until his eyes shone with the gleam of discovery. "You planned it? You were with me on this?"

She led him to believe it. "From the start. That investigator never should have questioned you at the hospital, not in the condition you were in. That was wrong."

"After that, they put that tall *chica* on the case. She's the one did me."

"Yes, she's the one. And we're going to beat her this time."

"I got Jesus on my side now. Don't want the needle any more, just Him. And you. Maybe you too."

"You've got me, Ramón."

Robbery is one thing. Murder another. Ramón shouldn't be doing twenty-to-life for murder. He'd been a drug-addicted victim of inexorable circumstance. Maybe not as deserving of clemency as Antoine, but still, a victim.

I'm going to make it this time, dear brother. Another win, another step toward the exit door. Justice will be restored.

9 »   FASHION

ERIC STOOD BAREFOOT in his boxer shorts at the open closet door, taking longer than usual to pick through his suits, shirts, and ties. Jessica, in cross trainers, padded softly into the bedroom and stood behind him. In deep concentration, Eric didn't seem to notice his fiancée. But of course he did. The pheromones alone would announce her presence.

"What do you think of these?" he asked, pulling out a shirt on a hanger and a tie from a peg on the tie rack. He turned around to face her.

Jess glanced at the clothing and pursed her lips against an urge to smile. The tie was cut in an outdated width, and the shirt was the peach-colored one he once described as "too girlish" and hadn't worn since. "It's shocking," she said.

"That bad?" His face fell.

"Not the clothes. I'm talking about your sudden interest in what you're wearing."

"I don't know about that." His voice was a little whiny. "I try my best. Maybe I'm not as concerned as *you* about clothes…" He eyed her outfit, top to toe. She was already dressed for work in a fuchsia moisture-wicking tee-shirt with large, open arm holes, revealing the black sports bra underneath, and skintight microfiber capris bearing the manufacturer's logo in relief on her left thigh. Shiny mocha brown hair in a ponytail. Even a dab of perfume. Sometimes he worried about how good she looked when she went off to work as a personal trainer at the gym. Wasn't that where he first noticed her? The muscles in her arms—and elsewhere—flexed attractively as she instructed a client on the elliptical machine next to his treadmill. He stumbled a bit and nearly fell off.

"So, you don't see the connection between your behavior and the late Loránd Kallay?"

Eric's eyes went to the ceiling and back to Jess. "You should've seen the fabric on those pants. And the *fit*..."

"On a dead guy?"

"...was *perfect*."

"Amazing! Even after he took three in the chest and crashed to the floor." With a big smile, she took the tie and shirt from him and put them back in the closet. "I'll take you shopping next weekend. But we won't be buying any Kallay designs. A little out of our price range." She pulled out another shirt and tie and handed them to Eric. "Here." Then she pulled out one of his nicer summer suits and laid it on the bed. "Come eat breakfast first."

"Like this?" He glanced down at his boxers, shirt hanging from one hand, tie from the other.

"Yes, just like that. I prefer skin to anything else you wear."

He laid the shirt and tie on top of the suit on the bed.

"I made you a smoothie," she said. "Banana, yogurt, and mixed berries. You don't want to ruin your perfect look with purple berry stains."

She turned to go but he grabbed her first. It had been a great weekend. Some mornings, especially Mondays, it was difficult to get out of the apartment.

At the office, Eric reviewed the evidence in the Kallay murder. On the night of the crime, after seeing Frances Kallay at Lenox Hill Hospital, Eric was convinced that she was the killer. Her story made no sense and conflicted with the physical evidence. She also had a motive to kill her husband. Although she wouldn't admit it, Loránd was a batterer. The evidence was all over her body. And there was no reason to believe there'd been a struggle or that she'd acted in self-defense. Everything in that killing den pointed to a stealthy, intentional act. She was a woman with means who could have sought protection instead of resorting to self-help. Past abuse wasn't a defense to murder, although a jury might take a detour around the law as an act of mercy and find her guilty of the lesser crime of manslaughter.

Immediately after leaving the hospital, Gilbert swore out an affidavit, and they went to the night judge, who issued an arrest warrant and an order for a buccal swab and photographic evidence. The order permitted them to take photos of her arms, upper chest above the sternum, and back above the pelvic girdle. Friday morning, Frances was arrested in her hospital room, the photographs and DNA sample were taken, and she was transported to a prison hospital ward—not nearly as nice as Lenox Hill. She asked for an attorney by name: Xavier Asante. He was expensive, but she could afford his fee. Although this was the first time she'd ever needed a criminal lawyer, she was aware of Asante's reputation through his partner, the attorney who represented the Kallays in civil matters, Rajani Choudhary. With Asante and ADA Eric Trumble at bedside, and a judge presiding by video connection, Frances was arraigned on the charge of murder. The court remanded her without bail pending the action of the grand jury.

Reviewing everything they knew so far, Eric wasn't so sure that the grand jury would indict. He and Gil needed to fortify the case before Thursday, which was "one-eighty eighty day." Section 180.80 of the Criminal Procedure Law allowed him only six days from the arrest to obtain an indictment, otherwise, the court would be compelled to release Frances on her own recognizance, without bail.

Linking her to the murder weapon would be a start. Everyone assumed that the Browning semiautomatic was the one, but it wasn't confirmed. The ballistics report wasn't in yet. The victim was the registered owner of the Browning, having purchased it about three years ago. Frances also had access to the gun if, indeed, her husband kept it in the unlocked desk drawer, as she said. Of course, many things she said were suspect.

On Friday afternoon, Nicki had called Eric to give him the fingerprint analysis. A few latents on the wall safe matched Loránd Kallay. She found a single print of value on the barrel of the gun that matched the victim's left index finger and a few partials with points of comparison to the victim's fingerprints, but the match was inconclusive. Nothing else. Nicki's theory was that the grip and trigger of the gun had been wiped. Either that, or Frances had worn gloves. A search of the house yielded the kinds of gloves one would expect to find in that type of home: winter gloves in storage, dress gloves for the opera, rubber gloves used by the servants. All very carefully put away and undisturbed. Judging by her appearance that night, it seemed unlikely that Frances would have had the presence of mind, after shooting her husband, to carefully return a pair of gloves to its usual place. Eric was hoping against that possibility. He was hoping for some DNA deposited on the wood grip of the gun if, indeed, it was the murder weapon.

Something else didn't quite fit. Kallay was left-handed, a fact they'd confirmed through interviews with acquaintances. A left-handed person had placed the gun, right side down, on the desk. Frances was right-handed. She may have thought that she could mislead investigators by wiping her fingerprints off the gun and placing it on the desk in a way that her husband— or another left-handed person—would have laid it down. But this also would require a good measure of control and presence of mind as her husband lay dying on the floor. Unlikely. It was also an improbable ending to her story about an intruder who struggled with her husband over the gun, overpowered him, and shot him. Why would the intruder leave the gun so nicely on the desk?

The answer: the Browning couldn't be the murder weapon! Kallay was forced to lay his gun on the desk before he was murdered with another weapon. Frances used another gun, and must have found a good hiding place for it. They'd have to go back to the house and search again.

Bottom line, Eric needed the results from the DNA and ballistics tests. Immediately. He called Nicki to find out the status.

"Hey, Nicki."

"What's up? How's Mrs. Fashion?"

"Resting comfortably in her City-issued nightgown. Actually, I'm going to call Rikers to ask if they've released her to the general population. She wasn't in such seriously bad shape over the weekend."

"You sound tired," said Nicki in that way she had.

"Who isn't tired? It's Monday and I worked half the weekend."

"Oh ... so that's what you call it? Anyway, don't stress. I have the ballistics for you. I'll send the report."

"Let me guess: the Browning isn't the murder weapon."

"Sorry, bad guess."

"Hmm…"

"The bullets in Kallay's body were discharged from that gun. He was killed with his own weapon."

"Sounds like an ad for gun control. If you buy a gun to protect your home, a family member is bound to get killed— by another family member."

"Yeah, like an angry spouse. Maybe you want to rethink getting married."

"Ha, ha. Maybe I want to rethink my case. I didn't figure the Browning to be the murder weapon."

"You thought the wife had another gun?"

"Let's just say this puzzle isn't fitting too neatly together. So, what about the DNA?"

"Sorry, not yet."

"Sorry again? What do you mean, sorry? It's expedited!"

"I was going to call you about that. The lab is backed up and your case came off the expedite list."

"But Inspector Bitters put the order in."

"Maybe so, but open cases have priority. If there's an arrest, it comes off the list."

"Fuck! Don't tell me—"

"The system picked up the arrest and automatically downgraded your priority."

"I never heard of this policy."

"It's pretty recent. Limited resources, you know. Everyone wants DNA analysis and people have to stand in line. If the rapist or murderer is still on the street, those cases are more important."

Eric swore a dozen times under his breath.

"Now, now," said Nicki.

"I wish you'd said something before we arrested her."

"I'm a mind reader?"

"You've been known to show that talent."

"Gee, thanks."

"And you also have the talent to move things along. I've seen you do it before. Try to get my case back on the expedite list."

"I'll see what I can do."

"Thanks. Gotta go."

"All right. Good luck with the fashion queen."

Eric shook his head and muttered curses as he hung up the phone.

"Hope it was good," said a raspy voice at the open door.

Eric looked up. "*What* was good?"

Gilbert walked in and took a seat across from Eric at the desk. "Just heard you say you screwed yourself."

"Very funny. We're both screwed."

"Glad to be included."

"I called Nicki, and the Browning is the gun."

"Well, okay ... another gun made it easier to see. But now we figure it another way. It doesn't do us in."

"No, but they got us with the new DNA rules. When we arrested Frances, our test went to the bottom of the list. Lower priority."

"Doesn't change anything. We weren't gonna *not* arrest her, were we?"

"We could've waited..."

"But we wouldn't've gotten the judge to order the photos. Bruises don't last forever. And she might've hopped a plane to Europe."

"She's not the type to run."

"Everyone's the type to run. Anyway, you're crying over nothing."

"How's that?" Eric turned sideways to Gil and pretended he wasn't listening as closely as he needed to.

"It's no big deal. If there's DNA, it proves she touched a gun that was in her house. Doesn't prove she fired it."

"With DNA on the grip?"

"Helps a little. But the main thing is the way she buried herself with that story."

"It's all circumstantial."

"But it's an obvious cover. That's where you sell it,

counselor."

"All right," said Eric. "What've we got?" He started to review the highlights of the brainstorming session they'd had on Friday. "When we talked to Frances at the hospital, she repeated the home invasion story. She claims it happened shortly before midnight. Already that's questionable. The M.E. says the time of death could be earlier, so she might've delayed calling the police. She says she was on the fourth floor when she heard a scuffle on the ground floor. That's impossible. We tested it. You can't hear anything from up there except the doorbell, and she denied hearing a doorbell. She says her husband wasn't expecting anyone, and there were no signs of a forced entry." Eric pondered a moment. "All these circumstances point to her, especially since we haven't come up with any known enemies of the victim…"

"Not yet," said Gil, "but we'll find one. Everyone's got an enemy…"

"Every cop maybe…"

"…and every prosecutor. But so far, this peacock Loránd is a saint. Everyone loves him."

"Tell me you're working on it," said Eric. "Check out every competitor and every associate…"

"We're lookin' at damn near everyone in the fashion industry and the social contacts too, including the people the dame knows."

Eric laughed. "The 'peacock' and the 'dame.' I didn't know you were a fan of pulp!"

Gil hunched his shoulders and scrunched his craggy face. "I don't drink OJ," he said, but his eyes were shining. "I'm just thinkin' of every angle here, another possible suspect … or an accomplice."

"If you're thinking it could be someone that Kallay let into the house, it doesn't make sense to me. It's not likely he would let a known enemy in the front door, and it's not likely that a friend would shoot him in cold blood. Frances still comes out on top as our suspect. She was already in the house, living with a man who didn't treat her too kindly. Those finger bruises on her arms and the purple bump on her chest were fresh marks."

"And I bet we woulda found more under that hospital gown…"

"…if the judge hadn't limited the order for photographic evidence."

"…a *whole* lot more."

Eric winked and said, "Sweet dreams, Gil."

The senior investigator responded with a swipe of his hand.

"Okay, what about the gun?" Eric asked. "It doesn't fit her home invasion story. She claims she didn't touch it when she came downstairs. The intruder must have put it there. Sure. A burglar comes in, shoots Kallay, and drops the gun on the desk. I don't think so. And what about the fashion drawings in the safe? A street thug wouldn't be interested in something like that. Of course, a burglar could've thought he'd find something better in the safe."

Gil shook his head. "Ain't no drawings, baby. The wife made 'em up. Let's search the business offices. If there's any drawings, they'll be there."

"I'm already on it. Get a team together this morning. I drafted your affidavit for the search warrant. Here." Eric pushed the papers across the desk. "Go sign it in front of a notary." He pointed. "It's that line at the bottom where it says 'Senior Investigator Gilbert Herrera.'"

"Ha, ha," said Gil.

"I'll take the papers to the judge and get the warrant after I talk to Dana."

"Dana, Dana, Dana. Always Dana." Gil stood and

grabbed the papers off the desk. "Give the Dane a kiss for me."

"Get lost. You can go kiss the 'dame.' But sign the papers and leave them on my desk first."

In a flash, Gil was out the door. Eric pushed up from the desk, ready to seek out Dana for advice, when the phone rang. The caller ID alerted him that it was a call he should take, but he answered as if he hadn't looked and wasn't aware of the caller's identity. No reason to encourage the swollen ego of the defense attorney on the other end of the line. "Assistant DA Eric Trumble," he said.

"Eric!" So condescending. "Xavier Asante."

The voice brought to mind that scene in the prison hospital ward before the arraignment, Eric's first encounter with this legendary figure of the defense bar. Asante made his entrance looking like a Latin fashion god, filling the dingy room with color. Lavender handkerchief in breast pocket, sharp edges to his black hair, gleaming briefcase and shoes. He needed only a few minutes with his new client to size up the situation before he pulled Eric aside and began his rantings: "This woman's husband was just murdered. She's traumatized and hospitalized. And you interrogate her? Without reading her rights? Without a lawyer? *Everything* she said is inadmissible. A judge will throw it out. You have no evidence. Arrested her on a mere hunch. It's unethical to say the least. You're going down, young man. You're going down!"

All bluster. Eric knew the law and knew he was within it. At the time of the questioning, Frances wasn't a suspect or under arrest, and Eric had done nothing to overbear her will. She wanted to talk. She'd called the police to the house in the first place, just to give her story.

Now, as he took Asante's phone call, Eric tried to match, or maybe even outdo, the tone of his adversary. Difficult, if not impossible. There were times when Eric still felt like the new kid on the block. "Xavier. I suppose you're calling to say your client's ready to confess?"

"It's more like this. I'm calling to say we're suing you for false arrest—*after* we get through this circus in the grand jury. We'll make our record there. I'm giving notice that Mrs. Kallay plans to testify."

"As is her right," Eric said. He gave Asante the scheduled time for the proceedings.

"We'll be there. And look out, young man. This is my advice. Talk to Hargrove about this case. It isn't going to look pretty for her."

The mention of Dana's name fired up Eric's protective instincts. Hardly aware of the words he spoke, he ended the call, replaced the receiver, and stared out into the distance beyond his open office door. *What* was *that* all about?

While Eric was talking to Asante, Dana was in her office with Deputy Bureau Chief Ernest Chin, briefing him on the cases he would oversee while she was on vacation. She laughed and said, "I'm just crossing my fingers that Ellen Fortier doesn't steal half my vacation away."

"What's going on?"

She explained her predicament.

"Tough luck. Who's handling it for us?"

"Jared assigned someone from the post-conviction unit in the Appeals Bureau. ADA Weingarten. Don't know him. Jared says he's good."

"Hope he's good enough to get an adjournment. Anyway, you'll do fine at the hearing. What could Ellen possibly have on this case?"

"I saw her motion papers this morning for the first time. Weingarten sent me a copy. She's claiming I withheld something in a forensic report that might have exonerated

Pineda."

"Knowing you, that's impossible."

"No further details were given. She's keeping her secrets until the hearing."

"The surprise factor! She wants to trip you up. Catch you off guard."

"Well, I don't have the time this week to speculate about what she has up her sleeve. My priority is getting this bureau in the best possible shape before I leave."

Eric knocked on the doorjamb and stepped in. "Sorry to interrupt, Dana. Hi, Ricky."

Ernest acknowledged the greeting. He was known by his nickname, a vestige of his youth. "Ricky" was a name given to him by bullies in the rough, mixed neighborhood where he grew up. The pejorative allusion to degrading, peasant labor was clear to him. As he got older, he decided to keep the name, embrace it, and wear it as a badge and a reminder of what his ancestors and immigrant forebears had endured.

"Come in," said Dana. "We were just wrapping up. How's it going with the Kallays?"

"That's what I wanted to talk about." Eric stepped in and sat down.

"You want me to stay?" asked Ricky.

"Yes, if you have the time." The two men were close colleagues, having shared an office for several years. In 2000, Dana considered both of them for the deputy spot, but Eric bowed out, claiming he preferred the trial work. The unspoken understanding was that he might have difficulty working so closely with Dana.

Eric filled them in on the current state of the evidence. He didn't mention Asante's warning—not yet—although it was circling in the back of his mind.

"The circumstances point to Mrs. Kallay, no question,"

said Dana. "But it isn't the strongest case. The DNA will help if you get it. Other than that, you need to develop the battering evidence. Signs of what's going on at home usually creep out into the open. There could be friends, family, or coworkers who saw his behavior."

"We're talking to people. But so far, all we've got are the photos. Finger bruises on her upper arms and bruises on her chest. We can't subpoena the medical records. There's no exception to HIPAA, so we'd have to get her consent."

"Out of the question for now. Okay. Let's go over the possibilities once more," said Dana. "Maybe I'm missing something. We know it's not a break in. No signs of forced entry. First possible shooter is Frances. She's already in the house and has a motive to kill. Second possible shooter is someone Kallay let in the front door without his wife knowing it. No witnesses to this. It's unlikely, but possible, since there's no reason to think that Frances knows all of her husband's plans. Also, she wouldn't be able to hear a knock at the front door from someone he was expecting."

Both men nodded in agreement.

"But I didn't hear your thoughts on the third possibility." Dana looked directly into Eric's eyes and didn't waiver, as her deputy looked on with a knowing grin. Ricky's mind was in sync with Dana's, while Eric searched and floundered. "The third possibility," he repeated under a furrowed brow.

"Yes. There could be another person that *she* let into the house when her husband was behind the closed door of the den."

"Holly shit," Eric muttered. How had he missed *that?* The word 'accomplice' floated in the nether regions of his consciousness. Gil had said something about that too, while Eric's mind had been elsewhere. "You're right. That's a possibility."

There was a moment of silence. Ricky broke it. "Is contract murder a possibility here? The woman has money, doesn't she? Maybe she hired someone and let him into the house."

"She doesn't seem the type."

"Based on what?" Dana asked.

"Based on the way she acted after the murder. She could barely get the words out of her mouth. The woman is spineless—certainly not very businesslike or methodical. I don't think she's capable of arranging anything as devious and complicated as a contract murder."

"Appearances can fool," said Ricky. "We all know that." The three lawyers exchanged knowing looks. "When the body is lying on the floor in front of you, even the person who arranged it could be rattled."

"Yeah."

"She was shaken up. Anyway, it doesn't hurt to follow up on the contract angle, does it? You could subpoena her bank accounts and financial records, see if there've been any large withdrawals of cash lately."

Eric was skeptical. "For all we know, the money was in the vic's name or in joint accounts. He was the one with the business, and she has no separate source of income that we know of. It could take weeks to unravel their finances."

"Maybe we could ask Bruce Reichert for advice on how to get those answers quickly." As Ricky made this suggestion, he shot a look at Dana. Even now, twelve years after Dana's stint in the Financial Crimes Bureau, her colleagues still tiptoed around any overt reference to her harrowing experience. Her onetime nemesis, ADA Bruce Reichert, had been her supervisor on that investigation into the money laundering crimes of the Colombian narcotics cartel. He was recently appointed to head the Special Investigations Unit, but his years of experience in FC made him an expert on financial investigations.

"I'll call Bruce and ask his advice on the best way to investigate their finances," Dana said, without betraying any sense of unease. She and Bruce and long since made peace and had developed a collegial working relationship over the years. "But," Dana went on, "apart from the contract theory, the accomplice could be one of Kallay's competitors or someone else with a vendetta, happy to kill him for Mrs. Kallay without being paid. Ask Gilbert and his crew to keep checking on potential business competitors, and also have them check out Mrs. Kallay's social contacts. Get phone records from the house and any cell phone. Did she have a phone in her hospital room?"

"I believe so."

"Check the records. She might have contacted an accomplice when she still thought she was in the clear."

"Will do," said Eric.

"It would be interesting," added Dana, "if anyone she keeps company with also happens to have a reason to dislike Loránd Kallay or his business, House of Loránd. That person would be a likely collaborator with Frances."

"The inspector has a team at the precinct making a list of potential enemies, and Gil is working with them. So far they've come up with no one in particular, but I understand that competition in the fashion industry is ruthless."

Ricky sat up taller and repeated, "*ruthless*," while straightening his jacket and tie, twisting his torso from side to side, examining himself in an invisible mirror. They all laughed.

"Maybe this really is about stealing his fashion designs," Dana suggested. "The shooter could have been acting with or without Mrs. Kallay's help. If our investigation leads us there, we'll have to reevaluate the charges against her."

This talk of other possible scenarios was making Eric panic about Asante's threats. *A lawsuit for false arrest. It isn't going to look pretty for Hargrove.* Had he made a huge mistake? Was the arrest going to drag Dana's name through the mud?

"But," Dana continued, oblivious to Eric's anxiety attack, "if this is about a woman who wanted to kill her husband to stop the battering, it's going to be a tough case. Defendants in these cases are sympathetic, even someone like our suspect, a woman smart and wealthy enough to figure a way out of her situation without resorting to murder."

Ricky turned to Eric. "Your description of the room where Kallay was found isn't consistent with a theory of self-defense."

"Except for a body oozing blood," said Eric, "the den in that townhouse was as tidy as Ellen's desk in the quad!"

Dana looked hard at Eric, as if she couldn't believe her ears.

"Unfortunate comparison," Ricky observed, eyeing the two of them.

"What're you talking about?" asked Eric. He was, as yet, unaware of Ellen's subpoena, and his comment was truly a coincidence. In their rookie days, when Dana and Ellen shared a four-person office with two other attorneys, Eric was their trial preparation assistant, with dreams of going to law school. Back then, like the rest of them, he used to call Ellen "Mary Poppins" behind her back.

"It's nothing," said Dana. "I'll tell you later. Back to Frances, like you said, the law isn't on her side if she shot her husband in cold blood. But even in cases of premeditated murder, juries have been known to acquit or to vote a compromise verdict of manslaughter where battering is involved. Any jury is free to exercise mercy. If it turns out that this is a desperate act of a battered woman, I can't say that I'll be unsympathetic. Bottom line, we have to be guided by the law that fits the evidence."

"Maybe that's what Asante was alluding to," Eric muttered.

Dana and Ricky aimed quizzical looks at him, demanding an explanation.

"He said something at the end of our conversation that wasn't very nice," Eric explained. "Actually, nothing he said was very nice. He threatened a lawsuit for false arrest, and then he said, 'Talk to Hargrove. It isn't going to look pretty for her.' Something like that."

Ricky sat up in outrage. "He has the balls to threaten us? To threaten Dana?"

"It's okay," said Dana, putting a hand up in the air. "I know this guy. It's all show. He's trying to throw you off balance, Eric. Did he succeed?"

Eric's face was drained of all color. "Course not. I'm just concerned about you, Dana. If I acted too quickly..."

"Don't worry about me. I'm a big girl. And I think your instincts about Frances Kallay's involvement are correct. We just don't have a complete picture yet. So, get to work!"

The two men took this as a directive to do just that. They stood up, said a few parting words, and left the room.

Once they were gone, Dana was left with a troubling thought she hadn't shared with them. This was the first time a defense attorney had used one of her assistants as a messenger. What was behind it? Connections came to mind: Asante ... Darren Tripp ... Evan. She would have to talk to Evan about this tonight. No, better yet, she should call him now, before his settlement conference this afternoon.

And after that, she'd call the DA. She was obliged to keep Patrick in the loop on this high-profile case, and besides that, any advice he could lend would be invaluable.

10 »   SCAMMED

EVAN FINISHED HIS conversation with Assistant U.S. Attorney Phillip Neary and hung up the phone. In the lobby of Belknap & Rose, Henrietta Edmonds was waiting for him. He went out to the lobby now. He could have asked his secretary to escort Mrs. Edmonds to his office, but he never delegated this responsibility. Not for this client. Respect, affection, compassion, and a special affinity—he felt all of these things for Mrs. Edmonds. At the edge of awareness, there was something else to complicate his feelings. A hovering cloud of forsaken duty and denial.

As he walked up to her, his mind was still sorting through AUSA Neary's update of the criminal case in federal court. The news wasn't good. The next court appearance was scheduled for Wednesday and they were under pressure to report to the judge regarding their negotiations. But the hoped-for settlement with a guilty plea wasn't materializing. Darren Tripp continued to maintain his innocence and was fighting the case all the way. This would thwart and prolong the negotiations in the civil class action lawsuit.

Evan held out a hand, ready to assist his client up to standing. "Mrs. Edmonds. How are you doing today?"

"Not too badly," she replied. In the milky eyes that looked up at him, he could see that the story might be otherwise. Her good nature always supplied a valiant smile in the lined face, a mask on her pain. She made no move to stand up. "It's a beautiful day!" she said brightly.

There was something uncomfortably familiar in her words. Or maybe it was the way she expressed herself. "It certainly is!" he agreed. "A shame we'll be in a courtroom this afternoon instead of outside."

He could have told her, again, that her presence wasn't absolutely needed during these meetings between the attorneys and Judge Evelyn Friel in the commercial division of the state trial court. The effort that Mrs. Edmonds expended in making an appearance, every time, was clearly a monumental undertaking for her. But this case was her pet project, and the court dates were the building blocks. Her interest in the case wasn't entirely personal but belonged to the plaintiffs in the class. The objective was to open Darren Tripp's eyes to his many victims, and to make him compensate them for the misery he had caused, hers included. From the perspective of trial attorneys like Evan and Joel, her presence in court was an asset. She put a face on the litigation and brought it to life.

"Let's walk back to my office and talk for a bit. We still have a few minutes before we have to leave for court."

She lifted a hand, and he grasped her by the bare forearm at the edge of her three-quarter-length sleeve. "Ooo, I sink right down into these chairs!" He reached for the second forearm. The skin was flaccid and warm. Bones could be felt. Evan had always thought that B & R's lush upholstered furniture in the waiting area was comfortable, until he met Henrietta Edmonds.

They made their way back. The pace was slow enough that they lost only a step or two when Evan spoke to his secretary along the way. "We'll need the car service to the courthouse in about fifteen minutes," he instructed. For Mrs. Edmonds, the subway or a yellow cab wouldn't work.

"Will do. Dana just called again. She had one last chance to catch you, but now she's going into a meeting and can't talk."

"Okay. Thanks." They'd been playing phone tag all morning.

"That's your wife?" Mrs. Edmonds asked as they continued their journey—another five steps into his office. On previous visits, she'd commented on the two framed photos on Evan's desk, Dana in one, the two children in the other.

"Yup. My better half."

"I feel bad now. Coming between husband and wife!" They stopped just inside the threshold, and she turned to show him the chagrined expression of a comedienne. The joke was hiding there, the delivery delayed. He loved this about her.

"Oh, don't feel bad! She'll just have to pick up the milk on the way home instead of asking *me* to do it."

"You're terrible!" With the force of a breath of air, she swatted him on his right biceps.

Inexplicably, that old camp song came to mind again, the one that Dana and Mom had been singing this morning in the kitchen. Maybe it was the mention of milk that sparked the connection. Of course, Dana wouldn't be calling about milk, but now it was too late to find out what she wanted to tell him. He made a mental note to call her when he got back from court.

Evan helped Mrs. Edmonds into a straight-backed chair, then rounded the desk and sat down. With shaking, knobby hands, she smoothed out the wrinkles on her lap, a dress in a pattern of spring flowers, lavender and pale green. Nestled in the thicket of white hair on her head was a small hat, with a demi veil gracing her forehead.

"Can you tell me about that again?" she asked. "What you said on the phone?"

"About the offer? We're very disappointed. They offered five million for the whole class. It's ridiculously low when you think that he made about a hundred times that amount from his sales of Life Source."

"Just a couple of pennies for each of us?"

"Not much more than that. About five bucks apiece." A five dollar bill, or even two cents, might have been worth something in 1919, when Mrs. Edmonds was born.

"Our losses are much greater than that," she said. "I bought those pills two times and paid $79.99 each time! Many people lost more than I did."

And that's just the purchase price of the product, Evan thought. What about the real costs? Life Source multiplied the health problems and medical bills for many of the plaintiffs, not to mention the emotional pain and anguish of lost hope, and the humiliation of being tricked. "That's why my recommendation to you, as the class representative, is to say 'no' to the offer."

"I give you my 'no.' You don't even have to ask!"

Wow! He liked this lady. The fire still burned hot. "Good," he said. "Let me get Joel in here and he'll lay out the details of our counteroffer. Then we'll all get in the car and go." Evan lifted the phone receiver.

In the modern, blond wood courtroom of the commercial division, the players assembled a few minutes ahead of time. Court officers, clerk, and stenographer. At the plaintiff's table, Evan, Henrietta, and Joel, in that order. At the defense table, Rajani, Xavier, and an empty chair. Darren Tripp had never made an appearance in this case, although he was permitted to do so under the terms of his bail agreement in the criminal case. He had posted cash bail of $750,000 and was confined to house arrest, tracked by ankle monitor, allowed to leave the premises only for court appearances. House arrest wasn't exactly cruel and unusual punishment for Tripp. He lived on a ten-acre suburban estate with rolling hills, sculpted gardens, a stable with three thoroughbreds, indoor and outdoor swimming pools, a helicopter pad, and a tennis court.

When the parties first entered the courtroom, the attorneys exchanged cordial greetings, nothing more. A week ago, Rajani Choudhary had called to convey her client's offer. Evan told her it wasn't even in the ballpark, but he didn't reject it outright, mindful of his obligation to discuss the offer with Mrs. Edmonds first. Implicitly, everyone knew there wouldn't be a deal made today. Evan was betting that, after a brief discussion, there would be a stalemate, and the court would set a discovery schedule to move the case along to trial. Most likely, they'd all be out of here in ten minutes, fifteen tops.

At precisely two o'clock, Judge Evelyn Friel ascended the bench, prepared and eager to move forward. She was in her mid-seventies, no more than seven or eight years younger than Evan's client, but the comparison between the women was stark. Judge Friel exhibited a healthy glow, vigor, and sharpness of mind that gave her an aura of youth, augmented by an impeccable elegance.

The judge greeted the attorneys and addressed the plaintiff directly: "Good afternoon, Mrs. Edmonds."

"Good afternoon, Judge Friel."

"I think this makes your attendance record a perfect one hundred percent. Certainly better than many of the attorneys who appear before me."

"Do I get a gold star?"

Everyone laughed. "Perhaps you should," said the judge. "I don't know if you're going to get much else out of this case for a long time to come. Where are we with settlement negotiations, counselors? Is there an offer?"

Rajani stood, her posture erect and stately. "My client authorizes me to offer five million dollars in exchange for a stipulation dismissing, with prejudice, the claims of all identified class members." The suggestion of a British accent embellished her voice. No matter how impressive she looked and sounded, however, the packaging didn't compensate for the lack of content in her offer.

"How many class members so far, Mr. Goodhue?"

Evan got to his feet. "Approximately one million, Your Honor."

The judge pretended to count on her fingers. "Gee whiz. That makes it about five bucks each. Three and a half or four after fees. Very generous." The judge bypassed Evan and looked directly at Henrietta. "How does that sound to you, Mrs. Edmonds?"

"Not very fair," she said in a shaky voice.

"I agree," said the judge. "As you know, it's my obligation under the law to pass on the fairness of any proposed settlement in a class action lawsuit. Even if you told me you were accepting this offer on behalf of the class, I would have to reject the deal. It's a no-brainer."

"Thank you very much, Judge. I told my attorneys I didn't think it was a very good idea."

"A wise decision." The judge turned to Evan. "Do you have a counteroffer?"

"We do, Your Honor. The counteroffer is three hundred fifty million. That's down from the five hundred million demanded in the complaint, a hefty discount for avoiding the time and expense of discovery and trial. My associate has the facts and figures to support the counteroffer."

With an indignant expression, Rajani pulled off her half-size glasses and said, "That's completely out of the question. We may as well stop right here—"

Judge Friel held up a hand. "Hold on a minute, counselor. I want to hear this. What do you have, Mr. Bachmann?"

Joel grabbed his chart and jumped up from his seat. "We surveyed a random sample of the class members, tallied their expenses, and averaged them out to find the out-of-pocket expense per victim—"

"Victim? These are customers, not victims," objected Rajani.

"All right, Ms. Choudhary, you've made your point. Go on Mr. Bachmann."

As Joel launched into his presentation, Evan glanced at him over the top of his client's head. Joel's suit jacket was unbuttoned, his shirt was loose and puckered at the beltline, and a slender streak of white saliva rimmed the corner of his mouth. Perhaps no one else noticed these details which, suddenly, made Evan shudder. Joel's other attributes were more important—a gregarious and enthusiastic manner, a logical, well-reasoned presentation. The judge was looking at him intently with an appearance of complete concentration on what he was saying.

Xavier Asante was the only attorney to remain seated. Evan sensed that he was biting his tongue. Xavier was not a quiet man, but he knew his place. He was just along for the ride today, to lend support to Rajani. Questions about the status of the criminal case would arise, and he was there to answer them. While he remained remarkably silent, his presence was felt in other ways. It was impossible to ignore him. How did a man find something like that to wear? The fitted summer suit was light gray, with a slight sheen to the material. The shirt was a peculiar shade of blue. Dana had a dress that color and she called it "periwinkle." The tie contrasted with the shirt. It was a very pale gray, almost white, with a matching triangle of fabric in the breast pocket of the jacket. His hair seemed perpetually wet, incapable of drying out.

Looking down at the table, Evan pressed a palm to the crown of his bald head and ran it down to the nape of his neck. He supposed that Xavier's thick, wet, sharp-edged black hair might be attractive to some women.

When Joel finished, the judge said, "Makes sense." She turned to Rajani. "How do you respond to that?"

"These figures are pie in the sky. Mr. Bachmann is adding in medical expenses and lost wages that can't be proved. Are the plaintiffs going to get the medical records for a million people? Prove causation for a million people? These are customers, Your Honor. They were added to the plaintiff class simply because they purchased Life Source. For all we know, nine hundred and ninety-nine thousand are perfectly happy with the product."

Joel countered, "I'm simply giving a reasoned basis for our counteroffer. At trial, we don't have to prove the exact amount of loss by every class member. We have to show that Tripp profited from false advertising, and that his product does *not* cure cancer, obesity, diabetes, arthritis, and everything else he claimed in his infomercial. We have that proof."

"And the proper measure of recovery," Evan added, "is the figure alleged in the complaint, which is the amount that Mr. Tripp reaped from consumer fraud. His net worth is approximately five hundred million, and all of that was derived from sales of Life Source. This money should be returned to the victims."

The judge turned to Rajani and said, "Go back to your client and see what you can come up with. There must be a middle ground here. Otherwise, you're in for a long, expensive ride, and we're going to get to know each other a little too well."

"Your Honor, at this point I can report unequivocally that Mr. Tripp isn't prepared to offer anything higher than five million until the criminal case is resolved."

"If you're asking for a stay of the proceedings in this case, I'm sorry," said Judge Friel. "The law is settled. A party facing criminal charges can be compelled to defend a related civil case. He can be called to testify, and if he takes the Fifth, the plaintiffs are entitled to an adverse inference against him."

"I'm not asking for a stay, Your Honor. I'm talking about a weakness in the plaintiffs' case. They don't have a case without a criminal conviction. If our client is acquitted, they have an uphill battle—an impossible burden, I submit. Mr. Tripp isn't going to pay a huge settlement here when there's a chance of full exoneration in federal court."

Evan's eyes danced with laughter. "I'm afraid Ms. Choudhary is mistaken. We don't need a criminal conviction. Deceptive advertising was already established in the FTC lawsuit. Our plaintiff class was lured into buying the product by the infomercials that were the subject of that lawsuit. After that, Mr. Tripp was enjoined from making any more advertisements. He defied the order, and now he's being prosecuted for contempt. This is just more of the same."

"I would agree with you there," said the judge. "Ms. Choudhary, it's time for you and your client to be reasonable here." She turned to Xavier. "And maybe you want to be reasonable in federal court, too. When is your next court date?"

Xavier rose to his feet. "Wednesday, Your Honor." His voice dripped with eminent courtesy.

"A criminal conviction looks like a foregone conclusion to me, Mr. Asante. Why aren't you negotiating a plea so you can limit your client's sentence exposure?"

Finally it was Xavier's turn for center stage, every inch of his façade in place. With a dramatic flourish he asked, "Make a deal? Should I advise my client to accept punishment for exercising his freedom of speech? Mr. Tripp is entitled to put the government to its proof. Beyond that, he's innocent of the charge. He's a businessman who believes in his product. He conveys this belief on television. Perhaps we should prosecute General Mills for saying that Cheerios is heart-healthy. This is free speech and entrepreneurship. This is America."

Asante paused for effect, and somehow, they gave it to him. The other attorneys were seated again, the result of a slow descent that began the minute he started talking. Before they could blink their eyes and see behind the glimmer, he continued his speech. "There will be no plea bargain. He's fighting this. Mr. Tripp's success has made him a scapegoat. He's the fall guy for every jealous populist, just because he earns more money than the average Joe. He's prosecuted for speaking his mind. Prosecuted on a whim to satisfy that base desire to find a villain behind every unfairness in the world. Any person who speaks his mind runs that risk. Put yourself out there, speak up, and get arrested. Report a home invasion, a murder, and get arrested for it!" Asante shot a look at Evan. *What was this about?* "Case in point. My new client, Frances Kallay. You've read the news. It's another example of prosecutorial whim. Like Darren Tripp, she spoke up, and look what happened! A prosecutor saw fit to target her on a hunch."

"We have a little more than a hunch here, Mr. Asante," said the judge. The color had been slowly rising in her cheeks during his soapboxing. "What does the Kallay murder have to do with our case?" She waved her hand in the air to stop him. "No, no, no, don't answer that! You made your point. Now, *you* get *my* point!" The judge turned to Evan's client. "Mrs. Edmonds, would you care to take the stand? I'll put you under oath and you can give us a better idea of what you're alleging in this lawsuit."

Henrietta's eyes sparkled at the suggestion. "Why, I'd be very happy to do that, Judge Friel!"

Rajani jumped to her feet. "Your Honor, I have to object." She maintained her civility, a dignified sort of indignity, as she spoke. "This is highly irregular. Maybe if this was a fairness hearing. But there's been no meeting of the minds on settlement."

The judge didn't seem to hear her. "Mr. Goodhue, would you kindly help your client to the stand please?"

Evan rose and put out a hand to Mrs. Edmonds.

Rajani kept talking. She hadn't been told to stop. "It's fundamentally unfair to allow the plaintiff to testify without permitting Mr. Tripp to put on a rebuttal witness. We can produce hundreds of satisfied customers, the people who got amazing relief from their symptoms by taking Life Source."

Actors, all of them. Evan had seen them in the infomercials. He'd love to cross-examine any witness that Rajani might call, and he said so now, as he assisted his client on her slow walk to the witness stand. "I have no objection to that, Your Honor. Bring them on."

The judge finally put a stop to Rajani's voice. "Take your seat, Ms. Choudhary. You want to talk fundamental? This is going to be half a dozen questions, no more. No direct or cross-examination. *I'm* doing the questioning. It's part of my *fundamental* duty as the supervising judge. If this case settles— and it *will*—I need to evaluate the fairness of any settlement in light of the alleged injuries."

Mrs. Edmonds was now on the stand, and Evan took his seat. The oath was administered, and the questioning began.

"Mrs. Edmonds, would you please give us some background as to your reasons for purchasing the product known as Life Source?"

"Certainly! Let's see..." The witness paused, collecting her thoughts. "It was about ten years ago, more or less, when I started to feel the symptoms of my rheumatoid arthritis..."

This would be anything but brief. Evan was pleased. But part of his mind was caught on a snag, whirring with thoughts of Xavier's bizarre ramblings and what Dana might say about it.

11 »   FAMILY

SHE HATED THIS. The man was playing them against each other, Evan against Dana, or vice versa, hard to tell. Any way you looked at it, he was making it personal. What was the endgame?

That afternoon, all attempts at phone communication failed. There was no chance to talk about it until they got home from work, and then it was only a brief exchange squeezed into the corners of family life. They waited until the kids were in bed and Brenda was behind a closed door, in her makeshift bedroom, before they hashed it out.

"What great luck," said Dana. "How did we both land cases against the same adversary?"

"Xavier Asante, no less. He's top of the heap. And his clients are two of the wealthiest people in New York."

"He must be thinking he struck gold."

"I'm not worried about him," said Evan. "He's full of himself. And he sure didn't win a merit badge from Judge Friel today. If anything, it was completely whacko the way he went off on a tangent…"

"Evan." She stared him down. "It wasn't whacko, and he wasn't trying to impress Judge Friel. He was directing his comments at *you*. It was a veiled threat."

"How do you call that a threat? He was stating his opinion that the police had no grounds to arrest Frances Kallay. He's going to make the same argument in criminal court. So, what else is new?"

"He knows you're going to tell me what he said in court, and he knows *I'm* going to tell *you* what he said to Eric on the phone, and you'll put two and two together."

"Tell me again what he said to Eric. I didn't think it sounded so bad."

"'Talk to Hargrove. Tell her to watch out, it isn't going to look pretty for her.'"

Evan paused to consider. "So, you're thinking..."

"He wants to make you worry about me and rile up your caveman instincts, so you'll want to protect me..."

"He knows how much I love you."

"That's part of the equation."

"Not necessarily. For all we know, he's under the impression we're just a power couple, sleeping in separate beds."

She smiled. "I don't know about you, but *I'm* in this marriage only for the power."

"Yeah, baby. Look where I got you." He gestured around their living room, lights low, ten o'clock, past their bedtime, little ones asleep down the hall. Dana sat on the couch that had the cranberry juice stain Natalie made when she was three, and Evan sat across from her in the easy chair that was a magnet for crayons and plastic GI Joes pushed deep into the cushions. Their eyes met and held.

Dana started to laugh. He put on a hurt expression. "What's so funny?" But she only laughed harder until he melted and laughed along with her.

She stopped for a minute, caught her breath and said, "You're all the power I need, darling."

His manly ego was appeased. He cleared his throat. "So. Let's get back to the point. What's Asante got up his sleeve? He knows you run the show in your bureau. Does he want you to order a dismissal of the charges against Frances? Or does he want me to lower the counteroffer in the class action? Who's he interested in helping more, Frances or Darren?" Evan punctuated each name with a toss of a hand, right, then left. This one or that?

"Neither one."

"How so?" Evan raised an eyebrow in exaggerated fashion. "What about every defense attorney's favorite ethics rule? A lawyer shall zealously advocate on behalf of his client within the bounds of the law."

"Oh, he'll zealously advocate. But the main person he's interested in helping is himself."

"Of course." Evan was on her wavelength. "Money speaks the loudest. It always does."

Two wealthy clients. Two fat attorney's fees. Asante stood to gain more if the settlement in the class action was lower, leaving more money in Darren Tripp's bank account. On the other hand, the more hours that Asante put into the Kallay case, the more his fee grew.

"He doesn't want me to dismiss the murder charge. He wants *you* to back down."

"Sorry, no chance. I'm sticking to my guns."

"Good for you, and good for Henrietta Edmonds. But ... I guess that means you don't love your wife very much." She put on the best pouty face she could muster.

"Good try, my love. You forget—I know that you're tougher than a million Xavier Asantes."

"I'm not feeling particularly tough these days."

"You need a vacation, that's all."

They fell silent for a moment that stretched into a full minute.

"Come on," said Evan. He stood up, walked over to her, and offered a hand. "Let's go to bed."

She placed her hand in his and allowed him to pull her up

into his arms. Pressed against him, she felt the beat of his heart and found that niche under his shirt collar, where her nose liked to nestle in the crook of his neck. She loved the smell of him.

"Shall we?" he whispered.

Next morning, Eric took a trip to the basement of the Criminal Court building, which housed the headquarters of the DA's squad, an area affectionately known as the "Dungeon." Gilbert sat on his ancient rolling desk chair while Eric propped himself in a partial sit on the edge of the battered metal desk, reviewing the list of Kallay's competitors.

"Any hits?" Eric asked.

"Not one. A couple of 'em have misdemeanor records, nothing serious."

"I guess they're all too busy designing clothes that no one's gonna wear."

"Oh, someone's wearing those rags, better believe it."

"Yeah, the stick girls walking the runways. I don't see any normal people dressed like that on the street."

"You don't hang with the right crowd, man. They wouldn't let you onto that street. The right street. Madison Avenue."

"Talking from experience, are you?" Eric laughed. He put the list down and started flipping through a pile of photographs of the Spring 2001 collection, taken during fashion week in September 2000. Designs by Kallay and other designers on the list. "I don't get it. Are these clothes or Halloween costumes?"

"Don't knock it," Gil retorted in his tough-guy voice.

Eric nudged him and flashed a photo. "I guess you like this chick with the blouse unbuttoned down to her waist."

"I said don't knock it."

"Ooo ... getting sensitive?"

"I wouldn't be so goddamn cocky. These fashion people blow us out of the water. They're rolling in dough. You gotta respect their money."

"I'll remember that next time you talk about scum-of-the-earth billionaire drug lords. I guess I'll have to start respecting *their* money too."

"This is different."

"Money is money."

"Depends how you make your money. This is art, not cocaine."

"Art! That's a good one!" Eric was searching for a clever rejoinder when he glanced at Gilbert and noticed, in those eyes that could be hard as black ice, a subtle glow of joviality. Gil was pulling his leg. "Okay, enough joking around. I'm going into the grand jury tomorrow. We need something to cross-examine Frances about. We have diddly-squat so far."

"There's time. Tomorrow's Wednesday. Isn't Thursday one-eighty eighty day?"

"Yeah, but in the morning. We arrested her Friday morning. Six days. I need the grand jury to vote a true bill before the end of the day tomorrow so I'll have it in court Thursday morning at ten."

"Well, you already have her on cross. There's double motive. Revenge for the beatings and money. He died without a will and she inherits everything. There's opportunity. She's alone in the house with him and the gun. And she's a liar. Made up that story about hearing a tussle in the den."

"The jury can find an explanation for that. A trick of the mind, brought on by the traumatic event. No question the gunshots were loud enough to hear upstairs in the bedroom. She's shocked and scared. She creeps down three flights of stairs while her mind is filling in the blanks. She tricks herself into thinking she heard an intruder minutes before."

Gil blinked his eyes and shook his head. "What are you? A Xavier wannabe?"

"I'm just anticipating his arguments. I have to be prepared for anything they come up with. We have no fingerprints, and the DNA isn't in yet."

"Stay on track, Boy Wonder."

"I am on track, looking for explanations. There's no explanation for the fashion sketches, except hers. You didn't find them at Kallay's business offices. They're still missing. That's consistent with her claim that someone stole them and shot Kallay in the process. The sketches are worth a lot of money. Like you said, 'Respect the money.'"

"I don't buy it. This home invasion story was bullshit from the get go. Someone helped the little lady. Dana's with me on that one."

"'Dana, Dana, always Dana.'"

"Okay. I eat my words. But isn't the Dane gonna hold your hand in the grand jury tomorrow?"

"She'll be there, but it's *my* grand jury."

"Yeah, but if Frances gives you an opening and you miss it, Dana will be there to whisper in your ear."

"Thanks for the confidence in my ability. I'm not going to miss anything. I'm going to figure this out. Let's get back to the theory that someone was working with Frances. Why haven't we found this person?"

"So far, every contact seems legit except the one phone number I told you about. She made a couple of calls from her cell phone to that number, and one of the calls was from the hospital, before we arrested her. But we can't trace the number. It was a burner phone."

"That makes it doubly suspicious. Let's assume that's the accomplice. What's their motive? It can't be to steal the sketches. She inherits everything anyway. Of course, the law won't allow you to inherit from someone you murder. But that's not what she's thinking. If she planned it with someone, the two of them are thinking they'll get away with it and she'll inherit everything, including the drawings."

"The theft is just part of the cover story."

"So the drawings are somewhere else. We have to find them. She must've picked a good hiding place."

"Or maybe there aren't any drawings at all. Hubby's creative juices weren't flowing."

"Another reason to kill him." Eric paused, his mind at work. "Hey, what did you find out about their son? What's his name?"

"Luther."

"You're kidding. Luther?"

Gil shrugged. "College kid, twenty years old."

"About the age when you want to kill your father."

"Speak for yourself."

"I'm talking about a father who named you 'Luther,' who does those awful things to your mother."

"Well, maybe the kid wanted to kill him, but he didn't do it. I checked out his alibi. We've got witnesses putting Luther in his dorm room at Cornell on the night of the murder."

"Kids who would lie for him."

"Don't think so. One of 'em's the son of the chief administrative judge. *He* wouldn't want to be caught lying."

"Maybe Luther drove down to Manhattan and back again without anyone noticing."

"Take a look at a map. It's impossible. Four hours each way."

"Maybe he hired someone. What else do we know about him?"

"Not much. He's a spoiled rich brat and he's smart, but

not the way you're thinking. Not the contract murder type of smart. He's number one in his class, a biophysics major, whatever the hell that gets you."

"It gets you to a nicer place than the Dungeon, that's for sure. Don't knock it."

"Not."

"Maybe the wife hired someone, but she doesn't seem like the type to me."

"Don't go by looks."

"What about one of the competitors on that list?" Eric turned his head and nodded at the paper on top of the heap in the middle of the desk. "Maybe, if there *were* sketches, Frances used them to get someone to do the dirty deed."

"Murder contract. Sign on the dotted line. Payment in fashion designs." Gil picked up the list. "We haven't found any connections between Frances and these people." He swatted the piece of paper with the back of his hand.

"In fact, you haven't uncovered *anything* about her."

"Not true, not true."

"Are you even looking?"

"Day and night. We found out a few things."

"Tell me."

"People say…"

"What people?"

"To be particular, Loránd Kallay's administrative assistant, a fruit named Cedrick Cougar, and one of his pattern makers, Miranda Carlton. They loved the guy. Said he was a saint, wonderful to work for. But they didn't have much nice to say about Frances. They've seen her around the office. Cedrick even had dinner with them a couple of times. I talked to Cedrick and Miranda separately, but they agree on a few things about Frances."

"Like what?"

"Like she didn't seem to have much interest in her husband's fashions and hardly wore his designs unless she was at a huge media event. When she was at the office, she would make little cutting remarks to him in front of other people. She didn't seem to care if anyone was listening." Gil put on a squeaky female voice: "'There's no *sex appeal* to this, Loránd.' Sir Cedrick thought she was way out of line. Kallay was a 'genius' designer. A 'real woman's designer' he called him."

Eric picked up two photos and examined one, then the other. "Compared to the other designers, his stuff is more conservative, if you could call it that. So why's she berating him? What's that all about? The guy made a lot of money."

"Miranda said the wife wanted him to design something racier."

Eric brought an image of Frances to mind, a slight woman, pale and hunched over, clutching the overlapping sides of her Kallay robe. A mess. Hard to imagine but, under different circumstances, she might look good in something racy.

"And another thing," Gil went on. "They say Loránd defended his designs when she made these little comments. He was kind of pathetic about it, but said he couldn't design any other way. It was … you know…"

"His art?"

Gil cracked a crooked smile. "Yeah, his art. Cedrick and Miranda said he was a strong businessman but different when Frances was around. Always ready to do anything she asked, trying to get on her good side. She didn't pay any attention to him half the time, like he was nobody, and he was always sniffing after her…"

"Sniffing?"

"You know, heeling like a dog she owned."

That fragile-looking, bruised woman … a dog trainer?

"That doesn't sound like the woman we saw."

"You can't tell a dead body to heel."

"What about wife beating? Did they have any suspicions? Did Kallay have a temper?"

"Nothing to report. He was a 'saint' over and over again."

Eric thought a minute. If Loránd was beating Frances, wouldn't that come out somehow? Why wasn't she using the battering as a defense instead of the unbelievable home invasion story? Eric was aware that battered women often blamed themselves and were ashamed and sought to hide it. That could be the reason. But maybe Frances was smart enough to know she wouldn't win with this defense. Shooting someone in retaliation for a beating, even if the beating was inflicted only seconds before, was not a defense to intentional murder. Deadly physical force was justified only to counter the threat of deadly physical force. She would have to prove that she grabbed the gun and shot him in the midst of an attack that threatened her life. Not very believable. She was noticeably weaker than her husband.

Eric glanced up at the audibly ticking second hand of the industrial-strength wall clock. "In ten minutes I've got some people coming in. Loránd's sister and brother-in-law. Maybe they can make some sense of this. Can you come up and sit in?"

"Yeah, no problem."

Eric tossed the photos aside and stood up from his half-sit on the corner of the desk. "Argh! Remind me not to sit here again." He limped toward the elevator.

Gil called after him: "I'll be up in ten."

The sister and her husband looked to be in their late forties, younger than the deceased. Her name was Greta, his name was William. She'd given up her maiden name, Kallay, and had taken her husband's last name, Sperry.

They sat side-by-side in the two guest chairs, pushed close together. Eric was behind his desk, and Gil sat in a corner of the room, behind Eric, quietly observing. To some people, Gil's appearance could be both startling and oddly reassuring. There was something wise in his asymmetrical, pock-marked face. From the start, the guests knew he was on their side when Eric introduced him as the senior investigator, and Gil shyly acknowledged them with his winning, crookedly innocent smile.

William Sperry was well put together in business-casual attire. A hint of curly masculine hair edged the opening at his collar where the top button was undone, and the glint of a gold wristwatch peeked from under the starched cuff. He held Greta's hand on top of their conjoined armrests. He was dry-eyed but furrow-browed and solicitous where his wife was concerned.

Greta Sperry's eyes were red-rimmed, her hair unwashed and messy, pushed behind ears with empty piercings in the lobes. She wore an expensive, form-fitting sweat suit which, in her case, would be called "athletic wear." Something her brother might have designed had he been in the business of exercise clothing. The sudden tearfulness and random quaver in her voice bespoke genuine emotion. Greta adored her older brother, and she was grieving sorely.

William squeezed and stroked her hand as she spoke. "He was a gentle, loving husband to her. He did everything for Frances. Everything!" Here, her voice faltered. "I ... I couldn't stand that woman, and this just proves how horrible she is. How absolutely horrible!"

This was delicate. Eric might venture a hint that, maybe, Loránd had done horrible things as well. Perhaps Greta had seen a few things that she wasn't facing up to or willing to admit. Perhaps Greta found her sister-in-law so despicable that anything Loránd might have done to her was well-deserved and something to be tacitly ignored or forgiven. But, at this moment, even the slightest suggestion of a dark secret in the Kallay marriage could backfire in a big way. Greta Sperry didn't appear to be in the mood to contemplate even the smallest imperfection in her murdered brother. Eric decided to stick to open-ended questions.

"How often would you get together with them?"

"I saw my brother at least once a week, sometimes more often. Last Wednesday we had lunch. It was the last time I saw him."

"And Frances?"

"Never. Not if I could help it."

William Sperry interjected, "We weren't in the habit of socializing with them as a couple, but Greta had a very special relationship with her brother. I have to say, he was a fantastic gent. Very talented too."

"When I was with him," Greta continued, "I didn't even like to talk about her. I would change the subject if he mentioned her. Whenever he spoke of Frances it was always something nice. She had wonderful taste in decorating their home, or she looked classy in his designs, or she was a great mother to Luther, or she was the new president of some charity or other. Always something nice, and it just sickened me that he was so snowed by her. She was very controlling and would just walk into a place and take it over. People at his office talked about her behind his back, and he didn't even know it."

Eric was having difficulty reconciling this description of Frances with his image of her from the night of the murder. He asked Greta, "So, you knew some of the people at your brother's office?"

"I would visit from time to time, and I would hear things.

Little jokes about Frances ordering Loránd around, telling him to design dresses for half-naked strumpets. She was beneath him! A complete lowlife! He couldn't see her for what she really was, a money grabber and a name-dropper."

"I understand they got married twenty-three years ago, before your brother was wealthy or well-known."

"We all came from nothing. But she married him when he was on the rise. She could see where he was going." Greta's lip was quivering again, and she brought a handkerchief to her nose. William gave her hand an extra squeeze and whispered, "It's okay. Take your time, baby."

Baby. William didn't look like the sort of "gent" to use that word. "Mr. Sperry, did you have the same impression of Frances Kallay?"

"Absolutely. I hardly knew the woman, but I can say that Greta's instinct about people is always on the mark."

Greta finished blowing her nose and was ready to talk again. She had more to say. "I'm glad you arrested her. There's no question in my mind she did it. She wanted the money, every penny of it. She wanted it all for herself."

Eric could see he wouldn't be getting much more out of this interview.

Harry Potter was a good way to get her mind off things, including tomorrow's grand jury in the Kallay case and ADA Weingarten's news that he'd been unable to adjourn the Pineda hearing. Dana opened the volume at the bookmark, and by the time she'd finished reading the first paragraph, she'd vanquished the last, lingering worry in her head. *(Wouldn't a bit of wizardry come in handy to unravel the Kallay case?)*

Eight o'clock: story time for the entire family. Brenda was in the living room, sipping her chamomile tea and reading a cozy mystery. Evan was in Tally's room, reading a Dr. Seuss book to her, and Dana was in the master bedroom, reading to Travis. She sat on the bed with her left arm around his shoulder, their backs propped up on the pillows and knees bent, the book held between them, half on her lap, half on his. These were the wonderful moments she lived for.

"Quality one-on-one time" they liked to call it. On occasion, the more cynical term Evan and Dana used was "divide and conquer." Because of their age difference, the children seldom enjoyed the same books. It was a shame. Dana loved to be snuggled between them, the girl in teddy-bear PJs on the right, the boy in baseball PJs on the left. There were times when it worked. Travis would have to be in his ultra-patient, big brother mood to tolerate a simplistic fairy tale at Natalie's level. Or Natalie would have to be so droopy-eyed with fatigue that she didn't care to understand a story at her brother's level, taking satisfaction in the comfort of closeness and the sound of a parent's voice.

Dana was reading the first Potter tale to Travis. The story was at the point where Hagrid was explaining to Harry that the Dursleys had lied to him. They'd failed to tell Harry that he was a wizard and had made up a story about the way his parents had died. Halfway through this passage, Travis started fidgeting. Abruptly, he sat up taller, turned to his mother and said, "Mom. Have you ever lied to me?"

The question was a punch in the stomach. He must have discovered her in a lie. Why else would he be asking? Children knew. They understood so much. But maybe this was a small thing. Every good parent lied. What about Santa Claus and the tooth fairy? She couldn't remember any big lies she'd ever told her children, the kind that, when discovered, would do serious damage to her credibility and engender a profound sense of betrayal. The real lies were the kind she dealt with every day at work. Was the witness consciously fabricating or innocently recounting the "facts" from a unique perspective? There were days when she believed that objective "facts" didn't exist— only perceptions. She'd come to expect that different people simply perceived and described the same event differently.

"That's a tough question," she said to Travis. "Lying is wrong, so I try very hard not to lie. I don't remember ever…" She stopped herself before giving a politician's answer. "Maybe we have to decide first what we mean by a 'lie.' Sometimes, people say little things that are untrue and it's considered good manners. If you ask me 'how are you?' and I say 'fine' even though my tooth is throbbing from a toothache, do you call that a lie? I might be trying to protect you from hearing about something that would upset or worry you."

"Okay, Mom. Okay, okay. I get it. But just because you're being so good and everything with this great reason to lie doesn't mean it isn't a lie."

Oh, my. She wasn't going to get away with anything. This kid of hers was so smart and so ethical. "You're right. There's a big difference between the actual words that come out of your mouth and the motive behind them."

"Yeah, kind of, you mean the reason for lying isn't the same as telling the truth. So you could be saying you *have* to go to work when really you don't *have* to. We have Dad's work, so you don't *have* to make extra money but maybe you just say that because you don't want to upset or worry me."

Double punch. Where was this coming from? Maybe Travis was remembering that year when he was so little, only two years old. 1995, when she took a full year's leave of absence from the DA's office. The family had been through a tough time at the end of 1994, not to mention the guilt Dana suffered as a consequence. She couldn't shake the thought that, if she'd only been home with Travis, none of it would have happened. That was the genesis of her idea to take a break from work, and soon after that, she learned she was pregnant with Natalie. Staying home meant she didn't have to worry about going to court looking huge as a house. In August she gave birth, and that same month they celebrated Travis's third birthday. By January, Dana was more than ready to get back to the office. She realized how much she was missing it.

Was Travis nostalgic for that time? He rarely mentioned it. He'd been so young, and it was best not to talk about it: there were some things she didn't want him to remember. But when she returned to work and Grandma Brenda came to help, Travis never asked Dana to quit her job and be a stay-at-home mom. Not that she could remember. Perhaps she'd volunteered an explanation by way of justification. *I have to work.* Or was he putting his own interpretation on what he heard, so many mornings, when she was leaving the house? *I have to get going now. Have to get to work.*

She closed the book, laid it on the bed to her right, and pulled Travis closer. "If I've ever said anything to make you think that I have to go to work for the money, then I've given you the wrong impression. That's one reason to go to work, but you're right, we could live well enough on Daddy's salary. Maybe we'd have to live in a smaller apartment or cut out some extra expenses, but we could live just fine."

"Or we could live on your money if Dad didn't want to go to work."

"Right. We could. So if I ever said I have to go to work, I'm not lying about it, but I'm saying it for other reasons."

"Like what? Are they forcing you?"

"Who do you mean?"

"Your boss, or whoever."

She smiled. Patrick forcing her to come to work? At the end of her year off, he *did* strongly suggest that he wanted to see her back in the office. "No, sweetie. No one's forcing me."

Not even myself. And she stopped for a minute to let that truth sink in. She knew her reasons and had discussed the subject with herself many times. Maybe she'd never expressed it adequately to her children. But it was something she wanted them to know, to internalize, to have for themselves when they were adults. She was proud of her career, and why not? "The biggest reason I go to work is that I enjoy it. I can use my brain and my skills in interesting ways, and it's very rewarding."

"So, you like it better than being here."

"Nope. No way. I love being here with you. But the two things can't be compared. There's a time and a place for everything. And I don't think I could be your mother unless I also had my career. After a while, you'd begin to notice that something was missing in me."

Travis considered this with a very serious look on his face. They were quiet for several seconds until she asked, "What about you? Aren't there things *you* like to do away from your family?"

"Sure, but that's different."

"How is it different?"

"I'm just a kid. We're supposed to have fun."

She laughed and said, "You should see all the fun *I* have at work! But right now, I can think of something more fun." She started to reach for the book, but Travis shot over her and grabbed it first. They settled back into place with the book on their laps, and Dana started up where they left off. Soon, Harry was making preparations for his first semester at Hogwarts.

12 »   JURY

IN A WAY, it didn't help that Dana was in the room. She was there to offer advice if he needed it, but her presence made him nervous. Eric wouldn't admit it, and he certainly tried not to show it. When he was a rookie, things were different. He wanted to cling to her, to walk in her shadow. But by now, as a senior trial attorney, he'd acquired his sea legs. It didn't matter. For big cases, it was common practice for the bureau chief to come into the grand jury. He reminded himself that this policy applied equally to all assistant district attorneys in the bureau.

It wasn't personal.

The grand jury room reminded Eric of the smaller lecture halls from law school days. With a full house, twenty-three grand jurors sat like students in a classroom. There were three rows of stadium seating, each row formed by a narrow, semi-circular desk, with chairs well-spaced along its length. The focal point was at the front of the room, where a professor would stand if it was a lecture hall. There was a table with two chairs, one for the witness and one for defense counsel, if the witness happened to be the defendant. A pitcher of water, paper cups, and a box of tissues were placed at a corner of the bare table. There was a chair a few feet to the side of the table for the stenographer. At the beginning and end of the presentation, the ADA acted as the "legal advisor" of the grand jury, standing at the front of the room to instruct them on the law. When a witness was called in, the ADA switched hats, became

148

a lawyer again, and went to the top of the stadium seating, behind the grand jurors, to question the witness.

This day, it was Eric standing at the back of the room doing the questioning, and Dana was standing a few paces behind him, near the back wall.

Critics of New York's grand jury system liked to say that it was the prosecutor's instrument, a mere rubber stamp. Felony indictments were returned in a very high percentage of cases. The state's chief judge once commented that even a "ham sandwich" could be indicted. In the days when Eric was assigned to lower level felonies, the place did seem like a factory assembly line. Cases were run through, one after another, and indictments voted every ten minutes. Buy and busts, purse snatchings, grand theft auto, burglary.

But the critics ignored a few things. The grand jury was the voice of the community, which made the final decision whether to charge the accused with a felony. The grand jury was secret, protecting the identity of witnesses and allowing them to speak freely without being cross-examined or intimidated by the defendant. The grand jury transcript was reviewed by a superior court judge, who looked for abuses in the process and sufficiency of the evidence. And the grand jury was the defendant's last chance to stave off a felony indictment. Every defendant had a right to testify.

In Eric's experience, the grand jury was not merely his rubber stamp. Not in the big cases, anyway. And if he was wrong about this one, the grand jury would tell him he was wrong. That wasn't such a bad thing either. The grand jury was there to protect the unjustly accused from the prosecutor's mistakes. If he was wrong about Frances Kallay, she was entitled to walk out of here a free woman.

It wasn't personal.

No doubt, many of the men and women in this room had

heard about the Kallay murder. There were no rules against grand jurors reading or listening to the news during their term of service. When Eric first walked into the chamber that morning and announced "The People of the State of New York against Frances Kallay," he noticed a glimmer of recognition in several faces. Many of them were older faces. It was easier for retirees to interrupt their lives for the full month of the grand jury term—the required length of service. They also didn't mind the measly juror fee, which gave them some extra cash along with their pensions. A few other segments of society were represented here: unemployed people who collected benefit checks, and employees with civic-minded bosses who continued to pay their full salaries while on jury duty.

In this jury, no one had raised a hand to beg off of the case. It was up to them to report any perceived inability to remain objective. Everyone wanted to hear this case. There was only one empty spot today in the middle of the room. Mr. Hannigan had called in sick that morning. The remaining twenty-two jurors would suffice. A quorum of sixteen was the minimum, but with fewer grand jurors it became more difficult to get an indictment. Twelve votes were needed to charge Frances Kallay with intentional murder.

Police Officer Martin Smith was sitting at the witness table. The stenographer's fingers were moving. Eric felt Dana at his back as he spoke. "Please tell the grand jury what happened when you responded to the Kallay residence shortly after midnight on Friday, June 22 of this year."

"A woman who identified herself as Frances Kallay answered the door. She wasn't dressed ... I mean, she was wearing a robe, like a bathrobe only nicer, and she had it wrapped around her, clutching her stomach. I asked if she was the person who called and if she was all right."

"What was her answer?"

"She said yes, she was the person who called 911. She said her husband had been shot by an intruder and he was dead."

Already a grand juror's hand was up in the air. It was Ms. Whitely, a very vocal corporate executive who was always on her cell phone during breaks. She was the most fully employed, the most in-the-world person on the jury, and for that reason, she thought she was entitled to run the show. Grand jurors were free to ask questions during the proceedings, but part of Eric's job was to keep the interruptions under control, without cutting off their right to participate.

Involuntarily, he glanced over his shoulder at Dana. Damn! He kicked himself for reverting to his childhood. He knew exactly what to do but was still looking for approval. Dana gave him a slight nod, showing that she agreed with his instincts. Allowing a single question now might satisfy this particular juror and keep her quiet for a little while.

He looked at Ms. Whitely as he announced, mostly for the stenographer's benefit, "A grand juror has a question." Whenever possible, he refrained from saying their names in front of a witness.

"Isn't that hearsay?" she asked. "Everything that Officer Smith said to her and what she answered—I don't think we're allowed to consider that."

No, but maybe you should consider that I'm trained in the exceptions to the hearsay rule—res gestae and party admissions. "Thank you for the question. As your legal advisor, I instruct you that this testimony, and any additional testimony you might hear today about conversations with Frances Kallay, is properly admissible and should be considered in making your determination." How did that sound? Eric didn't turn around again, but he felt—or imagined—the warmth of Dana's approval on his back. He also noticed a couple of the jurors directing mildly-veiled dagger eyes at Ms. Whitely. Their patience was being tested. It was difficult to be confined with certain people in a windowless room for a full month.

Eric continued his questioning. "What happened next?"

"Frances Kallay led me and my partner into the den on the first floor and showed me her husband. He was sprawled on the floor, face down, on the opposite side of the room. There was blood on his shirt and pooling under him, on the floor. The paramedics were right behind us. They checked the body for vitals and declared him dead."

"Did you have any further conversation with Frances Kallay?"

"Yes. I asked her what happened. She said she was upstairs on the fourth floor in the master bedroom getting ready for bed while her husband was working in the den. He was alone, and she didn't think he was expecting any visitors. It was close to midnight, maybe fifteen minutes before. She heard voices and some noises like furniture banging around, and then she heard gunshots. She was scared. She waited a minute before she came downstairs and found him. She said she called 911 immediately and left everything as it was. A wall safe in the den was open, and her husband's fashion designs for the 2002 season were missing. He was the owner of a fashion business, House of Loránd, and his designs were quite valuable."

"Did you check the front door to the residence?"

"Yes, there were no signs of forced entry, nothing broken."

"Did the house have a security system?"

"No. I mean, we noticed that a new system with video equipment was being installed, but it wasn't operational yet."

"Please describe the den as you found it."

"There was a desk, and the safe was on the wall behind it.

All of the furniture seemed to be in place except for the desk chair. It was tipped over and lying next to the victim."

"Was there any evidence of a struggle?"

"Not that I could see. Everything was neat except for that chair. It looked like the victim fell on it when he was shot, making it tip over. The weapon was exactly in the middle of the desktop. A handgun. It was a Browning semiautomatic, .22 caliber."

"Did you ask Frances Kallay about the gun?"

"No, but when she noticed me looking at it, she said, 'That's my husband's gun. He keeps it in the desk drawer.'"

Eric continued the examination, covering the chain of custody of the gun after Nicole Verona tested it, the recovery of three shell casings and the bullet from the wall, and the search of the house. Before dismissing the witness, he asked the jury if they had any questions for Officer Smith. "Raise your hand and I'll come around." This was the better way to do it, to screen the questions first. As predicted, Ms. Whitely's hand was up. As Eric made his way over to her, she gave him a cold stare, like a boss displeased with her subordinate. "You forgot something. There was no sign of a break in. So the front door must have been left unlocked before she went to bed, or maybe someone knocked or rang the doorbell and her husband let him in."

"Is that a question?"

"Ask him if he asked her those things. About the door being open, or hearing a doorbell."

Eric had avoided these topics because he knew that Officer Smith hadn't asked Frances about them, and he planned for Gil to clarify these points. Now that Eric thought of it, maybe he was trying to shield Smith from possible criticism for his oversights. Despite Ms. Whitely's condescending attitude, he was grateful for her questions and the self-awareness they brought. This was an example of the grand jury keeping him honest with himself.

Standing next to Ms. Whitely, Eric said, "A grand juror has a few questions. First, did you ask Frances Kallay if she left the front door unlocked before she went upstairs?"

"No, I didn't ask her that."

"Did you ask her if she heard a knock or a doorbell before she heard the other noises downstairs?"

"No."

"Did she ever volunteer any information about hearing a doorbell or someone knocking on the front door before the shooting?"

"No."

"Thank you, Officer." Eric paused and looked around the room. No other hands were raised. "You may step out."

As Officer Smith made his exit, Eric walked to the back of the room, where Dana was getting up from her chair. They came within inches of each other. "So far so good," she said in a low voice.

"No major gaffes?"

"Nope. All good. Who do you want next?"

"OCME. Kei Tajima."

"I'll get him," Dana volunteered.

When she left the room, Eric went over his notes. He had three witnesses planned before Mrs. Kallay made her appearance.

Tajima would give the details of the autopsy and his opinion about the time and cause of death, the distance between the shooter and the victim, the trajectory of the bullets, and the order in which the wounds were sustained.

Nicki would testify that she found the Browning placed in the middle of the desk with its left side facing up, that the bullets recovered from the victim's body had been fired from that gun, and that the identifiable fingerprint matched the victim, but DNA testing had not yet been completed.

Gilbert would testify that when he spoke to Frances Kallay at the hospital, she said they "always" kept the front door locked, and she didn't recall hearing any knocking or the doorbell that night. Gil would also testify that, after conducting tests, investigators determined that knocking on the front door and other noises on the first floor, including voices, physical fighting, and banging or falling furniture, could not be heard from the fourth floor. The doorbell could be heard, and most likely, gunshots as well. Of course, this theory couldn't be tested by firing a gun on the first floor. Gil would also testify that Loránd Kallay's sister confirmed that the victim was left-handed. At the time Gil arrested Francis, he confirmed that she was right-handed, and he collected a DNA sample by buccal swab and took photographs of her upper chest, arms, and back.

Although Officer Smith was with Gil at the time of the arrest and could have answered questions about the photos, Eric was saving the strongest evidence for last. Minutes before Frances Kallay was scheduled to testify, the grand jurors would be passing around the photographs of those bruises on her body.

Gilbert finished testifying a few minutes before Frances was due to arrive, and the jury stepped out for a break. Eric and Dana spoke quietly in an empty corner of the ante room to the grand jury chamber. It was the moment of truth. What did Dana think of the case?

"Sorry, Eric. Not much here."

"Is it that weak?"

"If I were on this grand jury and had only this much to go on, I would vote for dismissal. What do we have? A story that doesn't make sense. She has access to the gun, and she's the only one in the house with him. She has injuries that aren't explained. Possibly the jury could deduce that she's a victim of battering, but there's no expert testimony on that..."

"Patient confidentiality. I couldn't get the evidence..."

"Right, I know."

"But I'm allowed to argue reasonable inferences. If they infer that these are battering injuries, she has a motive, and then it makes sense that she made up the story about the intruder. The time of death is likely earlier than 11:45, so she delayed before calling 911. She was getting her story together and prepping the scene. She wiped the gun, pressed Kallay's index finger on it, and put the gun down like a left-handed person because she's right-handed and was trying to cover her tracks."

Dana looked skeptical. "That's a lot to infer. Maybe things will look different after she testifies. Then again, maybe she'll be a no show. If I were Frances Kallay, I wouldn't be walking into this grand jury. She can only hurt herself."

"How would she know that in advance?"

"Oh, I think Xavier is smart enough to guess, and that's what worries me. Something isn't right here. He knows that her statements don't make sense, and he knows about her injuries. So, he can guess our theory of motive and opportunity, even if he's unclear whether we think Frances acted alone or let an accomplice into the house to do the dirty deed."

"*He's* unclear..."

"Just as we are. Either way, Frances can only make it worse by coming in here and sticking to her discredited story about an intruder."

"And she knows I'll be cross-examining her about the photos."

"That's dangerous. I'm debating whether you should stay away from that tactic. If she repeats her story, she won't be testifying about her physical condition. She won't open the door to cross-examination on that subject. A judge could throw out the indictment for prosecutorial overreaching."

"But we already introduced the photos in *our* case. And I think that was the right thing to do." Even Eric could hear the defensiveness in his own voice. "Look what would happen if we *hadn't* put the photos in. A judge might say it's just as much a reason to dismiss the indictment. Xavier could argue that we withheld exculpatory evidence of a defense—justification or extreme emotional disturbance."

"Hmm. It does cut both ways. Tends to show a motive to kill and a defense to intentional murder." Dana crossed her arms, leaned against the wall, and dropped her gaze to the floor.

"Isn't that what you said? Even if it isn't an absolute defense to intentional murder, she can play the sympathy card and hope for a manslaughter indictment. Maybe she's hoping for ten years in prison instead of twenty-five to life."

"That sounds just as strange. Hoping for manslaughter." Dana was still looking at her shoes, and Eric felt the intensity of her thoughts. This wasn't easy. He made a suggestion. "Before I question her about the photos, I'll look over my shoulder at you and raise an eyebrow. You can give me the nod, yay or nay."

"All right. It's a plan." She looked at her watch and scanned the large waiting area. "Only a few minutes to go, and I don't see them yet." A half dozen witnesses and police officers were scattered throughout the room, a few of them talking to ADAs. Like airplanes in a holding pattern, several cases were scheduled to go into the grand jury, back-to-back, as soon as the Kallay presentation was over.

"So, tell me," Eric said. "What's your gut instinct on this?" He was still nervous about every decision he'd made along the way, the biggest one being the decision to have Frances arrested in the first place.

"You mean, what's my vote if I ignore the lack of hard evidence in this case?" She looked at him with smiling eyes.

"Don't be too polite, now."

She became serious again. "To be honest, my instincts are dormant right now. I don't think I'll have a sense of guilt or innocence until I see her face and hear her voice."

From across the room, a subtle wave of energy emanated. They turned to look. Frances Kallay was entering the waiting area, accompanied by her attorney, Xavier Asante, and two uniformed correction officers.

It didn't take more than a fraction of a second. With the stealth of a heat-seeking missile, Asante's dark eyes shifted, aimed, and found their target. Dana returned the gaze.

Eric hardly recognized her. The transformation in appearance was startling. With a straight spine and shoulders pushed back, Frances Kallay walked steadily on three-inch heels into the grand jury chamber. Self-assured, in control, she could have been a CEO of a major corporation, walking into a business meeting. Asante was her giant monkey loping along behind, his elegance eclipsed by hers. She was a petite woman, and her heels barely brought her up to the level of his shoulders.

Eric had seen enough of the Kallay clothing line in photographs to know that Frances was wearing one of her husband's more conservative skirt-suits, designed for the businesswoman. "Conservative" only in comparison to his casual designs. The suit was far from conventional, something that would turn heads in the midst of grays and pinstripes on Wall Street. It was high fashion, plum in color, with a tight skirt, sculpted jacket, and a blouse showing a bit of white lace above the lapel, under her collarbone.

How did she manage to spring out of Rikers Island? Of course, she couldn't have. She'd been remanded without bail. That meant she must have bribed a few correction officers to ensure delivery of the right cosmetics and clothing to Rikers, as well as several hours of privacy in front of a mirror.

Her preparations involved more than cosmetics. On the night of the murder, her hair had been a sort of non-color, so bedraggled it might have made a fitting nest for vermin. Today it was auburn, clean and shiny, professionally tinted and styled.

And the skin. No bruises were visible or even imaginable under the clothing. The old-fashioned touch of lace on her chest accentuated the milky softness of the skin on her neck and face, like an air-brushed photograph. She was a beautiful woman of fifty.

Asante was dapper as always, but all eyes were on her. Frances took her seat at the table in the front of the room, with her attorney at her elbow, keeping his mouth shut. The rules of the grand jury limited his role to conferring privately with his client whenever she needed his assistance or advice. He was not allowed to ask questions, to make objections, or to address the grand jury.

Before Frances said anything, the first order of business was the waiver. Every witness testifying in the grand jury automatically received immunity from prosecution for any crimes that were the subject of the testimony. Statutory immunity was designed to compel reluctant witnesses—even those who might be involved in the crime under investigation—to come forward and testify truthfully. It was useful whenever the prosecution needed the testimony of the small fish in order to hook the big fish.

Francis Kallay, like any target of a grand jury investigation, was required to sign a waiver of immunity before testifying. Eric had placed a waiver form on the table in front her, and a pen alongside, before she came into the grand jury room.

The oath was administered, and Frances Kallay swore to tell the truth. "A charade," some of the more cynical prosecutors might say, those who casually referred to the defendant's right to testify as the right to commit perjury. Eric had seen many defendants caught in verifiable lies under oath, but in this case, he was putting his cynicism on hold. What was the truth here? No one really knew except Frances Kallay.

"Ms. Kallay, the grand jury is considering evidence against you in connection with the homicide of Loránd Kallay, which occurred during the night of Thursday, June 21, into Friday, June 22, 2001. You are not obligated to provide testimony in this matter and have the right to remain silent. Do you understand?"

"I do."

"Have you consulted your attorney, Xavier Asante, with respect to making your decision whether to testify?"

"I have."

"Do you understand that you are required to sign a waiver of immunity, stating that you voluntarily give up your right to remain silent and that everything you say in this chamber may be used against you in a court of law?"

"I understand."

"If you'd like to continue, please read and sign the waiver of immunity. You may confer with your attorney if you wish."

"I don't need any further conferences. We've discussed this fully, and I'm aware of my rights." As she spoke, she looked at Xavier briefly and they exchanged dignified nods, as if they were longtime colleagues presenting a planned front. In silence, she started to read the form, taking her time.

While she was reading, Eric glanced over his shoulder at

Dana. In a quick movement, she raised her eyebrows to convey surprise. No one was more surprised than Eric. He turned back just as Frances picked up the pen and signed the document. Her demeanor was so businesslike and aloof that she might have been signing a document at a real estate closing. *She was very controlling and would just walk into a place and take it over.* Yesterday, Eric had doubted Greta Sperry's words. Now, he was beginning to see.

Frances replaced the pen on the table, sat up straight, and placed her hands in her lap under the table. Not a trace of emotion or weakness. The trembling, sick, vulnerable, inarticulate woman he'd seen five days ago had vanished, replaced by her confident sister.

"Ms. Kallay, at this point, you may testify regarding the crime under investigation. You have the right to make any statement you wish to the grand jury, and then I will have the opportunity to ask you questions about your statement. Do you understand?"

"Yes. I do. I've prepared a statement I wish to read." She turned to Asante. He extracted a document from his briefcase and handed it to her. Another part of their plan.

Frances looked down at the document and started to read. "Ladies and gentlemen of the grand jury…" She lifted her head and glanced around the room, pausing on many of the faces, one by one. She dropped her eyes to the page and continued. "On the night of June 21, 2001, I shot and killed my husband, Loránd Kallay."

A collective gasp sucked up the air and immediately released it. At full attention, the grand jurors came quickly to their senses, feeling the weight of their obligation to keep an open mind. They resumed their neutral expressions as best they could.

"I will explain how it happened. I have a complete defense

of justification. I'm not asking for your mercy. I'm asking you to apply the law to my case and dismiss the charge against me. I understand the law, as it was explained to me by my attorney, Xavier Asante."

Lawyer and client exchanged another nod. Eric debated whether to interrupt, but he let it go, wanting to avoid any further attention cast on this flagrant maneuver. This wasn't a beauty pageant or personality contest to decide which lawyer was better looking or more impressive. Eric was the legal advisor of the grand jury, not Xavier, who was improperly trying to advise the jury through his client.

She continued.

"My husband was a very talented, creative man. But he had a side to his personality that the world never saw. He saved his dark side for me … when we were alone." Here, for the first time, her voice dropped and broke on the last word. Rehearsed? She recovered quickly.

"As much as you may think that I'm a person of wealth and means, my husband controlled all the money in our marriage. Every asset was held in his name, and I was denied access to everything except one joint bank account which he managed, keeping the balance as low as possible. These facts can be verified, and I consent to a full investigation of our finances. Loránd repeatedly threatened that the consequences would be dire if I revealed anything about the brutality he inflicted upon me. He would cut off all support. Beyond that, any disclosure of my plight could have ruined his business, leaving me penniless and without a home. I had no other family to turn to.

"During the early part of our marriage, he was on his best behavior. Gradually, his cruelty was revealed. By that time, we had our son Luther, and I felt it was too late to get out of the marriage. The abuse was occasional at first, but in recent years it was constant. My husband was vicious but very methodical, careful not to make any marks on my face or my legs. You see, I was also a show wife in many ways and had to look good in his clothing.

"I understand that the prosecutor may have shown you photographs of my physical condition five days ago. If the grand jury orders it, I will undergo a complete physical examination. You'll find that I've suffered, on two occasions, broken ribs that are now healed, and a broken ulna that I blamed on a skiing accident two years ago. As embarrassed as I am to say this out loud in a room full of people, a medical examination will also reveal scar tissue indicating healed injuries to the private areas of my body.

"The cellar of our townhome was the torture chamber. It was accessed through a door that was hidden under a wall panel in the library, which could be opened by pushing a button. Anyone desiring to open the door would have to know the location of the button, which was concealed inside a bookcase. The police missed it when they searched the house, and I didn't direct them to it, as I will explain in a moment. The grand jury should order a search of that cellar, and you'll see exactly what went on down there. Loránd had no trouble forcing me down those stairs when he wanted to. He was much larger and ... stronger than me."

Her voice broke again. Asante touched her shoulder and said, audibly, "Take your time."

Eric wasn't letting this one go. "If you need to confer with your attorney, Ms. Kallay, you may do so privately." He tried to catch Asante's eye as he spoke, but the defense attorney wasn't having it. He knew he was out of line.

"I'm all right," Frances said. "I'd like to go on."

"You have the right to finish your statement and to speak to your attorney at any time, but Mr. Asante must refrain from offering any comments that can be overheard." With that, Asante shot Eric a cold look, intensely directed and gone the next instant. Any obvious discourtesy wouldn't do him or his client any good.

Frances flipped the page over and started on page two.

"I was deathly afraid of my husband and took every opportunity to get out of that house on my own, when I could manage it. On the night of June 21, I was scheduled to attend a function for a charity organization, Covering our Kids. Loránd allowed my participation because it looked good for him. Also, as the wife of a fashion designer for the wealthy, I took special interest in charities that provided essential clothing for the less fortunate."

Along with her special interest in prodding Loránd to design racier clothes for women, Eric thought.

"The event was to start at eight, and I was already dressed to go when the phone rang. Loránd picked up the call, took a message, and told me that the event was cancelled. There was an electrical problem at the building where it was to be held, and there were no lights, elevator service, or air conditioning. All of these facts can be confirmed for the grand jury." She looked up at Eric and back at the paper again. "I was forced to stay home, and the night was long. I'd been looking forward to getting out because Loránd's abuse had been especially brutal in recent days. He was extremely frustrated in his professional life. He had nothing ready for the 2002 season. His creativity had dried up. He lacked confidence, and every sketch he drew ended up in the wastebasket.

"That evening, I was at the end of my rope. I'd been thinking that I might find a way to escape in the middle of the charity function and never return home. I was disappointed to have lost that chance, because I thought I'd finally found the courage to leave. If I simply walked out the front door, with nowhere particular to go, he'd be sure to find me. He'd done it before, many times. But if I was out at a verifiable event, I could get a head start before he sent someone to look.

"From seven thirty on, I stayed in our bedroom on the fourth floor, crying for hours. Loránd was in his studio on the third floor, trying to draw. At some point, I changed into a robe he designed. I thought it would please him to see me wearing it when he came upstairs to bed. At about ten o'clock, he walked into the bedroom. I knew from the look in his eyes that I was in for more punishment."

Frances stopped and said, "Excuse me a moment." She pulled a tissue from the box on the table, dabbed her eyes, and started to reach for the pitcher of water. In a swift, dramatic move, Asante rose up like a giant, walked behind her to the other side of the table, and swept up the pitcher. With the other hand, he grabbed the short stack of paper cups, letting them fall to the table with a clatter when the top one came loose. He poured the water, and with an elegant bend at the waist, he served Frances like a waiter at The Four Seasons.

She nodded at him and drank. Xavier went back to his seat.

The grand jurors shifted uncomfortably in their seats.

Frances continued. "He grabbed me by the wrist and dragged me down all three flights of stairs to the ground floor. On the way down, he was cursing me, blaming me for his inability to create new designs. He accused me of disliking his work. He said he could barely tolerate my presence in the same house. I was leeching his drive and his ideas, leading him to ruin. He said, 'I'm going to end this once and for all.'

"I assumed he was going to drag me down to the cellar, but instead, he pulled me into the den. His grip on my wrist was strong. I couldn't break away. With one hand, he dragged me over to the desk and opened the top drawer with his other hand. He pulled out his gun.

"I was in a panic. He'd never used that gun to threaten or beat me. In fact, I don't remember him ever taking it out of that drawer in my presence. He bought it about three years ago and always kept it in that desk drawer, as far as I knew. He said he just felt safer with it there because he kept his sketches for the upcoming season in the safe behind the desk. The originals. They were very valuable."

Frances grabbed another tissue and dabbed at her nose before flipping the page over. She started up again at the top of page three.

"I screamed at him to tell me what he was doing. 'We're going to the cellar,' he said. Then—I'll never forget the way it felt—he stuck the barrel of the gun into my cheek and said, 'This is for you!' I was sure he would kill me once we got down to the cellar, and he'd find a way to hide my body. He took a step, and suddenly, he was on the floor. It was so unexpected. He was acting so crazy and excited that he must have caught a toe on the edge of the desk and toppled forward. Instinctively, he needed a hand to break his fall, so he let go of me. It was the chance I needed to get the gun away from him. He was still holding it, but his grip had loosened. I grabbed it quickly and backed up, pointing the gun at him.

"He pushed himself up from the floor and said, 'Give me the gun.' He lunged forward, grabbing for it. He was much stronger than me, and I knew that he could easily pull it out of my hand. He came for me and I pulled the trigger. He stumbled backward, into the desk chair, but he still seemed all right. He stopped and stared at me for a minute, and then, he was ready to come for me again, so I shot twice more. He fell on the chair, tipping it over, and fell on his face. He twitched a few times and was still.

"I went over to him and felt for a pulse. He was dead."

Frances stopped and took a deep breath. Her voice had become wispy and breathy toward the end. She took another sip of water from the paper cup and resumed her reading in a deeper voice.

"I didn't call the police immediately. I wasn't aware of the time. Looking back on it now, I believe I didn't call for about an hour. At first I was stunned at what had happened. I did nothing but stand there, looking at him. I couldn't believe he was gone. I awoke at some point and decided that no one would believe me if I told the truth. Everyone loved Loránd, and no one knew his secret. Besides that, I was too ashamed to tell anyone what he'd done to me."

Her glistening, red lips were full and trembling. Her voice shook.

"It was humiliating what he'd put me through all those years, and I was well-trained in myth and secrecy. The thought of explaining the truth to anyone at that moment was too much. Just too much. He lay there dead, completely still and innocuous. The simple question that everyone would be asking came to my mind. Why hadn't I left him long ago, or at least left the house earlier that night? I didn't quite know how to answer that question."

Frances flipped the page over, looked up, and glanced around the room. "Ladies and gentlemen of the grand jury…" She faltered, and looked at Asante, then up at Eric. "I'd like a moment with my attorney."

"You may confer privately," Eric said.

As Frances and Xavier leaned toward each other, Eric turned around and stepped over to Dana. "Don't need to cross with the photos anymore," he whispered.

"But you have a hundred other ways to impeach her. All the inconsistencies with the physical evidence. I've jotted them down." In her hands, she held a pen and a small pad with scribbled notes.

"Right. A lot of it doesn't make sense, but even if the jury believes her, she hasn't established a justification defense. I'll instruct them on the duty to retreat and argue..."

"We're not going to get to instructions and arguments. You can't submit this to a vote today."

"We have to!" His whisper rose a notch, and Dana warned him with her eyes. He lowered his voice. "Tomorrow's one-eighty eighty day. She'll be released..."

"I'm ready to continue," came a voice behind him. He turned around and looked down at Frances over the twenty-two heads of the grand jurors, some of them looking up at him with questions in their eyes.

"Please continue with your statement," Eric said.

"I needed to ask my lawyer a question about psychological evidence, and he advised me..."

"Ms. Kallay. You must refrain from telling the grand jury any of the advice Mr. Asante has given to you."

"All right. I simply want to tell the grand jury what I now believe to be true, but didn't realize at the time. I believe I was suffering from a syndrome that made me incapable of breaking free from this man. I'm willing to undergo a psychological evaluation in addition to the medical examination. I understand that the grand jury has the authority..."

"Please, Ms. Kallay. Continue with the narrative of the events of June 21 and 22."

"All right." She looked down at her paper again. "In the minutes after the shooting, as I stood there, the idea came to me that the more believable story would be that someone had broken into the house, or perhaps Loránd had let someone in while I was upstairs. That person wanted to steal the drawings or any other valuables in the safe. Loránd would have taken out his gun to protect himself, and they could have struggled over it. The murderer forced Loránd to open the safe, and then he shot him. He put the gun down to get the drawings, and he ran. In my state of shock, I thought this story would be believable, at least more believable than the truth about the long history of physical abuse.

"I used my robe to wipe the fingerprints off the gun. I understand that one of Loránd's fingerprints is on the gun, so I must have missed it. Since I'm right-handed, I laid the gun on the desk as a left-handed person would do, to make it look like someone else. I opened the safe, and wiped off my fingerprints. Of course, the safe was empty. As I said, Loránd hadn't been creating any new designs. I see now that all of these acts on my part created an unbelievable scenario. I didn't realize at the time that I would be taken to the hospital and that the fresh injuries on my body would be revealed and photographed. Later, after my arrest, I made the decision to tell the truth. I've spent the last few days building up my courage to do just that.

"I'm asking the grand jury, if you see fit to indict me for my previous false statements, if you think my actions amounted to obstructing justice, I will accept that charge. But do not charge me with murder or manslaughter. I'm telling the truth now, and I have a complete defense of justification. As you can see, I was the victim of abuse. My entire married life with Loránd, and everything I knew about him, led me to believe—indeed, made it clear to me—that when he took out that gun, he was about to use deadly force against me. He was going to drag me into the cellar and murder me. With every fiber of my being, I feared for my life. Only by sheer luck was I able to get the gun away from him. I had only one way to prevent him from grabbing the gun again and murdering me with it. My only recourse was to shoot him in self-defense."

She stopped. Apparently, her statement was at an end. A hush fell over the room. She took the time to scan the faces, going along each of the three rows. She brought the tissue to her nose once again, and her cheek glistened from a slowly descending teardrop.

At last, she said, "Thank you."

It was time for Eric's cross-examination.

13 »   FORSAKEN OATH

DANA'S HEAD WAS spinning as she walked out of the grand jury room. She couldn't shake the picture of that unsettling look. Xavier's eyes pinning her down. What was in it? *Watch out!* Something new was headed her way. Wasn't it only a few days ago that he was ranting about an innocent client being arrested for reporting "a home invasion"?

Then there was Frances. This had to be a first. In Dana's experience, defendants who were talkers usually gave stories that were chipped away, little by little, until they fell under the weight of their inconsistencies. Never had she seen something quite like this. A complete turnaround. I didn't do it. Well, no. I did it, but I was justified.

Neither story felt like the truth, although both versions rested on select pieces of reality. To a criminal defendant, indisputable facts were like money in the bank. Sprinkle a few into the narrative and maybe the jury will believe that the fabrications are also true.

Dana was inclined to think that Frances Kallay's latest story, along with its dramatic delivery, was an act, designed with one purpose in mind—to beat the charge. If so, Frances certainly had a high opinion of her acting skills, if not her ability to manipulate the emotions of the people who would be determining her fate. The weaknesses in her new story were obvious to Dana. But would the grand jury believe it? Dana couldn't take that risk, especially not now, when the truth lay somewhere in the distance, and so many questions remained unanswered.

Frances had looked sincere enough. Her voice faltered and trembled at all the appropriate moments, and the tears welled in her eyes until they spilled over the rims, leaving a trail over the professional makeover on her rouged cheeks. It was too perfect. The package as a whole didn't ring true. Only five days after shooting her husband (truth or fiction?) this woman was too well put together. She could have stepped out of a magazine.

Battered wife? She didn't seem to fit the profile. She was too strong and sure of her opinions, down to her self-diagnosis as the victim of a "syndrome." If the grand jurors were to believe her, today marked the fifth day of her freedom from years of physical abuse. A remarkable snap back.

If this was an act, the real person had to be more like the woman that Eric observed at the townhome, mere hours after the murder. This didn't make much sense either. The way Eric and Gil described it, Frances Kallay had been the exact opposite of what she was today. Meek, inarticulate, disheveled, and submissive. How could a person like that summon the strength to pull off the performance they'd witnessed today, especially after the trauma of arrest and days of incarceration? It seemed more plausible that the meek, submissive woman had been an act.

The turnaround was a surprise of enormous magnitude. Although put on the spot, Eric had delivered a forceful cross, considering the circumstances.

"Did you chamber the bullet before you fired, Ms. Kallay?"

"Chamber ... what is that? I pulled the trigger."

"When you took the gun from your husband, was the safety on or off?"

"I don't know. I've never fired a gun before..."

"Are you saying that you didn't disengage the safety before firing?"

"I have no idea where the safety is. I pulled the trigger and it fired."

To make sense of this testimony, they'd have to suppose that Loránd's semiautomatic was "locked and cocked," ready to fire. Not a very safe practice for a weapon stored at home, in a desk drawer in the den. But it must have been that way, if the tale was to be credited. Two hands were needed to work the slide, putting a bullet into the chamber, but Loránd was supposedly using one of his hands to hold his wife at the moment he opened the drawer and extracted the gun. If Frances didn't release the safety, then Loránd must have worked the release with his thumb when he was holding the gun. In this state, the gun would have been more susceptible to misfire, especially from the force of Loránd's supposed tumble to the ground, before Frances picked up the weapon and shot with a mere pull of the trigger.

There was another way to look at it. The state of the gun supported her theory of self-defense. A bullet was in the chamber and the safety was disengaged. Her husband was ready to kill her.

"What was the distance between you and your husband when you fired the first shot?"

"When he stood up, he was right on me, coming for the gun."

"So, there couldn't have been any more than a few feet between you?"

"I'm no good with distances. He was right there."

"The force of the first shot caused him to move backward, isn't that right?"

"Yes."

"Isn't it true that you fired the second and third shots as

your husband was turning away from you, trying to back up?"

"No. He was coming for me, reaching for the gun again."

Nonsense. Her story was disproved by the physical evidence—the autopsy, the position of the body, and the trajectory of the bullets. The first shot was fired at a distance of approximately ten feet, the second and third, as the victim turned, stumbled away, and fell.

The inconsistencies kept Dana's mind active as she walked with Eric to the elevator. He trailed behind, as if part of him remained in that grand jury room, presenting the magic evidence that would ensure an indictment. Dana was anxious to get out of there. Eric caught up just as the door opened on the elevator going down. They didn't speak. Crossing the street between the Criminal Court building and their office building, Dana became aware that he was still lagging behind, like a child. In her mind's eye Dana saw, once again, the shock that entered his buttery-brown eyes at the moment in their hushed conversation that she told him they weren't putting the case to a vote today.

He hustled to catch up and kept pace alongside, staring at her profile as he spoke. "Dana, I still think..."

"We'll talk when we get to my office." She glanced at him, caught his eye and smiled, just to melt the chill. He stumbled a bit and righted himself.

Did he think she was angry? She wasn't in the least. He'd handled the grand jury presentation well, although it was still debatable whether the arrest of Frances had been a good idea in the first place. If he'd come to her for approval at that stage, would she have given it? Unclear. Gil was the one who pushed for the arrest, and Dana, like Eric, relied implicitly on the senior investigator's judgment and instincts.

Was Eric angry at *her*? He wasn't happy with her decision, that much was clear, but he'd gone along with it. He had to.

She was the boss. No way could they submit the case to a vote in its current state. They were nowhere near the truth. If anything, they were farther from it, with two equally bogus theories thrown into their path. If the grand jury voted today and came back with "no true bill," they'd be precluded by double jeopardy from reopening the case against Frances.

They walked into Dana's office and she shut the door behind them. Before they could sit, Eric started spewing his thoughts like the gush of water from a hydrant. "We still have time! We can follow up on a few things this afternoon, then bring Gil back in for testimony by four o'clock, maybe even again at nine tomorrow morning. We can put it to a vote at nine thirty and be in court by ten…"

"There's too much we have to look into."

"You mean all of that stuff she told us to investigate? I counted at least four things." He slapped a fist into an open palm as he said each item: "Their finances, her medical records, the cellar, the Clothing for Kids function…"

"Precisely. A lot of things."

"But *she's* the one who's causing the delay! That means we have grounds to request an emergency extension of one-eighty eighty. There's authority for it, Dana! If a defendant's testimony raises new questions to be investigated, the judge can extend the time limit by a day or two for good cause—"

"Look, Eric," she interrupted. "Let's sit down and talk about it." She walked around the desk and did just that. He remained standing for another few seconds, unable to relinquish his readiness for immediate action. She didn't want to deflate *all* of that energy. "It's a good idea—an emergency application. It might work. But I have a better plan."

"Gee-zus." He sat down.

"We're going to let her go."

"*Gee-zus* again."

"Just for now. She's not getting away for long. She's going to lead us to the truth."

"The minute we let her go she'll be on a plane for Paris."

"I doubt it. She knows it looks much better for her if she pretends to cooperate. And in the process, she's going to give herself away."

"So, that means you're sure she did it."

"I'm sure she's involved somehow. She's definitely trying to cover up something or protect someone. She and her crafty attorney devised this plan. It started when she realized that her first story wouldn't hold up. Isn't that what she testified? 'I didn't know I'd be taken to the hospital and my injuries discovered.'"

"Right."

"What she really discovered during her hospital stay was that we didn't believe her. That became pretty obvious when we arrested her."

"She knew we had her with all those holes in her story."

"Exactly. So she figured she'd better come testify. That was the first step in her thinking. The next step was to develop a new story and make it work for her, no matter how we proceeded in the grand jury. If we put the case to a vote today, she as hoping to arouse the sympathies of the jurors with the photos and the battered wife syndrome, so she'd have a better chance at dismissal, or at worst, an indictment for manslaughter instead of murder. But I'm thinking that she and Xavier were guessing we would continue the case without a vote after she made such a stunning, unexpected turnaround."

"So we're just giving them what they want!"

Dana sighed and shook her head. "This isn't a game, Eric."

"No, but they're making it into a game."

"It's always like this. The objective of every defendant is

to beat the charge. You know that."

Eric shrugged. "Of course."

"Our objective is to strive for justice. Always. We can't lose sight of that. It's our job to look for the truth, not to indict and convict without the proper evidence. We were unprepared, and we haven't developed the case. Their plan is to buy more time, and they planted the seeds for that by consenting to an investigation. Frances knows we can't investigate her laundry list of items in the few hours we have left."

"Okay. But none of this stuff is going to lead us to the truth."

"You're right about that. Do you think she told us to investigate things that would disprove her so-called justification defense? Of course not. We'll look at the finances and her medical history and the charity event and find that it's all exactly the way she described. And we'll take a look in the cellar and find ... God knows what. Whips and chains."

Eric's square jaw flexed in mighty disappointment. "You know what we just did? We allowed her to con us into giving her a walk. We fell for it."

"Sure, we fell for it. And we want her to think that we fell for it. It's better for us. She'll relax a little and put her guard down. But we also have another plan."

Eric leaned forward in his chair and awaited the strategy that would lead to his redemption.

"We're not confining our investigation to the neat little areas she wants us to investigate. And while she's busy setting up the evidence to prove her story, she's going to slip up and reveal the clues that will lead us to the truth. I'm guessing it's an accomplice."

"Dana." Was that a parental tone in his voice? No longer Dorothy's Toto, Eric had suddenly grown up. "*Now* who's playing a game?" he asked. "You look like you're out to get this lady."

She smiled. "Sure, I'd like to see it. I can't deny it. As long as I've been in this job, I still can't stand to be lied to, especially when the liar is too sure of herself."

"She was convincing in a way, don't you think?"

"She was."

"Then why do we think it's a crock?"

"Just because of that."

"Because of..."

"Her self-assurance. She's a person who likes to call the shots."

"Or fire the shots."

"That too." Dana stopped and backed up. This conversation was reminding her that it was extremely dangerous to be too sure of *herself*. She could get into trouble that way. Predilections and assumptions always had to be checked. There was another theory that hadn't been considered out loud, one that fell into place with everything they knew so far. A theory consistent with innocence. "I'm troubled by just one possibility. We could be entirely off the mark, looking in the wrong direction and missing what's right in front of our eyes. Let's say she's not guilty at all, not even as an accomplice or a facilitator."

"Then why would she make up a story about shooting him?"

"She's under a death threat. The killer coerced her into giving the home invasion story and to change it to battering if the first story wasn't going so well. He gave her a compelling incentive: a credible threat that she was next on his list. She's been acting under duress the entire time."

Eric looked at Dana, and their eyes held in the silence.

Seconds passed as they considered this possibility.

Finally, Eric started to shake his head, slowly.

She nodded once and took up his rhythm, shaking her head right and left.

They stopped at once and smiled.

"Nah," he said. "Couldn't be."

"Yup. I don't see it," Dana agreed.

The reporters and camera crews started jockeying for position on the courthouse steps before seven o'clock the next morning. The 144-hour time limit of Criminal Procedure Law 180.80 was scheduled to expire at ten o'clock. On their way to court, Dana and Eric wouldn't have to face the news people. Reporters were banned from the DA's entrance at the side of the building.

It wasn't pure hand-holding that kept Dana at this level of involvement. Eric was more than capable of handling the brief court appearance, but she wanted to see the faces of the attorney and his client when Eric made his announcement: the grand jury investigation was still open and the People had no legal ground to keep Frances in jail. Would Xavier Asante give her that look again? Would Frances reveal any telling signs? Besides this, Dana had a more compelling reason to attend court: a direct order from the boss.

Dana figured something was up when she walked into the bureau at 8:30 and saw Lecia with a slightly stricken look on her face. She handed Dana a slip of paper. "The DA called ten minutes ago." Three of the boxes on the preprinted message slip were checked off: "Telephoned," "Please Call," and "Urgent."

Dana looked at the message and frowned. "Thanks."

The two women exchanged looks, enough to give Lecia a clue that Dana was worried. "He didn't really use the word 'urgent.' It was just his voice, you know. He wanted you to call back as soon as you got in. I guess it's about...?" Her eyes darted to the side as she flicked a neon-orange-tipped index finger in the same direction, toward the front of the building.

Dana's eyes followed, then looked skyward. She sighed. "Okay. I'll call him now. When you see Ricky, could you tell him to step in?"

"Will do."

She walked into her office and closed the door behind her. It didn't help that she'd been planning to call Patrick, first thing. She was one step behind, one step too late. Why so many mistakes? Why now?

She dialed his number.

In the many years she'd known Patrick, he'd never lost his cool around her. He was always eminently reasonable, persuasive, and self-confident, the source of sage advice and worldly wisdom. A well-respected administrator, trial strategist, and legal thinker. He wasn't any different now. But still, she heard it in his voice. She'd let him down. "Dana, what's going on out front? I was waiting for a briefing from you yesterday. I only heard about the grand jury secondhand."

Bad. There'd been so much to do yesterday afternoon. The meeting with Eric. The strategy session with Gil. The instructions to the DA's squad, getting everything on track for the continued investigation. At the back of her mind was the obligatory phone call to Patrick. So far, she'd been keeping him informed. She didn't need his approval for every step she took as the chief of this bureau, but it was a high-profile case, and the DA had to be kept in the loop.

Her intention to call Patrick was forgotten and didn't come to mind again until she got home. She could have called him that evening—the DA was available 24/7—but the thought was easily overshadowed by two children, eager to tell their stories of the day as she walked in the front door. Then there were leftovers to reheat and places to set for the dinner hour, with everyone around the table, Evan, Brenda, Travis and Natalie. Any trace of her plan to call the boss was thoroughly erased from her mind by the time she was reading another chapter of Harry Potter to Travis, snuggled up with her arm around his shoulder.

She was privileged to enjoy Patrick's deep trust. In this instance, had she taken it for granted? Had she been overly confident that he would agree with her strategy? Any major gaffes she made would find their way up the food chain and come to rest on his head. "I'm sorry, Patrick," she said into the phone. A simple apology was all she could offer. Excuses were worthless. *I forgot about it in the middle of deciding whether to serve leftover lasagna or chicken for dinner.* She strongly disliked the sound of excuses coming from the mouths of the attorneys she supervised. Why would Patrick want to hear any such nonsense from her?

"We are where we are," he said. "So, tell me if there's any chance for an indictment before ten o'clock."

"No. I directed Eric not to submit it for a vote. Frances Kallay raised a justification defense based on the battered wife syndrome, but it's inconsistent with the physical evidence. I'm convinced she's involved, possibly with an accomplice, but the evidence just isn't there yet. It was too risky to ask for a vote. Dismissal was likely, and we'd lose the chance to indict her down the road."

Patrick didn't respond immediately. She could guess what he was thinking. It would have been better if Frances hadn't been arrested in the first place. Less of a media circus. Better for the DA if they'd developed the case before arresting their suspect. But Eric hadn't come to Dana for approval, and she, in turn, hadn't gone to Patrick for approval. He knew all of this already. It was water under the bridge. "How did she look as a witness? How credible is the abuse allegation?"

"She tells a good story, and it's convincing because we have the photos of her injuries. She dared us to investigate further. She specifically consented to disclosure of her medical records and a search of the cellar of the townhome where all of this supposedly occurred. But somehow, it's too pat. She's too articulate and sure of herself. Even if she was abused, it still looks like intentional murder to me, possibly premeditated. We need to find out more about her life and contacts. It will be good for the case that she's out of jail. She'll lead us to the answer."

"Your instincts are telling you this?"

"Yes. She's involved, Patrick. The inconsistent stories give her away, and there's too much physical evidence pointing to intentional homicide."

Patrick considered this. She felt his mind accepting her instincts on faith. Airtight cases were the exception in this business, and when a case was entirely circumstantial, instinct and experience came into play. Patrick's instincts had always been unwaveringly correct. Hers had been, what, seventy-five percent? Maybe better than that. The cases in the minority had flung her into the gut-wrenching crises of her career.

His next question stunned her. "What do you predict Asante's going to tell those reporters on the courthouse steps?"

Odd that Patrick wanted her opinion on this, since he was far better at predicting anything that might happen in the public arena. He was more of a political animal than she. Was Patrick worried about Asante? He could expect that the outspoken defense attorney would take the opportunity to rail against the DA's procedures in this case. "You know Asante," she said. "We kept him as quiet as we could in the grand jury, so I'm sure he'll have a lot to say."

"He'll blow a lot of hot air about improper arrests and abuse of process. I'm not concerned about that. You had probable cause to arrest her. Legally sufficient evidence to indict is a different thing. If he wants to reveal their defense of wife battering and justified shooting, so be it."

"Usually it's a mistake for the defense to try their case in the press. Any statements or admissions can be used against her..."

"True, but I wouldn't put it past Asante. It may be part of his strategy. But there *is* one thing I want to prevent."

Dana's heart stopped with the thought that she was powerless to prevent anything.

"Just one thing," he repeated. "I don't want anything in the public court record to give him grounds for accusing our office of causing the interruption in the grand jury proceedings."

"How can we make sure of that?"

"I want you to go to court with Eric this morning."

"I was already planning on it."

"Stand at counsel table with him. Let him do the talking, but be ready to add anything we need to make the record I want you to make."

"And what is that?"

"That we were fully prepared to put the case to a vote, but we've adjourned it at the behest of the defendant. We're following up on areas *she* suggested we investigate."

"I see. Make it clear that the defendant is the cause of the adjournment."

"Yes. This is not a case in which we shortsightedly went into the grand jury and are now scrambling. The evidence, before she made a turnaround, was legally sufficient to indict."

"Okay. He has no grounds to criticize this office. That much we can make clear."

"More than that, we're indulging the defense. We're giving the defendant's version every consideration. In the interest of justice, we've acceded to her request for further investigation."

"Asante could blow that all out of proportion too," Dana suggested.

"Let him."

"I suppose it might help the investigation if she thinks that her testimony has given us pause..."

"It *will* help. And, as you say, she's involved somehow, isn't she? The investigation will lead us there."

"Yes." Dana gulped. This one better fall into her seventy-five percent category. She'd better be right.

"Okay. When you're finished in court, come up to my office. We'll watch the news together." It was understood that she and Eric would not be meeting the reporters on the courthouse steps. The DA himself always delivered the official word of the office, usually at a press conference. Any ADA who wished to talk to a reporter needed advance approval from Patrick. Defense attorneys, on the other hand, loved the opportunity to tell reporters that their clients were innocent and would be vindicated. The press delivered their words to the public—the pool of potential jurors for the trial. Any statement more specific was unusual because it was unethical for an attorney to reveal the confidences of a client.

"You want Eric to come up too?"

"Sure. Better if he sees the impact of his actions firsthand."

They said a few parting words, and Dana hung up the phone, suddenly aware of the tightness in her chest. The phone call hadn't been so bad. Still, she felt a profound disappointment in herself for letting her boss down.

There was a knock at the door. "Come in!"

Ricky walked in. "Morning, Dana," he said.

"Good morning. What time are you going over with Alissa and David?" These recently promoted ADAs were scheduled to give their first grand jury presentations.

"Nine thirty."

"So you'll be out of there around ten fifteen or ten thirty." The two cases to be presented were grand theft auto—the "ham sandwich" variety that took very little time in the grand jury.

"Most likely."

"Eric and I will be in court on the Kallay case and in Patrick's office after that."

Ricky pursed his lips in sympathy.

"Can you do me a favor when you get back?" she asked.

"Sure."

"Check in with Gil on the status of the Kallay investigation. Yesterday, Asante gave us the information we needed for the subpoenas, and they've been served. The team is also planning to do the consent search of the townhouse when Frances gets home, after her release. If Gil has any major developments, can you call me on my mobile phone?"

"Sure thing."

The minute Ricky stepped out, she picked up the phone. "Lecia? Round up Eric and tell him to get in here! Thanks."

Frances made another splash in a new outfit that gave her an air of innocence: a skirt-suit in eggshell white with a mandarin-collared blouse in smoky green. The shoes alone might have cost five hundred dollars. Again, it was mystifying how she'd managed this fashion show from her cell in Rikers Island. For all of her professed poverty and lack of access to Loránd's assets, Frances must have downplayed the value of that joint checking account she described in her testimony. Or maybe it was the strength of a promise that lined the pockets of the correction officers who'd gotten her dressed for court. *I'm innocent. I'll be inheriting everything.*

The Honorable Elbert Howell had excluded all cameras from his courtroom. Sketch artists were actively working, and reporters scribbled in their notepads. Dana and Eric executed Patrick's plan to the letter—almost. The first part went well. Eric was well-rehearsed and didn't need any prompting to convey the message Patrick wanted him to convey. Frances stood silently at attention, child size next to her attorney. A gentle smile graced her lips when Eric announced that no indictment had been handed up, and the People were granting her request for further investigation.

Xavier had a great time expounding at length about the travesty of this case, the improper arrest on "a mere hunch," and the humiliating days of incarceration at Rikers, endured by a delicate and sensitive woman. He went on to reveal the defense strategy: "Mrs. Kallay has a complete defense. She shot her husband in self-defense to repel his imminent use of lethal force with a deadly weapon." A few gasps could be heard in the audience. The newspapers, so far, had been printing her story about a home invasion. "The sad truth has come to light. For years, Loránd Kallay brutalized his wife. This time, he went too far. Before he could kill her, she acted to protect herself. Mr. Trumble heard my client's testimony and knows that he doesn't have a case. He didn't ask for a vote. Do we need any better proof that he doesn't have the evidence? If this case were tried today, there would be an acquittal. We demand that the prosecutor drop the charges immediately!"

On the elevated bench, Judge Howell appeared unmoved. "It's within the DA's discretion to keep the investigation open, counselor," he said, and turned to Eric. "Are these charges going to be dropped, Mr. Trumble?"

"No, Your Honor. Mr. Asante's demand is completely out of line. He's flat out wrong to suggest that the People don't have legally sufficient evidence to indict. The only reason we adjourned the grand jury proceeding was to accommodate his client's request." And here is where Eric went off script: "If Mr. Asante wants to test his theory that our case is lacking, he should consent to a forty-eight hour extension of the statutory time limit. In two days we'll complete the investigation his client requested and put the case to a vote!"

Dana was mortified. Should she jump in and risk making them both look like fools? They'd talked about this. Why was Eric still pressing for an extension? What if Asante took the bait? Most likely, the case wouldn't be much better in forty-eight hours, and they'd be going through this all over again.

Eric continued his argument, oblivious of Dana's agitation. "We've shown good cause for an extension. The defendant raised new issues that the grand jury needs to explore. In the meantime, the defendant should remain incarcerated. She's the cause of the delay."

He was making it worse! With "good cause" thrown in, it sounded like he was making an application to the court, not simply asking for the defendant's consent! Judge Howell could order an extension regardless of Asante's position.

Throughout Eric's argument, Frances wore a frown and a furled brow. Then, she turned to her attorney. Clearly, she wasn't going to allow him to consent to this.

Asante bellowed, "Preposterous! This is unprecedented!"

"*New York versus Griffin*, a Kings County case, 163 Miscellaneous 2d reports at 43…"

Dana was quaking. He'd even done legal research on this!

"We're going to be guided by a Kings County case?" Asante's voice was filled with indignation. "The statute is explicit! There's *no* room for an exception! Your time is up, Mr. Trumble! My client must be released on her own recognizance. Her suggestions for areas of investigation do not relieve *you* of *your* burden to submit legally sufficient evidence to the grand jury. You have failed. I will not agree to your end run around the statute."

"All right," said the judge. "I've heard enough."

Dana held her breath.

"There's no agreement to an extension, and I'm not granting one. This is a gray area in the law, and I'm not walking out on a limb."

She exhaled in relief.

"There's nothing more to do here. This case is adjourned two weeks for grand jury action. Put it down for July 12. Defendant is released on her own recognizance." The judge gave her a pointed look. "Mrs. Kallay, you are required to appear in court on that date or a warrant will be issued for your arrest." The gavel came down.

Dana didn't wait around to make small talk. She purposefully avoided Asante's eyes. He hadn't given her "the look" yet, and she wasn't going to invite one. "Come on, Eric," she said in a low tone. "Let's go upstairs."

They were out the swinging door first, not looking behind them. The defense team, when they came out, would be heading downstairs and out the front door of the Criminal Court building, into the waiting arms of the press. Dana made a beeline for the elevator bank and pressed the "up" arrow. This time, she really *was* angry at Eric. She tried hard to control that emotion.

"Not good, Eric," she said in a low voice as they waited for an elevator.

"It was a bluff."

"I know. But once you asked for a stipulation, you should've stopped. You stepped over the line when you involved the court."

"I was on point. I was saying we had a case, and I gave the reasons why the delay was her fault. Isn't that what Patrick wanted?"

"It could've backfired. Seriously. If Judge Howell was inclined to grant an extension, I would've jumped in there like an idiot and said, 'Mr. Trumble really didn't mean that, Your Honor.'"

Eric couldn't help showing a small, self-satisfied grin. "My argument was that good, eh?"

"Don't go there."

"I made it clear we had a case, that's all."

The corridor was filling up. Dana pressed the elevator button again. "The reporters in the courtroom took everything down." A half dozen men and women loitered along the walls, looking at their notepads, talking on their cell phones. "They're calling it in now. Patrick's gonna love this."

Come on, elevator. The defense team was approaching. She felt Asante's warm body and imposing stature fill the space next to her. He could have kept his distance. There were three elevators. Dana and Eric stood all the way right, and Xavier could have stayed left. Instead, he came within a foot of her and leaned slightly in front to press the down arrow under the lighted up arrow on the keypad between the middle and right elevators.

She found it impossible to remain concealed behind her blinders. Trying for a neutral expression, she glanced at her adversary. He returned her look with a contradictory countenance, cold eyes over a debonair smile. Mrs. Kallay was barely visible, on the other side of him.

Damn! Too late, she remembered the plan she'd scuttled by rushing out of the courtroom. She'd intended to have a civil conversation with Asante immediately after his client's release, to make arrangements for the consent search of the cellar at the Kallay townhome. But Dana wasn't going to say anything to him now, out in the hallway with people buzzing around.

As luck would have it, the middle elevator opened first, going down. Xavier and Frances stepped into the box and turned around to face outward. Dana avoided looking at them as the doors closed, just as the bell sounded for the elevator on the right, going up.

The door to Jared's office was open as they rushed past, but the room was empty. Inside the DA's ceremonial office, in a far corner, Patrick and Jared stood before a television screen. The two men glanced over their shoulders at Dana and Eric as they entered. Patrick's expression was grim. Jared's was apologetic.

Patrick quickly put a finger to his lips before silently beckoning them to enter. Dana closed the door behind her. She could hear the newscaster speaking as she crossed the room. "...and Judge Howell denied the prosecutor's emergency request to keep Frances Kallay behind bars..." Patrick gave an almost imperceptible shake of his head.

When the television screen came into view, Dana blinked and looked again. A trio stood behind the raft of microphones: Frances was in the middle, Xavier on the left, and on the right ... Ellen Fortier. What was *she* doing there?

Asante answered a reporter's question. "My client is not guilty. There's no indictment because the DA doesn't have the evidence. The charges should be dismissed, but that bullheaded prosecutor, Eric Trumble, refused. Then, he had the gall to petition the court for an emergency order to keep Mrs. Kallay in jail! There's absolutely no legal authority for his astounding request, and the court promptly released her. She has a full defense to the murder charge, but I'll leave it to her to tell you. Mrs. Kallay has a statement she'd like to make to the press." He looked down at his client, who was holding a piece of paper in her hand.

Speaking of gall. This was unheard of. A person accused of murder making a statement to the press?

Frances looked small, pure, and unthreatening, a halcyon vision of style, elegance, and humility. She spoke slowly and distinctly. "I've testified in the grand jury to rectify my earlier statement to the police. On the night of the shooting I was in shock. I had suffered many years of physical abuse at the hand of my husband and was mortally afraid of him. That night, I barely escaped with my life after he tried to kill me. I told the police there had been a home invasion because I was afraid that no one would believe me. My husband was a popular man, loved by many people who had no idea of his dark side. I provided every detail of what happened to the grand jury. The prosecutor has heard the truth. I have a complete defense of justification. I'm pleading with the prosecutor to dismiss the murder charge. But if this case does go to trial, I *will* be vindicated. It is my hope that my predicament will bring the plight of battered women everywhere more forcefully into the public eye than ever before. Thank you."

She politely refused to answer any of the questions shouted at her by the surrounding press corps. Next to Frances stood a petite woman of near equal stature—the director of Justice Restored. In stark contrast to the angel in white, Ellen wore her trademark black outfit, threadbare and frumpish, a complement to her dour and brooding manner. She started to speak into the nearest microphone, deflecting the focus away from Mrs. Kallay.

"You've heard Mr. Asante complain about a particular prosecutor on this case, Eric Trumble. I'm here to warn the public, and the DA himself, Patrick McBride, about the person who is really running the Kallay investigation: Bureau Chief Dana Hargrove. She's the supervising attorney, the person responsible for the decision to keep this unsupportable murder charge alive."

Around Patrick's television screen, the tension was palpable. Dana wanted to fly, to be somewhere else. This couldn't be happening.

"Frances Kallay has given compelling evidence that she was savagely beaten by the so-called victim. She was legally defending herself against his imminent use of deadly force. This is a case that should be dismissed outright, but Dana Hargrove is a single-minded prosecutor with one objective: to get a conviction at all costs. The Kallay case is just one example. My innocence project, Justice Restored, is representing a man who's been languishing in prison for a crime he did not commit, all because of the acts and omissions of this woman. We've subpoenaed Dana Hargrove to testify on Monday in the case of the People against Ramón Pineda. I invite the press to watch this one. You will see the lengths to which this prosecutor went to obtain a conviction against an innocent man. She's a woman who shuns her duty to seek justice. Prosecutor Dana Hargrove has forsaken her oath of office."

14 »   REPUTATION

PATRICK HIT "MUTE" and pointed to the small conference table in the middle of the room. "Sit down, everyone."

Dana feared she wouldn't be able to make it. Her legs were rubbery. The air rippled in a surreal wave, and there wasn't enough of it to breathe. *So wrong. So unfair.* She managed the few steps and sat down. Nowhere to hide. Patrick sat directly across from her, and Jared sat across from Eric.

Patrick's eyes went from Dana to Eric. Concern lined his face but didn't weaken the evident resolve. He was a leader, ready to meet the challenge. If he was seeing red at that moment, the emotion couldn't be detected. "You're going to tell me exactly what happened in court this morning. But before you do, remember that I've heard scores of defense attorneys making statements to the press. More often than not, they add a little color and exaggeration to the story. So I don't want to hear defensiveness, and I don't want to hear an attack on Ellen Fortier or Xavier Asante. That isn't going to help me out. I only need to hear it straight. Eric?"

Dana was grateful for the delay. She didn't think she could speak. Her cell phone buzzed and she looked at the screen under the table. It was a text from Ricky: "Call for an update." She couldn't call him right now, and she doubted that the renewed investigation of Frances Kallay, still in its early stages, had revealed anything earthshaking which could help her out in this meeting with Patrick.

Eric said, "Asante was right. I did ask the court to extend

one-eighty eighty by two days. But I started out making the record you asked us to make, and it went from there. I said that the People have a case, but we postponed the vote simply to accommodate her request for further investigation. After that, Asante started going on about how this is a terrible travesty, the People have no evidence, et cetera et cetera. I emphasized again that the defendant caused the delay because she raised new issues and asked us to investigate. I told Asante that if he wanted to test his theory that we didn't have a case, he should stipulate to an extension. We could finish the investigation she wants and put it to a vote in two days."

"If it was proposed as a stipulation between you and Asante, how did the court get involved?"

Eric's mildly confident look turned sheepish. "He started ranting again, so I cited case law to support the court's authority to extend the time limit for good cause."

"I see." Patrick turned to Dana. "What were you doing while all of this was going on?"

"I..." Her throat closed on the words. Never had her actions as a supervisor been so closely scrutinized. Awkwardly, she avoided Patrick's eyes and glanced at Jared, who gave her a small nod of encouragement. She straightened her spine and faced Patrick again. He was her mentor. He was her friend. He'd always believed in her. Always had her back. "I didn't say anything. Eric's application to the court ... well, it came as a surprise."

"I blew it, Patrick!" Eric interjected. "Dana told me yesterday not to go there. It started out as a bluff and I just kept going." He hit the side of his head with a flat palm. "When we walked out of the courtroom, Dana really gave me a dressing down—no pun intended."

Jared smiled. Patrick's expression remained the same. Dana started over again. "Getting back to your question, when

Eric took me by surprise, I considered stepping in but decided to hold back. Under the circumstances, it was the best option. If I had withdrawn Eric's request for an extension, we would have looked like fools, taking inconsistent positions. Also, the way things were going, I didn't think the court would grant such an unusual request. As it turned out, I was right."

"And if you'd been wrong? What then? I doubt we could finish this investigation in two days. Meanwhile, you can bet that Asante would be heating things up for us, filing an emergency habeas writ at the very least."

She had nothing to say to that. Eric slumped an inch lower in his seat.

"Look, Eric, without question, you put everyone in a difficult situation here. Next time, follow Dana's advice and don't tread where you're not allowed to go."

"I know. I'm sorry."

"Don't be sorry. Just don't do it again. As it turned out, we're okay on this one. The bigger question is"—Patrick turned to Dana—"what the hell was Ellen talking about? What are these 'acts and omissions' you committed in the Pineda case?"

Dana was now regretting her decision not to bother Patrick about the Pineda hearing. If they'd spoken when she first got the subpoena, he would have been better prepared for Ellen's unjustified ravings to the press. "I have no idea. My memory is that I did everything properly on that case."

"And did an excellent job," Jared cut in. "I remember that one."

Everyone at this table was trying to help her out. Did she look that bad? Hopefully, some of the color had returned to her face. The butterflies were settling. She told Patrick, "Ellen argues in her motion papers that I withheld exculpatory evidence in a forensic report. There's no way I could have withheld something like that."

"I remember we spoke briefly about this," Patrick said to Jared. "Did you assign someone to cover this hearing?"

"Ben Weingarten."

"Have you and Ben prepared for the hearing, Dana?"

"No. There's been so much to do before my vacation..."

"When's your vacation?"

"It starts on Monday..."

"The day of the hearing?"

"I'll be here. I mean, I'm driving back from the shore..." Her thoughts came out disjointed and incoherent to her ears. "Ben tried to adjourn it, but Judge Deal is going on vacation too ... Ben couldn't change the date ... the judge is trying to finish up his open matters before *his* vacation."

"So you'll be here on Monday?"

"Yes. To testify."

"You'll need to go over the file with Ben. Ellen can't establish that we knew about this alleged exculpatory evidence unless it's in the file. She must have gotten something from a FOIL request. Look through every piece of paper in that file."

"Yes, tomorrow. I ... I still have Friday. There's time." Suddenly, the week was gone and she'd done nothing to prepare. To her knowledge, neither had ADA Weingarten, except for his attempt to get an adjournment. Under the crush of other emergencies, they'd both conveniently downplayed the Pineda case, riding on the assumption that Ellen, a woman who lived in a different reality, had nothing to pin on Dana. She remembered Ben's nonchalant remarks when he called to say he'd been unable to get an adjournment: "I'll submit our reply papers by Friday. I'm sure the petition is meritless—the judge will deny it after ten minutes of testimony. You'll be driving back to the shore in no time!" He hadn't studied the case, but he was so sure. Based on what? Her reputation? Or was he one of those ADAs who operated under a misguided, entrenched sense of righteousness?

"Meanwhile," Patrick continued, "I have to decide whether a response is called for, and if so, whether I should respond now or later. Should I hold a press conference immediately to answer these distortions? What's your opinion on that, Jared?" Dana supposed that Patrick already had a good idea of what he planned to do. But it was part of his management style to ask the opinions of his top attorneys without disclosing his own opinion first.

"Honestly, I think it's better to wait," said Jared. "On the Kallay case, there's not much that can be said that wouldn't sound defensive. Without an indictment, you can't offer any opinion about the ultimate charge. You'll be coming from a much stronger position when the investigation is completed and Frances is indicted."

Patrick nodded. "And Ellen's accusations?"

"An immediate response would look like you're worried about her. I wouldn't dignify her accusations by responding to them. Ellen is somewhat off her rocker. You remember what she was like when she was here, particularly the last year, after her brother was arrested."

"I do indeed," said Patrick. "But she's had a few successes recently. She's built up some credibility. She's mounting a campaign against this office, alleging rampant prosecutorial misconduct."

"Yes, well today, it was all focused on Dana, the so-called 'single-minded prosecutor bent on getting a conviction at any cost.' It seems like a personal vendetta."

"This is personal?" Patrick turned to Dana.

"Jared and I have our theories." The buddies from rookie days exchanged knowing looks. "Ellen lagged behind us and never made it to homicide chart. The Pineda case was her first chance to prosecute a murder, and she botched the pretrial. You reassigned the case to me when I returned from maternity leave."

"So, this is about jealousy?" Patrick was incredulous. "She's a successful defense attorney now. Why would she care that she wasn't promoted to homicide chart?"

Jared said, "Dana is one of your top attorneys. If Ellen damages Dana's reputation, she builds up that much more credibility. But she isn't going to succeed. We know enough of Dana's work to be confident that Ellen's allegations aren't true and will be disproved. My guess is that the 'exculpatory evidence' will turn out to be a twisted interpretation of something that's entirely innocuous. After the hearing, you'll have some ammunition for a press conference."

Patrick had been listening with his fingertips pressed together, forehead resting on the spire of his index fingers. He kept this pose for a silent moment before raising his head. "Okay. It was my inclination to wait, and everything you're saying supports that course of action. I won't make any statement to the press until at least Monday, or maybe longer, when both matters are cleared up. If all of our instincts are correct here, the Kallay investigation will reveal the wife's involvement in the crime, and the Pineda hearing will clear Dana of any wrongdoing." He leveled his gaze at Dana. "Isn't that so, Dana?"

She swallowed through a tight throat and nodded in agreement.

An echoing refrain kept her company all the way back to the office. *Isn't that so, Dana? Isn't that so...?*

Keep moving, keep doing. Automatic pilot was best.

She directed Eric to call Asante or his people and make sure the message got through to him: investigators would be arriving shortly at the Kallay residence to conduct the consent search. She parted company with Eric at his office door and stopped at Lecia's desk. The phone was ringing. Lecia glanced at the display, ignored the call, and handed a small stack of message slips to Dana.

"News agencies?" Dana flipped through the little squares of paper, not seeing what was written on them. "ADA Weingarten" caught her eye on one of the slips.

"Mostly, and a few others. I gave them the usual line." Reporters knew the official policy preventing ADAs from giving statements to the press, but that didn't stop them from trying. Lecia's routine was to refer all inquiries from the press to a special phone number for that purpose in the executive wing.

"Thanks." Dana went into her office, closed the door behind her, and picked up the desk phone. She owed Ricky a call. He was next door, but she couldn't face anyone right now, not even her deputy. If she kept moving and doing without thinking, phone calls were possible. And she needed to involve Ricky completely in the Kallay case, so he'd take control while she was on vacation. Eric ... had she made a mistake assigning him to this case? He needed close supervision.

"Hi, Dana. I didn't see the news on TV but I heard about it. How'd it go with Patrick?"

"Just dandy."

"Hope it wasn't too bad."

"No worries. We'll get through it." She was the head of this bureau and had to project confidence. Quickly, she changed the subject. "What's the latest on Kallay?"

"When I spoke to Gil at 10:50, the team was on the way uptown to the Kallay residence. Since Gil didn't hear from you or Eric, he assumed that Asante was on board, but he said it didn't matter anyway."

"Didn't matter?"

"It's a consent search. No lawyer needed."

"Let Gil have his fantasy. She's got an attorney and we're not doing anything behind his back. Eric's calling Asante right now. Besides, if Gil questions Frances, we can't use it. Any waiver of her right to counsel isn't valid unless the waiver is made with her attorney present."

"Gil says he's not going to question her, just do the search. Any volunteered statements without police questioning are admissible."

"That's a gray area, and it depends on the judge. Would you call it volunteered or elicited when you blurt something out as the police are rummaging through your things? Call Gil and tell him to wait until he hears that we've contacted Asante." Suddenly, she didn't trust Eric to do this, and Ricky would drum it in. Oh, why was this case so messed up?

"Okay. I'll tell Gil to hold back until contact with Asante is confirmed."

"Good." Dana looked at the time display on her phone. It was 11:17. "Hope we're not too late. We finished in court at about 10:20 or 10:30. Frances might be home by now, depending on the traffic. Anything else?"

"No responses yet to the subpoenas they served yesterday afternoon for the medical records and financial records. Gil did confirm the information Frances gave you about the Clothing for Kids function. It checks out. Other than that, the squad contacted a few other people on the list of competitors, employees, and acquaintances, but they don't have any new theories about a possible accomplice."

"Okay. Thanks, Ricky." All of this was unchanged from the report Eric had given her at nine this morning.

"Oh, and one other thing. They're up on the trap and trace and pen register on her landline and mobile. The squad is getting live feed from the phone company on all incoming and outgoing numbers. They're dead so far."

"She's not home yet. We'll check later. Wouldn't that be a bonanza if she's dumb enough to call her accomplice?"

"It's not beyond imagination."

"We'll hope."

After ending the call with Ricky, she called Ben Weingarten. Voicemail came on, and she left him a message: "We need to prepare for the Pineda hearing. Have you looked at the file yet? Please give me a call." Only after hanging up did she focus on the notes Lecia had written on the message slip for Ben: "Leaving for U.S. Courthouse now, then going to the Appellate Division. Please call after four." Ugh. Her eyes weren't seeing. Her mind wasn't thinking. This ADA Weingarten was constantly on the go between federal court, responding to habeas petitions, and state court, responding to defendants' appeals. The anger rose in her chest. What a great choice Jared had made in the person to defend her.

Stop it. She shouldn't be mad at Jared. Ben's limited time was a feature of every ADA's job. On call, nonstop.

She stood up, circled the desk, and sat down.

She stood up again and looked out the window at the drab, concrete façade of the Criminal Court building. The third floor of that building housed the archives of the DA's office. Without delay, she should go across the street and request the file herself. Right now. But her eyes were stinging and her vision was blurry and the panic was rising in her chest.

Searching the desk, she came up with nothing to stanch the liquid streaming from her nose and eyes. Not a tissue anywhere. She never cried and rarely had a cold. Last fall she'd considered keeping a box of tissues on her desk after one of her rookies broke down in her office, but she never followed up on the idea. There were always coffee spills, however. She opened three desk drawers and found, in the bottom one, a small stack of paper towels kept there for such emergencies. The rough paper felt good on her face. She deserved rough.

No one should see her like this. She walked to the door and pushed the button on the knob. Locked in. Safe. The harder she tried to stop, the faster the tears came.

There was only one person to call. His number was a preprogrammed shortcut at the top of her list. She went over to the desk phone and pressed the code. He picked up after the first ring.

"Evan?" Her voice shook.

"I was about to call... Are you all right, my love?"

"It's okay. No, it's not okay..."

"I didn't see the news, I was in a meeting. But I have some idea of what happened. Mom called a few minutes ago—"

"Mom called? Are the kids all right?"

"Yes, nothing like that. They're still at camp. It's just that the doorman has been buzzing her from the lobby about the reporters."

Of course. She should have thought of it. The DA's office didn't disclose the home addresses of its employees, but there were ways to find out.

"I told her not to talk to them," Evan said. "And I called the lobby. Fred's on duty. I told him to make it clear to these people that they're not welcome. If he has any real trouble, he should call the police. Mom is staying inside until it's time to pick up the kids at three, but I don't think any news organizations are going to know who she is when she leaves the building."

"I'll call the DA's squad. They can send someone over..." Her voice made a little hiccup.

"Okay, do that, but you don't sound too good. Take a few deep breaths. Maybe I should come down there."

"No!"

"Should we meet? You want to go out for lunch?"

"I can't eat."

"You want to come here?"

Oh! There was nowhere to go, people everywhere.

When she didn't respond he said, "Okay. You don't want me to come there, we can't go out, so you're coming here. It'll do you good to get some air. Are you able to get out of the building?"

"Yes." The news vans were gone. She could escape.

"I'll lock us in my office. If you're hungry, I have a few things in the fridge. Yogurt and fruit anyway. Is it a date?"

"Okay. I'll be there."

"Good girl."

"Right. I'm just a girl today."

"You're my girl, and I love you. Get out of there now."

She hung up, dried her eyes, blew her nose, and looked in the mirror. A little red and puffy. Sunglasses were the thing, but she couldn't put them on in the office.

Five minutes later she dared to open the door. The sunglasses were in her purse. Stopping briefly at Lecia's desk, she stood at an oblique angle to her secretary, not meeting her in the eye. "I'll be out for a while. I'm going to meet Evan for lunch. You can reach me on my mobile."

"Okay."

With a quick glance and a forced smile, Dana walked away, taking with her a snapshot of Lecia's beautiful face wearing a look of concern and puzzlement.

15 » CELLAR

GIL HAD TO make this right. His instincts rarely let him down. In this case he'd been correct about one thing, Frances Kallay's involvement. But here was the state of it: no indictment, a media carnival, spotlight on the Dane, the top man pissed off. A mess.

Boy Wonder couldn't be blamed for the way it went down in the grand jury. There were some big holes to fill, now that Frances had changed her story. Self-defense was bullshit, Gil could see that much. The woman had to be hoping for a merciful jury—or a stupid one. The killing was intentional and unjustified. Maybe the peacock actually deserved what he got. If that was the case, Gil had no problem letting Frances go. But he didn't see it that way. There were too many people saying that Loránd Kallay *didn't* deserve it. Wife beater? Couldn't be. The fashion king was a saint. His public face anyway. No one had caught a whiff of the alleged cruelty going on in the cellar of their townhome on East 69th Street. That was the big mystery—how these society figures hadn't let anything slip. *If* there was anything to her story.

During the news conference on the courthouse steps, Gil was mobilizing the forces. He made arrangements to pick up Police Officer Martin Smith at the 19th and jumped into his beat-up Mercedes for the trip uptown. Investigator Manuel Colon from the DA's squad came along for the ride. The three of them would conduct the consent search of the cellar as soon as Frances got home. Their resources were limited. The team was spread thin, following up on other leads, and the Kallay case wasn't the only big investigation in town. Gil made sure that crime scene investigators and Nicole Verona's forensics team were on call if he needed photographs and analysis— depending on what they found down under.

On the way uptown, Gil got the call from Ricky to hold back until they confirmed that Asante was notified. "I coulda told you that," said Manny.

"No big surprise. We're dealing with lawyers here."

At the precinct, Smith hopped into the back seat of the Mercedes. "Nice ride," he said. "I see they pay you well at the DA's Office." Possibly a joke was intended.

In the front seat, Manny flashed Gil a look under raised eyebrows. In their book, Smith was a bit prissy, unschooled in undercover work, but decent and smart enough. Most likely, any forfeited vehicles in the fleet of the 19th were luxury rides of the swindling CEOs and inside traders among the well-to-do residents of this Upper East Side neighborhood. "I'm hoping for a raise," Gil deadpanned.

They headed for the Kallay residence, entered the one-way street, and double-parked in front of the townhouse. Yellow police tape was loosely strung across the front entrance, drooping in the humid summer air.

"Where's your man?" Gil asked Smith.

"How's that?"

"Don't you have some uniforms guarding the crime scene? Anyone could walk in there."

"We do a drive-by on the hour."

On the hour. Great. He should have expected as much. Until yesterday, they didn't know they'd be going in for another search. "I'll go up and ring the bell, see if the little lady is home."

A minute of ringing and knocking without response, and

Gil returned to the car. They sat and waited.

After a while, no more than five minutes, Smith asked, "You think she went somewhere first?"

"Nah. She wants to see us," Gil said.

"The feeling's mutual," said Manny.

"I'd find another dream girl if I were you," said Gil. "This one's going up the river when we're done."

"How long since the court released her?" Smith asked.

Gil looked at his watch. He was cool, not about to show the speck of annoyance he was feeling for his brother in law enforcement. Distant cousin, more like. "'bout an hour."

"It took her awhile to kiss her lawyer goodbye and find a ride uptown," said Manny.

"Yeah, I'm hoping it was a kiss-off," said Gil. "I don't wanna see him." He knew that the defense strategy could go either way, once Eric notified Asante that they were waiting for Frances. Asante might insist on being here in the name of protecting his client's rights. Or, he might think it best to stay away entirely, to give the impression of her full and unfettered cooperation. Gil was betting on the latter. Why send out an invitation to the cops for an open house only to put a lawyer in the way? "She must've gone to Police Plaza to pick up her personal effects. Needs the house key. Of course, we would've let her in without it."

"I bet she's making that stop," Smith interjected. "That'd be good for us. We took her cell phone when we arrested her. Maybe she'll make a call, and we'll pick it up on the pen." At that moment, investigators were eagerly standing by for activity on her mobile and landline.

"Our luck, the battery will be dead."

The radio under the dash squawked. Gil unhooked the handheld receiver and spoke into it. "Herrera."

"Got a message for you," said the dispatcher. "The lady's

attorney was called."

"He's coming?"

"Didn't say. But he was told you were there, and he didn't object or ask for more time. You're instructed to use your judgment."

"Roger." Gil's judgment told him to go in whether the lawyer came or not. They were after physical evidence, not statements.

Minutes later, a yellow cab slowly passed Gil's Mercedes on the right, pulled up in front, and came to a stop. The unmistakable backside of Frances Kallay's professional coiffure could be seen through the back window. She was alone. "Made good time at the Plaza," remarked Gil. "Look like that, and they put you at the head of the line." The smartly-dressed suspect alighted from the back passenger door, extending one high-heeled foot at a time. The eggshell white was spotless and crisp. She turned to them and let her eyes linger as she closed the cab door.

Gil stared back. What's going on in that lady's head?

Upright and poised in her heels, Frances walked slowly—reluctantly—toward the house, ascended the three steps and lifted the drooping yellow tape over her head, not mussing a hair. She removed a key from her purse and inserted it into the lock, just like it was any other day. If she felt their eyes upon her, there was nothing in her demeanor to show it as she let herself inside.

They were nice about it and waited at least thirty seconds—much less than the time it would take to do any rearranging in the cellar.

"You're very considerate," she said a moment later, after letting them in the front door. Gil, who stood a mere five-nine, towered over her. The thirty seconds had given her just enough time to remove her high heels and change into a comfortable, cushiony pair of house shoes that couldn't be accused of being slippers. "I don't know why you didn't just follow me in. Come right this way."

There was no use reciting the *Miranda* warnings. Let her talk, Gil thought. Let her dig her own hole. I don't have to ask her a thing.

She started to lead them to the library on the right side of the entry hall, but stopped. "I suppose you should see this first."

She led them to a narrow door in the entry hall, behind the lower sweep of the grand staircase. "This is the real door to the cellar. But my husband never used it." She pressed gently on the door handle. It didn't budge. "It's locked from the inside. He would always say, 'Let's go to the library, shall we?' and I would follow, because there was nothing else to do. If I didn't go on my own, it would be worse. He would drag me, kicking and screaming." She looked at them one at a time. Her eyes were tired and slightly bloodshot, her face drained of color. Maybe she wasn't as cool as they thought, and Rikers Island hadn't been such a carnival. "And then, it would be especially cruel downstairs." Her voice dropped, and she gave a little shudder.

It was a chilling exposition. Gil worked at an open mind, or as he liked to call it, a healthy skepticism.

She led them into the library toward a bookshelf adjacent to a blank wall panel of cherry oak. "There's a button in here." She reached into a shelf at shoulder level, and the wall panel released with an audible click. She grabbed the edge of the "door," pulled it open, and gestured. "Be my guest."

"After you," said Gil.

"I'm sorry. I'm not going down there. Too much to remember."

Gil hesitated. The lady told the grand jury that she'd shot

her husband. She looked far from dangerous at the moment, but she'd already displayed at least three personalities since he'd met her a week ago. Her aversion to the cellar raised the problem of choosing a man to saddle with an unglamorous duty. Gil didn't want to offend Smith. It would get back to Inspector Bitters. That left Manuel to spend some time with his dream girl. "Manny, stay here with Mrs. Kallay while we go down."

Manny didn't look too happy as Gil stepped through the secret door, followed by Smith.

A light automatically flicked on, illuminating the stairway. Motion sensor. It must be difficult to find a light switch in the dark while struggling with an unwilling wife. The stairs were narrow and steep, enclosed by walls on both sides. The wall on the right extended the full length of the stairs; the wall on the left ended about halfway down and opened into the cellar. Gil imagined what it might be like to carry or drag a kicking, screaming woman—even a petite one like Frances—down this treacherous passage. Impossible not to inflict damage on her or the walls. Too bad they hadn't gotten a look at her legs on the day he and Smith arrested her, but the court order allowed photographs of only the upper chest, arms, neck and head.

Gil descended slowly, examining the walls carefully on the way down. They appeared to be made of drywall, plastered and painted. Nothing impermeable or mar-proof. The light was dim. Gil could make out a few black marks and superficial scratches, normal wear and tear. "See anything?" he asked Smith.

"On the walls you mean?"

Gil turned and looked at his partner for the day. Smith had taken Gil's lead and was making a show of looking at one of the walls. Clueless.

"No obvious holes or indents that I can see," Gil

explained.

"Yeah." Said with a little laugh.

"Took her high heels off before he carried her down."

Gil counted twelve steps. At the bottom, as they made the sharp turn to the left, an overhead light flicked on, illuminating the cellar. On the wall opposite to them was another steep staircase leading up to the locked door that Frances had shown them. The two walls on opposing sides were covered floor to ceiling with well-stocked wine racks.

The men took a few steps in.

"Mother of God," muttered Smith. Stretched out in the middle of the floor was a rustic, medieval, rough plank table about six feet long. Straddling its center was a metal bar on hinges, capable of being lifted or lowered and locked into place, tightly, around anything on the table no larger than a slender human body.

They pivoted around to look at the other side of the half wall encasing the stairway they'd just descended. It was fitted with several large metal hooks. Ropes, pulleys, and chains dangled. Two pairs of handcuffs. Something white on the cement floor: a cloth with dried, rust-colored splotches. Blood. Or could it be red wine?

They walked slowly around the room, looking, not touching. A sudden flash stabbed Gil in the eye—a glint cast from a dangling cuff as it caught the overhead light from a certain angle. He halted, walked closer, and examined the cuffs. Kallay liked to keep his equipment shining. Was it new?

He walked over to a wine rack and peered at a bottle. "Hmm. Does that really say 1938?"

"Sell one of those and you could get yourself a new car," said Smith, still hoping to make a winning quip. His voice trembled slightly.

The table was next. Gil scrutinized it, imagining what he

thought it meant. He couldn't remember every detail of the parts of Frances's body he'd seen. Later, he would have to look at those photographs again. Strapped into this contraption mid-body, arms pinned underneath, wouldn't that leave marks of a certain width?

Smith was crouched on the other side of the table, looking at the device at eye level with the hinges. He started making little noises, as evidence of his analytic prowess. "Hmm," he pondered once, twice, three times. Finally he said, "Look here."

Gil came around, lowered himself to a squat, and saw what Smith had discovered. Finally, the man was proving that he had an eye. "Now, ain't that strange?" Gil mused. "This sucker is loose." He could tell, even without touching it.

"I don't think it's attached or screwed in place at all. Just laid on top, made to look like it is."

They both stood up, knowing what had to be done. "I'll go up to the car and call this in," said Gil. "Crime scene and forensics promised to be here in fifteen. Plenty for them here to bag and superglue."

Smith couldn't contain it. His face beamed with childish glee.

16 » ARCHIVES

THE SUBWAY RIDE did the trick and plugged her tears. Half an hour on the New York City subway in the middle of the day can do wonders to alter reality. The noise obliterates most rational thought, and the people are not the kind to be concerned whether a prosecutor named Dana Hargrove has forsaken her oath of office.

On the first car she boarded, a homeless man was stretched out for a nap, leaving a stench that compelled her to change cars at the next stop. After that, she was surrounded by an ever-shifting mix of passengers: a sprinkling of businesspeople like herself, mothers with young children, teenage truants, senior citizens, and tourists speaking Dutch. Dana recognized the sound, and even a few words, from the time she had a Dutch au pair.

It was summer, and young women with colorful toenails were dressed in tank tops and very short shorts. Men reeking of sweat wore tee-shirts and jeans with dirt pushed into the denim. The train experienced a brief, inexplicable loss of power, stranding them in a tunnel for the longest five seconds of anyone's life.

Up on the street in midtown, she blended in with the business lunch crowd and was beginning to feel like herself. When she got to the building, there was no need to hide her face as she stepped out of the elevator and into the reception area for Belknap & Rose. She was a respected attorney, the wife of a partner at B & R. The receptionist waved her through after calling Evan to alert him that she was coming. Along the way, Dana exchanged cordial greetings with a few of Evan's colleagues, convincing herself that their faces betrayed no suggestion of harbored secrets or recently circulated rumors. Why would any of these people have the time to watch the TV news on a Thursday morning?

Behind Evan's closed door, she fell into his arms for a long embrace. It would be so wonderful to remain like this, forgetting everything. Gently, he pulled away and led her over to the small couch next to a coffee table, where he'd set up the food items he was offering for lunch. They sat down.

"This *is* a date," she said, looking over the spread. Containers of blueberry yogurt, two bananas, and two granola bars.

"I only serve the best."

"I'm feeling better, but I don't think I can eat. These two cases are killing me."

"The cases or the attorneys? We predicted something like this. A few days ago you weren't very worried about Asante. Does this change things? Because I'm telling you, it isn't changing my game plan in the Tripp case. Not unless there's something more sinister under the surface. I don't see it. It's all bluster."

"It doesn't feel like that. It's a personal attack. And Eric gave Asante some extra fuel when he attempted his own power play." She explained what had happened in court, and followed up with a detailed rundown of Patrick's dissatisfaction with Eric's performance. Although the boss's displeasure with her own performance was less than clear to her, she quoted his question with acerbic emphasis: "'What were *you* doing while all of this was going on?'"

"So, you're feeling bad about letting Patrick down."

"Well, yes. There's that."

"Seems to me you did the only sensible thing."

"I like to think so. Yesterday, I told Eric to stay away from that tactic and he didn't listen to me. What can you do when someone doesn't listen?" She hated the sound of her own voice. Weak. She hated the subscript in her question. A thinly-veiled excuse. It *was* her fault. She hadn't been forceful enough in directing her subordinate.

"He ignored you and did his own thing. It's past history, so stop kicking yourself. What I'm worried about is whether Asante has taken on a new significance. Whether you're feeling threatened or scared."

"I wouldn't go that far. It's my reputation that's threatened. Not me. Patrick's got my back. The damage can be controlled, and Asante won't be able to go any further with his public complaints, unless…"

"Unless it turns out that Eric authorized an arrest of the wrong person—on your watch."

Dana nodded and looked off into the distance.

"In which case, it'll be your neck as well as Patrick's," Evan guessed.

She nodded again.

"But, from what you've told me, I think your instincts about Frances Kallay are correct."

"We've been jumping over huge blank spots to connect the dots. We need harder evidence."

"Well, you just gotta do what you always do. Keep working the case. The troops are in place, and they'll carry on very nicely without you when you're at the shore."

"I have to keep on top of it. I can do that by phone, and I'll be coming back for the Pineda hearing anyway, so—"

"I forbid that thought. I granted only a single day's leave of absence. Sunday evening to Monday evening. You're going to clear up this thing with Ellen and be back for more sun and fun."

Without a word, Dana leaned forward, elbows on knees, and stared at the brown spots on the banana in front of her on the table. Evan rubbed her upper back affectionately. "Go ahead. Don't be shy. That banana has your name on it."

She smiled, still looking down at the ripe fruit. "I don't know how anyone could eat that thing. Tomorrow it'll be close to liquid."

"Okay, be like that. I don't care. More for me. Pure honey."

She turned to him and put a hand on his cheek. "You're the sweet one. Thanks for lunch, but I've got to go now."

She made a move to stand up and he pushed her back down. "Whoa! You've been here five minutes, and we just got to the sore spot. And I'm not talking about the banana. You're dodging the issue, counselor."

"Come on, Evan."

"Come on yourself. How long have we been married? Forever."

"Eleven years."

"Almost forever. And you think I don't know this about you?"

"Know what?"

"That you like to pretend that the toughest thing doesn't exist."

"I'm not really worried about Ellen. She's a mental case."

"But she put on a good show today. 'Prosecutor Dana Hargrove has forsaken her oath of office.' Sounds almost poetic."

"I thought you didn't watch the news."

"I confess. I watched it while you were on your way up here. That little bit of her statement is a favorite clip. They're looping it on the all-news station."

She dropped her head and started to shake it.

"Sorry." He rubbed her back again.

"Who's dodging now?"

"I didn't want to alarm you."

"Denzel thinks she's making it a personal attack to enhance her credibility. If her cleanup campaign is successful, Justice Restored will be taken seriously. People love crusaders against public corruption, and they love to put a face on the evildoer. Ellen picked me as her scapegoat. If she brings me down, if she ruins me…"

"That's impossible. Ellen's allegations are just that—allegations. You couldn't have withheld anything significant. I know your litigation strategy. You always disclose more than you need to. An open file is the best policy, you always say. So what could she be relying on? What's in the case file that could back her up?"

From under a lowered brow, Dana looked up at her husband guiltily. "I haven't looked at the file yet. And the ADA assigned to represent me hasn't looked at it either."

Evan raised his eyebrows. He withheld his thoughts, but she saw his surprise. He'd assumed that she'd been preparing. She explained, "Earlier this week, when I spoke with Ben Weingarten on the phone, the only thing he'd done was to try to postpone the hearing. We've both been too busy to do anything else. His comments made me think that he's planning to wing it at the hearing. He said there couldn't be any merit to Ellen's petition. I don't know if his plan has changed since … this morning." Her voice broke. Was she really so scared?

"And now, you're afraid there might be something there? Something you forgot? Why don't you pull the file and take a look?"

"You're right, but…"

"But what?"

"I wanted Ben to do it. He's unavailable today. If I order

the file from the archive room, I'll leave a footprint."

"You mean the clerk will make a note of it."

"I don't want my name in the log. Not now. Not when I'm accused of withholding evidence. I don't want to invite any new accusations based on speculation that I tampered with the file."

Evan looked skeptical. He opened his mouth to speak but stopped. He was walking on eggshells with her, she could tell. If she wasn't acting so damn fragile right now, he might just tell her how ridiculous she sounded. All of a sudden she knew it, even before he gave her the hint: "Couldn't the same accusation be made against Ben if his name is in the log? He's representing the People at the hearing."

"Of course."

"Then, maybe you should reconsider."

"You're right. I should."

"You're ripping yourself apart for nothing."

"I can do a quick search. I know what I'm looking for. The forensics and lab reports. Ellen claims there's exculpatory evidence in a report."

"What kind of reports were in evidence? Remind me what this case is about."

Dana cleared her throat and sat up taller. "Ramón Pineda was convicted of felony murder. You remember. The arresting officer was Aurelina Vargas—"

"Our favorite cop! She's the one who helped with Anneke's case. Is Ellen accusing you of withholding evidence to protect Officer Vargas?"

"There's no possibility of that. Pineda committed his crime in July of 1992. I didn't know Aurelina until 1994."

"Right. This is the case that got her transferred."

"Didn't *get* her transferred. She asked for a transfer to a precinct with a lower crime rate."

"And she wound up in our old neighborhood."

"Yup. She didn't have to transfer. She wanted to. The investigation cleared her of any wrongdoing in firing her weapon. But still, it spooked her. She was just a rookie at the time."

"Damn fine cop."

"She was, and she is. In the Pineda case, she was riding with Sergeant Habberly when they were called to an armed robbery in progress, a bodega in Spanish Harlem. When they pulled up, they could see the defendant through the front window. They ordered him to drop his weapon. There were shots fired on both sides. The store owner was killed, and the defendant was wounded in the shoulder."

"What was his defense?"

"He claimed he was surrendering when Officer Vargas started shooting. She fired off two bullets. The first one hit his shoulder and supposedly caused him to fire his gun accidentally toward the front of the store. The bullet ricocheted on the security bars over the window and hit the store owner."

"That's no defense."

"I know."

"He's still guilty of felony murder."

"He was going for the only thing he had, trying to make it look accidental. If he got the jury's sympathy, he had some hope for a mercy verdict, no worse than robbery. But the evidence clearly pointed to a different scenario. I argued that the defendant was the one who shot first. He was a drug addict and very volatile. He had the gun aimed at the store owner and was about to pull the trigger when the police arrived. He panicked and fired off the first bullet at the owner but missed, hitting the shelves behind the counter. Then he spun around to the police, fired toward the window, and the bullet ricocheted."

"So there's no question that the victim was killed by a bullet from the defendant's gun that ricocheted?"

"No question. But, of course, I also argued that it didn't matter who fired first, or even if the defendant's gun went off accidentally. Under the felony murder statute, he was guilty either way."

Evan thought for a moment. "Ellen's accusation doesn't make much sense. This isn't the kind of case where you would have a motive to withhold a lab report. The forensics are going to be pretty standard. You've got autopsy, ballistics report, and trajectory analysis. His bullet hit the victim. It really doesn't matter if he shot first or second, or if he didn't intend to kill anyone."

"Yes, I'm telling you."

"Then go take a look at the file and prove her wrong."

"I'm going right now." She leaned over and kissed him. "Thank you, darling."

This time, he let her stand up from the couch. "Banana for the road?" He held up a soft fruit and pointed it at her.

"Knock yourself out."

"I'm glad you're going. Now I can eat in peace." He winked at her and started to peel it.

Headed downtown again, Dana had a single objective in mind. She wasn't going to wait for Ben. She needed to see that file now.

Her plan could derail if the file wasn't found—a possibility that wasn't beyond imagination. The archive department of the District Attorney's Office comprised half the third floor of the monstrous Criminal Court building. Thousands of cases were indicted each year, and the DA's internal files for the most recent ten years were stored here, organized by indictment number. Older cases were kept at a remote location, where a project was underway to scan every piece of paper in every file for digital storage.

The files ranged in size according to the complexity of the case. Some warranted no more than a slim manila folder, while others generated enough paper to fill multiple cardboard boxes. A misplaced file was not uncommon. The folder might be shoved to the back of a shelf, or eaten up by its larger neighbor.

To give herself a fighting chance, Dana called ahead from the lobby of Evan's building. She took out her cell phone, dialed the main switchboard, and asked for archives. As she waited to be transferred, she prayed that the file could be located before she got downtown. In the final moment of silence, before the clerk came on the line, her mind groped at a thought: *the indictment number.*

"Archives," said a man with a worn-out voice. Dana identified herself, and without hesitation, asked him to pull the file for "indictment number 2456 of 1992." Her certainty surprised her, but she had no doubts. Ellen's subpoena, and the information written on it, had made an indelible impression on her memory.

Half an hour later, Dana entered the archives department and walked up to the counter. The place looked like a prison. Fortified chicken-wire glass over the counter separated the clerks from the rest of the world, closing them in with their crumbling papers. There were locked doors on either side of the counter. Three arch-shaped openings in the glass provided a means of communication and a gateway for the exit of any average-sized file, which could be pushed on the countertop through the opening. Anything larger, like a box, required a meeting with the clerk at the door.

All of this was vaguely familiar to Dana, who remembered taking a couple of trips to archives several years ago. Now, if she wanted a file, she would ask someone on her support staff to retrieve it or to photocopy certain papers and bring them back to her office.

At the moment she walked in, the only person in sight was behind the glass. Perhaps there were others hidden in the labyrinth beyond. This clerk was a slight, stoop-shouldered man of about middle age, wearing a short-sleeved business shirt, open at the collar, revealing the neckline of his undershirt. "I called a short while ago," Dana said, pushing her identification card through the slot.

His eyes went from the picture on the card to her face, comparing them. At the same time, her eyes were drawn to the red patches of skin on his forehead—a slightly raw look, with flakes of skin around the edges. Eczema? Or maybe bits of paper. She was finding it hard to breathe. The air was heavy with ancient dust.

"Ramón Pineda," said the man. His mouth squiggled into a funny little smile, indicating that he was unaccustomed to receiving a visit from such royalty.

"Yes, that's the one."

Trying to control the squiggle, a corner of his mouth got away from him and developed a small twitch. "I have it right here." He pointed to a spot on the counter where he'd placed two large accordion folders. A piece of her life was inside of those folders, yet they rested there aloof and indifferent to her, like fat cats after a meal, gorged and complacent.

The man didn't move to get them but turned to a computer keyboard and looked sideways down at her ID card, his fingers poised over the keys.

"Just a minute," she said.

He froze and looked up at her in surprise.

"I'm not checking out the file. I just need it for a few minutes. I'll be sitting right here." She motioned behind her to

222 « V.S. KEMANIS

the wooden table and chairs in the area reserved for those who were not allowed inside the locked sanctum.

"Well, but I have to...," he started to explain, but suddenly lost the words.

"I don't want you to bother." She smiled at him, and his mouth twitched again. "The file isn't going anywhere," she assured him. His eyes darted around the edges of her face, not daring a direct look, as she reached through the slot for her ID card and put it back into her purse.

He turned toward the file, hesitated, and turned back again. "One of the folders has the motions and exhibits, and the other has the trial transcript."

"Both, please."

"Both," he repeated with a nod, as if to convince himself. He hesitated once more, then retrieved the folders and pushed them through the hole, one at a time.

"Thank you!" she said brightly and stacked them one atop the other. A few paces away, she unloaded this weight onto the table, causing it to react with a wobble on uneven legs.

"Keep everything in order," the clerk whined at her back. A phone started to ring, calling him away and relieving her of his further scrutiny.

She set to work. Pulling the elastic band from one of the folders, she opened the flap and saw that she'd chosen the right one to open first. No trial transcript here, just a hodgepodge of papers. These would be the motion papers, exhibits, reports, and photographs of the physical evidence introduced at trial. The physical evidence itself—the two guns, the bullets and shell casings, the defendant's clothing, and squares of wall panel from the bodega—had been stored at Police Plaza, and by now, were most likely destroyed. Perhaps the police weapon had been returned to Officer Vargas, Dana wasn't sure. Immediately after the arrest, the officer had been placed on desk duty for a month during the investigation, and later, the NYPD issued her a new weapon when she was transferred to the 20th precinct.

Is Ellen accusing you of trying to protect Officer Vargas? If any such accusation was lurking, it would be baseless. Dana didn't even know Aurelina at the time of Pineda's arrest, and they met only a few times before the trial to prepare the case. A few years later, Dana got to know her better. The petite, plucky cop with lively brown eyes and a thick, black ponytail was known for her remarkable intensity and dedication. When working a case, her single goal was a search for justice. She was fair to everyone, whether victim, neighborhood resident, accused suspect, or fellow officer.

On the night that Aurelina wounded Ramón Pineda she was a rookie, fresh out of the academy. Every cop knew that, whenever an officer fired a weapon in the line of duty, an internal investigation would be conducted. But that didn't make it any easier for Aurelina, being the target of an investigation so early in her career. Ultimately, she was cleared. There was no reason to think that anything negative about her performance would be found in this file.

With a beating heart, Dana pulled out the first set of papers in the folder. The packet consisted of a couple dozen pages stapled together at the top. The cover sheet was a familiar form letter issued by the Records Access Officer of the DA's Office, responding to the Freedom of Information Law request submitted by Ellen Fortier, executive director of Justice Restored. Right underneath it in the packet was Ellen's letter containing her FOIL request, and under that were photocopies of the items actually sent to Ellen.

This set of papers would answer all of Dana's burning questions, without any need to dig further. The fact that she'd found it so easily wasn't strange in the least. The latest activity in any case went into the file last and was usually on top of everything else. The most recent documents—Ellen's post-conviction motion papers and the subpoena served on Dana—were not here because Ben Weingarten still had them.

She stared at the form letter on top. "What's the number again?" asked the clerk, talking into the phone. The hallway door opened on creaking hinges. Dana's eyes darted to the young man striding in. The door banged closed behind him. Too young to be an ADA, he was most likely an intern or a trial preparation assistant. As he passed her and walked up to the counter, Dana resumed her inspection of the form letter.

It was dated February 15, 2001. Various blanks and boxes on the form were filled in by hand. Written on a line near the top was a reference to Ellen's FOIL request dated October 11, 2000. Below that were several short paragraphs, each with a small box next to it, which could be checked off if the description applied. Interesting. Only one box was checked, and it appeared next to these words: "The items you requested under the Freedom of Information Law are enclosed. No further items responsive to your request are on file in this office."

This was unusual because it indicated that Ellen got everything she asked for. On most FOIL responses, the second box on the form was checked: "The enclosed items are responsive to your request under the Freedom of Information Law. The remaining items you requested are exempt from disclosure and have been withheld for the following reason(s):" Listed underneath were a plethora of privileges and statutory exemptions. For example, if the request potentially encompassed thousands of documents, it would be denied as unduly burdensome. For another example—something that might be relevant to the Pineda case—the prosecutor's handwritten notes on strategy and theories of the prosecution were privileged.

Ellen was smart, and she knew the rules. Dana guessed, even before flipping to the FOIL request in the packet, that it was specifically directed at discoverable items: "Please provide the OCME's autopsy report for the victim Felipe Bedoya, the medical records of the defendant Ramón Pineda dated July 25-27, 1992, all evidence voucher forms, and all investigative and forensic reports regarding the testing of the physical evidence and the crime scene."

Nothing could be more specific than that. She'd identified only the items which were admissible at trial. The exactness indicated Ellen's belief that she would find something in these materials. Or maybe her request merely proved her pragmatism. Everything else in the file, other than the trial transcript, was privileged and protected. And she didn't need the DA's copy of the trial transcript because, most likely, she'd gotten a copy from Pineda's attorney on the direct appeal from the conviction.

"Thank you," Dana heard. She glanced up as the young man walked to the exit with an accordion folder under his arm. The patchy-skinned clerk had efficiently retrieved the requested item, duly checked it out in the computer log, and sent the man on his way. The door opened and closed loudly, with a shudder in its frosty glass pane.

She lifted the page. The first item under Ellen's letter was the autopsy report, just as Dana remembered it. Cause of death: single gunshot wound to the head. Entry point, Bedoya's right temple. Nine millimeter bullet extracted from deep within the victim's brain. Bits of the expert's testimony came to mind: ricochet ... loss of velocity ... lodged in the brain ... any direct shot with this caliber at close range ... greater likelihood of an exit wound...

Next, the defendant's hospital records. Bullet wound to

the right shoulder. Entered front, exited back. Trajectory ...
broken jar of enchilada sauce ... lodged in the display case ...
second bullet lodged in a wall panel ... deformed nine
millimeter...

Both guns had been loaded with 9mm bullets, a common
type of ammunition. *Pilot program.* In the area of weaponry, the
early nineties had been a pivotal period for the NYPD. For
decades, the .38 caliber revolver had been the NYPD's
mainstay. By the eighties, it was getting ridiculous. Every
criminal on the street had a semiautomatic, while New York
City cops defended themselves with their slow, clunky
antiques. For years, the Commissioner fought politics and bud-
get constraints, demanding that the force be given a fighting
chance. In 1989, the NYPD started a pilot program, and a
complete changeover in weaponry was made by January of
1994.

On the day that Pineda was robbing Felipe Bedoya,
Sergeant Habberly and Police Officer Vargas were partici-
pating in the pilot program, carrying nine millimeter Glock
semiautomatics.

Two guns. Four bullets recovered. Brain, wall panel
behind the counter, display case and wall panel behind Pineda.
Copies of the vouchers for the weapons and for the bullets had
been sent to Ellen, along with the ballistics report. The
defendant's gun, a Beretta 9mm semiautomatic, serial number
defaced, and the officer's Glock, serial number YZ194V33,
had been tested and found to be operable. A separate report
contained the "ballistics fingerprinting," which analyzed the
striations on the bullets to determine which gun had fired
them.

All of these papers looked familiar, just as she
remembered them. What could Ellen possibly have found?
There was nothing here. Nothing at all...

Voices and laughter came to her from far down the hallway, growing louder, until the door suddenly swung open on its creaking hinges. In a flurry of movement and sound, three people burst into the room, a woman and two men. Dana looked up at them. Kids, really. The door banged shut.

"I can't believe he said that to you." The boy who spoke wore a business suit that was too tight, like the only suit his mother had bought him as a teenager.

"Yeah, the man is a real…" The girl caught sight of Dana and held her tongue, giving the boy a roll of her eyes instead of the words she withheld. The boy knew what she wanted to say.

Their companion was ahead of them, already at the counter. "Hello," he said to the clerk.

"Appeals Bureau?"

"Yup." He showed his ID.

"Rhonda!" The clerk yelled in his loudest voice yet. "You have those files for the Appeals Bureau?"

Dana tried to ignore the noise and focus on the ballistics fingerprinting analysis. In the report, each gun and bullet recovered from the scene was identified by voucher number and description. A bullet under voucher number X had been fired from the gun under voucher number Y—except that the voucher numbers were far more complicated. Each one was composed of a distinct combination of seven numbers and letters. She had to keep flipping back and forth between the report and the voucher forms. The strings of numbers and letters were identical except for the last number. It looked like the officer who'd prepared the vouchers had simply picked up a stack of blank ones in numerical order and randomly assigned an item of evidence to each one.

And that's when something unexpected caught her eye. She looked, and looked again.

The three kids, each carrying an armful of folders, noisily loped past the table and out the door. Her brow and underarms grew damp. The dust-laden air was suffocating, the room unbearably warm. *This doesn't make sense.* Now she would have to look at the trial transcript.

"How's it going?" She gasped. The clerk's voice was magnified, as if he stood directly behind her. Perhaps he was speaking to his colleague. She turned around and met his gaze. There was no Rhonda in sight. Swiftly, his eyes shifted away from her face, and his mouth twitched as she answered him. "Just great." Her own smile was harder to muster this time, but she brightened her expression and gaily assured him, "I'll be done in a few minutes." She didn't know if that was possible.

After pulling out the trial transcript, she suspected it would take far more than just a few minutes. A thousand pages, printed on whisper-thin paper, were divided into two volumes. She thumbed to the end and looked for the index, where each exhibit should be listed by number, description, and page reference in the transcript. Her find was disappointing. The court stenographer had been lazy, listing the exhibits by number only, without any kind of description. Twenty-eight People's exhibits. No way did Dana have the time to sort through the massive transcript and find the testimony she needed.

There was still tomorrow. Ben would have to spend a good chunk of his Friday on this. He would have to. There was no shortcut.

Dana put the entire contents back into the folders, exactly how she'd found them, closed the flaps and fastened them. Instead of allaying her fears, this little trip to archives had given her a new sense of foreboding.

This can't be what it seems.

She went up to the counter and pushed the folders, one at

a time, through the slot. "Thank you," she said to the top of the clerk's head as he busied himself pulling the folders through the opening. Without looking up, he slid them to the spot on the counter where she'd first seen them through the chicken-wire glass.

As she turned to go, she heard, "Any time," with a hiccup of a laugh. She hoped never to see this man again.

Slowly, deep in thought, she made her way out of that tomb and down the corridor. Self-doubt plagued her more than ever before. Ellen's subpoena now loomed with a ruinous power that topped every other bad thing in this hellish day. There'd been the release of Frances Kallay this morning, the media circus on the front steps, the meeting in Patrick's office, and now this, a puzzling discovery. In times of trouble, she often went to Patrick for advice, but the image of his stern countenance gave her pause. He hadn't been pleased with her, and it was difficult to accept. In their thirteen years of working together, this was a first. Her easy claim to his precious time, his insight and sage advice, her reliance on that special accessibility, their friendship ... all of that was put at risk by a single case about a fashion designer and his troubled wife.

To be sure, Patrick was displeased with her supervision of Eric in the Kallay investigation, and maybe he didn't want to be reminded of that again, just now. But the Pineda case was a different matter. He wanted her to keep him informed. He'd told her as much.

She repeated this thought enough times to become convinced of it. This was her justification for returning to the executive wing without delay. She quickened her steps. Now, more than ever, she needed Patrick, needed to explain what she'd just seen and to talk about it. There was nothing to do but swallow her shame, don a mask of strength and self-assuredness, and go to him with her problem.

17 »   BLUE

EARLY FRIDAY MORNING, Evan set off for work in his running shoes. The wingtips were waiting for him in the closet at the office. He usually walked from the apartment on West 65th Street to Belknap & Rose on East 47th Street, especially on mornings like this, when there was no time for a run in the park. He looked forward to better days. In the next two weeks, there'd be plenty of early morning jogs on the cool, packed sand along the edge of the surf.

The day before a vacation was always the worst. The challenge was to anticipate and prepare for every contingency that might arise, to avert disaster and minimize the need for long-distance supervision over his cases. The goal for any vacation was a complete escape. This was the vision. A clean separation from the daily rat race, a gentle drift into an alternate reality, a worry-free state of mind. In his law career of nineteen years he hadn't fully achieved that vision. Not yet, but he'd come very close. Especially during the good times with Dana.

But this time, nirvana would be difficult to achieve. Too much had been thrown at his wife. This morning, she was foremost on his mind as he approached Columbus Circle and took a path along the southern edge of Central Park.

Dana was a worrier on a grand scale, far more than he. But it was always a healthy sort of worrying, the kind that prompted action toward a quick resolution. Every funk could be risen above, and every problem had a solution. But this mood was a bad one. In the years they'd been together, he'd seen her this way only a few times. Yesterday, as she sat on the couch in his office refusing to eat, there'd been a quiet desperation in her voice and a slump in her usual upright posture. Last night at home, she was trapped inside her internal landscape.

Everyone in the family sensed and reacted to her preoccupation. The children grew clingy. Natalie started to whine. Travis asserted his demands. He wanted to hear the next chapter of Harry Potter—in his mother's voice. Unable to meet their eyes, Dana responded absently. Grandma diverted the children and lavished them with extra attention and warm affection. She read the next chapter to Travis in the living room, while Evan took Natalie into her bedroom for story time. Dana was off on her own, ruminating.

That trip to the archive department was eating her alive. She'd hinted at it when she first came home from the office. At ten o'clock, in bed, she lay with her back to him, wide awake. He was almost afraid to touch her, not wanting to offend, to get too close, to invade the deep introspection she seemed to need. Cautiously, he placed a hand on her crown and stroked the wealth of thick, silky hair.

A voice emerged in the dark. "Could I have made such an error?"

Evan was convinced that, if Dana had made an error, it couldn't be as egregious as she feared. She mentioned that she'd gone to see Patrick McBride after her trip to the archives. The District Attorney was fully supportive and was personally looking into the matter, certain that he'd get to the bottom of the discrepancy Dana had found. But even with the prospect of eventually setting things right, the added pressure of Ellen's media campaign was too much for Dana to bear. What an astounding shock—those two muckrakers of the defense bar secretly teaming up. And that bastard Asante! Blatantly accusing Dana of the lowest motives in the Kallay prosecution. It was an abominable gutter tactic. A back alley route to Evan, an attempt to rile up a husband's primal instincts. Negotiation by threat. The connection was too clear to ignore.

Evan was itching to deliver a blow. A devastating response. He risked humiliating himself, unless he crept in for the attack underneath a credible cover story. He had no legitimate reason to contact Asante directly. Anything that had to do with *Edmonds versus Tripp* should be raised with the defendant's counsel on the civil side, Rajani Choudhary. But the usual protocol didn't absolutely forbid him from making a phone call to the man, now, did it? He could make a call and give Asante a piece of his mind in a way that wasn't an obvious surrender to emotion. It wouldn't be about a husband protecting or defending his wife. It would be about business, *their* business, with a clear message that gutter tactics wouldn't work.

Still, a direct contact would look strange. Evan already received regular updates about the criminal case from the federal prosecutor, Phillip Neary. Wednesday morning, Neary reported that the parties had attended a pretrial conference in the U.S. District Court. There'd been no deal made, and the case was still crawling along. Tripp was determined to go to trial, to put the prosecutor to his proof. The process could take months, maybe more than a year. In the meantime, Evan wasn't about to let his class action lawsuit molder. He would just give that scoundrel Asante a call and remind him of the five hundred million that Tripp had stolen from the victims. It was time to remind Asante of Henrietta Edmond's tenacity and Judge Friel's mandate. It was time for Tripp to dig deep into his bottomless pockets. Evan wasn't backing down. He was just gearing up. *That* would be the message.

In his mind, Evan started to compose opening lines and

rejoinders, laced with clever innuendo and suggestive intonation.

He may have been muttering out loud. A person on the street gave him a wary eye.

Okay. Stop it. Rehearsal rarely worked anyway. Carefully planned words always came out differently when repeated in the midst of the situation.

Maybe all of this was getting to him. Maybe all of it *was* about Dana. An image of her face floated before his eyes, erasing the city street. Last night, after story time with Natalie, he walked into the bedroom and saw Dana sitting on the edge of the bed, fully clothed, immobile, all the rituals of bedtime forgotten. The only light in the room shone from the small fixture inside her closet, casting a long, pale triangle from the open doorway. With half of her face in a blue-gray shadow, the oblique line of her profile was stunningly beautiful. Her head was tilted in thought with her eyes cast downward, allowing him to gaze upon and appreciate the strong line of her nose, the thick dark lashes, sensitive lips parted slightly, intelligence flowing deep within a curl of her magnificent brain. His wife. The mother of his children.

I love you, Dana! I love our family so much! The silent scream was visible on Evan's features, enough to draw another guarded look from a stranger. Suddenly, his surroundings came into focus. He was already on the East Side, a few blocks from the office, unaware of how he'd gotten there.

It came to him, suddenly, that he could make a greater show of strength by ignoring the "threat." Asante wasn't a threat at all. Any direct response could be taken as a sign of fear. Rajani was the only one to call. Evan's business was with her. If she chose to impart the details of their conversation to her partner, so be it. There were ways to be forceful without malevolence. There were ways to be himself, powerfully good and positive. Puffery, threat, and bluster weren't in his character, or even necessary. Rajani and Evan had a long history, and she would be able to see through any act. In the past, he'd been on the losing side with her, but for this one, he was in the right, and his strength was in the evidence. His plan was, simply, to litigate this case to the end. Rajani would know that much about him and wouldn't doubt the strength of his commitment to his clients. There was nothing to read into it.

Hard work and solid evidence always won the day, and this day was sunny, with the prospect of an infinite shoreline on the horizon.

At the office, Evan settled in quickly and surveyed his "to do" list. *Edmonds versus Tripp* was at the top, but he had a dozen other cases in various stages of litigation. There were complaints to write and to answer, interrogatories to draft, depositions to schedule. Meetings with his team, especially Joel, the person he counted on the most to guard against oversights, missed deadlines, and lost opportunities in the coming two weeks.

During the course of his very full day, three phone calls stood out as the most significant.

First call. Evan to Rajani. At first, her tone was strongly dismissive, gradually yielding. "Judge Friel really topped herself on that one," she said, "putting your client on the witness stand. The judge had no authority to do that without a proposed settlement on the table."

"Maybe it's unconventional, but she's not without authority," Evan countered. "She has to evaluate the fairness of any settlement we come up with. How is she going to do that unless she gets a sense of the evidence?"

"Come on, Evan. Your client was making a pure play to the court's emotions. Rheumatoid arthritis. Really."

"That's what this case is all about. These victims..."

"Plaintiffs…"

"…suffered from your client's deception, both physically and financially. And if you want to talk about a pure play to emotions, your partner takes the prize, bringing up the Kallay case out of nowhere. It had nothing to do with this."

"He had a point…"

"Based on a lie about a home invasion…"

"…and you can't ignore it. Xavier was making the point that police officers and prosecutors can be wrong, and that's why we all have a constitutional right to a jury trial. His point is that much stronger, now that the truth is coming out."

This was a not-so-subtle reference to Asante's exposition on the courthouse steps in front of the press corps. Evan ignored it. "Bottom line is, Judge Friel got it right—it's time for Tripp to make a reasonable offer and pay up. Using the criminal case as an excuse for delay is pure subterfuge."

They lapsed into haggling over numbers. Rajani claimed that "Darren doesn't have the kind of money you're talking about," to which Evan responded, "Our financial investigation says otherwise." Toward the end of the conversation he sensed a slight shift, a small concession on her part. She promised a new proposal for settlement by the time Evan was back from his vacation. But she didn't promise much. The figure would be "reasonable," nothing "remotely close to the three fifty" he was asking.

Second phone call. Evan to Mrs. Edmonds. It was a courtesy call he didn't have to make, but he felt compelled. He'd gotten into the habit of speaking with her frequently, more than might be expected or required by the code of professional ethics. He couldn't account for his level of involvement. Surely he felt compassion for her plight. He also sensed that Mrs. Edmonds was living on hope, and that this case was a big part of it. A lawsuit can focus the mind in an unhealthy way. Bitterness, revenge, obsession, frustration. Blind hope. Evan did what he could to steer her away from this trap, and he sensed that his voice had a calming effect on her. There was also a fun component to their conversations, a minute or two of low-key banter, which served as a reassurance that Mrs. Edmonds was keeping her positive outlook on life.

She answered the phone after several rings. He related the "progress" on the settlement negotiations in the best light possible, and she responded with a pallid "thank you." Something didn't seem right. Mrs. Edmonds wasn't her usual buoyant self. Her "thank you" was followed by a comment laden with self-blame: "I don't know why I ever bought that stuff." Her voice shook, and she spoke slowly, as she always did, but the chipper quality was gone. "Life Source. Doesn't the name sound phony?"

"It sounds like a brand name, like any other brand name. And the man selling the product was very persuasive. He sold it to millions. You're not alone..."

"Not alone. If you say so. But this house is very empty."

Evan's heart sank. His thoughtless use of a single word had touched on her loneliness. He didn't know much about Mrs. Edmonds' family. He did know that she was a widow. Bernard Edmonds had died twelve years ago. She lived alone, and her most frequent visitor was a favorite niece, who took on a big share of the responsibility in caring for her. Evan tried to deflect. "Is your niece coming over today?"

"Yes, but..." Her voice trailed off, and she didn't finish the thought.

"Mrs. Edmonds?"

She cleared her throat and forced out a chuckle full of sadness and embarrassment. "You're a good man."

"Thank you, but..."

"My sons. They should be the ones to come over and help

me, not Debra."

"Your sons…"

"Maybe you know how I can find them? I believe they live somewhere out west."

Oh no. What was this?

She persisted. "I'm being a nuisance, I know. But … you're a lawyer, so maybe you have ways to find things out. Ways to find people."

It was too late to turn back, to cut their conversation short. He inquired further, as decency required, and learned more than he wanted to know. Mrs. Edmonds had two sons who were, by now, in their early sixties. They had wives and families. Twenty-five or thirty years ago—she couldn't recall the year—Bernard had disowned them. Sent them away. Told his sons never to call or write or visit. The door was closed. He'd been irretrievably offended by an unspeakable transgression. His sons had refused to carry on the family business and wanted to pursue career paths of their own. After that, Bernard and Henrietta lived a progressively frugal existence. Their finances suffered, and Bernie gradually sank into an intractable depression in the years before he died.

This story of her married life bore no relation to the Mrs. Edmonds that Evan knew. Perhaps it was a relief to be living alone after years of dealing with such a man. Her natural sunny side must have bubbled up to the surface after Bernard died. Today, the forces worked against it.

"Matthew and Geoffrey. Those are their names. Maybe you can find them? I could pay you with the money I get from the settlement."

Her voice was at once full of hope and despair, revealing an awareness that her quest could only lead to further disappointment or heartbreak. Evan made no promises. He knew of agencies that specialized in such a thing, and he told her this, but he didn't say everything else that came to mind. More than likely, this kind of search wouldn't be difficult. Two men in their sixties, names, dates of birth, and parentage known, most likely well-established wherever they resided, with family and business ties. It wouldn't be difficult, but what would happen after he found them? He didn't want to speculate or to raise impossible expectations that might be crushed, with disastrous consequences.

"It might be expensive," he suggested, using the only excuse he could think of to discourage her. "I'll let you know the possibilities when I'm back from vacation." Another thing to weigh on his mind over the next two weeks.

"I'll pay anything I have."

Which, he knew, was very little. Maybe he'd just look for the sons himself. "Enjoy your time with Debra today," he said.

"Yes. Thank you. She's a good girl." A good "girl" in her late fifties.

The third phone call of significance that day was the one he least expected. Late in the afternoon, Cheryl Hargrove called.

"Sorry to bother you Evan. I know you're trying to finish things up and get out of there."

"Not a problem. You can call anytime. What's up?"

"I tried calling Dana first, but she's in a meeting. I told her secretary not to bother giving her the message. It's really you I should talk to."

The sound of this wasn't good. What on earth could Dana's sister want to tell him a few hours before the start of his two-week vacation?

"It's about your mother, Evan."

Oh no again.

"I called her this morning to say I wanted to go with her to pick up the kids at their day camp and maybe spend a little time with them this afternoon. I felt bad that I told Natalie I might be able to make it to the shore, but I really can't swing it, even for a day. We're having tech problems, a new cast member, and other issues in the show that require extra rehearsals."

"We'll miss you."

"Yes, I'll miss all of you too, and I wish I could come. It'll have to be another time."

"The busy life of a Broadway star."

"Well, it isn't all chocolate and roses! Anyway, I was a little early getting to your apartment. After Brenda let me in, she offered me some tea and became flustered because the dining room table was cluttered. She said, 'Just give me a minute to clear these papers away.' I offered to help, and I saw some of the documents."

"She's been working on her personal finances, she told me."

"Yes. I could see she'd been busy. And maybe someone else has been busy working on her personal finances as well!"

18 »   LINK

NOW THERE WERE two DNA results he needed, and the crime lab was still putting up roadblocks. Friday morning, twenty-four hours after the court had released Frances, the Kallay investigation still hadn't been marked off the "closed case" list, that fictional repository for crimes that were "solved" with the arrest of the prime suspect.

Eric's powers of persuasion had seen better days. No amount of cajoling impressed the urgency of the matter on his contacts at the lab. Maybe their hands were simply tied in red tape. The situation called for the intervention of people more important than ADA Eric Trumble. He had to involve the boss.

But he wasn't going to walk down the hall to her office. He dialed Dana's extension. Ever since the disastrous court appearance and Patrick's gentle lecture, he'd avoided a face-to-face with his mentor. Yesterday afternoon, he briefed Dana by phone on the outcome of the search at the Kallay residence. She'd asked about the status of the DNA tests, and he'd answered, a bit too confidently, that he was "on it." Now he worried that he'd given her the wrong impression.

Lecia answered. "Good morning, Eric."

"Is the chief in?"

"She is. She's on the phone. Is this about Kallay?"

"How did you guess?"

"I'll ask her to call you right away. She's busy preparing for the hearing on Monday, but Kallay is top of the list."

"Or top of the line."

"What's that?"

"Never mind. A stupid joke."

"Oh, I get it. Maybe you can use your connections to swing me a discount at House of Loránd. I need ninety percent off or more."

"I'll see what I can do. Thanks, Lecia."

Eric looked through the papers that Gil's team had delivered to him this morning. The financial records corroborated Frances's testimony—for the most part. All the major properties and accounts were in the name of Loránd Kallay: House of Loránd, townhouse on East 69th, beach-front property in Montauk, ski lodge in Vail, JP Morgan brokerage account, American Express card, on and on. Also as testified, Frances had a debit card for a joint checking account that she could access for her personal needs. Perhaps, from a certain point of view, she wasn't lying when she testified that her husband had kept the balance "as low as possible." From Eric's point of view, and that of any middleclass working stiff, the dollar figure in the account was astronomical, and Loránd had made a generous deposit on the day of his death. The account records, which dated back several months, didn't completely dispel the contract-murder theory they'd briefly entertained. There was no single suspicious withdrawal, either by size or payee, but there were frequent, relatively large withdrawals of cash. Mrs. Kallay had a very expensive lifestyle, with needs that were beyond the ken of people in Eric's socio-economic class. Perhaps. Or ... something else was going on.

The medical records were another story, but they were still incomplete. When Asante tendered a list of doctors and hospitals, along with his client's HIPAA authorization, he warned that Frances needed to check her files at home to complete the list. The records they had so far didn't confirm her testimony about two instances of broken ribs. There was only one such record from 1997, noting broken ribs and facial abrasions that Frances attributed to a car accident in which the air bag deployed. DMV records confirmed that a vehicle registered to Loránd Kallay had run off the road and collided with a utility pole. He was driving, and she was a front seat passenger. Unless Loránd deliberately wrecked the car to hurt Frances, this couldn't be called a battering injury. Did she think they wouldn't verify the car accident? Or would she come back with a story that the accident was staged to cover up the battering?

Eric also found an emergency room record from a Colorado hospital, dated 1999, regarding a broken ulna Frances claimed to have suffered in a skiing accident. As yet, there was no other evidence to confirm or contradict the accident story. As for Frances's willingness to undergo a physical examination to prove that she had healed injuries to her "private areas," the grand jury had ordered the exam, which was yet to be arranged and performed.

The phone rang. It wasn't Dana calling back, but another call he was expecting. Nicki. As of last night, she hadn't collected any useful identifying information on the handcuffs, hooks, metal bar, and other items collected from the Kallay cellar. He'd asked her to try again.

"I've used every method at our disposal," she reported. "UV light and fluorescent powder, blue light, superglue."

"Still nothing?"

"This is just really bizarre," she said. "No useful prints on any of this. I'm not saying that it could never happen this way, even with people handling the items normally. But it sure looks like there was an effort to leave no trace behind."

"It appears to be a setup is what you mean."

"Good possibility."

"The question is when and how. Frances was locked up from the night of the murder until the search."

"You could subpoena all the sex shops. Some of these items look new, and they're the type you can find in any sex shop."

"Can't do that. Do you know how many such establishments thrive in this city?" Even as he spoke, he was aware of his subliminal avoidance of repeating the word "sex" in a conversation with Nicole Verona.

"I can guess."

"It's impossible to track it down that way."

"At least we got the blood-type match for the stains on the white cloth. Frances Kallay. That's not to say we won't find Loránd's DNA on that cloth, or on the porous surfaces we swabbed. Did you call my contact at the DNA lab?"

"Yes, more than once. No help."

"Sorry. I know how backed up they are."

"You did your duty. Thank you, Nicki." He was getting a beep on the line, indicating another call coming in. "Gotta go."

The caller ID never worked when a second call was coming in while he was on the phone. Blindly, he clicked on the line and gave his standard greeting, "Assistant DA Eric Trumble."

It wasn't Dana.

"Hello. I'm trying to find someone to talk to about Frances Kallay. The operator forwarded my call to you."

The voice was female, strong but wary. Eric's heart quickened with the hope he was about to get the break he needed. "You've been directed to the right place. I'm conducting the prosecution."

"I heard in the news yesterday that the woman was released." There was a familiar quality to this voice. A bit of indignation underlying the inconsistent pace, a contradictory flow of urgency and hesitance.

"Yes, but the charges are still active. Do you have some information about the case?"

"I do, but—" She stopped cold.

"If you know something, I'd urge you to tell me. This is an important case. I'm sure you've seen the news. We're trying to get to the truth."

There. It was the best he could do. Still, she didn't speak.

"Hello," he said. "Are you still with me?"

"I'm … not usually someone to get involved…"

Yes! Suddenly it came to him. The face that went with the voice. Even if she hung up now without giving her name, it would be easy enough to track her down through employee records. "Would it be easier for you to come here to talk? Or maybe we can send an investigator up to Lenox Hill."

"Oh, no, please don't! I'm not at work anyway."

Got her.

"I'll come to your office," she offered. "Are you available today?"

"Yes. You can come right away. How long will it take you to get here?"

For a week now, Susan Tipple had been obsessed with her predicament. At first, it was easy to hide behind rules of patient confidentiality and her misguided impression of the facts. Those justifications were now gone. Curiosity killed the cat, so they say. It was her own fault.

She wasn't the kind of person to come forward, but she was a brave person in other ways. Without flinching, she'd cared for victims of gruesome accidents and crimes. This was in her training. This was in her nature. She'd never had a problem with involuntary reactions, fainting or lightheadedness or indecision. Bright red blood was merely a liquid that kept a corporal body alive when properly contained. It threatened life when allowed to escape from a body that was slashed, punctured, or brutalized. There were sutures, coagulants, pressure, transfusions, and other methods to restore containment.

This was different. This was something that, rationally or not, struck at her instinct for self-preservation. This involved a rich woman and her near-celebrity husband. There were aspects of money and power here that she didn't quite understand. The rich woman had access to resources, possibly dangerous people. This could lead to trouble for Susan. If she talked.

The past several mornings, after finishing her night shift, she'd stopped at a newsstand on the way home and picked up every newspaper in sight. She now knew every reported detail of the case, although she'd learned about the home invasion story even before reading it in the papers. Standing just outside the hospital room door, she'd heard bits of it from Mrs. Kallay's own mouth as the two men questioned her. Not all of it. Only some of the words were projected into Susan's straining ear, whenever the patient's weak voice swelled with emotion.

Two days ago, there was wild speculation in the news about what might be going on in the grand jury. All secret. Susan tried to cull the falsity, speculation, rumor, and opinion from everything she read. It was difficult. But then, yesterday, Frances Kallay changed her defense and disclosed it to reporters on the courthouse steps. She had a new story about being a battered woman, acting in self-defense. She claimed she was justified in shooting her husband. The new story intensified Susan's dilemma. It now felt very wrong to withhold what she knew.

Mrs. Kallay should have come out with her battering

defense from the start. It was the story Susan believed to be true when she first saw the patient. She had no moral aversion to such a defense. Killing a batterer could be justified, depending on the circumstances, if the situation was dire enough.

When those two men came to the hospital in the middle of the night, Susan wasn't in any mood to help them. Her patient was a pathetic little thing, completely worn out, frazzled and on edge. In shock. She'd just discovered her husband's dead body, Susan knew that much. But when she saw the injuries, she believed Mrs. Kallay had been beaten by that man. None of the doctors or nurses had been able to get anything out of her. Susan often had better luck. She had a way of listening with a nonjudgmental composure that put her patients at ease. So she made an attempt. As she pressed her warm fingertips to Mrs. Kallay's wrist, checking the pulse, she asked, "Who did this to you?"

"It's not so bad, really. I don't know why they even brought me here."

Susan touched the woman's forehead and smoothed her hair back. There was a slight reaction of fluttering eyelids and a shudder of release. The magic of physical contact. "Everyone's concerned about you, that's why they brought you here. It must have been very shocking for you tonight, making such a discovery."

"Shocking, yes."

"But it looks to me like someone hit you," Susan suggested, still stroking the woman's forehead.

"I just bruise so easily. It's nothing at all. Please tell the doctor I'm ready to go home."

"You rest up now. We'll see."

Susan tried again later that night, to no avail.

There could have been a home invasion, or there could

have been something else going on in that house. The injuries were not terribly severe. There were finger bruises on the upper arms. A man had grabbed her and squeezed her there, maybe shook her around a little. There was a bruise over her sternum and a bruise near her navel. She'd been punched twice. The punch in the belly had caused a hint of internal bleeding that would resolve on its own. The swelling and coloring indicated that these injuries were fairly recent, had been inflicted perhaps early in the evening, several hours before.

Other than these things, the woman was intact. There were few medical records available in Lenox Hill's computer system. Only an MRI report from 1999, following the removal of a cast on her arm, which had been applied by a doctor in Colorado after a skiing accident.

When Susan heard the men finishing their conversation with Mrs. Kallay, she padded quickly away from the open doorway and took up a position down the hall, at the nurses' station. It was quiet, about three thirty or four in the morning, and all of the patients on the floor were stable. She examined a chart on the desk, not looking up as the men walked by.

As soon as they'd gone, Susan returned to check on the patient. She was concerned that the men had overexcited her. Nearing the room, she heard Mrs. Kallay speaking in a rasping whisper. She was talking on the phone, either the bedside phone, or perhaps a mobile phone that was in the purse she'd brought with her to the hospital. The intensity and desperation in her voice carried the words more clearly than the enfeebled sound she'd assumed for the investigators. Susan paused at the edge of the doorframe.

I don't think they believe me…

Cliff…

I *did* tell them that…

I couldn't say no. They just wheeled me out of there…

D'you know what I look like? You went too far this time...

I can't tell them that. I can't change the whole thing...

[A very long silence.]

Okay. We'll talk when I get out of here. I have to go, someone's coming...

But it wasn't Susan that she heard. Another nurse was walking down the hall, not caring to step silently. Susan gave her colleague a smile and went back to the nurses' station.

Gil and Eric strode down the broad corridor on the tenth floor of the Criminal Court building, on their way to the judge who was presiding over the current term of the grand jury. A freshly-typed search warrant application was in Eric's hand.

All at once, the case was starting to come together.

"You got lucky, Boy Wonder. I think Nurse Tipple was really looking for me—"

"Are you kidding? That face of yours scared her off for a week!"

"Huh. Your looks sure didn't get what we needed. It took the Dane only five minutes to get the DNA."

"Don't be so cocky. Who forgot to ask Cedrick about the cellar?"

"There wasn't any cellar when I first talked to him."

"And what about Clifton Vaughn? You missed him."

"Kallay's records only went back to '97. He left in '96."

"An ex-employee... They're always the most unhinged."

"This ain't the U.S. Postal Service, baby."

"Just as bad. It's the *ruthless* fashion industry." Eric pushed the swinging door to the courtroom. "Come on, let's do it." Gil followed.

Their trip to the judge was the culmination of a very busy day. It had gone something like this (all times approximate):

At eleven o'clock, Dana blasted through the red tape and got the crime lab to start working on the DNA.

At noon, Eric interviewed Susan Tipple, who gave them a new mystery person of interest. The man named "Cliff." Susan signed an affidavit of the facts and agreed to testify in the grand jury.

At one, the pen register on Frances's cell phone showed a call to the same number she'd called while in the hospital. The burner phone. There'd been only one call from the hospital, the call to "Cliff," so the burner had to belong to him. Frances and Cliff were still in touch.

At two, Gil asked Cedrick Cougar if Loránd had ever shown him his wine collection. With tearful emotion, Cedrick recalled the intimate wine and cheese parties Loránd used to host in the cellar, treating his closest friends to rare vintages as they stood around that rustic, rough plank table. There were certainly no torture devices visible on those occasions. Their host liked to say that the medieval furnishings and humidity of the cellar created an ambience of antiquity, enhancing the flavor of his deep reds.

At three thirty, the crime lab called with the results. Viable samples of human cells were recovered from three items: the wood grip of the Browning, the porous surface of the cast iron bar on the table in the cellar, and the dried blood on the white rag. The DNA profiles were entered into the Combined DNA Index System, known as CODIS, and came back with two hits. The samples taken from the gun and the metal bar matched the profile of Clifton Vaughn, a registered sex offender. The profile from the blood matched the DNA sample Frances Kallay had given at the time of her arrest.

At three forty-five, Gil researched their new target while Eric drafted an application for a search warrant. "Lady Kallay got herself a younger man," Gil commented. Vaughn was thirty-nine. In 1996, at the age of thirty-four, he was convicted of rape in the third degree, a lower level felony. The victim was a former girlfriend who'd gotten an order of protection against him. He wasn't taking their breakup graciously. He stalked her, forced his way into her apartment, slapped her around, and violated her. He served a year and a half of an indeterminate prison sentence and was required to register under the newly-enacted Sex Offender Registration Act. His DNA profile was entered into CODIS, and his address was posted on SORA's public database.

Did anyone at the House of Loránd know this guy? For the second time that day, Gil called Cedrick, couldn't reach him, and called Miranda Carlton. She remembered Vaughn, who worked for Loránd as a pattern maker for a couple of years and was an aspiring designer in his own right. In 1996, his work started going downhill. He became unreliable, failed to show up for stretches of time, and then he simply stopped coming to work at all. Loránd sent him a letter telling him that his job wouldn't be there if he tried to come back. Miranda didn't know anything further until a few years ago, when she heard that he opened a vintage clothing store in the Village. "I never liked him much," she said. "He was a pretty boy, always doodling on his own sketches, and he had a grand opinion of himself. Thought his work was better than Loránd's or any other designer out there. Liked to complain that he could make it big if he only had the money for some fabric and seamstresses and models."

A lot of this information was of interest to the investigative team, but only the most important bits were thrown into the search warrant application: the phone calls to the burner, Tipple's affidavit, the DNA results, Vaughn's conviction and SORA status.

At four forty, they took the application to court, and the

judge signed the warrant. Out in the corridor, Eric handed Gil the warrant and said, "Collect the men. I'll meet you in ten minutes out back, in the parking lot."

"You think you're coming? It's too dangerous."

"It's just a search."

"Of the apartment of a killer. Don't get me wrong. I don't care about *you*. I just don't wanna be on the Dane's shit list if anything happens to you."

"Thanks a lot."

"Stay here and maybe another mystery witness will show up while I'm gone."

"Call me the minute you have something."

"Don't I always?"

They parted ways. Eric checked the time. Almost five. Dana would want an update. He had a lot to tell her, and it was the kind of stuff that would make her a happier person before she left on her trip, especially since part of her vacation was already ruined by Ellen's subpoena. Today, Dana had been busy preparing for the hearing on Monday. Almost every time Eric tried to catch her, she'd been on the phone or across the street in the executive wing with Patrick and Ben Weingarten.

But when Eric got back to the office, he was too late. Missed her by a few minutes. A little unusual, maybe, for Dana to leave this early, but maybe not so unusual for a Friday evening before a family trip.

"You could call her at home," suggested Lecia. "I know she wants to hear the latest on your case."

"I'll do that," said Eric. But maybe not just yet. Better not to bother her until later. Although Dana always made herself available, she preferred no interruptions in the evenings during family time, until after the children were in bed. This was no emergency, and he'd have more to tell her in a few hours, after he found out what Gil was digging up at Vaughn's apartment.

*   *   *

Clifton Vaughn lived in a very sterile-looking doorman building all the way east, in the neighborhood close to the U.N. Gil always found this area of town to be the least Manhattan-like of Manhattan. Slightly dead. There were no clubs or nightlife to speak of, and the streets were eerily free of pedestrians after dark.

Six o'clock was well before nightfall on this early summer evening. Gil arrived at the building with his team of investigators, including members of the DA's squad and Officer Smith and his partner from the 19th. To avoid drawing attention, Gil left the others behind and went into the vestibule, alone. At the sight of Gil's face, the doorman grew bug-eyed. His name was Clark.

Gil showed his identification and the court order—a "no knock" warrant—and urged Clark to give him a copy of the key to apartment 5F. "Keep your finger off that buzzer," he instructed the uniformed employee.

"Won't touch it," said Clark.

"Anyone home right now?"

"Not that I know of. My shift started at four."

Just then, a woman entered the 'vestibule with a Pomeranian on a leash. Clark opened the inner door for her, and they exchanged pleasantries as the woman unsuccessfully tried to conceal her curiosity about Gil. She averted her eyes, but they came back to him before she stepped into the lobby.

Gil continued his instructions. "If anyone's up there, we're not letting 'em know we're coming." He planned to leave two men downstairs with Clark, just to be sure there were no tip offs, and to handle Vaughn if he came home. "Have you seen this woman before?" Gil showed him a photograph of Frances Kallay.

"Sure," said the doorman. "That's the lady in the news."

"Besides the news, have you seen her anywhere else?"

"Hmm." His eyes shifted away from the photograph, to the glass door, the ceiling, the floor—everywhere but Gil's face. Perhaps he had an aversion to Gil's asymmetrical features, but more likely, his behavior was a sign of reluctance to part with certain knowledge he possessed. He was a man well into middle age, set in his habits and loyalties to the residents, the little acts and omissions that might influence them to open their wallets and part with a few dollars.

Gil made an assumption about what he was seeing in Clark's face. "Where, exactly, did you see her?"

"Here. Yeah. Here, I think."

"In this building? You think?"

"Yeah, I've seen her here. She comes to see Mr. Vaughn."

"And you've let her in?"

"Sometimes they come together."

"I guess I missed that."

Clark looked puzzled. "Her coming here?"

"No, the tip you gave my brothers on the squad."

"What tip?"

"When you saw her picture in the news, you must've known we were interested in where this lady's been, so you gave the police a call. Am I right?"

The man repeated his shifty eye movements. "Wha' for? People go places and know other people. I have to tell the police?"

Gil responded with a disgusted grunt and pulled out his radio to call the others in. They invaded the vestibule, filling the tight area with purpose and authority. The doorman's eyes went wide again and he buttoned up. Gil instructed two members of the team to stay with Clark. The rest of them entered the lobby, passing a few curious residents on the way, and took the elevator to the fifth floor. They found 5F in the middle of the long hallway.

Gil turned the key quietly. They entered with caution, weapons drawn. Vaughn might be waiting for them inside. With Gil and Smith in the lead, they crept through the short entryway, listening for any hint of movement, mindful that their target could be lurking around a corner. In a sudden burst they were in the living room, pivoting right and left. "Police!" A quick sweep of the apartment. No one home.

It was a modest-sized apartment, three little rooms: kitchen, bedroom, and living room. Four, counting the bathroom. But anyone could see it was an upscale building and an expensive neighborhood. Did the ex-jailbird make enough money in the vintage clothing business to rent a place like this? The rent would be high, unless Vaughn had managed to scam the system, taking over a longtime rent stabilized apartment of a relative or a friend. Or maybe his lifestyle was subsidized from other sources. Crime. A rich girlfriend perhaps. Who could that be? Loránd would turn over in his grave if he knew what Gil was thinking just then.

Smith and his partner took the living room, while Gil and Manuel scoped out the bedroom. The obvious things immediately drew their attention. The handcuffs. The ropes. A nice little display on the bed.

"Look familiar?" Manny asked.

"He forgot the torture rack."

"I guess something like that goes best in a cellar. Just a little fun and games here in the bedroom."

"Okay, we've got him!" yelled Smith from the living room. He sounded as excited as a seven-year-old at his first Yankees game. "This is it! This has to be it."

Gil and Manny exchanged looks. "I guess the man wants some attention." Gil twitched his index finger, a signal to follow him.

Smith was in a corner of the living room, standing over a desk. Pinched between the thumb and index finger of his right hand was a large, blank piece of textured artist paper, eighteen by twenty-four inches. "I just lifted this up and these were underneath." He'd uncovered a stack of similar sheets. The top one had a drawing of a woman—an angular, fleshless, long-legged woman—wearing an orange miniskirt and cream-colored, ruffled blouse. The bottom of the sheet bore the signature *L. Kallay*.

"Hit the jackpot all right," said Gil. "Sorry Frances. Looks like your hubby's creative juices weren't all dried up like you said."

"Yup. We're the lucky dogs who get a sneak preview of Kallay's 2002 collection," said Smith with pride. He followed up with a little laugh that conveyed he wasn't overly impressed with the distinction.

"Second only to the two thieves," added Manny.

Gil let Smith revel in his discovery for a moment, not suggesting, just yet, that they go into the bedroom to discuss what had been going on in there. "Looks like all of these sheets underneath are also drawings," Smith said, "but we won't just yet..."

"Right," said Gil. Smith gently lowered the cover sheet, mindful of his duty. The drawings must be properly preserved and vouchered as evidence.

Inspecting the area around the desk, Gil found another item of interest. A shredder, standard household size. He squatted and took a closer look. Shredded papers, strip-cut, were in the attached basket. This kind of shredder was pretty useless for even the lowest level of security. Gil would seize this baby and take it back to the Dungeon, where the papers would be put back together again.

Standing up from the squat, Gil noticed it took him a

fraction of a second longer than it used to. Field work wasn't getting any easier. Next year he turned fifty. Even his jeans didn't fit the same way. Or maybe they still fit the way they always had, but he no longer liked the feel of tight clothing. Too constrictive. At once, a picture came to mind: the perfect fit of those tailored pants on the barefooted legs of the dead guy in the den. If he were alive today, the famous designer would agree. Tight wasn't the right fit for men of a certain age.

Fit. Gil's eyes went to the stack of artist's drawings on the desk. Standard size, eighteen by twenty-four. They were lying flat, wrinkle-free, no sign of ever being folded, rolled, or bent. Where would these drawings fit? Maybe in that large flat drawer in Kallay's drafting table on the third floor of the townhouse. Where would they *not* fit? In that small safe, hidden behind a painting on a wall of the den. Kallay must have been using his safe for something else.

19 » MOM

BRENDA RESISTED EVAN'S coddling the more he tried. Really! To insist on driving her home when he had more than enough to do, to help Dana pack for their vacation. A waste of precious time. The round trip from Manhattan to New Rochelle would take a good two hours, maybe more than that on a Friday evening in the summer because of the usual weekend exodus from the city.

Dana and Evan had arrived home earlier than usual, bursting in the door with a strange kind of energy. Dana was clutching her briefcase in one hand as she balanced that big cardboard box in the other. The family congregated for "Pizza Friday," the usual lineup around the dining room table. There was a lot to do, Brenda could tell. Not a stitch had been packed, and they were leaving in the morning, so everyone just shoved that cheesy crust into their mouths and gulped it down, inviting gastric distress. Mama mia! Brenda had sense enough to nibble on hers.

Then the talk of driving her home began. Evan insisted.

"I'm perfectly happy to get on the train, dear heart," she said, meaning it sincerely.

"You've had a long week, Mom. I just can't put you on that train tonight."

"It's very comfortable. That's what I keep telling you. Move up to Westchester. The kids can have a backyard, and for you, it's an easy ride down to the city and back."

"Mom, let's not get off the point." He glanced at the kids,

not because he disapproved of the grease on their faces, but to remind her that he didn't like it when she raised this topic in front of them. The idea of moving up to Westchester. She was unaccountably annoyed. Why shouldn't the children hear about green grass and trees?

He redirected the conversation. "Maybe the train isn't so bad, but the car is much better. You don't have to sit next to a stranger, and I'm offering door-to-door service. Can't beat that!"

"Of course, but..."

He pushed back from the table and stood up. "Is your bag ready? Let me help you." He started for her "bedroom" as he spoke.

"No, no, I'm perfectly capable, dear!" Unlike the rest of the family she was all packed, including the extra satchel with all of her financial documents. The satchel was no better than an open-mouthed bag, stuffed to the brim with papers. This week she hadn't made much progress on her organization, and now, after opening most of the previously unopened mail, the volume inside of the bag seemed to have expanded. She didn't think it would spill, however. It was good and stuffed. She *had* made some progress in reviewing the brochures and voluminous paperwork that Mr. Lane had given her, the agreements and conditions and releases and provisos and heaven knew what else. After several hours with these papers and a few cups of strong tea, she finally understood what it all meant, giving her a big head start on their upcoming second meeting, this Sunday. No more sandwiches. A proper Sunday supper at five. She would be roasting a chicken this time.

"You're sure I can't help?"

"Please don't bother."

"Okay, I'll go get the car."

While Evan went down to the garage to extricate the car,

Dana started to clear the table, and Brenda retrieved her things from her room. She placed her small suitcase and satchel near the dining table and sat down with the children again. There was time for a few parting words, her best wishes for a fun trip. Natalie and Travis were buzzing with excitement, listing all the activities they were planning to do at the shore.

"Bring me a sea shell with the ocean inside of it," she told the children, and started to sing: "*By the sea, by the sea, by the beautiful sea...!*"

"I can't, Grandma," Natalie protested.

"*You and me, you and me, oh how happy we'll be!*"

"Quiet, Grandma!" She was tugging on Brenda's arm. "I *can't* bring you a shell. It'll spill out!"

"What will spill out?"

"The ocean inside of it."

Travis looked mildly disgusted. "Nats! She doesn't want you to put water in it! She wants one of those big shells, don't you Grandma?"

"If you find one."

"It sounds like the waves when you hold it next to your ear."

Still confused, Natalie was about to speak when Evan burst in and said, "Okay, Mom. Let's go. I'm double-parked." Before she could protest, he picked up her suitcase and the bag of documents.

Everyone stood. Her knees were so stiff. She gave Travis a squeeze and a kiss on the head. Natalie ran up for a prolonged hug around her thighs. Even Dana came out of the kitchen and walked right up for an embrace that lasted a good three seconds. Her daughter-in-law was not a demonstrative person, but on this occasion, her arms felt strong and the emotion ran deep. Dana pulled away, still grasping Brenda's shoulders. "Enjoy your vacation," she said. *Enjoy your break from us*, might have been the buried thought behind her deep brown irises. But there seemed to be more in her eyes, and they lingered a bit too long. Heavens! Why was everyone acting so concerned and ... and intimate? It made her feel old.

"I will, I certainly will! So much to do! Goodbye everybody. Have a good trip now!" She loved them all very much, but she did look forward to a full two weeks on her own.

The first few minutes in the car were peppered with Evan's exasperated comments about the traffic. There were pockets of congestion ("Let's walk, shall we?"), barely missed green lights ("Flaming blazes!"), and errant cab drivers ("Are you *blind?*"). Her baby boy really was quite funny, even when annoyed, but she didn't dare say out loud what she was thinking—that all of these problems disappeared when traveling on the commuter train. Not wanting to fuel the fire, she sat quietly, content with her own thoughts and plans for the weekend.

Just north of Manhattan, with the traffic easing up, they were both ready for conversation. "It's been a tough start to the summer," he remarked. "We're more than ready for this vacation."

"You certainly are. What a shock it was to hear Dana's name in the news. So awful. Once you get away for a few weeks, everyone will forget about it."

"That's the hope. It's hard to sit by and listen to these false accusations, repeated like a broken record. Newscasters always love to stir up a big sensation."

"Yes, well, these news people don't like to tell you everything. It's so awful, and it just leaves you wondering where the truth is." She didn't admit that a small worry had crossed her mind when she watched the news report last night, after the children were in bed. Those attorneys on the courthouse steps did sound rather convincing. They said just enough to raise a doubt in her mind about Dana. Not much, of course.

"You can't believe everything you hear on television," Evan said.

"No, not everything I suppose." There had to be *something* to it, surely. Otherwise, why would they report the story? But she had sense enough to know that the people being quoted might be wrong. That woman accused of murder could be lying, and those two attorneys could be distorting the facts. She'd learned plenty from Evan and Dana about the drama in the courtroom, how attorneys loved to hurl accusations back and forth. All part of their contentious legal system. To her mind, cooperation seemed like a much nicer way to do things.

But Evan wasn't interested in any more discussion of this unpleasantness about Dana's adversaries. His comment about what could and could not be believed was the opening for a new topic. Brenda didn't see the connection right away. "I don't know how much I've told you about the case I'm working on," he said. "The class action lawsuit."

She turned briefly to regard his face in the orange-tinged light of sunset. He was her son, and she didn't need to study his expression to know a few things about him. She'd been hearing about this class action lawsuit off and on for quite some time. Tonight, suddenly, the case was important to him, maybe almost as important as all of this hubbub about Dana. "A real big case, I know that," she said. "Millions of clients. I don't know how you have the time to talk to all those people."

"I have one main client, and she represents the class of people. They were all scammed by a telemarketer."

"Right. Something to do with health products?"

"Yes. Supposedly, it was an 'all natural' dietary supplement. The telemarketer made outrageously false claims about the product. He said it could cure just about everything from arthritis to cancer. People wasted their money, and worse than that, some of them got sicker when they took the supplement for a long period of time."

"What a shame."

"It just goes to show that you really can't believe everything you hear, Mom."

Like it was her fault! "I know, I know. Of course you can't! That's why I always investigate *everything* before I spend my money! You have to read every bit of information about the product, or if it's on television, you have to see the customers who used it."

"You're talking about the customers in the commercials on TV?"

"Yes. Any legitimate advertisement always has them."

"The testimonials."

"The satisfied customers. You can tell they're real people, like you and me. They give the whole story about what happened when they used whatever it is they're trying to sell. If the commercial doesn't have those people, I don't buy the product. Especially any of those pills for arthritis. I've tried them all. I know! Most of them are no good. It's too bad all those clients of yours didn't do their homework."

Her point was well taken, she could tell, because Evan needed a moment to think. Then he said, "They were tricked. The man in the commercials was very charismatic. Very convincing."

"So are you, dear heart. And I have to say, I do believe *almost* everything you say." She laughed to let him know it was a joke, but he only smiled. Politely.

He dropped the subject, even though it felt unfinished. For the rest of the ride, they talked about the children, and before she knew it, she was home. But was it really her home? Forty-four years had gone by, and nowadays she was staying somewhere else most of the time. Her boys had grown up here. Everything was so familiar. As they drove into the driveway, two lights were on: the one over the front door, and an indoor hallway light deep in the house, barely visible as a glow behind the curtains. A pretext. Al Jr. had installed automatic timers on just those two lights, making them click on every night at seven.

Evan parked in the driveway, ran around to the passenger side, opened the door for her, and went back to the trunk for her suitcase and satchel.

"Whoa," he said. "Papers all over the place."

She came up behind him. "Oh, never mind about that."

"I got it." He started to stuff them back in.

"Never mind! Let me do it." But he was too quick for her, and really, he'd been exaggerating. The papers weren't all over the place. Just the top layer had come sliding out halfway, and it was only a matter of pushing that layer back in again.

They got inside and he set the suitcase in the entry hall but kept the satchel hanging from his shoulder. "I guess this must go in the study with all of your financial stuff."

"Just leave it here, Evan. You have to get going. What about Dana?"

"What about her?" He was walking toward the study.

She followed him. "You need to get back and help her prepare for the trip."

"You know Dana. She's on top of it. Everything will be packed before I get home."

Just inside the door to the study, he flipped the switch for the overhead light. Brenda was right behind him and could see the moment of hesitation. He hovered just inside the door, eyes directed toward the desktop—or lack of it. She didn't have to step inside to know what it looked like and what he must be thinking. Al Jr. had always been somewhat messy, but Evan didn't like disorganization.

"Mom," he said, without finishing the thought.

"Really, don't bother. You can just set that bag on the floor..."

He didn't seem to hear her. He walked up to the desk and placed the satchel on top of the folders she'd stacked on the chair. "I've been meaning to review your finances with you. Let me help straighten this up a bit before I go, and then we can really get into it again in a couple of weeks." His eyes were scanning the topmost layer.

"Heavens, no! This has gone far enough!" She was alarmed at her tone of voice and the unexpected emotion that tightened her throat.

But it was too late. He'd already found something that interested him in a far corner, on top of the stack underneath the computer monitor. She couldn't even remember what that stack was all about. He picked up the paper, and his eyes went wide.

Well, what for? It was just a paper, like all of the others that came in envelopes that she opened up, tried to read, and placed on the desk in the area that seemed the most appropriate. Just a paper that confused her and might become clear after another reading under a bright light with a strong cup of tea, like all those other papers she'd brought with her down to the city this week.

Still holding the paper, Evan looked up at her. "Did you read this notice?" He held it up, but the writing on it was tiny, and he was standing a good eight feet away from her.

She felt the moisture in her eyes, threatening to spill.

He came over, put his arm around her shoulder, and gave her a reassuring squeeze. "Let's go into the living room and talk for a minute."

*   *   *

Dana was so busy packing that she didn't stop to wonder at Evan's delay. The children were "helping" to gather their clothing and the indispensable toys that must accompany them to the shore. They piled everything in the middle of the living room, where Dana would organize it all and pack the suitcases and duffel bags after the kids went to bed. By nine o'clock, she insisted that they brush their teeth and put on their PJs. It was too late for story time, but she promised to make up for it when they were down at the shore.

Travis was allowed to read in bed for another half hour and expected to turn off his bedside light at nine thirty. Honor system. In Natalie's room, Dana turned on the night light that was plugged into a wall socket and turned off the overhead light. She tucked Natalie in.

"Where's Daddy?"

"You know. He went to take Grandma home."

"He's taking too long."

He *was* taking a long time. "I'll tell him to come in and give you a kiss when he comes home."

"Even if I'm asleep," she insisted.

"Even if you're asleep." Dana kissed her forehead and smoothed her hair. "Nighty-night."

Out in the living room, the apartment was entirely too quiet, allowing suppressed thoughts to resurface. Her busy evening with the kids had merely interrupted her vivid imagination about Monday's hearing, when she would take the oath and give testimony. She'd never been on the witness stand before.

She thought back on the events of the day. Ellen had served Ben with a witness list for the hearing. Dana, of course, was the star witness. In preparation, they went over the evidence in the file again and did some further digging. There'd been strategy sessions with Patrick. Now, his words resonated deep within her, allaying her biggest fears. He'd come up with a theory and a course of action. Ellen had a plan, and Patrick had a counter plan, and Dana was at the center of both. It didn't help that she was confident of the outcome. The unpleasantness of the task weighed heavily on her.

To ease her mind, she almost preferred the anxiety created by her second thoughts about the arrest of Frances Kallay. There'd been new developments in the investigation today, but she'd run out of the office early before finding out the latest. No doubt, Eric would fill her in, but for now, she had a new, overriding source of worry—Brenda. Evan's phone call at four thirty had started it. After that, they both left work as soon as they could manage it, so that Evan could drive Brenda home. He needed to have a talk with her.

Cheryl hadn't seen very much—just enough to raise a worry. Sales literature about a reverse mortgage. Brenda's signature on a document, and a pen laid next to it. Fresh ink, it seemed. Cheryl was alarmed, but she was prone to embellishment. It was in her nature to make everything overblown and dramatic. She was an actress, a personality, a beautiful shining star. Dana and Evan were grateful for her care and concern, her love for the children, and the sense of responsibility that had driven her to call Evan about Brenda. But Dana wasn't jumping to conclusions just yet. It would turn out to be a very fixable problem. Evan would talk to his mother, straighten things out, and come home.

All of that should have been taken care of in the car ride up to New Rochelle. He should have been home an hour ago. Where was he?

Her mobile phone started its distinctive, rhythmic "ping" on low volume. Her ears were trained to hear it. The phone was lying on an end table next to the couch in the living room. She picked it up, expecting Evan. But it wasn't him.

"Dana, have I caught you at a bad time?"

"No, it's okay."

"Are the kids in bed?"

"All quiet here."

"Sorry, I tried to catch you at about five but just missed you."

"What's up, Eric? Give me some good news."

"It's all good. What's the last thing I told you?"

"Right after I called the DNA lab, you told me about your new witness. The nurse who overheard a phone call with someone named Cliff. Anything else turn up after that?"

"Plenty. Thanks to your pressure on the lab, we got the results. A former employee of the House of Loránd, a man named Clifton Vaughn, left his DNA on Kallay's gun. Vaughn has a record for sexual assault, and his DNA was in the CODIS registry."

"Wow. That had to be the 'Cliff' she was talking to."

"No question about it. And she's still talking to him. This afternoon, the pen register picked up a call to the same number she called when she was in the hospital. We got a search warrant for Vaughn's apartment. Gil and his team went up there about six o'clock. They made some interesting finds."

"Tell me."

"Bondage and sex toys in the bedroom, and—you're gonna love this—the Kallay 2002 collection. A stack of original drawings, all signed by the man. We also seized a cheap paper shredder with strip-cut documents we can put together."

Links between the evidence started to fly in her brain. "So this means ... hmm ... what does this mean? Frances says she shot her husband in self-defense when it was really Clifton Vaughn who pulled the trigger? Evidence of bondage in Vaughn's apartment *and* in the Kallay cellar? Frances and Cliff are in this together all right, in more ways than one."

"I think we're thinking the same thing."

"What are you thinking?" Dana asked, ever the teacher.

"Vaughn's the batterer and the setup in the Kallay cellar is phony."

"Exactly." That much was obvious, but Dana didn't want to rub it in.

"Her injuries were inflicted by Vaughn."

"Yes, it seems that Frances and Cliff have a very special relationship. Lovely." But there were a hundred other mysteries and interesting possibilities. Dana posed some of those questions now. "When and how was that setup put in the cellar? How did the murder go down? Was it spontaneous or planned? Even if Vaughn handled the gun at some point, could Frances have pulled the trigger? If Vaughn did the deed, is Frances still a full partner in the crime or just a facilitator, covering up for Vaughn after the fact? If she's just providing the cover story, why would she do that?"

"Like you said, they had a very special relationship. I think…"

"Hold on a minute, Eric." She was getting a beep on the line. It had to be Evan. "I have to hang up. Can I talk to you later?"

"Sure thing, Dana. Call anytime."

She pressed a button to switch over to the incoming call. At least, she thought it was the right button. The call was lost. Her lips moved with muttered curses. But then, a minute later, the phone rang again.

"Sorry, Evan. I hung up on you. Are you almost home? Don't talk on that thing when you're driving!" He didn't have a headset. She kept telling him to get one.

"I'm not driving. I'm still at Mom's."

"You're still there? I need you back here."

"Something came up…" His voice was low. "Can you

hear me?"

"Yes."

"I'm out on the front porch. Mom is up in her bedroom. Listen, I found some papers in her study. The first one completely blew me away. She's a member of the class in *Edmonds versus Tripp*."

"You're kidding."

"I kid you not."

"Shouldn't someone at B & R have noticed?"

"From a million names? No one has any reason to go looking for a Goodhue buried in there. The class members are gleaned from the Life Source sales records. All the notices in the lawsuit are spewed out by the computer."

"For all we know, there could be a few Hargroves on that list too."

"When I asked her if she remembered this product, Life Source, she said she bought a single order but stopped taking the capsules because they gave her gastric distress."

"How fortunate. That she stopped taking it, I mean."

"But apart from that, she's the willing victim of a thousand other scams. Every con artist in the country has her on his mailing list. Sweepstakes and so-called investments. She's under the impression she won a grand prize of ten thousand dollars because she already paid the 'taxes' on her prize money."

"Oh no. How much did she pay?"

"Five hundred dollars."

Dana shook her head. "Poor Brenda." But as she said this, she was really thinking of the children and of herself and Evan. Their choice of caregiver was called into question. Again. Was this so awful? Leaving the children in the care of a gullible senior citizen? She was their loving grandmother, so good for them in so many ways, a woman with excellent judgment,

except in this one respect. Untold numbers of people fell for
these kinds of scams. They looked legitimate on the surface
and tapped into basic human needs and desires. To feel unique,
to be shined upon by good fortune and deserving of material
pleasures. To quell anxieties about financial security. "I feel bad
for her, Evan, but this will get better. We just have to teach her
how to look out for these scams. A lot of people fall for them.
We can spend some extra time with her when we get back…"

"But it's worse than that, Dana."

She didn't want to hear this. She wanted Evan to come
home. Now.

"There's a man coming to the house on Sunday. She set
up an appointment with him for five o'clock. He's selling her
a reverse mortgage. I'm worried about her. We can't go away
and just leave her here. I can't let Mom stay in this house this
weekend. She's upstairs packing."

Dana heaved a huge sigh. A couple of days of her vacation
were already lost to Mary Poppins, and now this, an
unexpected guest on their trip to the Jersey shore. There would
be the awkwardness, embarrassment, and regret at the lost
opportunity for their hoped-for brief separation. A small break
from one another. Brenda's chance to enjoy her independence.
As a woman with a family, Dana knew the importance of that
feeling, the need to hold on to a life of one's own, apart from
the family members who were constantly pulling at your apron
strings.

Well, maybe it would still be a vacation. Brenda would
have a good time with Dana's parents, and everyone would be
rejuvenated by the new surroundings, the fresh air and miles
of sand and surf…

"I just got off the phone with Al," Evan explained. "He's
going to take Mom in while we're gone, and if she needs to go
to the house, he'll be with her. I'm taking her over to Al's just

as soon as she's packed."

Another deep exhalation. "Thank you, Evan."

"And ... don't worry. We can still leave in the morning."

Still?

"I'm pretty sure I can take care of this on the phone—my plans for this scumbag who's coming over on Sunday."

Immediately the guilt set in. Dana hadn't thought of catching the scumbag. It would have occurred to her, but she hadn't thought of it on her own, before he mentioned it. She only wanted Evan to come home. And now, she was grateful beyond words for all of the conscientious plans he was making for his mother while remaining ever mindful of his commitment to his wife and children.

"Thank you, darling," she said, full of sweetness. "Thank you so much for everything you do."

20 »   SING

ANTOINE WAS READING in the common area of the honor block when Victor came to get him. "Let's go, Frenchie. Big sis is here to see you." He twitched a finger with the "Love" hand.

They walked freely, side by side, out of the honor block, down the long linoleum corridor of the B block, on the way to the visiting area. There'd been many Sundays like this. It was the day of the week Ellen usually visited, and one of the days of the week in Victor's work schedule.

Over the years, a sense of trust had grown between this correction officer and inmate. Antoine supposed that, in the beginning, the task of building that trust was easy enough for Victor, who was half a head taller and fifty pounds heavier, all of it pure muscle. But soon enough, it was clear that Antoine wouldn't be a problem, verbally or physically. He was also not the type to snap. Some prisoners came into the system relatively compliant, their behavior under control, and then things happened to them. The hours, days, and nights never ended. Their anger and regret simmered, ready to explode. A constant vigilance had to be maintained against certain inmates—gang members and men who were more suited to a mental ward. And there were those who liked to prey on the physically weak, a man like Antoine, handsome and slightly effeminate.

Antoine had lived through many days of despondency, but he'd never snapped. And he'd never become suicidal.

"What do you think, Victor? Do I have a chance?"

"I've seen it go so many ways, I'm not gonna predict. If it was up to me ... well, I'm not on the parole board, so don't even ask."

Seconds passed with just the sound of their rubber-soled shoes squeaking on the floor, echoing down the length of the corridor. The days were dragging—only a month to go until the hearing. If Antoine waited much longer, he might never ask. He got up the courage now. "Would you put in a good word for me?"

Victor flashed one of his big smiles. "Waddaya think? I already did. I wrote a letter. All of it good. Signed, sealed, and delivered. Even had my wife check it. My spelling isn't the best."

Antoine was astounded that this well-respected officer had written a letter recommending his parole. Correction officers were obliged to fill out certain forms, ticking off checkboxes and ratings. But a separate letter to the parole board? It was more than Antoine expected, and he didn't doubt that the content of the letter, coming from Victor, was all positive. "Thank you."

"Like I said the first day I met you: 'Welcome to Sing Sing. I don't know what you've done, and I didn't get you in here. But you're here now, and what you make of it is up to you.' Did I say something like that, or what?"

"I remember it like yesterday," said Antoine.

"I've said it to hundreds of inmates. The years go by, and they look back, and most of them have nothing to show for it except wasted time. For you, something was made of it. You helped the men who were taking high school and college classes, and you were an example to a lot of the others. I've seen you straighten out the habits of more than a few men."

Pride swelled in Antoine's skinny chest, although it failed

to obliterate the kernel of skepticism that remained, his insecurity about what he did and did not deserve.

"But you can't ignore a few things," Victor continued, reading his thoughts. "If your time here was the only thing they considered, you'd be on your way out the door. But the board is also gonna look at everything you did before you got here. *That* I can't help."

And that was something Antoine couldn't change, no matter what Ellen chose to believe, no matter what kind of spin she tried to put on it.

"Whether you get out of here now or after the next review, I don't see you going back to the same line of business. Am I right about that?" Victor turned his head to look Antoine in the eye, but this time there wasn't a big smile on his face. It was the expression he used when meting out discipline. Delivering a message? *You'd better not be tempted.*

Antoine didn't have a quick answer, and then it was too late to say anything. Victor's hand was already pushing on the door to the visiting area, and they stepped inside. Ellen was sitting in her usual corner, apart from the other emotional meetings that were going on throughout the vast space. "There she is, the Lady Esquire." Victor nodded and winked at her, then backed out of the room, closing her brother inside.

Antoine walked over to his sister and gave her a hug. "Thank you for coming," he said. He never stopped being grateful for her visits. She could have given up on him years ago, starting with that day when they met in his trial attorney's office and looked through the box full of evidence against him, piles of fraudulent documents bearing his signature. The look on her face still haunted him. The alarm in her eyes steadily grew into full-blown shock as she reluctantly scanned one paper after another.

"I've been working on my letter to the parole board.

Here." She pulled it out of her jacket pocket. "Take a look and tell me what you think."

Antoine took the letter, consisting of four single-spaced, typed sheets, folded into thirds and in half again. He opened it and pretended to read. Knowing Ellen, and knowing what she believed about him, he already had a very good idea of what the letter said. His eyes were glassy with resignation as they moved quickly over the lines. Certain phrases jumped out: "a devoted brother," "a promising intellect," "top of his class in business school," "first offense," "under the influence of a devious scam artist," "just as much a victim," "innocent," "no criminal intent," "paid for his mistakes," "model inmate," "a thousand good deeds." The final lines: "Antoine has proven that he's a man of good character. Release him to society and let him continue to make valuable contributions in its midst."

As Antoine "read" the letter, the sounds in the room swelled and receded: cries and laughter and conversations of a hundred people, young and old, of every race and nationality. This congregation of displaced persons had been brought together at a moment in time, in this room, by a few irrevocable mistakes of the past—those acts of rage, greed, lust, and revenge that ran like silent films in their heads, the actors driven by emotions that had gone cold and were now inexplicable.

Finally, when Antoine thought she would believe he had read every word, he said, "It's a very good letter."

"Are you sure? What have I left out? Are there parts I should give more emphasis to?"

"It's perfect the way it is. I couldn't have hoped for anything better. And Victor says he's also written a letter to the board."

"He's a great guy."

"He's been the best."

They fell silent for a moment. Her mind was incessantly at work. He could see it. Why did she spend so much of her waking day obsessing over him? Why was he worth the effort? He knew that some of the things he'd said over the years—and some of the things he'd left unsaid—had contributed to her continued drive to save him.

Finally, she said, "I have an important hearing tomorrow in the case I told you about. The post-conviction motion in that felony murder case from 1993. It's actually going to be a benefit to you."

"How can a completely unrelated case be any benefit to me?"

"When I win it—and I know I'm going to win it—my credibility will be enhanced. Everything I say in my letter to the parole board in your case will take on a greater significance. They'll see that I'm a person who knows the law, knows the facts, and knows the signs of injustice. It won't be merely a letter from a sister about her brother. They'll have respect for the Director of Justice Restored. They'll know that I have the ability to uncover any bogus prosecution based on faulty evidence. My reputation will cut away any doubt that my opinion is the product of bias and emotion, based on our blood relationship."

She was intense and unshakeable in the glorification of her magnanimity. He rejected her fantasy but wouldn't say so. Out loud, he tossed her a mild test. "I'm sure you've done a great job on that case, and I don't mean to be negative or doubtful, but how do you know you're going to win? Nothing is for sure, especially not in a courtroom."

She smiled knowingly and stared pointedly at him. Antoine caught something in her expression that suddenly made him feel uncomfortable. It was the kind of feeling he got when he made the mistake of locking eyes with certain inmates in this institution, the ones who uttered bizarre statements of a distorted reality while they beamed an excited, fatal dare from a shining gaze: *Just see if you can prove me wrong.* Force was implied, whether you resisted or went along.

"I *know*," she said, "because I had access to the DA's file. I've laid the groundwork for a claim of undisclosed exculpatory evidence. I'll be able to show that an important piece of evidence was intentionally withheld. Evidence that would raise a reasonable doubt. I'm going to take her down—that assistant district attorney who prosecuted the case, Dana Hargrove."

"If something was so obviously part of her duty to disclose ... I guess I don't understand what motive this Hargrove has to hold things back."

Ellen looked at him, like she had so many times before, as if he'd said the most naïve thing in the world. He shrunk under her gaze. He was her little brother, the helpless victim who rolled over and let others take advantage of him. "I don't have to prove her motive! I only have to show something she can't deny—the DA's internal files have evidence she didn't introduce at trial. This is all about access. They control everything. They have the resources. They have the file rooms, the lock and key. The only place I have a small advantage against them is in Manhattan, because I used to work there."

They and them. Her favorite words. Now there was a new favorite word to add to the list. "Access. What are you saying?"

"I'm saying what I've been saying all along. I don't have access to your case file. I've been trying to get into the Westchester County DA's file room for years and haven't found a way. They hold things back, and I'm not able to see what's in there."

She was right. She *had* said all of this before, but never quite in the same way. He seemed to be hearing the words a bit differently today, the message burning through the external layer. "Don't the same rules of access apply to all prosecutors? The Freedom of Information Law?"

"It's not the same. It's not the same as full access, getting my hands on it and going through every paper myself."

"Your..." *Hands. Getting my hands on it.*

Antoine shook off a sudden chill. Ellen jumped to her feet and started to pace around his chair, like *she* was the caged animal, claustrophobic and volatile.

So, she wanted access. What would she find? Nothing that could help him. He mentally reviewed the evidence in his own case, remembering what Ellen had seen that day in his attorney's office when she examined dozens of documents. That big box had contained most of the evidence against him. The prosecutor had complied with the rules and disclosed all of it. Ellen had access to as much information as she needed to find out what Antoine's case was all about. That day, she'd asked him "why?" over and over again, and he'd given her his explanations, the construct he'd cobbled together. There were omissions but, in a way, everything he told her was true. In a way, Landers had been the orchestrator. Ellen chose to believe Antoine, and soon enough, she'd built his explanations into an elaborate story about "The Victim," that young impressionable lad who'd been manipulated by a seasoned con artist into blindly executing a far-reaching criminal scheme. Puppet and puppeteer.

Antoine never dissuaded her. She was the only person in the family on his side. She was the only one toiling away to maintain contact with his twin daughters, Brittany and Heather, while the mother of his girls did everything in her power to cut off all communication. Ellen was the only source of news about them, and the only person who could deliver a message from him. She was the only one fighting to get him out of here.

All his life he'd looked up to her. He didn't want to let her down. At the time of his arrest, she was a prosecutor. She'd seen plenty of bad guys in court, and he couldn't let her think he was one of them. He believed it would break him if he'd fallen that far in her eyes.

Their age difference had always shaped their relationship. He was four years younger. As children, and even now, she regarded him as less mature. In her eyes, he was still the little kid she used to manipulate in their backyard games.

Sure, he'd been young at the time of his arrest, but not *so* young. Not eighteen or nineteen but twenty-six. Yes, he was much younger than Mason Landers, who was forty-five at the time. Age and criminal experience were sources of control, but if those factors had been the only means of influence, Antoine doubted he would have gotten involved. He fell under Landers' control for a distinct reason, a particular vulnerability that might afflict an adult of any age. Its crippling effect was greater when it hit later in adulthood. Antoine was suffering the weakened condition of a person in the blush of an exciting discovery of an intimate fact of self, something buried deep within his psyche and emotional makeup from the time of earliest childhood.

Strange, but Antoine wouldn't mind being in that position again. He dreamed of it at night, staring at the vertical bars that imprisoned him. If given the chance—and there was now some possibility of it—he would repeat the more pleasurable aspects of that year leading up to his arrest, taking care, only, to be more discreet and cautious next time.

His hopes for this possibility had been raised two weeks ago. Would he tell his sister? Of course not. So far, he'd kept it to himself, and he wasn't about to reveal this secret. It was a new, previously unimagined prospect on the horizon, something to feed his dreams.

There'd been a visitor. His first visitor, other than his sister, in over three years. This man was a stranger, a man named Peter Goren, posing as an associate of Ellen Fortier at Justice Restored. Antoine tried not to show the puzzlement on his face as Victor pointed to the man waiting for him in the visiting area.

Goren extended his hand. Antoine accepted it for a brief clasp and a businesslike shake before taking a seat across from him.

"First thing to get straight, I don't know your sister. Someone else sent me."

Antoine was put on guard. Instinctively, he pulled back in his chair. "What's this about?"

"I'm here as a friend," Goren assured him in a low voice, motioning to come in closer. Antoine decided to trust the man. He pulled his chair in, dipped his head, and bent forward at the waist, elbows on knees. Goren explained. "Yesterday, I flew in from Las Vegas. I have a business out there. So does Mason Landers. Actually, we flew into JFK together. He asked me to see you."

Antoine's heart started to pound. "What do you mean?"

"He wants to say he didn't forget you. He never forgot you."

Goren was a slight, wiry man with intelligent eyes. Like Antoine, he had a certain sensitivity about him that made him the kind of man to fall in with Mason. That part of it was unpleasant to imagine. But the other message overshadowed that concern. *He never forgot you.* Antoine tried to focus on what Goren was saying about their businesses, to ignore everything else underneath that top layer of reality.

"It doesn't seem that way," Antoine protested in a low voice. "He skipped town. He didn't lift a finger to get me out of this."

"Sure, he went away. Wouldn't you?"

"I suppose I would."

"What good would it do if both of you wound up in here?"

Antoine saw the logic in this and nodded in agreement.

"He's been living in Nevada. But now that the statute has run in New York, he's back. They can't get him for any of that."

Funny, Antoine thought. Spend seven years in prison, and it's still hanging over your head, parole supervision for years to come. Spend seven years in freedom, and the case disappears.

"He says he's here to pay you back. To get the people who put you in here."

"How can he do that?"

"You'll know soon enough. And he knows what your sister has been going through. He promises that she'll be pleased with the payback he has in mind."

Antoine was astounded. He stared at the floor, shaking his head. A correction officer strolled by and gave them a look, maybe sensing that something was up. Antoine glanced up from under his brow and straightened up.

"Ellen was telling me about your daughters," Goren said a bit louder, pretending at conversation.

"They're getting big. They won't remember me when I'm out of here."

"I know they'll be glad to see you."

"I miss them so much."

The officer walked on, and suddenly, Goren was anxious to wrap things up and leave. "I have to go," he said. "We'll see you when you get out."

"Where? How?"

"Don't worry. We'll find you."

Antoine briefly examined Goren's face, the pointed

cheekbones, the small chin, the ears that protruded slightly, not quite as big as Dumbo's. He didn't want to see Goren again. But apparently they were a package deal, and he *did* want to see Mason.

"All right," said Antoine. "But you'll say nothing to Ellen."

"Why would I? Why would Mason? He knows how much she hates him. He's not doing this for her. He's doing it for you, because she's your sister. He's in the business of making money, and he might as well make that money from certain people. As a side benefit, he knows that she'll be pleased with the results. And so will you."

She'll be pleased. The memory of Goren's words floated just beneath Antoine's consciousness as the woman who would be pleased now paced around his chair. These thoughts mixed in with everything Ellen had been saying to him today, heightening his disturbing new insight into his sister's behavior.

After making a single orbit, Ellen sat down again and leaned toward him. One of her legs bounced up and down, jittery with nerves. "Next week, you'll see. I'll have good news for you after tomorrow's hearing in the Pineda case. They're going to sit up and listen to me then!"

Seeing her like this, Antoine didn't know how he felt about her anymore. He guessed at a deleterious element underneath her lament about lack of "access." He didn't want to ask. He didn't want to know any more about it. He said only, "You wouldn't have done any better if you'd gotten full access to the DA's file in my case. There's nothing in there that can help me. Nothing."

"How can you possibly know what they've withheld?"

"Because I know what I've done." There. He'd let it slip. In one little sentence, he'd pierced the protective shield they'd built together against the truth.

She still didn't see. "You were manipulated by a con man."

"I'm sorry, sister. You can't change the evidence against me, even if you got your hands on that file..." *Access. Payback. She'll be pleased.* At the moment, Antoine was not feeling very good about his sister. His eyes were open. Apparently, she was a woman given to underhanded tactics, no better than the dissemblers and swindlers he'd been housed with for seven years. No better than himself.

"I'm not trying to change anything," she insisted. "I'm working for justice and the truth!"

"Then I'll give it to them myself. I'll raise my right hand and swear an oath and tell the parole board what they want to hear, the absolute truth. It's the only thing that will get me out of here. They don't want bullshit and lies. They want to see me admit my crimes. They want to know that I've accepted responsibility. You want to give them the truth? Then change that letter you wrote to the board! Put all the evidence in there, everything you saw in those documents in my file..."

"But you said the letter is good..."

"The letter is very good, but it's about another man. Someone you made up! The truth has always been there, right before your eyes. Tell them your little brother was under the thumb of a con man. Maybe so. But also tell them that he knew what he was doing! Tell them he was knowingly in the business"—and wanted to make a killing, to live the easy life, and wasn't sorry for any of it! Not if he could live that life with Mason.

But Antoine didn't continue his thoughts out loud. The look on his sister's face stopped him, just short.

Next month, would it matter to him what she thought? The doors would be open to him and he would walk right out of here to the man who hadn't forgotten him. The man who was waiting for him. Antoine would do anything for that man, anything he asked. They would do it together again. Only this time, they would do it better.

21 » STAND

SOME VACATION. A day and a half on the beach, Saturday afternoon and Sunday, no chance to fully unwind.

Evan convinced Dana to stay away from her phone all weekend, to "leave the office in *their* hands." She noticed that he wasn't about to take his own advice. Evan spent a good part of Saturday leaving emergency messages and accepting return phone calls, plotting a trap for Brenda's scammer. But Dana complied with Evan's suggestion. She turned off her mobile phone and trusted that all of the attorneys she supervised, including Eric, would ably manage their weekend emergencies in her absence. She needed a break.

At the beach house, everyone had settled in by two o'clock on Saturday. The first to arrive were Dana's parents, Sidney and Marilyn Hargrove, followed by Dana's family, and a short time later, their close friends Noel and Melanie Avendaño with their three children, Patricia, Rafael, and Maria. The first hour was filled with bustling activity and excitement. The men unloaded the cars while the women tried to rein in the children, who raced from one room to the next, discovering the many quirky nuances of their two-week rental, an enormous six-bedroom house with wrap-around porch directly on the beach.

The weather was sunny and beautiful. For Dana, the picture-perfect panorama of seascape and dune held an unsettling undercurrent of anxiety. On the horizon was her inevitable solo trip back to the city, where she would spend a night alone and face Ellen Fortier on Monday morning. For much of Sunday, Evan was again unavailable, on the phone with the police and prosecutors in Westchester, coordinating the events that were about to transpire at the house he grew up in. That evening, as Dana was getting ready to leave, Evan pulled her aside from the other houseguests and conveyed the startling news. At that moment, Al was driving Brenda to the precinct to view a lineup with the man they'd taken into custody. "And you'll never guess who he is!"

With this bit of success to show for all of Evan's planning, Dana got behind the wheel and headed north for New York City. As she expected, the Garden State Parkway was jammed with people returning home after a weekend at the beach. She crept along at a snail's pace, surrounded by cars full of painful red faces, the surprising sunburns of early summer. At moments during their shimmering, metallic standstill, the captives awkwardly exchanged glances. Hadn't anyone heard of sunblock? Dana's own complexion had a deep olive glow that didn't burn easily, but she applied sunblock religiously to herself and to every inch of her squirming children—one of the biggest challenges of a beach vacation.

Back home, she crawled into bed after midnight, the apartment eerily empty and echoing. Her only company, as she lay in the dark, was the muffled sound of shuffling feet in the apartment above hers, something she normally wouldn't notice when Evan and the children were home. She tried to remember the faces of the upstairs dwellers, a childless married couple she'd met only once. They were doctors who worked odd hours, and despite the strange schedule, or because of it, they were politely quiet and unnoticeable to their surrounding neighbors.

After sleeping no more than five hours, she rose early Monday morning, took a shower, made coffee, and put on her business suit, nylons, and low heels. And something else she didn't normally do—she applied lipstick and a little eye makeup. She didn't doubt there would be sketch artists and cameramen—Ellen had literally invited the press corps to this hearing when she made her little speech on the courthouse steps. The "Forsaken Oath Sermon" is what Dana and Evan were now calling it.

Dana grabbed her briefcase, and minutes later, found herself sandwiched upright between strangers on a crowded subway car. Shoved up against a masculine barrel-shaped chest, Dana cast her eyes down and away. Here she was, on vacation! Just another day in court, but this time, she would be on the witness stand, the subject of an inquisition conducted by a righteous scandalmonger.

Although today was devoted to the Pineda hearing, Dana looked forward to getting an update on the Kallay investigation before she headed to court at nine fifteen. She hadn't spoken to Eric since the conversation she'd cut short on Friday night. Over the weekend, Eric had left a few messages on her mobile phone—only two, an amazing show of self-restraint. She'd listened to them while sipping her coffee, before leaving the apartment.

The first one had come in on Saturday night at ten fifteen: "Still no arrest, Dana. The suspect may be on to us. He hasn't returned to his apartment. We'll keep you posted."

The second call was made Monday morning at four thirty-five: "We got him, Dana! Vaughn's in custody! I'll fill you in later." He sounded ecstatic.

Theories of the Kallay murder were snaking through her mind as she emerged from the subway. As predicted, the television news vans were lined up in front of the Criminal Court building. She walked around the block and approached her office building from the rear, in the alley that was blocked off to the public. She was anxious to speak to Eric first thing.

But his office was empty as she passed by. Lecia handed her a few message slips. "A couple from Eric. He's with Gil and Manny in the Dungeon, questioning the guy they just arrested."

"Still?"

"Not coming up for air. The suspect is talking, and Eric's very excited."

"Gee, how can you tell?" The two women exchanged knowing looks and smiled.

"In his last message, Eric said, 'Don't let Dana go back to Jersey before I talk to her!'"

Ben Weingarten was waiting for Dana outside the courtroom when she walked up. It was only the second time they'd met in person, the first time being Friday, when they prepared for this hearing. As a senior appellate ADA, Ben was experienced in all kinds of post-conviction proceedings and appeals. In his early thirties, he was a man of the beanpole variety, six-four at least, with wrists dangling from jacket sleeves that could have used an extra half-inch of length.

A number of people were milling about. Dana and Ben stepped away from the courtroom door and found an empty corner.

"Everyone's inside," Ben reported. "Tons of press and random curiosity seekers. There's also a whole row of Ellen's groupies."

"Her law students?"

"Yup. A perky raft of awestruck interns. And her witnesses are all present and accounted for..."

"Including yours truly."

Ben smiled. His face and mannerisms bore no indication of nervousness. Dana had never seen him in action in court but had developed an intuitive trust. Despite the slow start last week, he'd quickly brought himself up to speed on Friday.

She pulled her mobile phone out of a jacket pocket and eyed the display. "Good signal out here," she said.

"I don't think it's as good in the witness room. You want to stay out here in the hallway until you're called?"

"Yes. Please." She didn't want to tell him that she'd go stir crazy if required to wait in that claustrophobic little anteroom reserved for witnesses. Besides that, her mobile phone played a big part in their plan for this morning. She had to be sure that her phone call would go through.

"I'll let the judge know," Ben said. "I'm sure he'll be okay with it."

"I've been thinking, we're lucky that Ellen's motion was assigned to Judge Deal. I've had several trials before him, and I know how he thinks." Along the spectrum, from those judges who most often favored the prosecution to those who favored the defense, Judge Deal was squarely in the middle, eminently unbiased, to the extent that his complete focus on principle and logic could, at times, render him oblivious to the reality of the streets. Far from what his name might imply, the judge was not known to be an easy deal maker. He preferred the trial setting, applying the evidence to the law. With an Ivy League background, he was an intellectual who thrived on complex discussions of legal theory. "He might just be the one to make it hard for Ellen. I'm having a premonition of one of his hypothetical sermons about what a jury would do with the information she *says* I withheld." Dana couldn't mask the acidity in her voice.

Ben nodded in agreement but didn't offer a comment. "Ellen walked in right before you got here," he said.

"It's early yet. She might have gone back to the lockup to talk to her client."

Ben looked at his watch. "Eight minutes."

Dana felt a flutter in her chest. She stood up taller and

asked, "How are you feeling about this?" The question sounded a bit arrogant, or maybe it was her tone. Sometimes, in especially tense moments, a haughty attitude crept into her voice involuntarily. A cover up. Or maybe she was only stalling. Under the circumstances, Ben could have asked her, "How do *you* feel about getting on the witness stand?" Of course, an ADA of Ben's rank wouldn't dare talk like this to a bureau chief.

He answered her question. "Good," he said. "It's fairly predictable how she'll present her case."

Predictable, yes. They'd gone over Ellen's case on Friday. There would be three witnesses before Dana got on the stand:

A clerk from the DA's office, Rhonda Oppenheimer. Most likely, she was the same "Rhonda" who'd been tucked inside that netherworld of dead paper when Dana visited the archives department last Thursday. Rhonda would testify that she'd responded to Ellen's FOIL request by sending her photocopies of various documents from the Pineda file.

A ballistics expert, Glenn Pearson. He would testify about the results of his tests on the evidence in the Pineda case in the summer of 1992 and the reports he prepared.

A court stenographer, Belinda Esposito. She would testify that her transcription of the Pineda trial in 1993 was accurate, including the absence of any indication that ADA Hargrove had sought to introduce certain documents into evidence.

Finally, to cap off her triumphant exposition, Ellen would call Dana to the stand.

In the hours between dusk and dawn, Ellen had considered many times whether her efforts of the past several years had been misguided and a waste of time, whether it would be easier to simply give up the cause right here and now. She could send a messenger to the courtroom at nine thirty with an affirmation, swearing to an unavoidable, unexpected circumstance. A serious illness of sudden onset, perhaps. And then, quietly, at a later date, she could simply withdraw the motion or submit it on papers, without a hearing.

Her heart had gone out of her.

Disappointment and defeat were nothing new to her, almost a way of life, making the victories that much sweeter. Over the years of toil and trouble with Justice Restored, each setback had provided another building block to her point of view. The case of Ramón Pineda was a confirmatory model. After his arrest in July of 1992, he was remanded without bail. To date, he'd spent nearly nine years in prison, paying for his past drug addiction by forfeiting his young adulthood to the state. That's how she'd come to see it. Poverty and childhood influences created a path to drug addiction. A heroin addict needed a daily fix. The drugs cost money. Crime was the only available source of income. A shivering, frail addict wouldn't be taken seriously unless he carried a gun. Pineda's physical and mental disabilities—the tremulous hands and chemically-induced volatility—had led to the unfortunate slip of the trigger finger and the death of the bodega owner.

A series of unfortunate and tragic circumstances. Wasn't nine years enough time to serve for all of these mistakes, half of them well beyond his control? Nine years, in which he'd been cleansed free of drugs, had come to rely on Jesus as his guiding light?

There was a core of rectitude in her fight for this man, despite her new disappointment—Antoine's apparent betrayal. Or maybe she was still fighting this fight for her brother's sake, and everything she chose to do today would really be about him.

What had the years of incarceration done to Antoine's perception? How could he possibly come to believe that his acts, under the direction of Mason Landers, had been volitional?

This was a new side to him, a transformation wrought from desperation. To get out, out, out. To convince the parole board of his contrition and personal responsibility. It was the only explanation she could find, but it wasn't good enough. Now, for the first time, she was troubled by a niggling doubt. Or was it merely a new form of anger and frustration? Antoine simply didn't understand himself. He lacked insight into his own behavior, and her task of redirecting his inner vision had grown impossible.

Her heart had gone out of her.

But, by morning, she was resigned to follow through. She'd made it this far, setting into motion every step of the plan for winning Pineda's freedom. It was going to work, even if— as she feared—her performance in the courtroom today might suffer from this low point in her mood and self-esteem.

In the minutes before the hearing, as she spoke to her client in the lockup behind the courtroom, Ellen kept an image of Antoine's lovely face in her mind, undisturbed by Ramón's black eyes pressing into her. She sensed the hardness that radiated from the core of this Jesus lover, and she ignored it. He bore no resemblance to her brother, although both men were caged animals. Antoine's eyes had remained soft and welcoming and vulnerable despite his inhospitable surroundings. Yesterday, his face was no different, even as he tried to convince her that he'd known exactly what he was up to when he completed all those transactions for the bogus mortgage lender Security National, that fabrication of an evil confidence man.

"What're the chances? Tell them I didn't mean it. I wasn't gonna shoot the man. The cops started the shooting."

She let Ramón talk for a minute before she said whatever

it was she said to him, and then they were seated at their table in the courtroom, without her knowing exactly how they'd gotten there. The intervening fifteen minutes had been sucked into a black hole.

Ellen's nostrils pricked at a faint whiff of prison, oozing from Ramón's pores despite his best-washed appearance. She stood and faced Judge Deal to announce their first witness, a clerk from the DA's office. Surrounded and queasy, she felt the intense heat at her back: scores of curious faces behind the bar, keenly focused on the proceedings. The courtroom was packed. Subtle noises gradually rose up, attacking the comfort of her oblivion. Coughs, rustling papers, the scratching sounds of artists' pencils, feet scraping the floor.

She'd scanned the crowd when first entering the courtroom but couldn't recall any details of that undulating sea. Perhaps Dana Hargrove's face was in its midst. But no, Judge Deal wouldn't be so sloppy as to allow the witnesses to sit in the audience during the hearing. It was proper to keep witnesses sequestered so they wouldn't hear the testimony of the others before they took the stand.

To her right, sitting at the prosecutor's table, was that gangling ADA with an earnest face. She didn't look at him, but sensed his loose limbs moving over and under the table. Her eyes were directed toward the judge as he looked down on her from his perch behind the bench. He was a mousy little thing, with eyeglasses in oversized frames, too big for his small head. Suddenly she hated the man. Behind those spectacles he was focused on her alone, studiously avoiding Ramón, the only life at stake in these proceedings. The judge peered without really seeing as the gears of his mind whirred and locked in their eager anticipation of his favorite game: the injection of cold evidence into the abstract legal precepts that so fascinated him.

Rhonda Oppenheimer, the archives clerk, wasn't on the

stand for very long. Ellen showed Oppenheimer various documents, one by one, and confirmed that a copy of each had been disclosed in response to the FOIL request: arrest report, hospital records, autopsy report, trajectory analysis, ballistics report, and voucher forms for each piece of physical evidence.

At the conclusion of direct examination, ADA Weingarten stood and straightened his spine in a show of superior elevation. He was at least a foot taller than Ellen. "No questions, Your Honor. The People stipulate to the admission of these documents into evidence."

"So admitted," said the judge. He twitched his fingers, beckoning to the court clerk to hand up the original documents.

Clutching her copies, Ellen felt dwarfed and knocked slightly off balance. She'd planned to seek the admission of the documents later, after linking them to other evidence. But she had no reason to complain. The stipulation, although unexpected, was all right. These were the documents that would win her case. Among them were the two that Dana had failed to introduce into evidence at Ramón's trial. Soon enough, that crucial fact would be revealed. Why, then, was she having trouble catching her breath? Weingarten seemed much too innocent and genuine.

The judge was still looking over the documents when she called her second witness to the stand, the ballistics expert, Glenn Pearson. In a few easy questions, she established his qualifications and his involvement in the investigation of the robbery that occurred on July 25, 1992. But when she pulled out his report, her heart started to pound. Words floated in her head, collided, and tumbled out in nonsensical spurts. "Looking at your report, Mr. Pearson, can you tell us which of the two guns you tested ... that is ... the bullet recovered from the victim's brain ... it was fired from one of the two..."

"Would you like to start over, counselor?" Judge Deal sounded like a high school debate team coach.

She glanced up at his small pinpoints under those outdated eyeglasses. "Yes, thank you, Your Honor." She cleared her throat, but just as she was about to speak, the lanky ADA pushed himself up to standing again. "Your Honor, the People are willing to stipulate to the contents of the ballistics report with respect to the bullet recovered from the brain of the victim, Felipe Bedoya."

Now Ellen was completely thrown. This was *her* case, and she was losing control over it. Quickly, she jumped into the breach. "I'm entitled to elicit this from the witness."

The judge raised his eyebrows, invisible underneath the top rims. "You object to a stipulation? In your favor?"

Too late, she regretted her clash with Judge Deal's logical mind. "Well, certainly not," she admitted. "But the prosecutor hasn't said how he's reading this report..."

"Then let's see what the prosecutor says. Mr. Weingarten, what is your proposed stipulation?"

From the witness stand, Glenn Pearson was looking on, his head ping-ponging back and forth between the participants.

The ADA picked up his copy of the report. "Mr. Pearson writes here that, based on his testing, the bullet identified under voucher number 23W9G12, which is the bullet recovered from Felipe Bedoya's brain, had been fired from a weapon identified under voucher number 23W9G06, which is a Beretta 9mm semiautomatic with a defaced serial number. The People stipulate that the ballistics report contains this finding."

"Well, Ms. Fortier, isn't this what you were getting at?"

"Yes, Your Honor, but..."

"Then you stipulate?"

"I stipulate, yes, but I have several more questions to ask this witness."

"Go right ahead." The judge sat back with a grin on his lips.

Oh, how maddening! She turned to the witness, who was patiently waiting. "Mr. Pearson, you tested two guns on the same day, did you not?"

"Yes, I did."

"When you received the weapons for testing, how were they identified?"

"Each firearm was in a plastic evidence bag marked with its voucher number."

"Did you open the bags one at a time and test them one at a time?"

"Yes. I could hardly fire two guns at once!" With sparkling eyes, the witness looked past Ellen into the audience. "Well, maybe I *could* fire two guns at once..." A few titters sprinkled the air.

"But this wasn't the Wild West. It was a ballistics lab."

"Right about that."

"So you opened one bag and fired test bullets from that gun."

"Yes."

"Those test bullets were used for comparison to the bullet identified under voucher number 23W9G12, the bullet from the victim's brain, to see if the striations matched."

"That's correct."

Ellen noticed the look that passed between the judge and the ADA. She'd been leading the witness, stating the essential facts instead of asking open-ended questions. But the ADA didn't seem interested in objecting. She was getting to the point quickly, and he didn't care. His eyes were wide open and interested, not a hint of distress in his features. Maybe he didn't predict where she was headed. But he had to see—it was written in the documents.

"Do you remember which gun you tested first?"

"It's been nine years. No, I do not."

"You determined that the bullet that came from the victim's brain had been fired from the Beretta under voucher 23W9G06, did you not?"

"That's right."

"Did you put that Beretta back into the voucher bag marked with the number ending in '06' when you were done?"

"Yes."

"Tell me then, where did you get the description for that weapon when you wrote your ballistics report?"

"I looked at the gun and wrote a description." Pearson's gently mocking tone elicited another few snickers from the audience. Let them laugh. They would see the importance of this point soon enough.

"Is it your testimony that you did not copy that description from the voucher form prepared by Police Officer Robert Sullivan?"

"Correct. I did not copy it."

"By the way, are you familiar with the NYPD regulations that apply when a police officer fires a service weapon in the line of duty?"

"Yes, in a general way. Internal Affairs conducts an investigation."

"Were you aware that, under those regulations, Police Officer Aurelina Vargas and her partner, Sergeant Dean Habberly, were not allowed to process the physical evidence in this case?"

"Yes, I was aware."

"They were precluded from filling out the voucher forms…"

Ellen's feelers were out, but still no objection from the ADA. His restraint was puzzling. Her method of questioning was improper, and she was delving into an area that was off topic, irrelevant. Weingarten's silence was killing her. This was the kind of subject—alleged police misconduct—that always provoked an objection.

"I'm aware of that protocol," Pearson answered. "But I have no memory of who filled out the voucher forms. I have no memory of seeing the voucher form for the Beretta. I received the gun in an evidence bag marked with the voucher number."

"You're saying you don't need the voucher form to write your report?"

"I know my guns, counselor."

Ellen glanced at ADA Weingarten and said, "Yes, I'm sure you do." She turned her back to him and faced the judge. "I have no further questions."

Behind her, she heard the scrape of a chair. The ADA was getting to his feet ... but wait! She'd missed something! She'd been so pleased with Pearson's answer, that she'd let a crucial point slip her mind. "I'm sorry, Your Honor. I have a few more questions."

"All right, go ahead. I'm giving you plenty of leeway here, Ms. Fortier. Watch your step."

A rebuke from that little man! No doubt he was displeased with her style of questioning, not to mention her last-minute change of mind. Well, he hadn't given any direct orders to clean up her questions, so she continued to lead, trying to make this short. "Mr. Pearson, just to be clear, since you know your guns, there was no need for you to refer to the voucher forms when you testified at trial, isn't that right?"

"Yes. The prosecutor on the case...," Pearson began.

"That would be Dana Hargrove?"

"Yes. ADA Hargrove questioned me about my report. That was it."

"The voucher forms weren't in evidence, were they?"

"I wouldn't know that."

"But ADA Hargrove didn't show them to you for any purpose, even to refresh recollection?"

"I doubt it, but you can check the transcript on that."

"All right." Ellen paused on this note, which wasn't as strong as the first one, her premature ending. But now she was done. "No further questions." She turned to the judge and made a show of respect—it could only help her client. "Thank you, Your Honor."

Walking back to her table, she captured a still frame of the man that everyone wanted to forget, that casualty of society and the criminal justice system. With shining obsidian eyes and deliberate effort, Ramón was sitting ramrod straight, attentive, looking like he deserved to be sprung.

This wasn't such a bad thing she was doing. No, it was not.

Again, ADA Weingarten stood and said, "No cross-examination, Your Honor."

So be it. No objections, no cross-examination. No defense for his colleague, the inviolable Dana Hargrove.

"Mr. Pineda calls Belinda Esposito to the stand," Ellen said.

The stenographer walked in from the side room and took the oath, looking a bit scared, worried perhaps about impending accusations of a faulty transcription. Nothing could be farther from Ellen's plan. Everything in the trial transcript supported her winning theory.

Weingarten was amenable to pushing that theory along. He stipulated to the admission of the trial transcript and allowed Ellen only a few questions before interrupting her again. She had just asked the witness to examine the list of exhibits admitted into evidence at Ramón's trial. "Do you see any entries on that list for the voucher forms corresponding to the two weapons, the Beretta and the Glock? Those numbers would be 23W9G06 and 23W9G08."

The ADA stood up. "Your Honor, we stipulate that the People did not introduce those two voucher forms into evidence at trial."

The judge looked at Ellen, inviting her response. His eyes permitted only one answer. Apparently, Judge Deal had no problem letting the ADA steal her thunder, just as the ADA had no problem implying that there was no thunder to steal. Weingarten was conceding every point in her case. Everything! Would he also stipulate that Dana Hargrove *knowingly* concealed this crucial evidence at trial? That she continued to conceal it for nine years while Ramón rotted in prison? "The stipulation is acceptable to me," Ellen said.

"So stipulated," said the judge. "Go on, Ms. Fortier. Let's get through this."

Weingarten sat down again, and Ellen continued. "Ms. Esposito, let me direct your attention to a portion of Police Officer Sullivan's testimony on page 352 of the transcript…"

"Your Honor." He was back on his feet! "The People further stipulate that, during the trial, ADA Hargrove refreshed the recollection of Police Officer Robert Sullivan by showing him, at different times, the voucher forms numbered 23W9G06 and 23W9G08. However, ADA Hargrove did not introduce those voucher forms into evidence."

"Is that your point, Ms. Fortier?" asked the judge.

"Yes, it is."

"Then you stipulate?"

"Yes, but I reserve the right to question ADA Hargrove about those sections of the trial transcript."

"We'll take up that issue in a minute. Are you finished with this witness?"

Ellen hesitated, wondering what "issue" could be involved in calling Dana to the witness stand. The judge didn't wait for her. He turned to the witness and said, "You may step down, Ms. Esposito—"

"But, Your Honor—" Ellen protested.

"—the court thanks you for coming today."

"—I haven't finished my direct examination."

Esposito's eyes darted between Ellen and the judge. "Shall I...?"

"You may go," said the judge.

"Ahh!" The sound escaped Ellen's lips, just loud enough for the judge to hear. She took a defiant stance, arms crossed over her chest.

The witness didn't budge. The judge instructed her in a louder voice this time: "Step down, Ms. Esposito. Thank you for your testimony." With a look of relief, the witness complied. She could tell who was in charge.

Artists' pencils scratched. Voices rose above a whisper. The judge banged the gavel, and a death pall descended over the courtroom. "*Now*, we'll talk about your next witness, Ms. Fortier."

"Mr. Pineda calls Dana Hargrove to the—"

"I'm considering preclusion."

Ellen couldn't believe her ears. "Preclusion?" The judge was threatening to take away her star witness!

"Any testimony from ADA Hargrove would be superfluous. I've looked at the documents and heard your witnesses. You've made your point. There's an apparent discrepancy between the numbers on the voucher forms and those on the ballistics report. We've got Officer Vargas's Glock under voucher form 23W9G06 and the defendant's Beretta under voucher form 23W9G08, but the ballistics report says the opposite. Pearson says that the number ending in '06' is the

Beretta."

"It establishes a reasonable doubt—"

"—that your client didn't fire the fatal bullet? Let's assume more than that. Let's assume it isn't just a reasonable doubt but an established fact that the fatal bullet came from Officer Vargas's gun. It has no consequence to the outcome of this case. There was a shootout during a robbery and someone was killed. Mr. Pineda was responsible in the eyes of the law, under the elements of felony murder, whether *his* gun or someone else's fired the fatal bullet."

"It *does* matter, Your Honor. Ramón testified that he didn't start the shooting. Officer Vargas started it, and Ramón's gun accidentally discharged in reaction to being shot in the shoulder by the police. If the jury had known that Officer Vargas killed the victim after shooting Ramón, they would have been very troubled by these facts. They would have acquitted Ramón of murder."

"Then the jury would have been acting contrary to the court's instructions."

"Juries are permitted to exercise mercy in favor of the accused. They're the eyes and ears of the community. I've shown a reasonable possibility of a different verdict..."

"You've shown no more than a mistake in a ballistics report which has no consequence under the law."

"Mistake?" Judge Deal was blind! So intent on his sterile legal analysis, he was clueless about the raw emotion and hidden motives that drove human behavior. "A police officer's career was at stake. The NYPD's reputation was on the line. This was no mistake! There was an intentional switch of the guns, a cover up—"

"Whoa, counselor. You have no support for that conclusion."

"It's written all over these forms. Why else would Glenn

Pearson receive the Beretta in a voucher bag with the number ending in '06'? Someone switched the guns in those bags before they got to him. If the jury had known about this cover up—on top of the fact that it was Officer Vargas who killed the store owner—the jury would have acquitted. No question about it."

"There's nothing to suggest anything more than a mistake. At most, you've shown negligence in the handling of the evidence, not an intentional switch and concealment."

"Even if it's negligence, the documents clearly show the mistake, and those documents have been hidden away! There's at least one person who knows of this concealment. That person is Dana Hargrove. She's the one who decided not to enter the voucher forms into evidence. She owes the court an explanation why the mistake remained buried in the DA's archive room for nine years."

The judge paused. Finally, she'd struck a chord. Five seconds passed while he considered her suggestion.

In the space of that pause, Ellen shuddered off a cold wave of queasiness. If the judge allowed her to go forward, everything depended on her skill in examining that darling of Trial Bureau 90, her former officemate, Dana Hargrove. Of course, Dana would deny everything, or say that she couldn't remember. But Ellen had to make her believe in the *possibility* of a mistake, something serious enough to elicit a look of doubt in Dana's eyes, and perhaps a tiny quaver or catch in her voice. These manifestations of guilt would prove her point. Yes, there was an intentional switch, or at least, knowing concealment. This is what she would argue to the judge, based on Dana's behavior.

Ellen was banking on a proven track record, having won two cases using this strategy. Most recently, in the Trevor Blakely case, she'd confronted the prosecutor on the witness stand, showing him the exculpatory information written in a police officer's notebook. He couldn't remember if he'd seen it before and couldn't say why it hadn't been turned over to the defense at the time of trial. He stumbled on his words and scrunched his brow in perplexity. Little signs of worry. It raised a reasonable doubt, and Blakely was released.

Confronted with the possibility of a grave mistake, anyone with a conscience would react this way. Dana would be no different.

The judge turned to the prosecutor. "What is your view on this, Mr. Weingarten?"

The ADA got to his feet. "The People agree with the court that the alleged discrepancy in the paperwork is no reason to vacate the murder conviction. As to preclusion, the People express no view, except to say that we have no objection to putting Ms. Hargrove on the witness stand. At great personal sacrifice she arranged to be here today, and she's more than willing to give the court a full picture of what happened at the trial."

"All right," Judge Deal said. "We'll see what she has to say."

"Thank you, Your Honor," said Ellen. "If I may, I'd like to question the witness with the original documents."

"Certainly." He handed the documents to a court officer and instructed, "Bring the witness in."

The officer handed Ellen the stack of papers before proceeding down the aisle to the back of the courtroom. The attorneys took their seats and waited. A word was whispered: "Good." Ellen turned and dipped her head toward her client, who was looking less than angelic. "Get the bitch," he rasped. She responded with a nod and the semblance of a confident smile. Her heart was beating fast.

A new sound broke the stillness. Heels clicked up the

center aisle, advancing at a deliberate, moderate pace. Their weight and sound and timing described a feminine gait. Ellen refused to turn and look, waiting until Dana passed through the opening at the bar and walked up to the court clerk, who administered the oath. She was tall and dark and poised and professional. Attractive, even handsome. Not beautiful, although some might say so. She had a regal presence. Already, Ellen could see Dana's resolve to remain unyielding.

Dana took her seat in the box, yet Ellen hesitated. The judge looked down on her and said, "You may inquire."

In the next instant, Ellen was on her feet, in a superior position to the seated Dana Hargrove. But the promise of control was clouded by a vision. It was 1988 again, and the two women were at their desks in the rookie quad. Their bureau chief, Patrick, came striding in like he always did, full of energy and authority. He grabbed and dragged a straight-backed chair along with him, placed it backwards in front of Dana's desk, and straddled it, draping his forearms on the top of the chair. He leaned toward her. His Dana. She was the person in their office he wanted to see. Always.

Shaking off the cobwebs, Ellen searched for, and found, her first question. "You conducted the felony murder trial against my client in January 1993, did you not?"

"Yes, I did." Dana removed her eyes from Ellen and looked at Ramón. Not a quick, shifting look or a nervous glance, but a slow, careful turn of the head. She regarded him for a full three seconds before turning back to Ellen. If it was speech, it would have been this: *I don't regret anything I've done.*

Ellen picked up the ballistics report and motioned to a court officer. She would not approach the witness. Not yet. The distance between them would gradually diminish, one step at a time, as her questions became progressively more direct. That was her plan.

The court officer handed the report to Dana. Ellen inquired: "Do you recognize the document you've been handed?"

"Yes. It's the ballistics report prepared by Glenn Pearson, which was entered into evidence at Mr. Pineda's trial."

"Do you see, on that report, a voucher number associated with a Beretta semiautomatic handgun?"

"I do. It says 23W9G06."

"Let me show you another document." Ellen picked up the voucher form and walked two paces toward the witness, but again motioned to the court officer, who handed it up. "Do you recognize this document?"

"I can't say that I recognize it. I can tell you what appears on this form."

"Okay. If you want to play a game of semantics..."

"Hold it there, Ms. Fortier," said the judge. "Ask a proper question." Perhaps Weingarten didn't care, but the judge was getting tired of her methods.

"All right," said Ellen. "Let me ask you this. What does this form *appear* to be?"

Dana raised her eyebrows and exhaled deeply. *I'll humor you,* her behavior seemed to say. In that moment, Ellen loathed this woman and her velvet, middle-toned voice. "It appears to be a voucher form. The voucher number is 23W9G06, and the item vouchered is a Glock semiautomatic pistol with the serial number YZ194V33."

Ellen took another step forward. "Is it your testimony that you don't remember this document?"

"I remember something like this, but not specifically this." Dana handed the paper back to the court officer, who handed it to Ellen.

"Well, do you recall, generally, that each of the weapons in this case was assigned a voucher number on a voucher form?"

"Yes, I do."

Clutching the voucher form, Ellen approached again. Two steps. "And do you remember that you failed to introduce those voucher forms into evidence at trial?"

"I didn't have to. The numbers were placed in evidence through Police Officer Sullivan's testimony."

"So, he remembered those numbers off the top of his head?"

"I refreshed the officer's memory first."

"Refreshed his memory." Ellen looked down at the floor and up again, meeting Dana's eyes. "Isn't it true that, under the rules of evidence, *anything* at all can be used to refresh a witness's memory?"

"Yes."

"So, before you asked Officer Sullivan to give the voucher number for the Beretta, you showed him a paper of some kind to refresh his memory, didn't you?"

"Yes. I showed him the original voucher form. He was the officer who prepared it. The '23' at the beginning of each number stands for his precinct, the 23rd."

Two more steps. "Whatever it was that you showed him..."

"The original voucher form."

"...was *not* placed in evidence. You got him to testify that the voucher number ending in '06' went with the Beretta. Isn't that so?"

"I asked him a question and he answered it, if that's what you mean when you say I 'got' him to testify."

"Well, after showing Officer Sullivan a piece of paper and eliciting the testimony you wanted, you decided not to introduce the original voucher form into evidence, isn't that right?"

"As I said, there was no need."

"No need. But didn't you have another reason to keep it from the jury?"

"There was no other reason."

"The number did not match the number on the ballistics report. Isn't *that* the true reason you concealed it?" Two more steps, and Ellen was at the box, placing her hand on the rail.

"That's not how I remember it. Everything matched. And that's why I can't say that I recognize that form." With a tilt of her head, Dana acknowledged the paper in Ellen's hand, as if it were no more than yesterday's New York Post.

Where was the quaver in her voice? The darting, evasive eyes? Ellen searched for the telltale signs, a look of dread, a tiny jolt of self-doubt. Nothing. The two women locked eyes in a stare-down, Dana cool, Ellen boiling over. Against her will, she retreated first.

With nothing left but a shot in the dark, Ellen risked it: "If that's what you remember, then how do you explain *this*?" She took her hand from the rail and slapped the document. "How do you explain that the ballistics results on Pearson's report were for a Beretta instead of a Glock under this voucher number?"

Dana's unashamed stare was interrupted by the briefest flit of her deep brown eyes to the left. In that movement, Ellen sensed the communication that passed between the two prosecutors, Hargrove and Weingarten. Buddies, compatriots, colleagues, conspirators, partners in crime. A silent question. What should Dana's answer be? There was a signal, a decision made. If only the judge could see it! If only he had Ellen's intuitive sense, he would know the truth.

A hundred people waited. Finally, Dana spoke. "At the time of the trial, the number on the voucher form for the Beretta matched the number for the Beretta on the ballistics report. That is my memory."

So cool. Not a blink.

For Ellen, the room shimmered in a mirage of heat and light. Words tumbled and spilled out: "You want us to believe your memory, from nine years ago, when *this* form was in the DA's internal file?" Dizzily, she swiveled to face the prosecution table. "After ADA Weingarten *stipulated* that it was in the DA's file?"

Before Dana could speak, Ellen pivoted again to face her. "When ... the ... People ... stipulated!"

Judge Deal cut in. "We have your point, Ms. Fortier. Mr. Weingarten, the People's stipulation is still good, is it not?"

Weingarten jumped to his feet. "Yes, it is, Your Honor."

The judge turned to Ellen. "I think you're done with this witness."

"Just one or two more..."

"I think you're done. Anything from the People?"

"Yes...," Weingarten started to say, but the judge was no longer looking at him, distracted by a sound at the back of the room. Heads turned. The judge, Dana, the court clerk, the court officers—all directed their gaze past the bar, down the center aisle. Weingarten turned halfway and looked over his shoulder. Ellen could barely move. In the grip of an invisible hand, she twisted just slightly and froze, seeing nothing but the brown wood of the judge's bench.

This time, the sound and weight and timing of the footsteps described a masculine gait, assertive, authoritative. The District Attorney himself, Patrick McBride, strode through the opening at the bar and took his place next to Weingarten at the table.

"As I was saying," continued the judge, "do the People wish to cross-examine?"

"We do, Your Honor," said McBride. "If I may?"

"Please do."

Weingarten sat down, allowing McBride to step forward as the People's representative. Ellen retreated to her table. Absently, she pulled her chair a few inches away from Ramón before she sank into it. The smell of prison sickened her. Anything could happen now. Anything at all.

The District Attorney stepped into the arena. "Ms. Hargrove, as an assistant district attorney in my office, are you familiar with the procedure for gaining access to archived internal files?"

"Yes, I am."

"Please explain the procedure."

In her lap, Ellen's interlaced fingers were squeezing hard.

"Only employees of your office have access to the internal files. All others must make a FOIL request or subpoena the records. A log is kept, recording every employee who requests a file from archives. Up until September of 1994, paper logbooks were kept."

A small shockwave hit. Ellen had prepared so carefully, but what was this? September of 1994. By all appearances, this line of questioning was entirely unrelated to this proceeding. Shakily, she got to her feet. "I object, Your Honor. This isn't relevant."

"Overruled. Proceed, Mr. McBride."

"How did things change after September 1994?" McBride asked.

"The log was computerized. The archives clerk signed people in on a computer screen. The record can be searched any number of ways, by case name, the date accessed, or by the name of the person accessing the case file. That wasn't possible with the paper logbooks, and they were kept for only five years. After that, they were destroyed."

Hah! Here was the confirmation. With her last ounce of

nerve, Ellen got to her feet and tried a second time to convince the judge that McBride's questions were way off the mark. "Your Honor, this really … it really…," she was nearly hyperventilating, "it has nothing to do with Mr. Pineda's motion."

"Overruled again. Ms. Fortier, I suggest you remain seated. I'm going to hear this out."

She dropped to her chair. Ramón tugged at her sleeve. She pulled away.

McBride continued. "Ms. Hargrove, when was Mr. Pineda sentenced in this case?"

"In February of 1993."

"What did you do with the file after the case was closed?"

"I sent it to archives."

"Have you had an opportunity to check the archives log with respect to Mr. Pineda's case, indictment number 2456 of 1992?"

"Yes, I checked the log this past Friday."

"How did you gain access?"

"As a bureau chief I'm authorized to access the internal computer records of the office. I have read-only access."

"Please describe how you conducted your search."

"I entered the indictment number for Mr. Pineda's case and the name of a former employee of your office to see if that person had requested the file."

Nothing. There would be nothing.

"Did you find that name for any date from September of 1994 to the present?"

Of course not.

"No, I did not."

"How about before September of 1994?"

"Yes, I found it."

Ellen's interlaced fingers were bloodless and numb. It was

too late. She'd been powerless to stop it. With unassailable command, McBride had flawlessly led the witness to this point.

Before the room started to go dark, Ellen noticed an alarming communication. The judge caught the eye of the senior court officer and delivered a silent instruction. Was it so very clear where McBride was headed? The officer took note and began a slow-motion advance toward her table. As the darkness descended, the pesky annoyance at her side grew to an intolerable pitch. There was a childlike tugging at her sleeve, the sound of angry words, and the stench of sour breath, hot against her neck.

"How can that be," the District Attorney was asking, "when the records consisted of paper logbooks before that date?"

"In January of '95, after you took office as the District Attorney, you had the archive storage system upgraded. As part of that project, all paper logbooks then in existence were scanned into the computer system."

"Tell us the results of the search you conducted last Friday."

Dana paused. McBride's imposing figure, a partial shield, slowly moved to the side and turned in profile, allowing Ellen a full view of the witness stand. But something strange was happening to her vision. It constricted to a pinhole of light framing Dana's face, miles in the distance, on the other side of an endless tunnel.

"For the date June 27, 1994, I found the name Ellen Fortier. At that time, she was an assistant DA in Trial Bureau 90." A murmur started up in the audience. "That date falls within her final week at the DA's office. She resigned on June 30, 1994."

"Was there any official reason for ADA Ellen Fortier to request that file?"

"None at all. On that date, Mr. Pineda had already lost on his direct appeal, and no other motions were pending."

The murmur swelled. Ramón's rasp was now well above a whisper. "Wha' the fuck!"

The judge bolted upright in his chair and banged the gavel. His other hand went up like a stop sign. "Hold it, Mr. McBride."

Ellen swiveled right and left in her chair. A wall of men created a barrier to flight. Three court officers, wearing white shirts with chevrons on their shoulders, stood with their hands resting on their respective utility belts, weapons holstered. A fourth person was a strange little man Ellen recognized. He wore jeans and a tee-shirt, had a craggy, pockmarked face, a ponytail, and a crooked, devious smile. Where had he come from? He looked at her with deep satisfaction in his eyes before casting a proud look in Dana's direction.

Dozens of voices stirred the air. "Look!" someone yelled. Ramón pushed away from the table. Dizzy with fear, Ellen stood up on jelly legs. The judge rose above them and pointed his gavel, here and there, at attorney and client. "Officers, take charge!"

Two court officers gripped Ramón's arms on either side. The third officer took Ellen by the arm. The scary little man just looked at her and said, "You're under arrest..." Suddenly, his name shot into her head. Senior Investigator Gilbert Herrera. One of Dana's favorites. He always did have a way of sneaking up on people. "...for obstruction of justice and falsifying official records." Perhaps no one but Ellen and her client could hear him. The din continued unabated. The judge banged his gavel again and again. Ramón started shouting at the top of his lungs: "I want another attorney! This is a fraud!" The two officers held him back.

But Ellen was drifting away into her own little world with

Herrera. He stood directly in front of her, inches between them. Shyly, she looked up at him. "You're not gonna run, are you?" His eyes were strangely kind. He took her arm gently and nodded at the court officer to release her other arm. The officer joined his brother officers in restraining Ramón and cuffing his hands behind his back.

"Order!" With a final bang of the gavel, the audience started to settle down. "Mr. McBride, do you have an application?"

"The People are prepared with a rebuttal case, Your Honor. Police Officer Robert Sullivan is waiting outside. He brought the true original voucher forms with him—the NYPD copies."

"I appreciate the effort, but there's no need for a rebuttal case. The court has all it needs in this proceeding. You can save that evidence for trial, Mr. District Attorney." He pointed the gavel at Ellen. "I'm talking about your trial against Ms. Fortier here."

Ellen's head drooped heavily on a limp neck. The investigator's warm hand loosely circled her slender biceps. In that moment, the distillation of her entire professional career was concentrated in that warmth, the single, tangible attachment that said, more than anything, *This is the law.*

"My motion!" yelled Ramón, struggling against the hold of the officers. "She said she'd get me out!"

With cold eyes, the judge gazed down at him, bestowing the first cognizant look he'd given the prisoner all morning. "In case you hadn't guessed, Mr. Pineda, your motion is denied."

22 »   PARTNERS

As Dana stepped down from the witness stand, her knees
started to buckle. The weakness caught her by surprise. It was
the first indication she'd had all morning of the emotion
stirring beneath her composed, professional exterior.

Sensing an imminent collapse, she summoned her innate
strength and stood tall, ready to face the unpleasant truth. Ellen
was under arrest. Not a happy ending, but a just and correct
one.

Judge Deal ordered the courtroom cleared. The entire
audience filed out while the attorneys, law enforcement
officers, and court personnel dealt with the aftermath—the
processing of two prisoners. Predictably, many of the curiosity
seekers from the audience would loiter in the broad corridor
outside, hoping for another glimpse of the participants when
they emerged. The reporters among them would be angling to
steal a comment, a photo, or a ten-second news clip when the
District Attorney and his entourage departed the scene, fresh
from the cauldron of legal mayhem. Ellen's followers—the
row of law student interns—had no reason to stick around.
Stunned and leaderless, they left the courtroom with tears in
their eyes and pale, stricken faces.

Dana stopped short next to the witness box, allowing the
court officers to cross in front of her as they escorted Pineda
to the lockup. After they passed, she stepped toward the
counsel tables, coming within a dozen feet of Gil and his new
charge. She paused to regard the incongruous sight of her

315

former officemate with hands cuffed behind her back. Dressed completely in black, docile and compliant, Ellen could have been mourning her own demise. She listened quietly to Gil as he recited her constitutional rights to remain silent and to have the assistance of counsel. Although Ellen didn't need a reminder of the law, her behavior gave no indication of this. With glassy eyes and a dazed expression, she answered "yes" each time Gil asked whether she understood.

When he finished the catechism, he turned to regard Dana with the shine of accomplishment in his eyes. The gentleness under the tough-guy looks was captured there, along with signs of his fatigue. It had been a busy twenty-four hours. He looked at her and said, simply, "Dane."

"Gilbert."

Their gaze fixed and held for just a second before Dana turned to Ellen. The defeated attorney avoided the eyes of her nemesis. Did Ellen know about yesterday's arrest in Westchester County? Most likely the word hadn't gotten to her. Notable events in suburban counties, unless extraordinary, were rarely newsworthy in Manhattan. If Ellen had heard about the arrest, Dana would expect to see an indication of that knowledge in her eyes or behavior. Instead, she'd seen only the signs of sinking hope and growing desperation in Ellen's performance during their tense exchange in the courtroom.

What Ellen had done was despicable, a violation of attorney ethics and a violation of the law. Several violations. She'd falsified evidence in at least three cases, Pineda, Blakely and Nazarov, and there was every indication that more would be found—log entries noting her access to more than a dozen case files. Ellen's timing provided additional proof of her scheme. Starting in 1999, exactly five years after she left the DA's office, the number of post-conviction motions filed by

Justice Restored dramatically increased. *No one will ever know. The tampering won't be discovered. Memories fade and the logbooks are gone, destroyed.* Ellen's misguided self-assurances were now easy enough to guess.

They'd narrowly averted Ellen's fraud in the Pineda case, but Blakely and Nazarov were already released from prison. Perhaps it wasn't impossible to undo what Ellen had done, to ask the court to reinstate those convictions and send the defendants back to prison. Such a request was unprecedented. The ultimate decision whether to take any action would be Patrick's to make.

Despite Ellen's egregious conduct, Dana felt compassion for her. She had a brother in prison, a young man recruited by a career criminal who'd gotten away. Almost. On Sunday, Mason Landers walked right into a trap of his own making. Funny, but Ellen had done a similar thing. Like Mason, she'd been operating under the delusion that the passage of time made her safe.

Not so funny for Dana. She was chilled to the bone at the thought of the uncomfortable intimacy her family shared with these two offenders.

Sunday evening, when Evan revealed the identity of the man arrested on the doorstep of his family home, it took Dana a minute to believe it. After seven years in exile, Mason Landers had dusted off his signature modus operandi, assumed an alias, and set to work in his old stomping ground, showing up for a chicken dinner and an opportunity to rip off the unsuspecting Brenda Goodhue. Was it pure coincidence that he'd chosen Brenda? How many others were on the new "client" list of "Mike Lane"? Luckily, he was now behind bars—but the investigation was ongoing. There had to be other victims. Landers was not a man to stop after victimizing just one or two.

Another alarming image: Brenda at police headquarters, viewing a lineup. She picked "Mr. Lane" immediately. Evan's brother had been with her, and Brenda was safe. Shaken, but safe, and much the wiser, not likely to be victimized again. Dana had to remember that. Uneasy but grateful, she assured herself that her family was safe. This wasn't like that other time. No blood or violence was involved, only greed and revenge, and in Ellen's case, a warped kind of loyalty to family.

Dana took a moment before she removed her eyes from Ellen's downcast face. So vocal only minutes before, she now stood mute and dejected. Dana thought of the man who'd sparked the sequence of events precipitating Ellen's downfall. News of his arrest would be especially welcome to her right now. Should Dana say something? *Mason Landers is in custody.* That single sentence could provide a safety net for Ellen's painful, headlong dive into the gutter.

But it wasn't Dana's place to say anything. The case they'd just battled in court was too closely connected to Landers. Ellen's motive for attempting to spring Pineda had grown out of her love for her brother and the unremitting blame she directed at his co-conspirator. Dana couldn't risk saying anything that might be perceived as an attempt to elicit a response from a shackled prisoner who'd just been advised of her constitutional right to remain silent.

Dana said nothing to Ellen, and their eyes did not meet. She turned to Gil once more. Businesslike, she said, "I'll touch base with Eric before I go."

"Everything's under control. I left him in the Dungeon with Manny." This was another accomplishment that Gil could be proud of, and his face showed it.

"Yes, thank you, Gil."

"I owed you one."

The prisoner at his side gave no indication of hearing their conversation. Her head was drooped, her gaze fixed on an imaginary spot on the floor. Dana looked at Gil and conveyed a message with a flick of her eyes toward Ellen and back again: *You owed me one, but you gave me two.* He seemed to pick up the thought and the gratitude that went along with it.

Dana stepped away from Gil to wait for Patrick and Ben, who were talking to Judge Deal. They finished their conversation and came up to join her. It was time for them to walk out of the courtroom, leaving Gil behind to finish up his business with Ellen. Just then, Dana noticed three members of the DA's squad standing at the back of the courtroom. No doubt, Gil had arranged for these men to escort them. The protection of the District Attorney and his assistants was always foremost on Gil's mind.

"Ready?" Patrick asked.

"Yes," said Dana. "There's a lot to do before I get going."

"And I have a press release to write. Call me before you leave."

"Sure will." It was understood that she would give Patrick an update on the Kallay case after talking to Eric. Patrick had also asked her to call Bruce Reichert, head of the Special Investigations Unit, to fill him in on the evidence against Ellen. Bruce would be conducting the prosecution, and this was a case right up his alley. Dana smiled at the thought of how she used to dread this man, so many years ago. At the moment, she looked forward to giving him a call. They hadn't spoken in months. She imagined a gleam of pleasure in his small eyes, bright as glass marbles under those fuzzy eyebrows that would squeeze into a single brown caterpillar, low in his tense brow. Today, her phone call might evoke one of his relatively lighter moods, separating that furry line into two shorter creatures high in his forehead. A strange, intense man, dedicated and serious. Single-minded at times—a quality that would serve

District Attorney McBride well in a prosecution against a former ADA.

With Patrick in the lead, Dana and Ben on either side, they walked out of the courtroom. As anticipated, a group of reporters eagerly sprang into action. The three men from the DA's squad formed a protective ring around Patrick and his assistants.

"No comment at this time," Patrick said. "I'll be releasing a formal statement and taking questions in the press room at one o'clock." They would have to wait. Above all, Patrick was a cautious man, mindful to avoid hasty remarks that might come back to haunt him.

The triumvirate and their escorts headed for the elevator bank. As they waited, Dana thanked Patrick and Ben for their support in the courtroom. "You made all of this a lot easier for me," she said.

"My pleasure," said Ben.

Patrick flashed a devious look. "The People would stipulate to that."

Big smiles burst onto their faces, but they held back the laughter as they stepped into the elevator together.

At their respective floors, they parted ways. Patrick and Ben had offices in the DA's wing of the Criminal Court building, while Dana went downstairs to cross the street to her building. One of the men from the DA's squad insisted on accompanying her. News vans and reporters were swarming out front. They took the side exit and successfully made the passage across the barricaded street.

After her call to Bruce it was only a matter of minutes before Eric walked into Dana's office, to give her an update on Clifton Vaughn. In shirtsleeves, with his tie loosened at the collar, Eric was jittery and excited, unshaven, eyes red-rimmed, and face aglow. This was a man who thrived on lack of sleep.

"Chill, Eric. Sit." She gestured to a chair across from her at the desk.

Eric sat and looked at his watch. "Eleven thirty. It's been a night."

"And a morning. When and where, exactly, did the arrest go down?"

"About four, at his vintage clothing store downtown. He must've thought all eyes were off of him at that time. Gil said he was looking over his shoulder, putting the key in the lock."

"He knew we were after him."

"That's what we figure. We had a man on his apartment building all weekend. Vaughn didn't come back. Maybe he noticed the police action outside on Friday night. Either that, or someone tipped him off. It could've been the doorman—I understand he was the type looking to have his palm greased, no matter who did the greasing."

"Where were you when they arrested Vaughn?"

"At home, getting an hour or two of sleep. I told Gil to call me the minute something happened. He called right after the arrest and told me to come down—he was having one of his intuitions, you know…"

"One of Gil's famous intuitions."

"Right. He said Vaughn was a talker and would keep talking. I jumped into a cab and got down here toot sweet. He's been talking this whole time, off and on, to me and Gil and Manny, except, you know, Gil went up to court at about ten thirty…"

"That's a long talk, Eric. Don't tell me that Vaughn is going to find grounds to complain."

"We did everything by the book, Dana. Even Thurgood Marshall would approve. The first part of it just shot out of his mouth at the time of his arrest—"

"Before rights?"

"They couldn't get a word in edgewise! The minute they said he was under arrest for the murder of Loránd Kallay, he started spouting off: 'You've got nothing on me! So what if the bitch wanted to off her husband? I didn't do it!' et cetera et cetera. Finally they *Mirandized* him, and most of everything else he said is on the videotape we took in the Dungeon."

"Most of it? Everything but the beatings, you mean." She smiled at her own joke, feeling light and heady. She'd survived her morning ordeal and was poised at the tip of an imminent, joyous getaway to the pristine sands and salty breezes.

But Eric wasn't in the mood for jokes. This was a serious matter. "Come on, Dana…"

"Okay. Tell me everything."

"We treated Vaughn like a king. Advised him of his rights more than once. Gave him food and coffee. He's a night owl. Didn't show the slightest bit of strain. You should see this guy, Dana. He's a slicked back little jockey type with these electric eyes. We were fading and the sonuvabitch was blasting away."

"Maybe he was on something."

"I think it's just *him* he's on. Said he didn't need a lawyer and kept running his mouth. Of course, he started out by denying everything."

"Talkers usually do."

"He was telling us off. He was smarter than everyone in the room. He was going to convince us how wrong we were. But it wasn't long before he started giving little hints of things he knew…"

"And you were careful not to lead him?"

"Totally."

"Nothing about the DNA or Nurse Tipple and the phone call to Frances?"

"Not a word. He started out by telling us that he'd never

been anywhere near the Kallay residence. He quit his job at the House of Loránd years ago and hadn't seen Kallay or his wife since. After he cooled down, you could see his mind working. He must've known about the search, and he had to come up with an explanation about the fashion designs. 'You think I stole Kallay's drawings, don't you? Well, you're wrong.' He was trying to judge our reaction, but we just stayed zipped and let him talk."

"What excuse could he possibly come up with?"

"Total bullshit, that's what. He claimed that Frances brought the drawings to his apartment a week before the murder. Supposedly, Kallay was worried that someone was after them, and he asked his wife to store them where they couldn't be found. Vaughn said he didn't take them to the police after the murder because he was afraid he'd be pinned for the crime. Convenient excuse, right?"

"I couldn't have thought of a better one." She rolled her eyes heavenward.

"So, this was his story up until about five thirty this morning."

Dana started to worry that Eric would take another six hours to describe, minute by minute, the next six hours he'd spent with Vaughn. She tried to hurry him along, "So you chipped away at his story?"

"He chipped away at it himself. He started to get nervous after telling us about the drawings. It was inconsistent with his first story, that he hadn't seen Mr. or Mrs. since '96, when he quit his job. So he backtracked and said, 'Well, yeah, this was the one time I saw Frances, when she came over with the drawings.' Then he had to think of a reason she would know where he lived. Naturally, he knew we were aware of his status as a registered sex offender. He laughed it off and said, 'Frances must've gotten my address from the registry.' At that point, I think it was Manny who made a comment, something like, 'So Mrs. Kallay decided to leave her husband's designs with a known sex offender.' Vaughn laughed again and made some crack about, 'She was a little kinky that way.' We just stared at him until he started fidgeting. In his eyes you could see those handcuffs and ropes. He knew we must've seen them in his bedroom. All of this eventually led to, 'Yeah, maybe I saw her a few times for sex, and maybe she liked it a little rough. No crime in that.' Then he started putting on an act, like he was more worried about a sex charge than a murder charge."

"I know where you're headed with this," said Dana. "The rest of it was pillow talk, nothing more."

Eric gazed at her in awe. "You're omniscient!"

"It's all pretty predictable. There's only one kind of smart murderer—the kind who gets away with it."

"And this one buried himself. His last shovel of dirt was this story about pillow talk. Or maybe we should call it noose talk."

"Pretty funny, Eric." His mood was lightening, she could see. "What did Vaughn choke out of his lady friend when he had her neck in the noose?"

"Her plan, as good as a confession. She supposedly told Vaughn that she hated her husband and would love to get rid of him. She mentioned that Loránd kept a gun in the desk drawer. She was thinking of using it to kill him some night when she had a good alibi. The charity fund raiser was the ticket. She could kill him, go to the charity function, come back, and discover his body. A perfect plan, but Vaughn pleaded with her, 'Don't do it, Frances!'"

"Let me guess. She ignored his pleas and did it anyway."

"Broke his heart. Especially since she foolishly abandoned her neat little alibi and decided to tell the police that she was in the house when she heard the gunshots."

"Okay, this is all very plausible," Dana said with a straight face. "Why didn't it happen the way he says?"

Eric didn't seem to notice the tongue-in-cheek. "After the way his story morphed? First it was, 'I haven't seen Frances since '96,' and then it was, 'She told me she wanted to kill her husband.' He was such a smartass, looking at us like he'd just given us the absolute proof of his innocence. He pointed out that we'd already suspected her and arrested her and got her to admit the shooting in the grand jury. Now this. Now we hear that Vaughn received a full confession of her plan in advance. It was Frances, acting all on her own. What more could we want? He was so sure of himself, but then he got carried away and stepped off the cliff."

"Good one. Cliff stepped off the cliff."

"Ha ha. This was the thing that did it. He said, 'Who else would be so dumb as to leave the gun on the desk? She must've been in shock. She shot him, panicked, and left the gun right where the police would find it. What more do you need?'"

"Oh boy."

"Yeah, oh boy. There's only one way he could've known about the gun. He must've been there. We never went public with that bit of info. It wasn't in the news. And Nurse Tipple didn't overhear anything about a gun when Frances called him from the hospital. Only the killer or an accomplice would know it had been left on the desk."

Dana nodded her head in apparent agreement, her features gradually tensing under a furled brow. "You're forgetting one thing."

"What's that?"

"She called him Friday afternoon. We have it on the pen, but we don't know what they talked about."

Eric's face fell momentarily and sprang back to life. "They wouldn't've been talking about the gun. That was old news.

She was telling him how it went down in the cellar Thursday afternoon."

"Plausible. So you think he talked himself right into a hole. But it took a while. There were layers of fabrication, a lot of it exculpatory."

"Eventually he led us to himself."

"Okay. Put it together with the other evidence we have. Add it up and tell me the real story. How did this crime go down?" She'd already deduced the facts, but she wanted to hear Eric's theory. He would be the one making the argument to the jury.

"Frances and Clifton were having a messy little affair. He liked to knock her around, and maybe she liked it too. They planned the murder together. Before that night, she gave Vaughn the gun and a key to the house. He would let himself in when Frances was at the charity function. But the event was cancelled, and Frances couldn't leave the house without attracting Kallay's attention. Vaughn wanted to go through with it. He let himself in with the key. Maybe she begged him to postpone the dirty deed, but he was hotheaded and ready for it. He grabbed her arms, pushed her around a little, and punched her a few times. Or maybe he did this after he killed Kallay. Maybe she was freaking out afterward and he got rough with her, told her to keep a level head. They had to get their story straight. He wiped the gun and pressed a few of the dead man's fingers on the barrel. He convinced Frances that they should leave the gun on the desk, to make it part of the home invasion story. The safe was already open, and the burglar was demanding the goods. Kallay defended himself with the gun, they struggled for it, and the bad guy won. Then he needed his hands free to get the contents of the safe, so he laid the gun on the desk." Eric pretended to hold a gun and place it on Dana's desk. "And guess what?"

"Vaughn is left-handed."

Eric looked at her with a mixture of admiration and chagrin. "Maybe *you* should tell the story."

"But you're telling it so well."

He made a comical grimace and continued. "To go along with their story, Frances opened the safe and emptied it. But here's another glitch in their tale. The safe was too small to hold the drawings. They were stored flat, probably in a drawer of the drafting table upstairs."

"Then what *was* in the safe?"

"We don't know. Maybe nothing. We didn't find anything at Vaughn's apartment that filled the bill. But he did have the drawings. His reasons for killing Kallay could have involved the drawings or Frances or both. If money was the only motive, Frances would be inheriting everything, so it looks like Vaughn might've wanted the designs for another reason. He was a frustrated designer. He might have planned to copy them or pawn them off as his own work."

"So, why did Frances change her story?"

"That started at the hospital. Her phone call really threw him. He didn't know that he'd left marks on her bad enough to put her under observation. She was frantic about the police not believing her, so they came up with a backup story, the battered wife syndrome. Vaughn convinced her that she could claim self-defense. After we arrested her, she knew we didn't believe her story, and she changed it. But Kallay was actually gentle as a kitten, so they had to plant some evidence. While Frances was still locked up, Vaughn used his house key to let himself in when the guard was down. He planted the bloody rag, the handcuffs and ropes, and the metal clamp on Kallay's rustic wine and cheese table."

"You're forgetting one thing, counselor."

"What's that?"

"Vaughn wouldn't have known for sure that she was going to switch stories. She was incarcerated and escorted by prison guard to the grand jury where she testified. It was a closed proceeding, and the world didn't know about her testimony until after she made a statement to the press on the courthouse steps. Very soon after that, our men were waiting for her outside the townhouse. Vaughn had no chance to sneak inside under our noses."

Eric beamed a big smile, his energy bursting through the pale-skinned exhaustion. "You're gonna love this. You'll never guess what we found in Vaughn's shredder!"

She smiled. "He was so sloppy, wasn't he?"

"You bet. There was a ribbon-cut letter from Frances that we had no trouble putting together. She wrote, 'Now I'm a battered wife. He did it in the cellar. Help me.' We found no envelope, but it couldn't have been mailed. There wasn't enough time, and besides that, correction officers read all the prisoner mail."

"Hmm... Did Gil check the visitor log at Rikers?"

Eric nodded. "Only one visitor—her attorney."

Dana felt slightly guilty at the shiver of excitement that passed through her. Now there was more than just the questionable delivery of clothing and cosmetics to the jailed woman. Asante may have done something very stupid which, if proven, was cause for disbarment or worse. Criminal charges. And it wasn't outside the realm of possibility. There'd been other notable attorneys who lived like they were above the law, relying on plausible deniability as they enabled the criminal lives of their incarcerated clients. For some, the impetus was simply a devil-may-care attitude. In Asante's case it might have been more—a deliberate building block of his defense strategy.

"I'll talk to Patrick about it before I leave," Dana said.

"This is good work, Eric. Send Gil my congratulations too."

"He'll appreciate that. He was feeling bad about letting you down, that we had to release Frances."

"As it went, everything worked out fine. Frances became a partner in the investigation when we released her from jail. Now there's enough evidence to indict both of them for murder. Send Gil my thanks. I really couldn't talk about it in front of Ellen this morning."

Eric dropped his head and let it bob a few times. "Damn! I can't believe Mary Poppins is behind bars!"

BEACH

Saturday, July 14, 2001

THE SUN HAD just set on their last full day of vacation. At the house, Noel and Melanie offered to watch the kids, "ours and yours," while Evan and Dana took some time for themselves on the beach. Before heading out, they grabbed towels and draped them around their necks to be prepared for any mood or whim or spontaneous urge. A moonlight swim? Or something else.

At surf's edge, the hard packed, wet sand felt cool and smooth under bare feet. "It's been perfect, hasn't it?" She took his hand. "I can't believe we're leaving tomorrow. I could use another few weeks of this."

"Or a lifetime."

She loved this time of evening, especially in summer, when the descent of night was subtle and so gradual that it seemed to last forever. They had little company along the strand but the sights, sounds, and smells of nature. Gulls squealed, waves broke and rushed at them, just missing their feet. Sea salt wafted in the mist. Warm bursts of wind buffeted the sounds, making everything far away and mysterious. From a distance, out over the water, a bell clanged, a fog horn sounded.

"But we'd go stir crazy after a while, wouldn't we?" Dana stepped on a gelatinous bulb of seaweed and skittered sideways.

Evan laughed. "You would, for sure."

She didn't need to think very long about that. "You're right." He knew her well. There was a time when she tried to walk away from her career. No one could possibly enjoy what she endured on a daily basis: high anxiety, moral dilemmas, courtroom combat, grit, and heartache. Was she crazy? After a year at home, she came running back. The rewards of her job were too great, her commitment to the victims too strong, the camaraderie with her colleagues too compelling. "But I wouldn't say 'no' to another week at the beach," she admitted.

"Or two."

She sighed. "All good things must come to an end." Despite the rough start, their vacation had been relaxing, full of carefree days with the people they loved the most. Sandcastles had been built, all of them washed away. A wonderful but imperfect escape, one foot in, the other out, for they hadn't ignored the call of responsibility. Guiltily, like closet addicts, they'd been managing their cases from afar.

For Evan, there were no clean endings in sight. The world of civil litigation was ruled by interminable papering and the blowing of hot air. Proceedings cranked along at the speed of a Model T. Mrs. Edmonds, for all her years, was anxious to move the class action faster, but she would just have to wait. Darren Tripp's settlement offer was still unrealistically low, and it promised to remain that way until the federal criminal case was resolved. Meanwhile—good thing—his attorney's strong-arm tactics and veiled threats against Evan and Dana had backfired. Asante had been neutralized. Any limited credibility he once had was now completely undermined in the wake of Dana's report to the committee on professional ethics that Asante had evidently provided messenger services for the criminal conspirators, Frances and Clifton. In addition to the ethics complaint, Patrick had opened a criminal investigation.

Did Asante knowingly aid the murderers in planting false evidence in the cellar of the Kallay townhome? If so, he was guilty of tampering or obstruction or worse.

To top it off, Asante was no longer representing Frances. She'd eaten up all of the funds in her separate checking account and was now a pauper, represented by a court-appointed attorney at public expense. The administrator of Kallay's estate, Greta Sperry, had successfully frozen all of her brother's assets pending the outcome of the criminal trial against Frances and her lover Clifton, who were both under indictment for murder. Eric, after all, had done a superb job during the second grand jury presentation, and Patrick was pleased. If convicted of murder, Frances was prohibited by law from collecting any inheritance from the estate of her victim.

Ellen was also under indictment and sitting in jail, unable to come up with bail money—a quarter of a million. Two Fortiers, brother and sister, were now incarcerated, suggesting the possibility of an interesting twist. If Antoine managed to win release at his upcoming parole hearing, the tables would be turned. Once he made it to the outside, would he take up the fight for his sister?

At the very least, Antoine wouldn't be tempted back into his former life of crime with Mason Landers. The master scammer—a confirmed flight risk—was locked up tight, remanded without bail. The investigation into his recent activities was uncovering a particularly vile scheme of retribution against the people who'd been involved in Antoine's prosecution: law enforcement officers, attorneys, and even the judge who sentenced him. Mason had carefully picked their most vulnerable family members to victimize. As icing on the cake, he'd targeted Brenda Goodhue, a family member of Ellen's nemesis Dana Hargrove. In his twisted take on the world, Mason was sending a sort of "thank you" to

Ellen for all of her hard work on Antoine's behalf.

In addition to his new crimes, Mason was still on the hook for the old ones. Despite best laid plans, he was now under indictment for all the crimes he'd committed with Antoine in 1992 and 1993, without any hope of getting the charges dismissed on the ground that the prosecution was untimely. His lessons in the law were coming the hard way. A surprise wrinkle did him in. He wasn't aware that the clock stopped ticking on the statute of limitations for any offender who was knowingly evading arrest. In Mason's case, this amounted to the entire period of his voluntary exile.

With Mason Landers safely out of the picture, Dana could relax. Or could she? That morning, Brenda moved back into her home after spending nearly two weeks with Al Jr. and his family. Shortly after she settled in, Evan and Dana each picked up an extension of the house phone and gave her a call. "Hello!" Brenda greeted them in her singing voice. "I'm so glad to be home!" And she also expressed, with joyful anticipation, that she was looking forward to resuming her days with her grandchildren, Natalie and Travis.

Everything was back to normal ... but a little reassurance never hurt. "Your mom sounded good this morning, didn't she? I mean, you know her better than I do..."

"Hmm ... not so sure about that. I mean the part about you versus me."

"But you would know if she was feeling nervous, wouldn't you? About being back in the house ... all alone."

"Nervous she is not. *That* I can tell you."

Maybe it would be better if Brenda *was* nervous, or even a little bit on guard. Dana was thinking this, but she didn't say it. Instead, she asked, "What are the chances of another Mason Landers stalking the neighborhood?"

"Zero. She's lived there more than forty years. It's a safe

neighborhood and she loves it there. The good feelings and memories are going to outweigh this one incident. And if you're worried about her doing something foolish again..." He stopped walking and turned to face her, still holding her hand.

Dana put on her innocent voice. "Why would you think that I would be worrying about that?" She reached for his other hand.

"Oh, I don't know!" He smiled big, and she could just see it in the fading light. His teeth seemed excessively bright.

"You're such a good son." She was delighted with the look of him in the gray twilight.

"Flattery will get you nowhere."

"How about the truth?"

"Truthfully speaking, we've had a wake-up call. Mom and I both learned our lessons. Nothing like this should ever happen again."

Dana squeezed his hands, accepting his reassurance for now—until the next time that she needed it.

They turned and continued walking in the same direction, moving farther away from the house. Would they ever turn back? Up ahead, a man and a woman were approaching. It was too dark to see their faces at a distance, but Dana sensed something about them from their shapes and movements. Like Evan and Dana, they were walking hand-in-hand at a leisurely pace. They wore baggy shorts, long to the knee, without any thought of fashion. Their gait was slow and measured. Knees and legs were stiff, heels came down heavily and flat-footed with a small reverberation into the hips. The man was a bit bow-legged. Now they were closer. Now they were showing the age on their faces.

"Hello," said the gray-haired lady pleasantly. The other three gave friendly greetings. In that moment, the two couples shared something, the pleasure of simply being.

They passed on.

Up ahead, no one else was in sight. Indeed, it seemed the beach was theirs, once that couple had passed.

Dana paused, and Evan did the same. They turned to face the water and remained still for several minutes, looking out to sea. The moon was high and slightly more than half. The waves were low and made small crashes into white ridges of foam, phosphorescent against the immense gray.

Mesmerized by the distant horizon, they were surprised by the sudden crash of a large wave. "Oh!" The water surged over Dana's ankles and she jumped back.

"It's warm though," he said, tiptoeing in.

"You call this warm?"

"Like a bath! Let's go for a swim!" He swung around to face her, and she saw what he had in mind. There was a gleam in her husband's eye. Could she see it? Or did she just know it was there? She crept backwards, moving farther away from the water. He followed slowly, in mock stealth. With a few quick steps, he ran up and grabbed her hand. In a tug-of-war, he pulled and she resisted, crying out in glee, losing ground one step at a time. At water's edge, she surprised him with a sudden slackening of resistance and a charge forward, planting a kiss on his cheek.

He stopped short, stunned and smitten. She grabbed the ends of the towel around his neck and pulled him in. This was something he wouldn't resist. Drawn into the kiss, Evan surrendered. His mouth was soft and welcoming, erasing everything else.

A breathless moment later, she pulled away, drunk with the night and giddy, so unlike herself. "I'm not swimming," she said in a playful whisper.

"Oh, no?" His voice was sleepy and desirous. "Why not?"

"I have a better idea."

She took the hand of her willing victim and led him away from the water into the fine, dry sand, still warm from the day's heat. In a cove under the dune, out of the wind, they laid their towels down.

ABOUT THE AUTHOR

V.S. Kemanis is the author of three collections of short fiction and the Dana Hargrove legal mystery novels. She lives and writes in New York. Learn more at www.vskemanis.com.

OPUS NINE BOOKS

All works published by Opus Nine Books are dedicated to the nine members of the family headed by John and Kate Swackhamer at 3 South Trail, Orinda, California – a large world under one small roof.

Made in the USA
Middletown, DE
30 April 2016